A GRIMM
DECISION

JEFFERY H. HASKELL

aethonbooks.com

A GRIMM DECISION
©2023 JEFFERY H. HASKELL

Aethon Books
www.aethonbooks.com

Print and eBook formatting by Josh Hayes. Artwork provided by Vivid Covers.

Published by Aethon Books LLC.

Aethon Books is not responsible for websites (or their content) that are not owned by the publisher.

This book is a work of fiction. Names, characters, places, and incidents are the product of the author's imagination or are used fictitiously. Any resemblance to actual events, locales, or persons, living or dead is coincidental.

ALSO IN SERIES

Check out the entire series here!
(tap or scan)

FORWARD BY THE AUTHOR

Thank you. None of this would be possible without you, the reader, buying and enjoying my books. I can't tell you how much this means to me, but I can show you by writing more books. Both in this series and others. Thank you, again. Enjoy A Grimm Decision.

CHAPTER ONE

The man known as *Mr. Falcon* stepped off the gangplank onto the soil of Cordoba. Heat wafted off the ground in waves, bringing sweat to his brow. He reached up with a kerchief and dabbed his face. He hated the heat. Custom-made technology in his nondescript blue suit went to work cooling his body.

Cordoba's primary starport rested in the bottom of an extinct volcano's caldera. On the flight down, he was told it had to do with the altitude of the mountain making take-off and landing more cost effective. It was an absolutely massive caldera. From one side of the lip to the other, they could park two battleships end to end.

"Mr. Falcon?" called a young woman in a bright red summer dress, with her dark hair in a bun.

She had an aircar waiting for him. The temperature-controlled interior was a welcome relief from the thirty-degree exterior.

"How long to the general's abode?" he asked.

The driver slid into the front and closed the door before answering.

"Fifteen minutes. Hang on," she said. The car lifted off under her skilled control. She banked the vehicle, giving him a good look at the spaceport and the small military portion where a squadron of orbital fighters were parked. Inwardly, he scoffed at their attempt to intimidate him. Orbital fighters were hardly a match for a real warship, especially the kind he commanded.

True to her estimate, fifteen minutes later she sat the car down on the roof of their military headquarters. A massive spiral-shaped structure covered in the orange tiles they preferred.

Three men in their overly dressy uniforms, carrying sidearms in gleaming white holsters, awaited him. His driver triggered the door, but she remained.

"I'll be here when you're ready to return, sir."

Falcon stepped out, ignoring the men who escorted him. All of it was a measured attempt to remind him that Cordoba had military power. They had no clue how much they were outmatched. The only thing stopping his people from simply conquering the backwards planet was their proximity to the Alliance. A sour expression covered his face as he thought of the failed attempt to take Zuckabar. Not to mention his company's new board of directors and partners wanted more subtlety from their operations. It bothered him on a fundamental level, knowing that they were no longer independent.

They marched silently to the lift. The doors opened, and he stepped in with them. All of it was a show. He knew that. The lift descended past the upper floors, picking up speed. Levels flashed by and Falcon realized they weren't headed for a top-floor office when it slowed down and stopped at a sub-basement.

He was pleasantly surprised to find her office was far more spartan than he expected after the show of the soldiers and squadrons. A flag of their world hung on one wall. It was a simple design. A shield with an eagle's crest over a background of yellow and red stripes spoke to their heritage. Another weakness Mr. Falcon didn't share. Traditions and heritage were useless concepts compared to efficiency and structure.

General Juanita Pérez sat behind a simple wooden desk.

"General, it's an honor to meet you," he said, holding out his hand.

Pérez, all smiles, took his hand in a firm grip—for a woman. Inwardly, Mr. Falcon understood what it had to take for two sisters to make it to the head of the military on a planet descended from barbarians. Her height and build were unimpressive, though.

"Mr. Falcon, welcome to Cordoba."

"Thank you, General. I'm honored to be here."

She waved for her servants. The rich aroma of coffee filled the room. A young man handed him a small cup of the powerful brew.

"What can I do for you, sir?" Pérez asked after sipping her drink.

"I believe the real question is what can I do for you? After all, from what we can see your plans are falling short—"

Pérez sneered, not quite slamming her cup on the desk. A cold visage instantly replaced the warmth she expressed a moment before.

"And why would you think that?"

Mr. Falcon felt the lack of protection, but he knew they couldn't touch him. Pérez might not know about the Sword of Damocles that hung over her planet, but even without that knowledge she wouldn't dare hurt him.

"Please, General. We have intelligence assets imbedded in your government and civilian infrastructure. There isn't anything we don't know. Including that your candidate, Franceska Divine, is trailing the incumbent president by over forty points. With an election later this year, that doesn't bode well for your... plans." Falcon leaned back, sipping his coffee. "This is excellent. Can I buy a few pounds for my office?" he asked, gesturing with his coffee cup.

She ignored his non sequitur. "There's still time to turn it around. The people are tired of President Santiago's isolationist policies. They see what is happening to the Alliance and they are afraid. It only makes sense for them to want to embrace the Terran Republic. We just need to do so from a place of strength to guarantee we don't lose our culture by joining them."

Mr. Falcon crossed his legs, steepling his hands and resting his chin on them. He looked at her, really looked, letting his examination of her be evident.

"Are you eager for war, General?"

That took her back. She shook her head sternly. "Of course not. Only a fool wants war, but a wise leader is always prepared for it."

"People who crave power also want war, General. War allows politicians to become gods. You get to decide who lives and who dies. Who is loyal, and who is a traitor... just like in the Alliance."

For a moment, he saw the truth on her face. The almost euphoric gleam in her eyes as she pondered the possibilities. Yes, there was no doubt in Falcon's mind who would truly be in charge if Divine won the election. It wasn't the sister, or Divine herself, but General Pérez. Either through a puppet like Divine, or if the puppet met with an unfortunate accident, the general herself.

"I don't know what you or your organization think of me, Mr. Falcon, but I want what is best for my people."

Falcon waved away her concerns. "Of course. Can't you do both? After all, who better to lead your people than you? And if there are those that can't see it, well, all the better that they can't disagree with you, right?"

He leaned back, sipping more of the delicious coffee with its rich aftertaste. He really wanted some for his office. They may lack the technology to compete with the military powers, but they certainly could grow coffee.

"What do I need to do?" she asked.

"First, I have some unfortunate news for you. Your president has decided that his isolationist policies are working against him. He's invited the Alliance to send military units here for a joint training exercise."

Pérez slammed her hands down hard enough the desk shook. "I'm the head of the military. How is it you know this and I don't?"

He smiled mischievously. "I told you, we have our sources. I know they will accept, and it just so happens the timing is going to be right. Allow our hackers to infiltrate your voting systems and ensure Divine's victory. You can then publicly dismiss the Alliance and embrace the Republic at the same time."

She stood, turning her back to him. Behind her were a row of plaques, pictures, and medals. Hundreds of photos showed her with soldiers in the mud, in vehicles, leaping out of airplanes. Pérez was quite accomplished, he knew. Her weakness was that she truly wanted what was best for her people, but she also wanted power. More than wanted, more than desired, she was drawn to it like an addict to narcotics. She had to have it and whatever she had would never be enough. Given the right push she would do anything, even murder, to gain the power she craved. His psyops people predicted a seventy percent chance this tactic would work. If it didn't, his backup would have a hundred percent chance of success.

Her entire body shuddered as she reached a decision. Falcon leaned forward in anticipation. He keyed his neural network, ready to signal his team to perform the hacking even as he sat there.

Pérez lifted her head. "No. I won't cheat, Mr. Falcon. Not ever. If he wins, he wins. I will just have to hope my people can see what I see: a coward hiding behind his own wealth."

Falcon sighed. Her reaction was disappointing, but hardly surprising. His mind flipped the network over to the secondary protocol and he sent out the message.

"If you don't, he will. Do you really think a man with such power, such temporary power, will stop at anything to hold on to it? Our operatives are already seeing traces of domestic hacking in the voting system..."

"Just because he is an honorless man doesn't mean I will resort to the same behavior. No one will fall for his nonsense. Franceska is too popular for that to work. No, I will not cheat my people."

"Even if it means you lose?" Falcon asked.

"What is winning if I destroy what we fight for?"

"I admire your commitment and integrity, General, I really do. I think that's all there is, then. I'm sorry we couldn't be of help," Falcon said as he stood.

"Wait, that's all? You offer nothing but empty words and lies?"

"My dear General, that's all any politician offers."

Falcon turned to leave, then stopped, reaching into his pocket. He carefully placed a slim black card with gold trim on her desk. The image of a falcon, claws out, embossed on the front.

"If you do change your mind, press and hold the falcon down and say your full name. I will get the message."

He spent the ride back to the spaceport carefully calculating the time and distance involved. They would have to move quickly and carefully. The Terran Republic wanted Cordoba and the Terraforming Guild wanted the Alliance destroyed. If he worked it right, they would both win.

CHAPTER TWO

SIX MONTHS LATER. ALLIANCE CAPITAL:
ALEXANDRIA SYSTEM

"Squadron orders, twenty degrees down bubble and commence firing." Even to Jacob's ears, his voice sounded insufficient. Commanding an entire squadron of four destroyers, including his own, weighed on him like no problem he'd faced before.

Spacer First Class Abbott relayed his orders with expert precision. "Squadron confirms."

The *Interceptor* shuddered as the four turrets opened fire. The enemy ships, marked as Tango-Alpha One through Four, on his plot were heading right for him. It was the kind of engagement destroyer skippers loved. Tin can vs tin can.

It was also unrealistic to a fault.

"Launch, launch, launch. Two minutes to impact," Lieutenant Brown stated evenly from his position at weapons.

"Coxswain, seven degrees port, increase acceleration to..." Jacob glanced down at the plot as the engagement window widened, the yellow circles showing their maneuvering arc. "Four-five-zero g's."

"Aye, aye, Skipper. Four-five-zero g's," Chief Suresh replied.

He had complete faith in his crew. It was the other three ships he wasn't sure about. Oh, their skippers were good, otherwise they wouldn't be in charge. It was one thing to run a ship, another to run it in combat, and even more complicated to run as part of a squadron. *Apache* and *Kidd* were on his starboard flank, and *Justice* to his port, pacing *Interceptor* as they cruised through space.

Or maybe Jacob doubted himself and the rest of the DesRon 12 was fine.

The ship hummed as it increased in speed. Gravity pushed back on the crew lightly, forcing them to lean into the momentum.

"Contacts changing course to keep their angle of attack. No change in acceleration. Maintaining three-five-zero gravities," PO Tefiti announced.

The air in Jacob's suit recycled every few seconds, keeping his body and mind oxygenated, but he desperately wanted to pull off his helmet and breathe the ships canned air.

What was wrong with him?

"Weps, task PDW #1 to deal with the torpedoes. Range to targets?" he asked.

"Aye, aye, sir. PDW #1 powering up," Lieutenant Brown said.

The last time they had used the PDW lasers, they almost melted their ship. The solution to that problem was both elegant and simple, and supplied by Lieutenant Kai. Only activate one turret at a time rotating them as needed and giving the ships internal heat management time to deal with the load.

"Range to contacts, six-zero-four-thousand klicks, about half that for the torpedoes," Tefiti said.

There was more than enough time for the PDW to deal with the torps.

Jacob's plot updated, showing the four enemy destroyers still heading right for them.

"Comms, relay to *Apache* and *Kidd*, adjust course fourteen degrees starboard, and accelerate to flank." Since the enemy committed to coming straight down his throat, maybe he could catch them in crossfire.

Though something about the way they were blindly flying right toward him made his gut react. He pulled up the radar scan showing their distance from one another. They were awfully close formation for a squadron. Only a few thousand klicks separated the ships. He admired their formation discipline, though.

"More launches. Call it, one volley every four-five seconds," Brown said.

That was interesting.

"Tefiti, there's just four, right?" he asked the PO.

"Sir?" Tefiti actually turned in his seat to look at his captain. With the helmet on, he had perfect noise cancelation and didn't need to wear headphones.

"If there was another ship with them, say right about here —" Jacob activated the plot editing feature and pointed to a spot a thousand kilometers behind and in the center of the formation. "Would you hear them?"

"No, sir. The other ships, and their torpedoes, would baffle any gravwake emanating from their stern."

Did that explain why they were shooting at him despite the impossibility of the shot? As a distraction?

"Carter," he said routing the call to his XO in DCS. "If you were a light cruiser hiding behind those ships wake, when would you show yourself?"

"When my Long 9s couldn't miss, Skipper. If it were one of

our LCs, then she would have a .5c weapon. I'd fire at 200,000 klicks."

"I concur. Thanks, XO."

Jacob went back to the plot, watching the distance roll down. With his squadron breaking up at flank speed, it wouldn't be much longer for them to trigger the ambush.

"Comms, squadron orders. All ships, load MK XIVs and hold fire until my mark."

"Orders relayed and confirmed, sir," Abbott said.

If Jacob was right, and he was pretty sure he was, then he needed to preempt their ambush. Firing the EW weapons right before they intended to shoot him, and then counterattacking in the window where his ships were hidden. Of course, their ships would be hidden from him, too, but... if they didn't change course, then it wouldn't matter.

"Load the Long 9s and aim for these coordinates," he ordered. If Jacob were over there, he would place his ship in the middle of the four gravwakes. Making sure to have as much concealment as possible. He calculated the coordinates and sent them over to Brown.

"Aye, aye, sir," Brown said. "Long 9, load the shot and prepare to fire."

"Sir," Abbott announced, "squadron confirms MK XIVs loaded."

Jacob absently tapped on his chair, waiting for the range to drop. If he was right, they would fire one more torpedo volley, and then immediately attack. He raised his hand in anticipation.

"Third volley in space."

"Mark," Jacob ordered. All four of his destroyers fired the latest generation of electronic warfare torpedoes propelled by magnetic coils at seven hundred g's before micro gravcoils kicked in and continued their acceleration toward the enemy.

They wouldn't hit, and Jacob didn't need them to. The wall of electronic noise slammed down in front of them like a tsunami.

"Fire the Long 9s!" He dropped his hand signaling visually.

The destroyers fired as one. Nine kilograms of nano-reinforced tungsten shot down the twenty-nine-meter-long barrel at 30% the speed of light. Once in space, the steel shroud broke apart, launching the hardened tungsten arrow down range.

At the same time, the enemy ships starburst, changing course into four different directions, revealing... not a light cruiser, but a heavy cruiser. With more firepower than both groups of destroyers combined.

Six Long 9s fired from the heavy, along with eight quad-barreled 20mm, and four double-barreled 40mm turrets.

Kidd and *Apache* vanished in a burst of fire that blinded the other two ships in the squadron before any of their crew could abandon ship.

Interceptor bucked and wailed as two of the 20mm rounds struck her starboard side, renting a long furrow in her ablative armor. Two Long 9 rounds missed her by mere meters.

Justice made it through unaffected.

The heavy cruiser, though, bucked under the impact of all four Long 9s fired by DesRon 12. Megajoules of energy exploded into the 500-meter-long ship, turning it into a shining star for a half second, and when the light was gone, so was the ship.

Exercise complete, flashed across all the screens.

The main viewer blinked twice, replaced by the blue-white gem of Alexandria. The planet's northern hemisphere shined white from the thick blanket of snow from her overly harsh winter. Jacob removed his helmet, wiping his sweaty brow. Actual combat had been less stressful than the training scenario and he had no idea why.

"Do you want me to set up an AAR with the other ships'

commanders, Skipper?" Carter asked from the screen connected to Jacob's chair. He stared at him for a moment, realizing this was the second time Carter Fawkes had asked the question.

"Yes, Carter, with my compliments. Would you ask the COs of the squadron to meet me at Frosty's at eighteen-thirty?"

"Sounds like a lot more fun than what I'm going to be doing," Carter said with a smile. "Will do, sir."

———

Frosty's bore the sign of the Alliance Navy motto in ancient Latin—*Officium, Decus, Virtus*—curving around the top of a representation of Alexandria, while the Marine Corps traditional motto, *Semper Fidelis*, curled around the bottom. In the middle, it simply said Frosty's. Its design purposely looked like a ship's badge. While Jacob had never met the owner, the retired Marine master gunnery sergeant was well known. No one called him anything other than Frosty. Despite owning one of the most successful bars on Utopia, the rotund man who was a long way from PT still worked the bar, mixing drinks and serving his customers.

As Jacob walked in wearing his day uniform, he instantly regretted not changing into civilian clothing. It was Friday night on Utopia and the place was packed. Virtually everyone wore civilian clothing.

Great. Way to stick out.

Frosty's layout forced Jacob to walk through a crowd before finding his table in the back. All his worry, all his concern, vanished when he saw the other three captains of DesRon 12, all wearing their day uniforms. They looked sheepishly around as if they should have known better as well.

Jacob was just glad his first squadron command got along.

While he eventually made it work with Captain Hatwal, he didn't want to go through that kind of breaking-in period again.

That was probably why NavPer sent Lieutenant Commander Kimiko Yuki and *Apache* to be in his squadron, which he would be forever grateful for.

"Skipper," she said with a wave and a cheer. Next to her were the COs of *Kidd* and *Justice*. Commander Robert Carlos and Lieutenant Commander Sabrina Marsh.

Kim looked the same: a teenager wearing her mother's uniform. Despite that, once you looked beyond her diminutive form and youthful good looks, she had the countenance of a seasoned officer.

Robert Carlos didn't stand, simply nodded and smiled. The sun-weathered features of the man marked him as a New Austin native, and while they had served together as part of DesRon 9, Jacob hadn't ever figured out how they knew one another. Other than Commander Carlos acted as if they were long-lost friends, which was fine with him since Carlos was also his XO for DesRon 12.

Lieutenant Commander Marsh sat opposite Kim. She was a native of Alexandria, and therefore had the mixed heritage of a hundred ethnicities. Brown hair, brown eyes, light brown skin. She was taller than Kim, but almost everyone was. As far as Jacob could tell, she was competent and executed her orders efficiently. As far as he could tell... since she never said much, he still hadn't gauged her character completely.

"I have to say, this is quite a bit better place to have an AAR than the *Interceptor*'s briefing room... no offense," Commander Carlos said.

"None taken."

Kim moved to hug him, then remembered they were still in uniform and settled for a handshake.

"I forgot to tell you congratulations on having the top score for war college," he said.

She blushed fiercely, her Asian features growing even darker as he heaped praise on her.

"I wish I could take credit for it, but some damn fool officer gave me the crazy idea that warships should be aggressive and sneaky."

"I can't imagine who that would be," Jacob replied with a smile. He sat down next to her, waited a moment for their drinks to arrive before placing his NavPad on the table. "I know DesRon 15 thought they had us with their little maneuver, and in a way they still won—"

"Sir, we took out a heavy cruiser at the cost of two destroyers. That's a bargain at twice the price," Sabrina Marsh said, speaking up.

"I agree with Sabrina, sir," Kim said. "Destroyers don't win fist fights against heavy cruisers."

Jacob leaned back, not wanting to step on their enthusiasm for a job well done. And it was a job well done because they were right. No one in the navy, hell, in the entire Alliance military, would see what they accomplished against DesRon 15 as anything other than a victory—except the families of the two hundred and sixty men and women receiving letters from him.

He pulled up the holographic recording of the tactical view. It wasn't exactly accurate, as it was impossible for the computer to show what they did in a three-dimensional space with any kind of detail. Instead, it showed the four ships of DesRon 12 and 15 heading toward one another. In retrospect, the trap they set up was obvious.

"I know that we pulled off a miracle here. Though I should have suspected the trap sooner. The problem with fleet simulated engagements is..." He gestured for his officers to finish.

Marsh spoke up first. "They're simulated."

"Right. No matter how hard we try to treat them as real, they're not. I kept us in the lane far longer than I should have. If this were a real head-to-head engagement, what should I have done?" he asked.

Kim looked hard at him. He could feel her telling him he was being too hard on himself, but if he wasn't, who would be?

"The orders and ROE were pretty clear, Skipper," Kim said, using his honorific even though he wasn't her captain anymore. "System patrol and engage enemy forces. I'm not sure we could have done anything else."

Jacob nodded at her and then looked at Carlos. "Robert?"

Carlos smiled jovially. "I agree with Commander Yuki."

"Sabrina?" Jaco asked.

"I'll defer to the captain's judgement," she said.

Jacob rewound the holo from the destruction of the ships to the point where the engagement started at one million klicks.

"Yes, our ROE allowed us to engage enemy forces. However, a one-to-one engagement is a loss for us. This is the point where I should have broken off and used our superior starting velocity to escape the engagement envelope, or switched to hit-and-run tactics."

Robert shook his head, clearly disagreeing with Jacob's assessment of the battle.

"Sir, that would have been against our orders," Robert said.

"I know. As the squadron commander it's my duty to keep the ships operational. At the end of the day, taking out one heavy cruiser wouldn't matter one bit to the Caliphate. Losing four destroyers and their five hundred plus crew makes a difference to everyone in the Alliance. We don't have the throw weight to go one-on-one with them. We just don't."

He made eye contact with each of them, making sure they understood. "Now, let's take a look at the crew performance—"

The rest of the makeshift meeting followed a predictable

pattern. There were rough edges he needed to sand down from his command, but nothing dramatic. In fact, all his criticism pointed squarely at himself. When it was over, they all stood, shook hands, and headed out. All but Kim.

"Skipper—" she started.

He held up his hand. "I know what you're going to say, Kim."

"Then why do I need to say it, sir?"

"You don't—"

"Jacob. You can't save everyone. It's a war. People die in war. Unfairly, unjustly, unevenly. But more people die if we don't win the war."

Her statement hit him like a slap in the face. Leaning back, he tilted his head to look up at the ceiling. Frosty's had a mural of the constellations as seen from Alexander. They moved, he realized. The entirety of the ceiling shifted as Utopia's orbit shifted.

Kim was right, of course. People died in war. They died in service. He knew that better than most. However, like his mother, if he could save them, he would. Committing forces to a futile battle for no other reason than to win, wasn't winning.

"I'll think on it, Kim."

Her eyebrow quirked up as if she could see through him.

"Sure you will."

CHAPTER THREE

"Lights on."

Midship Yua Watanabe didn't recognize the voice, which was no surprise to her. After all, in a military prison, there was a different guard each day of the week. Sunlight flooded into her prison cell. Enough that she would receive the necessary vitamins and mental health benefits before it switched to normal light.

"Prisoners will stand clear."

That was new. Yua leaped up, coming to parade rest in the center of her room. There was an odd dissonance in her position. She was still nominally an officer. As a prisoner, though, she had to obey the orders of the noncommissioned officers, and even the privates, who stood watch.

A tall, wide Army soldier appeared in front of her cell. He wore the dark green of their branch, his hair mostly shorn, and his uniform neatly pressed.

"Watanabe, Yua, Midship. You have a visitor. Do as you're told, or you will be punished. Understood?"

"Yes, Staff Sergeant."

What followed was her standard day. She stood in the

middle of her cell while two female privates entered and mag-cuffed her hands to her side. A quick search of her body revealed no weapons, and then she was walking.

Ten minutes of guarded doors and secured lifts later, she entered a room with six booths. Each one had a seat and intercom with a privacy shield. Whoever was there could speak and see her, but not touch. The privacy shield allowed them to use whatever volume they wanted without disturbing the other prisoners, but the military corrections recorded every conversation.

She sat down, the screen between her and the guest still black. Once the privates unlocked her hands and backed away, the screen faded to transparency, and Yua gasped. For an instant, she smiled, happy to see a familiar face. Then he spoke.

"How the hell am I supposed to get you out of this?" he growled.

"Father, I'm sorry. You don't have to get me out. I'm—"

He interrupted her as if she hadn't spoken. "You have dishonored your family. Of course I have to get you out. If you are found guilty, it would cause incalculable damage to my business dealings. I sent you to the Navy to be an asset to our family enterprises, not a burden."

"Father, my commanding officer told me I need to accept responsibility for what has happened, for what I've done. I won't allow you to rob me of that."

Her father leaned back. For all her bravado, Yua suppressed a shudder of terror. Despite what she'd seen and experienced on Midway, Miriku Watanabe scared the crap out of her. She hadn't cared. Her father provided her with money, clothing, and swank rich people to party with. Only when she joined the Navy had her father's money and influence failed to provide for her. She had to take matters into her own hands.

"He sounds like an idiot. Is he why you're in prison? Did he order you to do something, then have you take the blame? Is that it?"

"No. I made my own mistakes and people died. That's on me."

Her father switched to her native tongue, spitting out a dismissive epitaph at her. "I don't care who made the mistakes. I won't have you dishonoring me and ruining my business."

He stood.

"I was at fault," she said again.

He turned his back on her.

She fervently prayed for him to look at her one more time. Her prayers went unanswered as he left.

Yua put her hand on the screen, not realizing how truly alone she was until that moment.

CHAPTER FOUR

Jacob double-timed up the steps to the command hall at Melinda Grimm Naval Base. His XO, Lieutenant Carter Fawkes, ran behind him, pulling at his uniform as if he knew a drill instructor would leap out of the shadows and drop him for having his nameplate wrong.

"Carter, relax."

"Skipper, you might be used to the brass, but there are more stars on these uniforms than there are in the sky."

Jacob grinned at his response, half turning to clap him on the shoulder. "You'll be fine."

Once at the top of the stairs, massive double doors hung open and several Marines manned security scanners. Crowds of officers stood in lines, passing through the scanners one by one.

"Any idea what's going on, sir?" Carter whispered to him.

Jacob didn't turn back to answer him, just pitched his voice low. "If I had to guess, we're getting our war footing on. After Medial, we've given the Caliphate a one-two punch they won't soon forget."

They waited the next twenty minutes in line, observing

those around them. Carter was the only rank he saw below commander. Most were captains and admirals.

"Commander Grimm?" a familiar voice called out to him, but he couldn't place it. He turned to look where it was coming from and saw a smiling Captain Hatwal.

"Captain, so good to see you," he said, holding out his hand.

Hatwal took it and shook. "You remember my XO, Commander Ban?"

"No, not at all. Doesn't ring a bell," Jacob said with a deadpan expression.

"Funny. Look, same rank now," Archer said, tapping his silver oak leaf.

"Congratulations, it couldn't have happened to a nicer guy."

They laughed and shook hands, and Jacob drew the man into a quick hug and clapped his back.

"How's *Firewatch*?" Jacob asked as the line started moving again.

"Fully repaired and ready to get back in it," Hatwal said with a proud look.

"And the rest of DesRon 9?"

"Good to go. I heard they gave you a squadron as well?" Hatwal asked.

"So far, it's a training command. We've been playing OpFor two other squadrons."

Hatwal laughed. "You are very good at that."

"I have my moments, sir."

The line moved, and it was Jacob's turn. He showed his NavPad and the Marines carefully scrutinized it before letting him pass. He waved to Hatwal and Ban before collecting Carter and following the Marines' directions to the auditorium.

The circular building lay at the heart of the base. Large enough to house over four hundred personnel, it was used for mass briefings that needed to happen in person. Of course, orders could be sent over NavPad, and often were.

This was a strategy meeting, though, with questions possible, and Jacob was eager to be there. He'd only ever attended low-level ones in the past.

"Sir." Carter pointed at a row of chairs near the top, forty rows, each marked.

"Right, just a commander among brass," Jacob said to himself.

They climbed the stairs, taking their time as the giant room was still filling up. At the bottom of the amphitheater-like design, he spotted SECNAV DeBeck sitting next to the president's chief of staff, Leilani Kahale. Jacob only met her the one time, but the Ohana native seemed sharp and excellent at her job.

He found his seat and rested the NavPad in his lap, ready to take notes. The device blinked from an incoming call.

Jacob held it up and answered.

"Hey, handsome, where are you?" Nadia asked.

"High-level strategy meeting on base. You?"

"Trying on dresses with my mom. You don't know how thrilled she is that someone is finally making an honest woman of me."

Jacob blushed a little at her words. "Tell her not to get too excited. You'll never be honest."

"Oh, you're going to pay for that. I'll meet you there when you're done. We can grab dinner?"

"Sounds good," he said. Nadia's eyes took on a serious lilt for a moment, as if she wanted to say more, but then the moment passed.

The image vanished just as the lights in the auditorium went dim. Jacob placed it back on his lap.

A young woman with blonde hair and a crisp uniform

walked stiffly onto the stage. She carried nothing with her, but the stage was set up in such a way that anyone speaking on it would be heard by the entirety of the audience.

"Ladies and gentlemen, the SECNAV," she said.

Admiral (Ret.) Wit DeBeck rose, even though he wore a blue, two-button suit with a slim collar, as was the latest trend, Jacob still saw him in uniform. He wondered, if he ever retired, would he always look like a former Navy captain?

DeBeck took center stage and cleared his throat.

"Now that the war is official, voted on, and proceeding, I can bring you all up to speed on the latest of the goings-on of the Caliphate."

Wit spoke for ten minutes, laying out what had happened so far, the Alliance's successes and failures, equally dispassionate about both. He did not include the *Interceptor* in either of his descriptions of the raid on Medial or the disabling of the enemy's FTLC. Most everyone in the audience hadn't even known the Caliph Navy had FTLC. A hushed round of murmurs rippled through the room at the mention of it.

Wit held up his hands. "Please. I know it's a revelation and a half, but what's done is done."

An admiral Jacob didn't recognize, and who clearly had pull considering he was seated in the second row, spoke up, his voice amplified by the auditorium.

"Did you stop to think we could have used that information? How many sneak attacks did the Consortium endure that we could have prevented?"

DeBeck stared back at the admiral, his steely gaze unwavering.

"The answer is: none. We knew only that they had it, and that was all. They no longer have it, nor will they ever have it again. Or at least in our lifetime."

"How can we be sure?" someone shouted.

Jacob squirmed in his seat. If he were giving the briefing and his junior officers just shouted questions, he'd come down on them like a railgun. No, he wouldn't have to. His XO would have, and if it were enlisted, the Bosun would. Then again, FTLC was quite a stunning revelation.

"I'm not here to debate the past," Wit said. "If you have official questions, run them up the chain of command. I'm here to make sure we're all on the same page going forward." Wit paused, looking over the audience with his unshakable gaze. Jacob had met the man more than once, and he wouldn't ever want to be on the receiving end of that look.

"Utopia has completed construction of a new Legion-class battleship, USS *Whirlwind*. Plus a brand-new class of battleship we're calling Guardian. Her name is the USS *Pegasus*."

A flurry of whispers filled the auditorium.

"Two, Skipper? I had only heard of the *Whirlwind*?" Carter whispered.

"I think they did a good job of keeping it under wraps," Jacob whispered back to his XO.

The SECNAV continued, and if he was bothered by the commotion, he didn't show it. "The shipyards at New Austin, Weber's World, and Seabring are ramping up production on destroyers and cruisers, but they are lagging. Mostly because we're still recovering from the lack of manufacturing capability. Now that Blackrock, Novus, and Zuckabar are providing raw materials en masse, we expect that to change. This also makes them prime targets."

The screen behind him flared to life showing a dozen Alliance planets. Jacob recognized several: Vishnu, Blackrock, Zuckabar Central—an unconscious shiver ran through him at the thought of the frozen hellhole—Sebring, and Weber's World.

"These are the planets that we think are the most likely to

come under attack. Notice that Alexander isn't on the list. Our emplaced defenses and distance from the border would make it difficult for an assault force to make it here. Barring a *stealth* ship, we're safe. That brings you all up to date. I will now turn the rest of this briefing over to Fleet Admiral Villanueva."

Everyone in the room stood sharply, snapping to attention. There wasn't a single soul in the entire Navy that she didn't outrank.

"As you were," she said. The audience seated.

Jacob was glad to see her looking well. Even though the stage was far away, she had a spring in her step, like she'd had a good night's sleep.

SECNAV DeBeck nodded to her before brushing past to retake his seat.

"Thank you, Mr. DeBeck. I believe we're all on the same page. For OpSec reasons we're having this briefing here, and with a few exceptions, nowhere else. Let's not underestimate the enemy's intelligence capability, or who the enemy is."

Jacob glanced around to see if anyone else reacted to the odd way she phrased her statement.

"The Caliphate is bottlenecked at Praetor. With TF 16 taking Medial, and the Consortium's reinforcements coming online, they are spread thin. It appears they relied heavily on their FTLC tech"—Jacob felt like she looked right at him—"and without it, they've withdrawn to avoid attacks for the time being. This gives us breathing room, but no time to relax."

She waved her hand and the massive hologram of the planets shifted, replaced by a fuzzy image of a TRN battleship. The logo of the Terran Republic was still fresh on the side.

"This is the only physical intel we have on the Guild's new ships. If they're coming from the Terran Republic, we might have to worry about them as an ally. For now, exercise caution when encountering any of their ships. We don't expect this to be a problem, but... our intel has always been spotty where the Guild is concerned. We are actively working to correct that."

She paused, taking a sip of her water before breathing in to continue the briefing.

"This is how we're going to distribute the fleet, while assembling enough forces to go on the offense—"

Her screen spiraled out to show multiple new task forces and groups. Some were sent on long-range patrol, others stationed at new home ports. The most noticeable change was *Alexandria* and her consorts moving to Zuckabar. Jacob couldn't quite wrap his mind around Alexander as *safe* as the admiral thought. However, he had to guess if the Guild had another stealth ship, they would have used it by now.

The amassed collections of admirals and captains were briefed on their new orders, and then it was over. Lights returned and Jacob took a second to rub his eyes as they had adjusted to the dimmer conditions.

"Skip, we're not on their assignment list," Carter said.

"You noticed that, huh?"

"Commander Grimm?"

Jacob turned to see a startling young ensign waiting for him. "Yes, Ensign Colfax?"

"Sir, Admiral Villanueva requests your presence at her office in thirty minutes."

"Of course. Let her know we'll be there."

There was no doubt in his mind what waited for him. They were going to send him on another secret mission. And he'd just gotten used to the idea of commanding a squadron.

———

Melinda Grimm Naval Base had underground transit for moving from building to building and it took Jacob all of ten minutes to get to the command HQ. Carter silently followed, but Jacob felt the pressure from the young man.

"Go ahead and speak, Carter," he said as they ascended the stairs out of the tunnels.

"Sir, it's just... and mind you, I'm grateful for everything I've learned with you..."

Jacob understood what bothered him. Regardless of what branch of the military a person served, spy missions and secret squirrel business wasn't good for an officer's career. When huge swaths of your jacket were blacked out, it slowed promotion and made other officers unwilling to trust you.

Promotion wasn't an issue for Jacob. Commander was the highest rank he would ever achieve. Part of him wondered what his *junior* officers would think when they outranked him. Would he live to serve under Admiral Fawkes?

"Secret missions don't make promotions, I know," Jacob said. Carter seemed relieved he understood. "There's nothing I can do about it, though. I wouldn't worry about it. Admiral Villanueva is a good officer; she'll make sure those involved will be rewarded."

"Aye, sir, understood."

Outside the admiral's office, a chief petty officer worked diligently at a desk. He noticed the two officers and stood. "Commander, she's expecting you. Just you," he said.

"Thank you, Chief. Carter," he said, turning to his XO, "why don't you go see what the building's mess has to offer?"

"Aye, aye, sir." Carter grinned like a man set free from the death penalty. Scurrying off, he found his way out in a hurry.

"It will be just a moment. She's in there with Admiral Thomas—"

"No, I don't understand," a man bellowed. His voice loud enough to pierce the walls.

Chief Kim glanced down at his desk. A slight red flickered on his cheeks. "Sorry sir," he said.

"No need to apologize, Chief. Admirals are above our mortal understanding," Jacob said with a grin.

The chief understood and wisely went back to his work. A moment later, a tall black man with the rank of two-star admiral stormed out. He passed Grimm with an eye, as if he knew Jacob, but didn't stop to acknowledge his presence.

Jacob took a deep breath and let it out slowly as the furious admiral departed.

"She's ready to see you now."

Jacob steeled himself and marched in.

The admiral, as commanding as ever, sat behind a simple ubiquitous metal desk. Her NavPad projection lit up her face with blue and green light. He stopped in the middle of the office, came to attention, and spoke.

"Commander Grimm reporting as ordered."

"At ease, Commander," she said with a smile.

It hadn't been his imagination; she really looked better.

"You appear well, ma'am."

"Victory agrees with me. It's easier to get the sleep you need when you know your side is winning. By the way"—she pointed at her NavPad—"I spoke with Admiral Webster. He didn't mince words about your roll in saving TF 16, but your official report gave the credit to Lieutenant Boudreaux?"

Jacob stifled his surprise at the conversation. The battle for Medial was months before. Before the secret mission to Zephyr.

"Credit where credit's due, ma'am."

"You would say that," she murmured. "Regardless, well done. I also see your training command is performing well. Good on you for taking that seriously. I know some officers look at that situation as a punishment, and I hope you haven't."

Now he couldn't hide his surprise. "Punishment, ma'am?

I'm lucky to serve with some of the best, and we've only gotten better."

"Good. Those officers are the future of the Navy. Would you be surprised to learn that everyone who serves with you earns promotions at a higher rate than the fleet average?"

She implied it was somehow due to him, but he didn't think that was true at all. They were just good people who wanted to do their jobs. Even if sometimes he had to show them how and give them a little kick in the aft section.

"NavPer sends me good people, ma'am."

"NavPer," she scoffed. "If it were up to NavPer, you would be the only person assigned to *Interceptor*."

"Ma'am?"

"Jacob, I've told you before, your enemies are imbedded in the military and the political realm. You don't even know the toes you've stepped on by succeeding. The people you've crossed and exposed."

"I am so confused, ma'am. I'm just a Navy captain. I don't know how I could step on anyone's toes... other than the enemy that is."

She nodded, hitting a key on her NavPad. "When you uncovered the human trafficking ring in Zuckabar, there were arrests on every planet between here and the Iron Empire. Entire corporations fell and thousands of people lost their jobs. When the Guild was kicked out of the Alliance, hundreds if not thousands of politicians across the Alliance lost a significant amount of their campaign funding. The list goes on. I've hand-selected your officers since the beginning, trying to get you people who would thrive under your leadership."

That begged the question, in Jacob's mind, about Watanabe.

"Ma'am, if you don't mind my asking, how's Midship Watanabe?"

She leaned back, waving her screen over to show the image of the midship, telling Jacob she knew he would ask about her. He didn't know whether to be impressed with her foresight or upset at his predictability.

"On paper, she was exactly the kind of officer we needed in the Alliance. JAG is investigating what happened at the Academy to allow her through. I would like to say it was an isolated incident... I would like to." She frowned, as if seeing something Jacob couldn't.

"Having met her, ma'am, I can tell you she's quite persuasive. I haven't received a formal letter of notification, though, about the court-martial?" Even with the severity of her crimes, Jacob didn't want to see her executed, which was one of many punishments, since they were at war.

"I've heard of her powers of persuasion. JAG is still investigating and will proceed when they can. As for you, I wanted to tell you in person. I know there are a lot of ships in the area and they're all heading out on different missions. With the new fleet distribution, I didn't want you to think that I had forgotten you."

Jacob braced himself for bad news. Was she sending *Interceptor* on another secret mission? Ordering her to escort duty far from the front? He didn't crave combat, but he wanted to do his part to help win the war.

Villanueva glanced up from her NavPad. "For now, I need you and *Interceptor* where they are, training a squadron and playing OpFor."

He hid his disappointment, not well, but he hid it.

CHAPTER FIVE

A military court, and specifically the Navy, had their own traditions dating back a thousand years or more. Most officers only saw the inside of any legal wrangling when they were picked for the court. When Jacob and Nadia were finally let into the room, he was surprised at how many people were attending. Midship Watanabe wasn't a politician's daughter, her parents weren't in the Navy, yet as he walked in, he spotted no less than three captains, an admiral, and two senators. Along with several members of the media.

"Is this odd?" he whispered to Nadia. "I feel like this is odd."

"I've attended celebrity parties with less famous guests," she replied.

As the defendant's former captain, Jacob was ushered to the prosecution's side. Though he stopped in the middle of the aisle. While he firmly believed and acknowledged Yua's guilt, he also wanted to make sure she received a fair trial. He knew part of that was the fact that the Navy had given her a raw deal by allowing her to breeze through the academy.

While it was a custom for those on the accusing side to sit

behind the prosecutor and *vice versa*, Jacob wanted to show the court, and Yua, that her commanding officer stood with her.

"There," he said, pointing at an empty row behind the defense table. Nadia quirked an eyebrow at him but dutifully followed. There were days where she still used a cane, and today was one of them. It took them a moment to edge down the narrow pews.

Jacob figured, all in all, maybe a hundred people could fit in the room.

Ensign Brennan entered, her coppery red hair catching his attention while he looked around. A moment of shock hit him, but it passed as quickly. Brennan saw him and smiled. Her cheeks heating in the process as if she were embarrassed to be there. He was glad Yua had more support than just him and he nodded to the seat behind him and Nadia.

After a few moments of indecision, she took a seat behind her commander.

Jacob turned. "Good to see you here, Fionna."

"Thank you, sir. I can't imagine how scary this has all got to be, and I thought... well, I thought a friendly face might help."

Before Jacob could respond, the courtroom security officer shouted. "All rise for the honorable Admiral Silva, presiding judge."

If Admiral Silva had undergone the regenerative ageing treatments, Jacob couldn't tell. There was a subset of people who it didn't work on, or who refused to have it done for some moral or religious reason. Silva, though, had long salt-and-pepper hair wound into an intricate bun that rested atop her head. She wasn't much taller than Nadia, but her commanding presence demanded respect as she entered the chamber and took her place on the bench.

"As you were," she said, and everyone in the room took their seats. Her eyes caught Jacob's for a moment with a questioning look. The moment passed, and he wondered if he'd imagined it.

Silva motioned for the bailiff who opened the door opposite the main door. Two spacers first class with the armbands of shore patrol escorted Midship Yua. She wore her service dress black. They looked brand new and were probably fabricated that morning.

Yua marched to the defense table, eyes straight ahead, blocking out everything, and came to a halt. She made a left-face and stood at attention in front of the judge.

"Midship Yua Watanabe reporting as ordered, ma'am."

Admiral Silva eyed the young woman up and down, looking for any flaws in her uniform or countenance.

"I'm glad you're taking these proceedings seriously, Miss Midship. While this is just our preliminary hearing, it would go well for you to continue to show such professionalism and military decorum throughout. Understood?"

"Aye, ma'am, understood."

"Good. At ease and have a seat."

Only then did Yua turn and see Jacob for the first time. Her eyes went big as she looked at him and realized he was sitting behind her seat. She composed herself and walked behind the desk and sat down at attention.

Her lawyer barely noticed; his nose buried in his NavPad as he went over the case.

"CSO, read the charges," Admiral Silva ordered.

Jacob knew from reading about the court they would bring the charges from lesser to greater. He just hoped they weren't throwing *The Book* at her.

"Midship Yua Watanabe, you stand accused of the following crimes. All taking place aboard the USS *Interceptor,* or the planet known as Midway, during your time serving aboard the USS *Interceptor*. Do you understand?"

"Aye, CSO, I do," she said.

"Charge and specification one: Failure to Obey an Order or Regulation. During the aforementioned cruise, you were ordered to stand down and return to your cabin by Ensign Brennan, which you refused. Charge and specification two: Conduct Unbecoming an Officer. Though you served as a midship, your time is calculated as an officer. Your actions regarding yourself and deceased co-conspirator—Spacer Blachowicz—were in direct violation of your responsibilities as an officer."

The list went on, and with each new charge Jacob winced. They were all terrible. Any single one of the charges was enough to land her in prison for years. The last two, though, were the ones Jacob was concerned about the most.

"Charge and specification nine and ten: Involuntary Manslaughter. During your cruise and in the process of desertion, you unintentionally caused the death of Spacer Karl Blachowicz and Spacer First Class Maxwell Jean Cooper. While neither's death was by your hand, your actions, and yours alone, were directly the cause of their death."

A hush came over the courtroom and Jacob resisted the urge to say something, anything, in her defense. These proceedings were necessary to the wellbeing of the whole Navy, yet it put him in an impossible situation. Cooper's death demanded justice, and to a lesser extent, so did Blachowicz's, but Yua, while certainly responsible for both, wasn't entirely culpable.

"How do you plead?"

Yua Watanabe stood to attention. She had two options. Plead guilty and throw herself on the mercy of the court, or not guilty and hope during the proceedings to bring evidence to show mitigating circumstance. If Jacob could advise her, it would be the former.

"On advice from my counsel..." She took a deep breath. "Not guilty."

A murmur ran through the crowd, not enough to warrant the judge intervening, but to Jacob the current in the room was palatable. He'd hoped she would plead guilty.

"Midship Watanabe," Admiral Silva began, "do you understand that by entering this not-guilty plea, a trial by your peers will commence, and if found guilty of these charges, the penalty of death may be applied?"

Yua shook, squeezing her hands tight, her shoulder blades straining hard as she forced her back straight.

"Aye, ma'am. I do."

"Very well. CSO, enter the plea of not guilty. The trial will commence as soon as the convening authority and the JAG office can arrange for a twelve-member court that will hear the charges. The court shall convene not later than one month from today. Court dismissed."

Jacob reached forward and squeezed Yua's shoulder, letting her know she wasn't alone. She turned her head and mouthed "thank you" as the security team took her away.

He leaned back next to Nadia, letting out a long breath. "That could have gone better."

"Those are serious charges, Jacob. Are you sure you want to be standing with her?"

He glanced her way, surprised that she would say such a thing.

"She was a part of my crew," he said, as if that explained everything.

"I'm not saying you're wrong," she said, holding up her hands in mock surrender. "I'm saying the implications here run deep and some of this could rub off on you. It's not like you have a sterling reputation to back you up."

Jacob almost laughed, catching himself in the last second,

and it came out as a cough. The idea never occurred to him. Standing up for Watanabe was the right thing to do. Why would anyone who wasn't there care one bit about what he did?

"Captain Grimm?" a woman said.

Jacob looked up into the sad eyes of an older woman. She looked lost, alone, and he knew exactly who she was.

"Ma'am," he said, standing instantly and taking her hand. "I hope you received my letter, along with Chief Boudreaux's?" he asked.

Belinda Cooper smiled softly at him and patted his hand. "I did. Along with half a dozen others, including a list of foods my son loved from a PO named Mendez. That was sweet."

Jacob gestured to Nadia. "This is Chief—"

"I'm retired, just Nadia Dagher now," she said.

"Nadia Dagher," Jacob said.

"Did you serve with my son?" she asked.

"No, ma'am, but I can tell you he helped save my life," Nadia said reverently.

Mrs. Cooper looked away for a moment, watching Yua be escorted out of the room. "It's hard not to hate her, but my son wouldn't have wanted that."

Jacob stepped out of the pew, followed by Nadia. He still held Mrs. Cooper's hand and guided her out of the courtroom.

"Max was a good man. He died doing what he loved and serving his nation. I know those words don't bring comfort, but they're still true."

She looked up at him, a look that nearly broke his heart. He knew it all too well. Too well.

"From anyone else, I would think that, but from you... thank you."

Jacob walked her out of the building and down to a waiting aircar. She hugged him fiercely before departing.

The winter cold nipped at him as he watched her aircar disappear.

"Do you ever get used to it?" Nadia asked.

"The cold?"

"No, the letters."

He knew what she'd meant. As a man who took his duty seriously, and often relished the little things duty demanded, like the formalities and ceremonies, it was one thing he could do without.

"No. The day I do is the day it's time to retire. They are both a terrible privilege of rank and a punishment for failure."

Nadia studied him with her trademark poker face. He couldn't tell what she thought from minute to minute unless she wanted him to. It wasn't fair, he thought.

"You're a strange man, Commander Grimm."

"You wouldn't be the first to say that, just the prettiest."

"Flattery will get you everywhere."

He quirked an eyebrow at her. "Well then, my dear, will it get me to dinner with you?"

———

Petty Officer Josh Mendez held his NavPad up, going over the incoming order. Interceptor orbited above Alexandria, docked with a fleet supply ship as spacers and apprentices unloaded the foodstuffs and other provisions, he would need for the next six weeks.

"PO, looking good?" Bosun Sandivol asked.

"Aye, Bosun. Looking good. I've got everything I requested and then some. I feel like supply and logistics know something we don't," he said with a grin.

Bosun frowned, looking down at his NavPad and then back at Josh. "They just might. There's another ship coming in after this one with ammo and ordnance—" his NavPad alerted him again. "And one more with personnel. Don't get comfortable PO, I think we're heading out."

Josh frowned. He planned on taking some of his accrued leave to go home and see his family. He hadn't seen New Austin in years, and while vids to his family were nice, he was sure his mama would like to see him in person. Then there was the matter of Ensign Lopez's family. He owed them a visit as well. He would have done all of that if *Interceptor* had stayed in the dock another six weeks as planned.

"Aye, aye, Chief, no rest for the wicked."

————

Captain Paul Bonds looked up as the sound of his MarPad notified him new orders were coming through.

"What?" Normally he would have known this was happening long before it did. He'd spent the time since the fall of Medial with the logistics corps, doing a tour as an admin, which he hated. He was a fighting man. Filling out forms and sitting on his thumbs during a war was a waste of his time. He'd thought that after the conquering of Medial, he would be awarded with another combat tour, but Marine command wanted to groom him for higher rank.

Something he didn't want at all.

The notification sounded again. Paul placed his thumb on the reader, unlocking the MarPad. The holo function activated showing him a floating copy of his orders while the anthem of the Marine Corps played softly in the background.

"Well damn. Welcome home, Paul," he said.

CHAPTER SIX

Jacob rocked his squeaky command chair back and forth as he waited for the computer to spit out the results. He already knew the outcome. His ship, the entire squadron, was dead. Blown up by superior enemy forces in a worthless bid to defend Alexandria.

There were some things destroyers couldn't do. Stopping battleships was at the top of the list. However, it was a good object lesson for him and his training command. People died, just like Kim had told him before. He refused to believe there wasn't something he could have done better, thought of faster—some clever tactics that would win the day. Faced with overwhelming odds, though, the only victory was survival.

"Crew efficiency rating at 92%, Skipper," Carter said from the MFD attached to the command chair. The real challenge was keeping the crew going, keeping them performing at their peak even knowing that death was almost certain.

The screen split into four, three squares for each skipper of DesRon 12's destroyers and one for Carter.

"Our crews performed admirably, though in the end, it

wasn't enough," he told them. "What could we have done differently to impact the outcome?"

Part of his command involved training captains for combat. As strange as it was to Jacob, he had more ship-to-ship combat time than any other skipper in the fleet. Though the gap closed rapidly as the war raged on.

"I don't see how, sir," Commander Marsh said. "That was a battleship. We couldn't have known until we engaged and by then it was too late." Marsh glanced down, as if she suddenly remembered she didn't enjoy speaking. It was a challenge to get her to offer her opinion, and Jacob admired her willingness to speak first.

"Noted. Does everyone agree?" he asked. They did. He continued: "I'm sure you're right, Sabrina. However, I would like each of you to get with your command crew and brainstorm some ideas on how we could have turned that battle around. If not victory, survival. Agreed?"

"Aye, sir," they said. Their images vanished, leaving Jacob wondering if he made the right call.

"Sir," Spacer Abbott interrupted, "priority message from Fleet HQ. Order packet on your screen now."

"Thank you, Sean," Jacob said.

The seal of the Department of the Navy appeared on his screen.

Commander Jacob T. Grimm, USS Interceptor, *you and DesRon 12 are hereby ordered and directed to transport Ambassador Nguyen. You will depart no later than 24 hours from receipt of these orders and proceed at best speed to Cordoba. Render any and all assistance to the ambassador as duty allows. A more detailed Op-order will follow.*

-Fleet Admiral Villanueva

. . .

Jacob focused on the orders for a long moment. Confusion, followed by curiosity, flooded his mind. Why send *Interceptor* to escort an ambassador? Let alone all of DesRon 12. Why not tell him in person when he'd just met with the admiral?

"Sean, acknowledge receipt in the log and send a message back confirming the orders."

"Aye, aye, sir."

They were sparse to say the least. Normally, orders came with all kinds of flowery language to account for any situation. Maybe that would be in the op-orders? Jacob shared them with Carter.

"Can you find out what ship we are escorting?" he asked his XO.

"I don't know, sir, it kind of seems like he's going to be aboard *Interceptor*, doesn't it?"

Jacob read the orders again and, sure enough, they did read like he would be on his ship. But why? *Interceptor*'s size prohibited any guest accommodations and—

"Sir," Abbott interrupted. "A Corsair is requesting docking permission with the starboard airlock."

"That was fast. Is it the ambassador?"

In an emergency, the Navy could move with alacrity, but this surprised him.

"No, sir, he says he's the company commander of the Marine contingent."

"Marine contingent?" Jacob asked. Poor Abbott didn't know if he should confirm what his CO was asking or stay silent. "Never mind, give them permission. Carter, have Gunny meet me in the mess with you. Roy, you have the conn."

"Aye, aye, sir, Ops has the conn."

Jacob jumped out of his chair, legs powered by curiosity as

he hit the ladders and slid down to the next deck. By the time he entered the mess, the airlock cycled green and slid open. Jennings moved right behind him like his shadow.

Captain Paul Bonds, in all his Marine glory, entered with two Marines behind him.

He stopped, standing ramrod straight, and performed a parade ground salute.

"Permission to come aboard, sir?"

Jacob returned it just as well executed.

"Granted. Paul, it's good to see you. What are you doing here?"

Captain Bonds paused for a moment, glancing around like he'd come home. "You don't know?" he asked.

Jacob waved him to follow. "Carter, get with the Bosun and find these Marines a rack."

"Aye, aye, sir."

Paul fell in behind Jacob as they headed for the O-deck and the briefing room.

"Good to see you, Gunny," Bonds said.

"Thank you, sir."

"You know Captain Ferro still wants you for Recon."

"He has made that clear, sir. I'm fine where I am."

Paul remained silent while they ascended the ladders.

When they turned to go to the briefing room, he said, "All I know, sir, is that I received orders this morning to report to *Interceptor* and join DesRon 12 as their Marine company commander."

"How many marines?" Jacob asked as he took his seat at the head of the shark-painted table.

"Two hundred total once the transport arrives."

Had he heard him right? Two hundred Marines and transport? Marine Transport Ships (MTS) were speedy, lightly armored ships loaded with Marines and equipment. If he recalled correctly, they were basically a company in a can.

"Why?" he asked.

Paul snorted. "Hell, skipper, you know as much as I do at this point. Marine command says jump, I say what planet? The MTS is the *Jack Coughlin,* and it carries Charlie-Seven-Five... my company."

"Of course, I'm just playing catch up here," Jacob said.

Jacob tapped the table, bringing up the orders in a holo display, along with any information the computer had about Ambassador Nguyen.

"Is that the man?"

Jacob frowned as he read the bio. "It says here he's the ambassador to Terra, but the orders mentioned a place called Cordoba," he said.

"Skipper, Admiral Villanueva is on the line for you sir," Abbott said.

"Put her through."

The admiral appeared on his NavPad's holo function, or her head did anyway.

"I know you were expecting to stay in-system," she said with no preamble, "but the situation has changed. Ambassador Nguyen has called in a favor above my paygrade. I tried to keep you here, but Admiral Thomas made some good points and I need him on my side. Your squadron is the only one I've got to spare that meets his requirements."

Political favors and machinations were all too familiar to Jacob. He'd watched good careers die because of them and felt the effects on his own more than once.

"Aye, ma'am. Can do. Might I ask, though, why the troop ship?"

Villanueva looked at something off screen for a moment, her eyes scanning a document from what he could tell.

"Cordoba's president has requested a JTE with the Alliance ground and space forces. The ambassador thinks he can get them to join us in the war. While their army is small, their strategic location for trade would make them a valuable asset in the long run. Do whatever he needs and assist in any way possible."

"Aye, aye, ma'am." The line vanished, and he was left alone with his thoughts. A mission was a mission, and whether they were in Alexandria or Cordoba, it was all the same.

He keyed his comms to the bridge. "Roy, sound the return. It looks like we're going on a trip."

CHAPTER SEVEN

"Do you know when you'll be back?" Nadia asked. She sat on Jacob's bed, her Pad nestled in her lap, surrounded by his things in his room on the ranch, with his blanket over her shoulders to ward off the cold.

He looked up at her from the Pad, a perfect real-time image of him, even though he was in orbit.

"I'm sorry, I don't. I want to say no more than two months, but..." He shrugged. They both understood life in the Navy. Long deployments and absence weren't anything new.

"It's okay," she said with a smile, placing her fingers on the image. "I'll keep myself busy helping your dad with the ranch. Mom wanted to come see the land, anyway."

Jacob cocked his head to the side, as if he were trying to parse the meaning behind her words.

"You're working on the ranch? That's a sight I would pay to see."

"Hey, mister, I'm quite capable."

"I don't think anyone doubts that at this point."

He had to go; she could tell. Her own time in the Navy held a hundred similar conversations. They always felt too short and, at the same time, too long.

"I've got a favor to ask you," he said. She could tell he was hesitant to ask, almost reluctant to ask.

"Whatever you need, I'm here for you."

"It's about Watanabe. Yua is going to need someone looking out for her. If I were in-system, it would be me. Can you do that?"

"You mean give her moral support while snooping to make sure she gets a fair trial? Sounds like you need a spy for that."

"Or an ex-spy. Thank you, Nadia. See you soon."

"Goodbye, handsome. Hurry back."

She closed the call before he could respond, preferring the quick clean cut to the delayed, drawn-out farewell. They had said what needed to be said, anything more only added pain.

Before she could move, her NavPad beeped again. Surprise rolled through her. Had Jacob forgotten something?

She turned on the screen, frowning. "SECNAV DeBeck, how can I help you?" she asked.

CHAPTER EIGHT

Commander Jacob T. Grimm, Lieutenant Carter Fawkes, and Ensign Fionna Brennan were decked out in full mess dress and standing at the customary line designating the beginning of the ship. Behind them, Bosun Sandivol had five of his best spacers, also wearing their dress uniforms to add to the pomp of the moment. Off to one side, Gunny Jennings and Bravo-Two-Five were decked out in Marine glory.

"Boat bay, stand clear for arrival. Stand clear for arrival," Spacer Klaus said, his voice reverberating around the large room. Yellow lights flashed and the Richman Field's blue indistinct haze snapped to life with an audible crackle of energy. The massive doors cracked open like a clamshell, revealing space beneath them and the hovering Corsair.

"Detail," Bosun Sandivol said. "Atten-shun!" The gathered crew snapped to attention as the Corsair's thrusters pushed her up through the open door to hover inside the bay. Chief Boudreaux's unhappy visage manned the controls as she waited for Spacer Klaus to close the doors. Once they were sealed shut, she lowered the dropship down into a gentle landing.

PO Mendez shot forward as the side doors slid open. He placed the step stool down for the civilians disembarking the dropship. Navy or Marine personnel would have just dropped to the deck, but civilians, Jacob knew, preferred the easy life. Otherwise, they wouldn't be civilians.

Ambassador Nguyen exited first. He wasn't a tall or a wide man. Average would be how Jacob described him. Perfectly normal. His wife was next, and she matched him well. Four more people, aides, Jacob imagined, exited the boat. He frowned as they did so. They were young, otherwise they wouldn't be assistants to an ambassador. The oldest was maybe twenty-five. Two men, two women. One of them caught his eye. Call it a danger sense, or just his experience as an officer, but he knew she was trouble the moment she stepped off the Corsair.

She held out her hand for Josh to help her down and he practically fell over himself doing so. She was pretty, with the figure the young have. Her long blonde hair fell in twin braids and a few pieces dangled in her face. Her allure was undeniable, and it sent a shiver of worry down Jacob's spine. Destroyers were small, tight-knit ships. Having civilians aboard was bad enough. Having a woman aboard who would undoubtedly be showered with attention was worse.

Her eyes caught him looking at her, and a playful smile adorned her lips along with the barest hint of red against her cheeks. Jacob glanced away quickly, cursing himself for a fool. Now she would think he was staring at her.

That was a problem for future Jacob, though. He had to deal with the here and now. Ambassador Nguyen stopped at the customary mark, a good sign that he'd traveled aboard ship before.

"Permission to come aboard, Captain?" he asked in a light voice.

"Granted, Mr. Ambassador. It's a pleasure to have you aboard. I'm afraid *Interceptor* is a bit lacking in accommodations for civilians. I've had the Bosun fabricate more comfortable bedding for you, and we've outfitted my stateroom for your visit."

"That's fine, Captain. This is my wife Sara," Nguyen said.

Sara placed her hand on her chest and looked shocked. "Captain, we're putting you out of your own room?"

Jacob couldn't help but smile. "No, ma'am, it's the Navy's room, not mine. I'll be fine. We aren't outfitted for carrying VIPs, but while you're aboard, my crew and I will do everything in our power to make the journey comfortable and convenient for you. This is Ensign Brennan, if you have any issues or need assistance, don't hesitate to call her."

Brennan piped in, "Day or night, ma'am."

She smiled back at him and hugged her husband around the shoulders.

"Captain, I understand this is out of the ordinary, but believe me, you're saving me months of travel. Via civilian transport this is a two-month journey and I already spend four months out of every year in space. There and back in a month is a treat. Even if we have to downsize the staff to do it. Will my staff be a problem?" he asked.

Jacob wanted to say yes, especially with the way all the male crewmembers' eyes seemed to focus on the pretty blonde.

"No, not at all. Though, unlike a civilian ship, we segregate our sleeping quarters and heads. Please be aware that men aboard ship are restricted from entering female cabins, even with permission." He caught himself at the last moment. "With the exception of you and your wife, sir. Of course, you will bunk together."

They politely laughed and smiled.

"Now if you'll allow me, I'll have my Bosun escort you to your cabin, and his assistants will see to your people."

"Of course, and again, thank you," Nguyen said.

Jacob watched them go, Bosun taking the ambassador and Sara, and his two assistants guiding the other four down to deck six where they would be staying.

"Josh," he said as he saw the PO leaving.

"Sir?" Mendez said, jogging forward to stand at parade rest in front of his captain.

"At ease. I want you to find out if they have any dietary requirements. After that, set up a separate dining schedule for him and his personnel."

"You don't want them eating with the crew, sir?"

The question seemed innocent enough, and if it weren't for the nagging feeling in his gut, he would have dismissed the whole idea and let them eat with the crew instead of creating extra effort for one of his hardest working POs.

"Sorry, Josh. I know it's more on your plate, but I would rather separate out the civilians for mealtimes."

"No more work than usual, Skipper. I'm on it."

"Good man. Dismissed."

Josh turned and practically ran out of the boat bay, eager to get to work. The boy had a knack for running the galley that Jacob appreciated more than the PO could ever know.

"Skipper," Carter said, "if it's okay with you, we'll resume duty?"

"Of course, and thank you. I know dress uniforms aboard ship are inconvenient."

They left, leaving him alone with his thoughts as he walked back to his cabin, which he shared with Carter for the trip. The entire way there, he couldn't help but feel something was off. Maybe it was the unusual mission, the too-pretty girl, or something else, he wasn't sure. His gut told him danger was on the horizon. If Jacob knew one thing for sure, it was listen to his gut.

CHAPTER NINE

DesRon 12 waited at the starlane out of Alexandria for the MTS *Jack Coughlin* to arrive. Jacob's other three ships floated in tight formation. The lane led to an empty system dominated by a massive blue giant. The nav charts called it Blue Beetle, and while it experienced a tremendous amount of traffic, the sheer nothingness of it prevented any permanent bases there.

It was the first leg in the journey, Jacob noted as he went through the charts. Three more lanes heading directly for the Terran Republic, then they would change heading toward the galactic center. Two more lanes while still in Alliance space, then the final two lanes in unclaimed territory. Not that there were any settlements or colonies in those last two systems. Cordoba and a place called Port Ryba were the only inhabited systems in the area, astronomically speaking.

The database showed a tremendous amount of traffic coming from Ryba and through the systems he'd be taking to travel there. Ambassador Nguyen could have easily found a ship to take him. There wasn't really any need to task *Interceptor*, other than to keep the man from having to spend more time on travel. Which Jacob understood. Not every person enjoyed space travel as much as those in the Navy.

"Sir," newly promoted PO McCall said to get his attention. "MTS *Jack Coughlin* is in formation and ready for starlane embarkation."

"Pass my compliments along to Commander Estaban, Mac. Have them slave their computers to ours. Astro, when you're ready," Jacob said.

"Aye, aye, sir," Mac replied.

Ensign Brennan's fingers danced on her console as she laid in the coordinates for the lane. "Helm, come to zero-one-zero relative."

Chief Suresh repeated the coordinates as she edged the ship's shark nose in the right direction.

Most of the work to find the lane had already happened while they waited for *Jack Coughlin* to catch up. Now it was just a matter of fine tuning the angle of attack to match the drift that happened while they waited.

"All departments report ready for starlane. All lights are green," Hössbacher said.

"All ships are ready," Mac said to Brennan.

"Skipper, all ships report ready for starlane ingress," Ensign Brennan notified him. There was a formality to everything they did, every step they took. Space travel's inherent danger was made more so by lax skippers. Procedures existed for a reason. He would follow every single one.

Jacob paused for a moment, gazing out at the star field shimmering on the forward display. He never grew tired of the view. Never tired of the stars calling him home.

"Close the aperture," he said.

"Aye, sir. Aperture closed," Suresh said.

"Execute starlane ingress."

As one, four destroyers and one troop transport locked onto

the faint line of gravity, tying Alexandria to Blue Beetle. Gravity surged through their coils, and they shot off down the lane, vanishing from Newtonian space and traveling at superluminal speeds.

Everyone aboard leaned back as they crossed the threshold, unconsciously resisting the perceived fall. For the crew, it felt like standing on the edge of a chasm, then leaping off.

"Starlane achieved zero-point-zero-five-degree variance," Tefiti announced from his station next to Brennan's.

"Well done, Devi," Jacob said loud enough for everyone to hear.

"All in a day's work, Skipper," she replied.

Jacob seriously doubted there was any compliment he could pay the COB that would ever impact her unflappable nature. Then again, she was a coxswain. Unflappable was part of the job description.

———

Josh Mendez sped through his chores in the galley, trying to prepare the meal for the afternoon rush while accounting for six extra mouths to feed. He'd passed the skipper's mealtimes on to the civilians, and they would arrive any moment. A half hour after that, the crew would start their lunch rotation. In that two-hour window, the mess would feed 130 crew. A daily occurrence for his team.

"Who's that?" Perch asked from where he chopped onions.

Josh looked up in time to see one of the ambassador's assistants walk into the mess. Her long blonde hair was undone, and she showed more than a little skin in the dress she wore.

"Civilian, keep working. I'll take care of it."

He heard Perch and Zack mutter about how he had all the luck as he exited the galley into the mess.

"Ma'am, your meal's not ready yet. If you want to come back—"

Her smile could melt stone as she graced him with her full lips.

"Oh, that's okay, I don't mind waiting," she said.

Josh's heart raced and even though he had no interest in her, he couldn't help but trip over his own words as he gestured to a table for her to sit at.

"Can I get you something to drink while you wait?" he asked.

"Coffee, if you have it. Cream and sugar?" Her sweet voice held a musical quality that made Josh's ears burn.

"Right away," he said.

A moment later, he placed a steaming cup in front of her. She smiled, touching his arm as he tried to step back. "You can sit and talk, can't you?" she asked.

"I'm sorry, ma'am, I'm afraid I can't."

"What's with the 'ma'am'? You're making me feel old. My name's Gabriela. My friends call me Gabby. You're a friend, right?" Her big blue eyes looked up at him, pleading, and in that moment, PO Josh Mendez would've disowned his Abuela if he thought it would make Gabby pleased with him.

"Y—yes, of course, but I really have to prepare lunch. Maybe after?"

She pouted, her lips scrunching together. "Fine," she said with a dismissive wave.

Josh walked away, relief flooding through him. Gabby's allure couldn't be denied, but something about her bothered him.

"PO, are you stupid?" Perch asked. "We can handle lunch, go talk to her."

Josh glanced back at Gabby, not surprised to see her watching him, only for her to turn away the moment he looked.

"Duty calls, Spacer. Duty calls."

He worked with a variety of females aboard ship, from spacers to officers, but none had quite the effect on him that Gabby did. Well, maybe one. Josh's thoughts turned to a particular curly-haired redhead who, for the moment, was off limits. Maybe if she were reassigned, but then they would never see one another.

————

Jacob perused the public database on Cordoba, trying to get a feel for what the system was like. As far as he could tell, they were above average in wealth. The planet was large, and with the exception of the capital and a few population centers, sparsely inhabited.

Cordoba's main export was coffee and cosmic luck. They were perfectly positioned between the Terran Republic and the Alliance.

Astronomically speaking, Cordoba held a variety of interesting stellar phenomena. Two dense asteroid belts, for instance. Almost all of which were composed of gadolinium. A highly magnetic but relatively useless mineral that wasn't worth the cost of mining. Both asteroid belts were unpopulated. The money in the system was all on the planet. It would make for an interesting navigation challenge. Jacob packaged up the important aspects and forwarded them to his astro team.

Once he finished, he clicked off the light. If he could get right to sleep—

He was out before he finished the thought.

CHAPTER TEN

Cordoba had no history of violence against the Alliance, but Jacob learned long before that caution was better than confidence. They came out of the starlane from Rygel as one, all five ships packed in as close as the regs would allow. The feeling of lifting suddenly left Jacob's throat in his stomach, threatening to make him puke, but he held it down. It passed as quickly as it occurred.

If anyone on the bridge retched, their ELS suits hid the noise.

"Status?" he asked after several seconds, his voice thick with the fog of transition.

The system's primary planet floated off in the distance, farther than the ship could see. A half million people lived and worked on Cordoba.

While the system had its own government and security that didn't mean they were safe. However, there would be no Alliance vessels answering a distress call out here. DesRon 12's men and women were at action stations, ready for anything.

"Immediate space is clear," Tefiti said. "Passive is picking up moderate activity up to a million klicks. Gravwakes identified as light freighter traffic." PO Tefiti leaned closer to his console as if it would help him hear. Jacob didn't knock the PO's habits— whatever helped him.

The MFD attached to Jacob's chair flashed through several ships, each one the computer picked up. All were freighters or light transport ships. No military gravwakes detected.

"Go active on all sensors," Jacob ordered. "Helm, ahead two-five gravities."

"Aye, sir, active on all sensors," Ensign Brennan repeated.

"Two-five gravities, course zero," Chief Suresh said.

"Comms, send a packet to the Cordoba Space Patrol, alerting them to our presence and our intended course."

"Aye, aye, sir. Send to CSP course and speed," McCall said.

Jacob didn't have to order the squadron to follow, they would on their own. He checked the plot, and sure enough ten seconds after *Interceptor* accelerated, the other three destroyers and the lone Marine transport followed. *Interceptor* in the lead, flanked by *Kidd* and *Apache*, with *Jack Coughlin* sandwiched in the middle of the arrowhead, while Commander Marsh and the *Justice* brought up the rear. As he watched, the message came in that *Justice* dropped her towed array, keeping their six clear of anyone trying to sneak up on them.

"Comms, signal my compliments to DesRon 12."

"Aye, aye, sir," PO McCall replied.

Once they were clear of the starlane, and Tefiti continued to find no unusual traffic, Jacob ordered them to three hundred gravities acceleration. *Jack Coughlin* topped out at 350 g's for non-emergencies, 400 for flank. Of course, his Hellcat stomped all over with 560 as her max, faster than even the three more modern destroyers. Even with the new armor, they maintained the same mass as before since they had lost two forward torpedo tubes and the associated ammo reserves.

"ETA to Cordoba, eight hours, fifty-three minutes at current speed," Ensign Brennan said.

"Excellent. Well done. Stand down from Condition Zulu. Resume Condition Yankee."

A moment later, McCall's voice went out over the ship. Jacob only half listened as he studied the plot. There were faint sensor echoes in the distance along with several radar and lidar returns. Something about it triggered his gut, but what?

"Tefiti?" he asked as he pulled off his helmet. "Do we have any historical data on Cordoba?"

"I'm not sure. Let me check the database."

While he did that, Jacob stood and stretched, loosening his muscles. "Roy, call the relief so you can get out of your suits," he said.

It didn't take long for non-suited personnel to arrive and, one by one, relieve each station until everyone had returned wearing their standard shipboard uniform. Except for Jacob, who leaned over the still-suited Tefiti as they searched the data.

"What are we looking for, Skip?" Tefiti asked as he scanned pages upon pages of logs. Every Navy ship that had come through Cordoba kept a log going back to the system's founding some two hundred years before.

"Anything that sticks out. Something about this traffic pattern feels off. Maybe it's nothing." He clapped the PO on the shoulder. "Go get changed. I'll take a look later."

Only then did Jacob realize he was the last person wearing his ELS suit. "Austin, you have the conn."

"Aye, aye, sir, I have the conn," Lieutenant Brown said.

Jacob exited the bridge, giving June a nod as he headed for his cabin... only to stop and turn sheepishly around for the ladder as he remembered he wasn't living in his cabin at the moment.

Jacob entered the cabin he shared with Carter, already pulling at his suit's seams to get it off as fast as possible.

Most people aboard a small ship like *Interceptor* wouldn't even notice the hum of the gravcoil or the tiny gravitic changes as the ships surged. Jacob grabbed the bar on the overhead, as the ship accelerated to his orders. He leaned back, along with everyone else aboard ship until the secondary gravcoil caught up and normalized gravity.

His suit off, he pulled out his day uniform and—

"Emergency maneuvers, all hands brace," Austin's Voice bellowed over the ship-wide speaker.

Jacob had one foot in his trousers and couldn't untangle himself before lateral g's piled on. Hopping like mad to avoid falling, he failed and crashed into the deck hard on his shoulder.

Something inside cracked like a twig under foot. He grimaced in pain and rolled onto his back, cradling his now useless arm.

He breathed in deep, focusing through the agony in his shoulder. He eyed the comms button and narrowed his vision until he only saw that. It took him far too long to crawl along the deck to the button.

"Captain to the bridge, captain to the bridge," McCall's voice called out.

"What do you think I'm trying to do?" he spat out. His hand came down on the button and he practically collapsed with relief.

"Bridge, Captain, what's going on?"

"Sir," Lieutenant Brown answered, "a civilian freighter appeared on our long-range radar on an intercept course. I ordered the rapid change to avoid a possible interaction or collision with their gravwake."

Jacob bit back his reply. Instead, he pulled himself up to a sitting position and started working on getting his trousers up.

"Are we out of the danger zone?" he asked. If Brown noticed anything about his strained voice or heavy breathing, he said nothing.

"Yes, sir. It's an independent freighter that's large enough it might cause problems. They're pushing their gravcoil to the absolute maximum. If this were Alliance space, we would be justified in ordering them to heave-to."

Jacob heaved the last few inches of his trousers up around his waist before collapsing back down. He couldn't fault Brown for pursuing his duty with zeal. No one could predict a clumsy skipper.

"Pass the information on to CSP and let them handle it... and Brown?"

"Yes, Skipper?" his voice crackled over the comms.

"Have PO Desper come to my cabin. I seemed to have broken my shoulder."

Brown paused, the line open, but he didn't say anything. Finally, he managed to speak. "Aye, sir. Desper to your cabin."

———

Austin stared at the comm speaker in stunned disbelief. He'd thought nothing of ordering an emergency course change. It was good practice for the crew, and it would guarantee the ship wouldn't be in any danger. Instead, he broke the captain's shoulder.

"Damage control? Any casualties reported?" he asked.

"Aye, sir, about a half dozen minor scrapes and bruises."

He could shoot himself now and save the misery from the next couple of weeks. He would never, not ever, live it down.

CHAPTER ELEVEN

With his arm in a sling and wearing mess dress, Jacob and his officers lined up on the boat bay waiting for the ambassador. He felt foolish wearing his most prestigious uniform with the full complement of medals on display. The situation demanded it, though. Ambassador Nguyen requested the full service be performed for his taking up of the new post. Who was Jacob to deny tradition? Even if he could, he probably wouldn't have. While no officer enjoyed mess dress, it was an opportunity for life aboard ship to have some variance. Close to eighty crew were packed into the boat bay, all wearing formal attire.

He would, of course, accompany the ambassador down to the planet along with several of his people, including Captain Bonds and two of his Marines.

"Company, atten-shun," Chief Suresh bellowed in her best DI voice.

Ambassador Nguyen, his wife, and assistants entered the boat bay.

The ambassador, to his credit, was suitably impressed. His wife, though, stole the show.

"Oh my, what a lovely surprise. Your crew is so wonderful, Captain Grimm. I think they should all have an extra day of leave, don't you agree?" she said loud enough for everyone in the boat bay to hear.

Jacob smiled broadly at her, knowing exactly what she had done.

"Why, Madam Ambassador, you honor us. How could I say no?"

Out of the corner of his eye he caught his crew beaming. They were too disciplined to shout or move, but he could see the extra effort they put into standing straighter.

Jacob did an about-face and walked the couple to the waiting Corsair. He held out his hand to help Sara up, which she took gladly. Once the couple were aboard, Jacob waved Carter and Roy aboard.

"Austin, you have command until I return," he ordered.

"Aye, aye, sir. I'll take good care of her," Lieutenant Brown replied.

"Don't get too excited, Lieutenant," Chief Suresh said from beside him. "We're in parking orbit."

Brown's cheeks heated at the jab.

"On you go, COB," Jacob said with a jerk of his thumb toward the hatch.

Once they were all aboard, Chief Boudreaux began the launch procedures. She had a full deck with Stawarski running second. Jacob decided it was best for him to stay in the cabin anyway. Seated and strapped in, he tuned the small monitor in the front to show the nose cam footage.

Interceptor's crew departed, trundling through the double hatchway that separated the boat bay from the rest of the ship. Then the Corsair dropped, floating through the black.

Boudreaux's voice crackled over the internal comms. "ETA

to Polis Del Mar, seventeen minutes. There's a storm in the upper atmosphere so it will be bumpy. Maintain your harness."

Jacob noticed Sara holding her husband's hand hard enough her knuckles turned white.

"Ma'am," he said politely, "these things can literally fly with one engine and no wings. They are well designed."

"My anxiety doesn't believe you, Captain," she replied with a tight smile.

Paul took the seat next to Jacob and strapped in.

"I wanted to chat with you for a moment, Skipper. About the joint training we're going to be doing with the 1st and 2nd Soldados?"

"That's your bag, Paul. I'm just an escort. We're going to hang around in-system and do mock-war games with the CSP."

Paul had a look on his face, like he had an idea he wanted to share but wasn't sure.

"You have an idea?" he asked.

"Yes, sir, I do. But I need the Corsair and Viv— Chief Boudreaux," he corrected himself, "for it to work. Along with Bravo-Two-Five."

Jacob leaned back, thinking over the request. Nominally it wasn't an issue. As the Marine ground force commander, Captain Bonds was within his rights to request aid from the Navy commander of the system, which was Jacob. His only concern came from the appearance of impropriety. He knew Paul and Viv were an item. Off duty only and they kept it down low. There was a line to walk in the Navy, and it only grew thinner as rank increased. Paul couldn't date in his chain of command, and neither could Boudreaux. It left them perfect for each other, as long as they weren't on the same ship. The other request for his Marines was easier to say yes to, though Gunny Jennings wasn't going to like it.

"You got them. If we need a Corsair, I'm sure one of the other three ships in the squadron can loan us one."

"Roger that, sir. Thank you."

The internal speaker crackled to life. Boudreaux distorted voice came out. "Brace for plasma engine conversion."

————

The Corsair parted the clouds in a swirl of plasma engine exhaust, showing Jacob a clear view of the sprawling city below. Bright orange terracotta roof tiles clashed with newer industrial solar-paneled exteriors. The endless city sprawl flashed below him as they descended, allowing him to see individual buildings and streets.

"The solar panels seem odd," he said as the Corsair banked. On Alexandria, the only people who used them were those who lived far off-grid and didn't want to pay a premium for a microwave receiver.

"They're a few years behind us in technology," Ambassador Nguyen said. "Their fusion reactors are twice the size of ours and half as efficient. Because of problems they've had with containment, they only use them for shipping, not the general population."

That struck Jacob as inefficient, and he said so.

"It's not for us to judge, Commander," Sara said with a tsk-tsk motion of her hands.

"Of course not, ma'am. I don't always understand the ins and outs of other societies. Heck, I barely understand Alexandria and I'm from there."

She let out a laugh that surely charmed any who heard it. Jacob noticed the admiring look on the ambassador's face and decided he was a good man. Anyone who loved his wife that much couldn't be all bad?

"I take it fusion reactors fall under the military technology trade ban?" he asked.

Nguyen raised an eyebrow, as if he were reevaluating his assessment of Jacob's character.

"That is correct, Commander. Anything Congress has deemed to be 'integral to the defense of the Alliance' is illegal to trade. Though not for lack of trying on the Cordoban government's part. They have all but begged us for more military tech. This training exercise between our military and theirs is an olive branch in that direction. Their president has his own domestic issues to deal with, and he felt this would appease his critics in the military who wish he would be more... authoritarian."

Jacob found the entire thing fascinating. While he'd read up ðn the Caliphate, and their theocracy, even learned some of their language, he was woefully under informed about the dozens of little one-planet nations that dotted the fringes of the major powers.

"Why didn't they join the Terran Republic?" he asked.

"Well..." Nguyen glanced at his wife, then leaned toward Jacob. "There are complications to joining the Republic. For one, they have an exhaustive list of social requirements and ideals that are updated literally daily."

"The other reason?"

"Autonomy. The Republic assigns its own governors to oversee planets. The people of Cordoba are fiercely independent. You could easily describe them as loyalists. The idea of giving that away to the Republic would be at fundamental odds to who they are."

Jacob considered the information for a moment. Loyalty to one's nation was by no means a fault. There were far worse things to be. However, any ideology, regardless of intent, when taken to an extreme was dangerous. Hyper-loyalists might regard any trade or negotiations with a foreign power as a betrayal. Just as his own government had spent almost twenty-five years pushing their "peace-at-all-costs" belief. On the surface, peace was the goal. Peace required two parties willing to live peacefully, and clearly that wasn't the case with the Caliphate.

Jacob shook his head, clearing the thoughts from his mind. He needed to focus on the mission at hand. Tonight, they were attending a diplomatic gala, and tomorrow it was time to work.

The United Systems Alliance had many famous cultural contributions to the galaxy. Ronin's one-kilometer-tall statue of Buddha carved into the Sugoi Mountain. New Austin's famous Mustang Plains or Seabring's magnificent moon telescopes.

However, one thing the Alliance wasn't famous for was her architecture. Alexandria's buildings, in Jacob's opinion, were boring.

Not so on Cordoba. The bright orange terracotta shingles that covered the city also decorated the Alliance embassy. The multi-level, multi-winged complex was covered with artfully made roof tiles. Only the landing pad, which jutted out from the south side top floor was the dull grey of ceracrete.

Boudreaux circled the building once, banking the ship to port for a view of the surroundings. Once she finished circling the wings rotated up with a thunk of metal, the ship shook, and descended onto the landing pad with all the grace of a butterfly.

"Your pilot is very good," Ambassador Nguyen said.

"One of the best," Jacob agreed.

CHAPTER TWELVE

Jacob shifted the sling on his arm where the band bit into his shoulder. His shoulder throbbed even through the healing nanites. PO Desper assured him the pain would fade within a few hours, and another two after that, he would have the use of his arm again. By tomorrow it would be as it never happened.

He chuckled to himself. Brown's embarrassment would fade, and if the price of learning his lesson about overzealous course corrections was only Jacob's shoulder, then he would pay the price. Putting that out of his mind, he focused on the embassy.

Once a luxury hotel, Alliance engineers had converted it to an embassy, with walls, security, and flags. The landing pads' shiny metal surfaces had yet to be dulled by the weather, which led him to believe it was a new addition.

"Ambassador, welcome to Cordoba," said a man in a light-blue suit with multiple buttons and insignia on the breast.

Jacob watched the formality play out as they were welcomed to the planet. It interested him in the way any new cultural difference would. He found Cordoba instantly fascinating, from the uniformity of their roof tiles to the way they dressed.

"This is Commander Grimm, the head of the orbiting squadron and de facto leader of Alliance military forces in-system. Commander Grimm, this is Mr. Álvaro, my liaison with the locals who staff the embassy."

"A pleasure to meet you, sir," Jacob said, holding his hand out.

"The same," Álvaro said with a stiff formality. The man turned his back, spinning in place. "This way, sir." He led them to the exterior entrance of a lift with the doors held open.

Jacob shot an inquisitive look at Nguyen, who shrugged. Álvaro seemed less than impressed with Jacob, not that he needed the man to be, it was just... odd.

"The gala is in full swing. Everyone you invited is here, uh... with the notable exception of Lady Franceska Divine."

Nguyen frowned at the news.

Jacob had no idea who she was or the importance of her absence. He spent most of his free time studying the Alliance, Consortium, and Caliphate. There simply wasn't time left over for him to be familiar with all the single-system independent governments in the galaxy.

"She's the opposition leader. What we would call the minority leader. My understanding is she's in the running for president?" Nguyen asked Álvaro.

"Yes, sir, though her poll numbers aren't enough to give the current administration pause." His voice filled with reverence as he spoke about her.

"All the same, I'm glad that the rest of my invitees came."

The lift doors binged open and Jacob suppressed his surprise. The embassy looked nothing like he expected. Plush red carpet with gold inlay covered the floor, famous paintings from around the Alliance adorned the walls, and gorgeous crystal chandeliers sprayed multicolored light down from the ceiling. At first, he thought they were standard lights, but he quickly realized they were channeling natural sunlight through their crystals.

"Awe-inspiring, isn't it?" Nguyen asked.

"Yes, sir." Was all Jacob could manage.

Nguyen's wife perked up as she stepped out. A true stateswoman, she immediately headed for the nearest important figure. Jacob heard her thanking them for attending before she moved out of range.

"She's quite the companion," he said to the ambassador.

"You've no idea. Captain," he said. "Thank you for delivering us here in such comfort."

"You are too kind, sir, I've slept in that cabin."

They both laughed, shook hands, and parted.

Jacob genuinely liked Nguyen. He seemed a reasonable fellow with a good head on his shoulders. His wife certainly was in her element.

He, however, wasn't. Not even a little. The only "state dinner" he'd attended was aboard a Consortium heavy cruiser. This wasn't his bailiwick. His heart thudded as anxiety threatened him.

I wish Nadia was here, she would know exactly what to do.

Lacking his lovely spy, he channeled his inner Nadia and did his best to blend in and listen. All political situations were minefields, and if he kept his mouth shut and ears open... as hard as that would be for him, he would emerge unscathed. The urge to mix and speak to people pulled at him.

"Skipper, let's get a drink," Paul said, coming up beside him and touching his elbow to gesture at the wine table.

"Good idea," Jacob replied.

Paul spent a moment looking at the rack of wines, finally deciding on a Pinot Noir with a gold label. He held the bottle out to Jacob who raised his hand. The big Marine cocked his head at him.

"You really don't drink alcohol?" Bonds asked.

"Not a drop. I know, crazy."

"Not at all, Skipper. I just wonder how you keep sane."

"Maybe I don't," Jacob replied with a deadpan.

"Touché."

Jacob retrieved a decanter of water and filled a heavy crystal glass. He found his way to a small corner where he put his back against a wall.

"I'm not quite prepared for this kind of event," he confided in Bonds. "I didn't expect a full-on state affair."

"Marines spend a lot of time in embassies, since we're the sheep dogs for the ambassadorial types. Years back, I was on this little hole where angry locals overran the place. The ambassador got out, Lord knows how, but it wasn't with my men. We managed to escape via Corsair to an orbiting heavy cruiser."

Music picked up from the live band, forcing Jacob to raise his voice slightly. "I don't know how you do it, Paul. I'd hate this kind of assignment. I appreciated serving on *Enterprise*, but I'd pass it up in a heartbeat for *Interceptor*. Even when we're not in the action, we're in the action. This feels too much like being an admin."

"Oorah, sir."

Gunny Jennings appeared at Jacob's arm. He hadn't seen her walk up; she was just there.

"Captain. Skipper," she said nodding to both men. If not for her rows of medals adorning her chest, and the deadly serious expression on her face, the size difference might almost be comical. Compared to Bonds and Jacob, she was tiny.

"Good to see you're working on your verbosity, Gunny," Bonds said.

Her eyes moved slightly to acknowledge the captain's

remarks, but beyond that, Jacob couldn't even tell if she was breathing.

The evening continued with Jacob staying in the corner, watching and listening. Snippets of conversations made their way to him. A man in a dark suit with a red tie asked about trade problems with the Terran Republic. A woman in a low-cut red dress wanted to know where a man in uniform stood on the upcoming election.

Jacob managed to piece together a few things while standing in the corner with his growing crowd of Marines and spacers. The election, while not close on paper, seemed to be hotly contested. The current president was a staunch isolationist who wanted Cordoba to stand on their own, while his opponent wanted the planet to embrace their neighbors. Both seemed genuine in their desire to protect their people. If the president, though, was such an isolationist, what was the Alliance doing here with a company of Marines and a squadron of ships for a JTE? He couldn't be much of one if he agreed to the joint training.

Ambassador Nguyen made his way to Jacob and motioned for him to follow.

Jacob handed his glass to Jennings and stepped through the military personnel who had congregated around him.

"Ambassador?" he asked as he followed the man through the thickening crowd.

"Come, I want you to meet the president and we only have a brief window."

Jacob instinctively ran his hands over his uniform, making sure every pin, every stitch, was in place.

Ahead, the crowd parted as the main doors opened.

"Ladies and gentlemen, Presidente Santiago!" Muted clapping and murmurs of respect filled the hall.

Jacob stayed behind. The man who entered was short, bald,

with vacant eyes. He looked tired. Surrounded by large, burly security men with obvious guns. Who did he think would try to kill him at the Alliance embassy? Of course, if it was his president, he would insist security be with him. Jacob chided himself for his thinking.

"Mr. President," Ambassador Nguyen called. They shook hands and the man's disinterested eyes hardly moved. "May I introduce Commander Jacob T. Grimm of the USS *Interceptor*."

The president froze for a solid three seconds. His eyes twinkled with an inner fire. He pushed past the ambassador and held out his hand to Jacob. He couldn't help but take it. Their height difference forced Jacob to lean over to accommodate him.

"Commander Grimm! It's such an honor to meet you. I've followed your career since you busted the human trafficking ring. People in my government were involved and your action helped us root them out." Without waiting for an answer, and still having failed to release his hand, the president walked toward the buffet table, dragging Jacob with him.

Jacob was taken aback. One second the man looked like a zombie, the next his excitement was palatable. Jacob managed to extract his hand politely before they got to the table.

"It's an honor to meet you, sir. And our privilege to come and learn from your navy."

The president waved away his comment. "You and I both know that it is our navy that will learn from you," he said a little louder than Jacob would have liked. There was always a delicate balance when dealing with a less developed world's military. Yes, the Alliance ships were far more advanced, but he didn't want to throw it in their faces.

"Tell me, in Zuckabar, when you were suckering the pirates in for the kill, did you know they wouldn't be able to find the freighter you escorted?"

El Presidente's enthusiasm for the first battle of Zuckabar struck him as odd. He had written his after-action report, testified to the battle, and gone over the tapes, but to speak of it casually... felt disrespectful to the thirty spacers who lost their lives. However, the man was also a head of state and Jacob would oblige.

"We hoped the gravwake from our ship would hide them long enough to escape. It's an old trick, sir."

The president's smile threatened to engulf his face. "An oldy but a goody! Come, my friend. Let us drink and speak."

Before long Jacob found himself the center of attention at President Santiago's table. A half dozen middle-aged men, and two women who couldn't be older than their early twenties, circled the table as the president grilled him for details. No information was too small. He even wanted to know the recipe PO Mendez had used to make the stew that kept the crew alive while on their way back from Wonderland.

Of course, Wonderland was classified, all Santiago knew was that *Interceptor* had taken an extra-long patrol, engaged pirates, and been driven farther from Zuckabar... to the point they had to engage the same pirates on their return without having eaten for several meals.

The conversation, and the questions, went well into the night.

CHAPTER THIRTEEN

Jennings grunted as she lifted the pack onto her shoulders. Cordoba's gravity held less sway than her home, and the atmosphere wasn't as thick as Alliance standard, but her late nights since the gala were catching up with her. The rest of her squad, Corporal Naki, Lance Corporal Owens, and PFC June, were haggard as well. Their barracks were outside Cordoba's capital city of Polis Del Mar only a klick from the embassy.

"Bravo-Two-Five, ready to roll out?" she barked.

"Yes, Gunny." They replied in unison.

She looked them over as they stood at attention. Their normal gray-and-white fatigues were swapped for dark green and brown that matched the countryside of Cordoba. They wore their boots, fatigues, tactical vests, and all their regular field equipment: a bayonet, nanite-powered canteen, two days' worth of rations, seven training mags, and their MP-17s locked to training mode. At least they weren't using Cordoba's garbage gear. She would have liked to have more of their advanced gear, but this was a basic soldiering training exercise. Which meant they had to make do without all the hi-tech gear.

Groundside assignments weren't regular for the *Interceptor*. She would much rather be aboard ship than playing soldier on an alien planet while her primary responsibility flew around the system unprotected by her. However, they were in for a month of war games with Cordoba and the captain wouldn't need his Marines as much as Captain Bonds would.

Her three Marines fell in behind as she led them out of the small barracks and toward the CP. Cordoba's standing army was shy of a hundred thousand people spread across three branches. The army was who they were interacting with. While she did wish to be on the ship, if she couldn't, then thrashing grunts was the next best thing.

They marched in a line, the three Marines and her next to them, feet falling in unison.

"Listen up, people. You are to be on your best behavior. I don't care one wit about politics or who did what to whoever. I will not tolerate making the captain look bad, understood?"

"Yes, Gunny!"

Jennings scanned her surroundings as they marched, memorizing the route back and locking in familiar landmarks to make her way if she were cut off or lost.

Ten minutes of marching later, they arrived outside the staging area. Multi-wheeled trucks far less sophisticated than the Mudcat lined the area. Hundreds of soldiers lounged on their rucks, resting in the dawn light. Jennings spotted the officers next to a smaller vehicle with an open canopy and what looked like a coffee counter built into the back of it.

"Hunker down, I'll find out what we're doing."

Dropping her ruck, she headed for the coffee. Not that she wanted any. Jennings tried the local stuff and it made her tongue want to shrivel up and die from how bitter and thick it tasted.

"Sir, Bravo-Two-Five reporting as ordered," she said to Captain Bonds.

He turned to her and smiled broadly. "Gunny, I was just talking about you. This is Comandante Sofia Ruiz. She's leading the company of infantry currently sunning themselves."

A strong-looking woman with thick bushy eyebrows and possibly a few too many pounds, Jennings couldn't tell from the uniform, extended her hand. Her grip, though, was strong and warm.

"Ma'am," Gunny said.

"This lean, mean fighting machine here," Bonds continued, pointing at a slight man with a pencil-thin mustache who blushed under Bonds' praise, "is Capitán Javier Martinez. He's her 1st company commander."

"Sir," she said, careful to exert slight pressure as she shook his hand.

Ruiz gestured to what Jennings now realized was an espresso machine. "Espresso, Gunny?"

"No thank you, ma'am."

Bonds chuckled. "The gunny here is what you would call a traditionalist, aren't you, Gunny?"

Jennings' crystal blue eyes scanned the field as they spoke, taking in every detail. "If the captain says so, sir."

The three officers grinned at her proclamation.

"As I was telling your Captain Bonds," Comandante Ruiz said, "this is 2a Compañía, 3rd Battalion. Our largest single force."

Plasma engines roared overhead as five Corsairs buzzed the field five hundred meters up, burning through the sky shy of the speed of sound. Their tails were marked with the flag of the *Jack Coughlin*. Their formation broke, as they pulled a hard turn, two going left, three right. Jennings almost felt the g's on her as she watched.

Corsair wings flipped vertically, and the ships came to a sudden halt, spinning around and landing even as their rear doors descended. Just before touchdown Marines leapt out in rows of four, running behind the Corsairs to form up as a company. Plasma engines whined down and a silence permeated the field. In a matter of thirty seconds, there were two hundred Alliance Marines formed up with full gear.

"Well, Oorah," Jennings said.

"Impressive, Captain Bonds. Is this meant to instill us with confidence, or fear?" Capitán Martinez said.

Bonds side-eyed him before saying, "Is it too much to ask for both?"

"Very good, Captain," Ruiz said. "Let's move this inside the CP, and we can begin our planning operation. I know my troops are both eager to learn from you and impress you. You may not know this, but you Alliance Marines have quite the reputation."

"Oh, we know," Bonds said.

Jennings followed them into the tent and took a step to the right, standing next to the hatch and falling into parade rest.

Bonds glanced at her and shook his head, a wry smile on his face as he motioned for her to join him at the table. Confused as to why he would want her there, but not willing to voice her confusion, Jennings did as she was ordered and stood next to him at parade rest.

"We are going to break off into three groups, then," Ruiz said. She unfolded a *paper* map onto the table, using coffee cups to keep the edges down. "One, training. If your sergeants and junior noncoms would be so kind as to lead our privates through a mock boot camp, we could ensure some of your skills are imparted on the ones most likely to implement them." Ruiz glanced around the CP.

Jennings noted there were six other people present, four of them were officers, which she placed in the unimportant category. The other two, though, were NCOs based on the ranks on their sleeves. She had familiarized herself with their structure, as much as possible given the limited intel they had.

The taller man, well, tall for her, not the skipper, had a stout build and looked like he could wrestle a Seabring sabershark. If she were right about ranks, he was a brigada, their version of a gunnery sergeant. The other was Sergeant Primo, like a Marine staff sergeant. Neither looked pleased. The way they huddled together and whispered set her on edge.

"The second group, I would like to contain platoon level and comprise technical training. Small unit tactics, combat ops, that sort of thing," Ruiz said.

"And the third?" Bonds asked.

Ruiz pretended to hide a mischievous grin. "That's the group that will go into the field and perform combat operations against your—how do you say?—OpFor?"

Bonds barely contained his pride and enthusiasm at the proclamation. "Yes, ma'am, that's how you say it. Would you like some of your men to accompany my opposing force to see how we do it and if it's of use to them?"

Jennings thought that was a weird way to put it, but she shrugged the statement off. Of course, they could teach the locals a thing or two.

"Excellent. Let's give the men some time to train and begin our combat exercise in a week," Ruiz said.

Bonds leaned over the table, carefully examining the map and markings. Jennings followed his lead. The area marked lay a hundred klicks from the city. The western edge of the map was a fort and the eastern half a valley surrounded by tall mountains. The valley itself was easily a hundred square kilometers, more than enough room to fight.

"Choose your best people, and that's who can go with Jennings and her Marines."

Bonds hadn't shared his plan with her beforehand, not that an officer needed to. It was fine with her. She would rather shoot people than train them.

"Wait," the brigada spoke up for the first time. "You want to send ten people up against an entire company of infantry? I know you Alliance types are arrogant, but this is idiocy and a waste of time."

"Brigada Ortega," Ruiz interrupted him, "might I remind you we are all following orders here. Ours is not to question the validity, but to find the best way to carry them out."

In a show of insubordination that would have sent an Alliance Marine to the brig, Ortega glared at Ruiz and stormed out of the tent. Maybe she had read the ranks wrong after all? If she looked at an officer that way and didn't respond when spoken to, losing a mock battle would be the least of her concerns.

The other sergeant followed him out. At least he had the decency to look embarrassed.

"Forgive me, Captain," Ruiz said in a hushed tone. "Not everything on Cordoba is as... smooth as the Alliance."

"You'd be surprised, ma'am. However, might I ask, is he not in your chain of command?"

"Sofia," Martinez said, placing a warning hand on her shoulder. Jennings eyes and ears perked up. Her gut warned her of danger, and it had her fight or flight kicking in. Not an immediate danger, though, but an undercurrent of one.

"Thank you, Javier," Ruiz said, placing a hand on his. "There are divisions among my people, Captain. Technically the military is to remain neutral in any political discussion, but the upcoming election has everyone here a little on edge."

Now Jennings was all ears. She'd heard about the contentious campaign at the gala when they arrived, but all elections were contentious, so she paid no heed.

"We have such regulations as well. Can't have the military interfering," Bonds said.

Ruiz nodded her agreement. "Yes. Of course. Regardless, Captain, back to our plan. Will this work for you?"

"Aye, aye, ma'am, it will."

———

Brigada Ortega cursed himself for his foolish outburst. He couldn't contain his anger at having to play second fiddle to the Alliance marines. They were the problem, not his beloved planet. The only difference between them was technological. His people had a military tradition more than three thousand years old. They were true descendants of Hispania back on Earth. Not a mulatto of desperate peoples whose only advantage was based on sheer luck of where they had settled.

If his ancestors had gone another few hundred light-years, they would have had the Alliance worlds, instead of a barely sustainable rock that took nearly four hundred years to terraform.

He found his ground car and climbed in, waiting for Sergeant Vargas to catch up.

"Where to, Sergeant?" Vargas said as he climbed in.

"I need to contact the general, but on a secure system. She will know what we need to do next."

CHAPTER FOURTEEN

"And that about wraps it up. Questions?" Carter asked.

Crammed around the briefing table aboard *Interceptor* were three other captains, their execs, and four Bosuns. The Bosuns were involved to keep logistics ahead of the game. After all, DesRon 12 was about to expend millions of dollars' worth of ammunition and supplies, the people who had to account for it needed a say.

Kim leaned forward, her slight frame made her look more like a teenager playing spacer than the motivated, dedicated, and skilled spacer she was.

"Sir, they have what could generously be called destroyers, one maybe light cruiser, and a few dozen patrol boats... how exactly are they expected to compete against us?"

Jacob took a moment, mentally composing his response. He used silence in meetings like a tool. One that helped his people learn. While they waited for him to respond, it forced them to think about the problem.

"That's an excellent question, Kim. Does anyone have an answer?" he asked while looking at each of his captains.

Robert Carlos looked like he wanted to say something but

ended up staying silent. Jacob felt like he knew the answer but wanted to give less experienced people the chance to answer.

"Sir," Lieutenant SG Xavier Thompson, Kim's executive officer, spoke up.

"Go ahead, Xavier," Jacob said with a nod. Using the young man's first name caught him off guard and even through his night-black skin, Jacob saw him blush.

"Uh, we don't fight against them, we integrate with them?"

Jacob hated what he was about to say, mostly because he hated it when his SOs used it against him.

"Are you asking me or telling me?"

Xavier looked around for help, finding none, he squared his shoulders. "Telling you, sir."

"Very good. Yes, that's exactly what we're going to do. For the first two weeks. Then what do you think we will do?"

This time, Carlos did speak up. "Break the fleet, and us, in half and pit them against each other."

Jacob smacked the table in excitement causing Sabrina Marsh to flinch. "Exactly! We will use the system as a battleground and culminate in a massive live fire action"—he pulled up the holo on his NavPad displaying a barren moon—"here. We will blow the hell out of this thing and demonstrate the awesome power of concentrated fire."

The grins around the room told him he was right. There wasn't anything quite like firing the weapons for real, and especially when the targets didn't shoot back.

"May I make a suggestion, sir?" Marsh asked.

Jacob, not wanting to ever shoot her down lest her newly found confidence erode, waved for her to continue.

"We should take this one step further and bring a small portion of their spacers aboard. At the very least, we could do a tour or maybe even have some of their officers train on our equipment."

Jacob kicked himself mentally. He should have thought of that. There were regs, of course, for bringing foreign military personnel aboard ship, but as long as they kept them clear of the more sensitive areas, like the reactor room and Astro cartography, it should work.

"Excellent suggestion, Sabrina. Why don't you take point on that. Contact the ambassador's office and have them officially make the request. Now, return to your ships. We have one more hurdle to jump before we get going."

"Aye, aye, sir," they said as one.

"Kim, hang back, will you?"

"Aye, sir," she said. "Xavier, get back to the ship and I'll be along shortly."

"Aye, aye, ma'am."

Once the room had cleared, Jacob stood and walked around to sit on the edge of the table near her. "Bright young man," he said.

"Yes, sir. He's a little shy, but I'll break him out of his shell."

Jacob glanced at the hatch, thinking for a moment. "I have to fly down to the surface. Naval command wants to meet me. As squadron exec, I'd like you with me. Can do?"

Kim's eyes lit up. "I don't know, sir; I've got a lot of paperwork to do back on *Apache*..."

———

Cordoba Naval Command Station loomed before them. *Apache*'s Corsair aviator brought them in a lazy downward arc, leveling out a few klicks before the massive structure.

"That's a sight," Kim muttered from beside him.

He couldn't have agreed more. The building stretched high into the sky at least a kilometer tall and two klicks wide where it intersected the ground. Not that it stopped there. Signs aplenty showed underground access which meant the building went down, how far he knew not.

"They certainly have something on us with architecture. I would have never thought that building was military." Beautiful parks and fields of grass surrounded the building for kilometers.

CNC's structure spiraled upward, with orange terracotta tiles placed along the edge of the roof, giving the entire building the appearance of a drill rising out of the ground.

"You should come to Rōnin some time, you would love it," Kim said.

"It's on the list. As long as the war is on, though, I doubt will get sent that far from the front." Rōnin's location lay opposite Zuckabar on the far "northern" edge of the Orion's Spur. About as far from the Caliphate as it was from Terra. It took months just to get to it from Alexandria and was far and away, the single most remote planet of the Alliance.

The pilot's voice crackled over the speaker, "Sixty seconds to touchdown. POs make sure hydraulics are green."

Jacob loved flying in Corsairs. They were one of the smartest decisions the Navy had made in the last twenty years. True multi-role spacecraft capable of anything and everything the Navy asked of them.

Machinery whirred, sending the wings spinning up. Plasma engines screamed as blue fire hit the landing pad and the pilot put the ship down with barely any momentum.

"He's good," Jacob told Kim.

"Aye, sir. One of the best."

"I'll pretend I didn't hear that so Boudreaux doesn't make me lose my lunch next time I fly with her."

The side hatch whirred open, with a gust of warm air instantly bringing sweat to Jacob's brow. He groaned inwardly as he heaved up to exit the craft.

Outside the ship, a group of officers in their double-breasted high-collared coats made of bright reds and gold buttons awaited them. Jacob and Kim wore their SDWs, which were impractical for real work but looked impressive. Especially to anyone who knew what all the medals on Jacob's chest meant.

"I have to say," Kim told him as they approached, "I like their uniforms."

"Commander Grimm, I'm Capitán de Helena Castro. Welcome to Cordoba Naval Command."

Jacob saluted with great precision, wanting to make a good impression on the senior officer. Castro's lips split into a broad grin as he returned the salute.

"You're familiar with our ranks?" Castro asked.

"Of course, ma'am. I wouldn't want to be brought up on charges of insubordination," Jacob replied with a grin.

"Oh, I like you, Commander."

"This is an epic base, ma'am. How long did it take to build?" Kim asked.

"A lifetime, Commander. A literal lifetime."

Castro led the two through double doors tall enough for a Raptor suit and wide enough to drive a Mudcat through. Walking through the door felt like passing through an invisible barrier. Outside it had to be at least thirty-two degrees with high humidity, inside no more than twenty-one with normal levels of humidity. Jacob visibly sighed as the heat vanished. He and Kim removed their cover and slipped it under their arms as they followed the captain.

"That's some impressive atmosphere control," he said to Capitán Castro.

"Thank you. We do have a few areas where our technology may outshine even the Alliance."

"I have no doubt, ma'am."

They took a lift up thirty floors in silence, only the soft tones of local music filling the background. Jacob took the opportunity to examine their guide. Castro had a thick frame but was by no means fat. She had to weigh around seventy kilos and stood 1.6 meters tall if his judge of height was accurate. That was a bit suspect, though. At almost two meters tall himself, he wasn't the best judge of shorter people's height.

Floor 32 dinged and the doors slid open. Castro led them to the left and down a hall where a smartly dressed young woman sat behind a desk. Two men wearing combat uniforms guarded a door behind her. Jacob noted their sidearms, similar to Nadia's favored archaic chemical pistol. Old technology, but deadly all the same.

"Commander Grimm, USS *Interceptor*, to see the admiral," Castro said.

"One moment," the young woman replied.

Castro turned to Jacob and gave him what he thought was an apologetic smile.

"This is where I leave you, Commander. However, I will see you again."

"Oh?" he asked.

"Yes, I'm the fleet commander you will be training with. I look forward to finding out exactly where my people rank."

She smiled at Kim and walked away, head up, shoulders back.

"She's very confident," Kim whispered.

Jacob shrugged. "We are too."

"Commander Grimm, the admiral will see you now." As he stepped forward and Kim started to follow, the woman cleared her voice. "No, ma'am. Just Commander Grimm."

Jacob turned to Kim and held up his hand. "You did say you had a lot of paperwork to do."

"Touché, sir." She retreated to a nearby couch, pulling out her NavPad as she sat.

The soldiers opened the manual door as he approached, their grim expressions unreadable. He thanked them all the same, catching sight of their name tags in case it was relevant later.

The admiral's office looked more like President Axwell's office at the Palisades. Opulent decor with gold trim, and precious gems lined the long walls. From hatch to desk Jacob traversed five meters of what felt like a museum. Side tables made from a dark wood, shined to gleam, held golden models of ships he didn't recognize. Underneath the ships were plaques of marble, with the ships' names emblazoned in gold.

This is a lot of wealth for an admiral's office.

At the end of the office was a large desk, wide enough Jacob could lie down on it and still have room left over, deep enough it would take two long steps to traverse.

Behind the desk sat Fleet Almirante Lucia Pérez, in all her glory. Her bright red uniform had gold inlay, gold epaulets, and rows of medals that made Jacob's look like a first-year cadet.

"Commander Grimm, reporting as ordered, ma'am," he said. Just because they were in a foreign land, didn't mean he got to throw military protocol out the window. The only difference was that he wouldn't obey every order she could give. Obviously, he was the top of the chain of command out here, only answering to the ambassador—assuming no military crisis.

"Very good, Commander, I'm glad you know your place," she said. Lucia's eyes were steely grey that matched the streak in her otherwise thick black hair bundled on top of her head. "Other foreign powers have come to us and treated our navy as second-rate citizens. I'll be honest, I thought you would do the same. With your reputation for victory and state-of-the art ship

I—" Jacob tried, and failed, to suppress a chuckle. "What is so funny?" she asked with a stern, disapproving look.

"Sorry, ma'am. It's just... *Interceptor* is forty years old and hardly SOTA. However, she's reliable and crewed by the best. I would never dream of disparaging your accomplishments, Admiral. Regardless of tech level, blood, sweat, and tears are all the same."

Pérez leaned back, seeing him in a new light. The corners of her mouth twitched. She had a timeless beauty about her, a kind of elegance. Marred somewhat, but not substantially by her age. Jacob saw the iron in her, though, the strength needed to rise to the top.

"Thank you, Commander. I appreciate that. Now, let's go to the grain and plan out how the next three weeks are going to go."

CHAPTER FIFTEEN

CORDOBA GROUND COMMAND

General Juanita Pérez went over the report from her sister, the Admiral. Lucia had much to say about Commander Grimm. None of it she liked. The last thing they needed at such a critical moment was a competent Alliance officer in their system making waves. With the election drawing near, they were running out of time.

Unlike her sister, Juanita's desk was unadorned, small, with no pretense of wealth. The show of superiority was for people who needed their position reinforced.

Juanita pushed the reports about Grimm aside to go over the ones about the Marines on the planet. Grimm could put sticks in the wheels, but he couldn't stop what was coming.

The Marines could, though, and that was a problem.

She would either have to take them off the field or make sure their hands were tied when the time came. But how? The Marine Captain Bonds was sharp, and his technology was obviously superior. But they were just people. People who had weaknesses. Military people all the more. Drink and celebration were where they would fall, not on the battlefield.

Bonds' plan did the division for them, splitting up his Marine detachment into four teams of fifty each. Spreading them out to do the most training with her troops. Part of her, a small part, smarted from her planning the betrayal of people who considered themselves friends, if not allies. What was she to do? Her government refused to ally with the Republic, the one nation that guaranteed survival. The Alliance's doom was a forgone conclusion. As soon as the Caliphate fought against them in earnest, there was no way their tiny fleet could stand up to the might of the Caliphate Navy.

If Cordoba sided with the Alliance, then her people would follow. If they sided with the Terran Republic, became a member planet even, then not only would they have access to advanced technology, the Caliphate wouldn't dare attack them. The fool, Santiago, would have them be lapdogs to the Alliance, hoping for leftovers while they flatly refused to give them the tech they needed to compete.

She wouldn't see her people thrust into a war allied with those who wouldn't even share their most basic advances. The Terran Republic promised much. She wasn't stupid enough to think they would deliver it all, but if they only delivered a tenth of what they promised, it would make her people that much more secure.

No, an alliance with the Terran Republic was the only way forward. She shuffled the three photos on her desk, staring at each one in turn. The first, a tall man in a white uniform with brown hair and eyes: Commander Grimm. He looked every bit like the Alliance propaganda said he would.

Second, almost as tall but more muscular, a large black man in fatigues, Captain Bonds. He was dangerous. Their reports said he led the assault on Medial and had seen action in Zuckabar. This was a man who knew what it was to lead in combat. She was thankful that he taught her soldiers now.

The third picture puzzled her. Why her agent had elevated the short, blonde-haired Marine as a threat was beyond her. She was a mere sergeant. They had no file on her the way they did the other two. The woman looked somewhat unusual, with a thick neck and shoulders, but otherwise she appeared the typical soldier.

"Why?" she asked aloud to an empty room.

Regardless, she would make sure all three were watched whenever possible. They—she—couldn't afford any slipups. Santiago had to go. If the election failed to unseat him as the Guild predicted... she would deal with that tragedy when it happened.

"Ma'am," her adjunct interrupted her from the open door. "You have a *personal* call on line three."

"Thank you," she said.

Personal call was code for her liaison. They couldn't fund a coup with their own money. No one was that rich. It required equipment, intelligence, and money for bribes. Lots and lots of money.

"Yes?"

"General, it is good to hear your voice. How are things proceeding?" the man who only went by Mr. Falcon asked.

"I wasn't aware our deal included me answering to you?" she asked. Juanita played a dangerous game. She needed the outsider's money, but she knew keenly that his approach to her was entirely too coincidental. Despite his generous donations to their candidate's campaign, Franceska Divine hadn't closed within spitting distance of Santiago. The man was too popular with the commoners. If only they knew he was leading them to damnation.

"It doesn't. We're all friends here. I was merely making conversation."

She frowned. Falcon's slick tone and all-too-smooth words grated on her.

"Mr. Falcon, I don't have the time for *friends*, nor the inclination to explain to you what I'm doing at any given moment. If you have a question...?" She let it hang.

If her attitude perturbed him, he didn't let on.

"Do you need anything? I can't help but notice that Santiago got his joint training exercise. Perhaps we should wait for a while longer?"

She'd considered that herself, but ultimately dismissed the notion. The election was the perfect time. People expected a change of power, even if the prevailing consensus among the common masses was Santiago's victory. It would be much easier for them to accept the coup and not resist.

"No, we can't delay. If luck is with us, then we won't ever need these plans. If not, the only time we can strike is right after the election."

Mr. Falcon didn't respond right away. He let the silence linger for almost thirty seconds.

"I have means," he finally said, "means that could deal with them decisively, if you wished?"

Deal with four Alliance destroyers? The entire navy couldn't beat them unless it was a sneak attack.

"I appreciate your offer. For now, we are going to continue with my plan. Once we have control of the government, we will order them out."

"As you wish," he said and then hung up the line.

Juanita needed the man's money and resources—badly. She just wished that she didn't end every interaction with him feeling like she had traded a piece of her soul for his aid. At least, if things went south, she knew where to find him. Something he didn't know she knew.

———

Boudreaux liked Cordoba. She especially liked the bars. They knew how to drink and celebrate. Nearly every place she visited in the week she'd spent dirt side had a live band and a festive atmosphere. Their alcohol tasted almost as good as her home planet's, and the people were exceedingly friendly. The men, a little too much. Once they knew she was taken, though, they backed off, which was more than she could say for some of the places she'd spent time in. Zuck Central came to mind, where she carried a combat knife when out, to convince her would-be paramours of her commitment to returning home *alone*.

"I hear Navy pukes make the worst pilots," a baritone said from behind her.

"You must be thinking of the Marines," she retorted. "The Navy doesn't have pilots, only aviators."

"Fine looking ones at that."

She turned with a big smile to see Paul Bonds, wearing civilian clothing that showed off his impressive muscular forearms.

"Paul," she said as she leaped up to hug him, which turned into a rather long kiss. Once they were seated, she played with his hand and frowned. "I've cooled my jets for a week. When do you need me?"

"As an aviator, another few days. I want to hold you and Charlie-One-One in reserve. You're going to be using your bird to float Jennings and her combat team around the battlefield. Keep the locals in suspense as she pops up from one side of the training field to the other in less time than they think she can."

Boudreaux thought about the plan for a moment, examining it from multiple angles. "Don't they have surface radar?"

Paul's eyes twinkled as he cast an admiring gaze at her. "They do, but like most radar, it scatters below one hundred meters, and I happen to know you can fly NOE with your eyes closed."

Despite her years flying the Corsairs, his compliments tickled her belly and made her blush. Maybe it was how much she liked him, more than she had told him, and certainly more than she admitted to herself.

"You've got yourself a Corsair, then."

Paul scooted his chair closer to hers. "It's all part of the final war game. Should be a lot of fun."

"I can think of things we could do that are more fun..."

"Oorah."

CHAPTER SIXTEEN

J acob only had about one million and five things to do before the exercise kicked off at 1800 hours. The least of which was deal with last minute changes to the program.

Cordoba command was insisting that his squadron and only his squadron play the aggressors. He couldn't for the life of him understand why they thought it would be a good idea to have his destroyers trounce their navy time and time again.

However, it was their system. They gave the orders. It was damned peculiar though and not at all what he wanted. They also turned down his request to have officers come aboard to act as liaisons.

"Sir," PO McCall said over the comms speaker next to him.

"Skipper, go ahead, Mac."

"Call from *Apache*-Actual, patching you in."

"Kim, what can I do for you?"

"Did you see this shi—" She stopped herself from swearing over official comms at the last second. Jacob did indeed know what pile of excrement she referred to.

"Yes. What choice do we have?" he asked her.

"But sir, we're not going to get anything out of this, and they certainly aren't. At best this is about as useful as a drill. Our people already know how to run their weapon systems, we needed a *fight.*"

Everything she said was correct. Their month-long voyage to Cordoba went from a useful war game to a one-sided smash where the only thing Cordoba could hope for was a clean defeat.

"What do you think we should do?" he asked. He had his own thoughts on the matter. Breaking up the squadron into two, or even four units, might give them the fight they're looking for.

"We need an outer system patrol anyway. We're too far from reinforcements. Why don't I take *Apache* and *Justice* out to the rim and practice our stealth and ECM. Two destroyers are still more than enough to wipe out their whole fleet, but at least *Interceptor* and *Kidd* won't make it look too easy."

Jacob pulled up a holo of the system, zooming out until it was useful. Cordoba had a lot of outer system activity. It was a popular system to trade with and lay on the route between the Terran Republic and Alliance space. A quarter of all trade traversed the system. Having a pair of Alliance destroyers out there would help calm some fears. Show the flag during an uncertain time.

"Officer thinking, Kim. You have my permission. When will you get underway?"

Kim's professional demeanor barely changed; it was only that he knew her well that he detected the slight blush of her cheeks.

"Before the official start of the games. Call it 1715. I still have ten crew on planet. They're wrapping up and heading back within the hour."

The chrono in the corner of his NavPad read 1559. "Excellent. One week to the minute I want you back here. I'll let Capitán Castro know of the change."

"And Admiral Pérez?"

Technically, he would need to run any significant changes to the war games by her. Jacob, though, decided what was significant and what wasn't. "I will inform her personally the next time I see her. I think this would be best done person-to-person."

Kim saw through his thinly veiled excuse. "I've got my orders, Skipper. Time to execute them."

When the line died, he keyed the bridge back and asked to be connected to *Kidd*.

"*Kidd*, Spacer Malone speaking."

"Malone, Commander Grimm. Can you put me through to Commander Carlos?"

"Aye, aye, sir. One moment."

Jacob glanced idly at his NavPad as he waited. He really wanted to help train Cordoba's navy, not just lord over them how inferior they were to the Alliance.

"Commander Carlos speaking."

Jacob filled him in on the change of plans.

"I want a full accounting of our battles, weaknesses, mistakes, you name it. Even if it's me. Understood."

"Aye, sir. Understood. I'll stick to you like glue."

"Good man," Jacob said and disconnected.

———

Interceptor cut through space on invisible waves of gravity, accelerating at only half her maximum. Jacob could push his half-strength squadron to 500 g's, but then Cordoba's ships wouldn't stand any chance. As it was, he gave them an opportunity for success. The operational goal for DesRon 12 was simple: orbit the planet and bomb the major cities.

Capitán Castro had to stop him, which was much harder than one might think. Since he was the aggressor, he got to choose the time and place of the engagement.

Swinging the ships out wide, he set a course for the outer belts, then halfway there and outside detection range, he did a full-power turn and came back along the ecliptic, skirting the edge of detection. Castro's light cruiser and destroyers orbited Cordoba at the poles. Standard defense doctrine suggested her ships should stay at the planet to protect it.

Now, if Jacob wanted to be a real jerk, he could just launch a bombardment from outside their detection range. However, that would leave the planet an irradiated husk and useless to everyone. The assumption always was that people invading a planet wanted to take the planet, not render it lifeless.

"Helm, come about fifteen degrees to starboard and five degrees down bubble," Jacob ordered.

Chief Suresh reiterated his orders exactly before executing them.

"What are you thinking, Skipper?" Carter asked from his position in DCS.

Jacob pondered the map of the system. Most people thought of space as a big empty nothing. Jacob knew, though, that the key to any victory was using every advantage, terrain included. He manipulated his screen until it showed the small group of battleship-sized asteroids that followed the planet like a lovesick teenager.

"We're going to sneak up on them."

"Devious, Skip."

"If they didn't want to be caught unaware, they should have put a probe to cover their backside," he replied. "Comms, set a MK XIV to delayed activation. I want it flying right at their processing infrastructure on their moon, Iberia. Set it for random spurts of gravity." The blood-red moon was rich in nickel-iron and had extensive mining and processing plants. It was a valid target for any attack... it was also five hundred thousand klicks from the planet. If Castro was looking in the wrong direction when he made his approach, all the better.

"MK XIV ready, sir," Spacer Gouger replied.

"Weps, stealth launch," Jacob ordered.

"Aye, aye, sir. Stealth launch," Lieutenant Brown confirmed. Stealth launches weren't useful in battle, but under the circumstance, could be useful. He needed the Cordoban Navy to believe the torpedo was his ships accelerating toward the moon. If they picked up the EM spike of a normal launch, that was out the window. A stealth launch was the equivalent of them tossing the torpedo overboard and letting its engines do the rest. Long after *Interceptor* cleared the area.

The spacers in Torpedo Room One heaved the weapon into place. The tube inner doors opened and the PO in charge of the compartment ordered them to load. Two meters of grav drive and delicate electronic warfare components slid into the tube.

"Bridge, Torpedo Room One. Loaded and sealed."

"Ready, skipper." Austin's hand hovered over the fire button as he awaited the order.

Jacob watched the numbers on his MFD carefully. He wanted to fire at just the right moment. He'd ordered the ship to turn toward the moon, angling slightly "down" so that the torpedo would look as if it were coming from a different direction than where his ships were actually heading. It would take luck, but a quick astrogator might see through the ruse.

He raised his hand, preparing to give the order. As the line from his ship to the moon intersected, he brought it down swiftly. "Fire."

"Fire one," Brown said.

The outer doors blew open, expelling the torpedo at barely 1g of acceleration. Without the coils to shoot it along at 700 g's, the torpedo simply floated in space. In mere moments, *Interceptor* was nothing more than a fading dot. An hour passed while the torpedo moved a tiny thirty-five klicks toward the moon. At the same time, *Interceptor* was hundreds of thousands of klicks away when the small but powerful grav drive kicked in. The torpedo shot forward at 540 g's. The fusion battery packed into the fuselage powered the ECM spoof that began broadcasting a signal very much like *Interceptor*'s.

———

Capitán de Navío Castro hated waiting. She would rather be out in space, looking for her opponent, or doing something. Anything other than waiting for a blip on her screen to show her a possible attack. Her light cruiser, *Estrella*, was the most advanced her people could build. It had the tonnage to be called one, but not the firepower. They used high-energy laser emitters for turrets and missile batteries. In other words, she mused, it was useless against a modern warship. Great against pirates, which she had personally seen, too, but against *Interceptor*'s range? Not a chance. If they even scored a hit, she would be shocked.

"Ma'am, I think I have something," Lieutenant Ortega said from astrogation.

"Lay it on me," she said as she stood, heading for him.

Ortega pointed at his screen showing an intermittent signal. She squinted, trying to see what he saw.

"It's weak, but it looks like their ship and she's heading for Iberia's main production plant."

"You can tell that from this?" she asked, pointing at the almost invisible notation on the screen.

"Aye, ma'am. Uh." He seemed embarrassed. "I might have taken some pretty detailed readings of their destroyer as they departed the area... ma'am."

Castro smiled broadly at the young man. "Well done. Double-check the course, and if it remains true, let's plot an intercept to get them right before they intersect with the moon. We might not win the fight, but we can give as good as we get."

"Aye, aye, ma'am."

———

"They fell for it, sir," Ensign Brennan said. The blips on her screen moved away from the planet.

Interceptor had maneuvered behind the following asteroids. Only popping out long enough to update passive sensors before dropping back behind the rock. At flank speed, they would achieve orbit of the planet in less than ten minutes. More than fast enough. He just wanted to make sure the enemy had taken the bait. It was entirely possible they were playing him. He wouldn't easily fall for a trick like the one he played on Castro.

"Let's give them another fifty thousand klicks, then we'll move in for the kill. Brown, keep a running update for our turrets. If we have to shoot, I don't want a delay. Devi, same thing for helm."

"Aye, sir," they said in unison. He loved the way his crew worked, efficient and on target.

Jacob held his breath as the Cordoba ships continued to

move toward the moon Iberia. Part of him tinged with guilt. Subterfuge and guile were his thing, he knew that. It was one thing to beat an opponent because the tech was superior, an entirely another thing to outsmart them. Here, he was doing both. He hoped Capitán Castro would forgive him. She certainly gave off the vibe of wanting to learn more.

"Five-zero-zero-kilo klicks, sir," Ensign Brennan announced.

"Helm, execute maneuver delta-four," Jacob ordered.

He had worked out several specific approaches to the planet. Delta-one was the quietest, four the loudest.

Interceptor rose above the asteroid it hid behind, her grinning shark maw looming like a predator. The gravcoil powered up and she shot through space, leaving the asteroids behind her. Ten thousand klicks off her port beam, *Kidd* followed, staying just ahead of *Interceptor's* gravwake. The two ships accelerated at an easy 250 g's. At the two-minute mark, they cruised at over 290 KPS toward Cordoba.

"Will they be able to make it into engagement range when they see us?" Jacob asked.

Ensign Brennan punched in the calculations on her computer, running through several different scenarios. "No, sir, even if they started now, they couldn't get back to zero before we achieve orbit."

Then he'd won, all without firing a shot. In a real fight, though, it wouldn't be over until one side couldn't shoot anymore. Orbiting a planet wasn't the same as controlling a planet. It certainly made it advantageous, though.

"Gauger, notify Capitán de Navío Castro that we will have control of her planet shortly. Better luck next time, Commander Grimm out."

———

"I see it, Ortega, I see it," Capitán de Navío Castro said to her dejected astrogation officer. They thought they'd seen through the *Interceptor*'s deception. Only to find out they detected what the ship wanted them to.

Castro sat back in her chair hard, but she managed to bring a smile to her face. "The good news is, they can't pull that trick again."

"No, ma'am, we'll see through it next time."

That was the point of the exercise, to learn. She couldn't be mad at him for that.

CHAPTER SEVENTEEN

Jennings wiped the sweat from her brow, flicking the droplets onto the ground beside her. If not for the nanites in her uniform, sweat would cover her. The heat on Cordoba was tolerable, but only barely.

Naki, Owens, and June were behind her, crouched as she was, in a classic wedge. Out to either side of them were the eight local soldiers who had volunteered to train with them.

"Capitán," she whispered.

Capitán Javier Sanchez moved silently to kneel next to her. He held his slug throwing rifle in an approximation of how she carried her MP-17, tight to the chest and barrel down.

"Yes, Gunny?"

Their position overlooking the FOB for the main force had several advantages. One, it was heavily wooded. Lots of animals baffled thermal readings. Two, it was twenty meters up the side of a ridge that ran three klicks long. They had rappelled down the night before under the cover of a summer downpour.

They were dry by 10 hundred and wet again from sweat by 11. She didn't know what was worse, the extreme cold or heat, but she decided she hated them both.

"If this were a Marine FOB, we'd put the CP in the middle. Is that true for you people?" she asked.

Javier and his five men seemed like decent soldiers to Jennings. They listened, did their best to imitate what the Marines did, and treated all her people with respect. She couldn't ask for more from the situation. Despite their difference in rank, he treated her as the expert she was.

"No, Gunny." Javier knelt down and crawled to the very edge of the lip. Jennings followed him and ended up next to him. He pulled out his electronic field glasses and scanned the makeshift base. "The army decided that if there was going to be fighting, it made sense to disguise the—CP as you call it—as something else and put it in the back. That way, no snipers or sappers could decapitate the unit."

Javier stopped and pointed. Jennings used her helmet to zoom in on the location. Sure enough, toward the back of the tents and fabricated structures, she spotted it. The CP.

"That's our target, then," she whispered.

Javier hesitated. "Gunny, I know you Marines are well trained, but the entire reason we put it in the back is to keep this very thing from happening. You can't walk through an entire camp of soldiers, into the CP, and declare yourself the winner."

Naki chuckled from behind. Jennings slowly turned her head to Javier, a deadly gleam in her eye. "Javier, that's exactly what we're going to do."

———

Captain Paul Bonds looked over the *paper* maps on the CP's large desk. The local army had impressive knowledge of the area and the maps were detailed. They were paper, though, and lacked the finesse of holograms.

"Work with what you got, Paul," he muttered to himself. A glance at his MarPad showed him the time, 0530. Despite his warnings that attacks were most likely to happen between 0500 and 0700, the army officers didn't want to rally the men out to 100 percent security. They insisted to him that no one would dare attack their HQ. Ruiz had wanted to push things, but that wasn't how the army operated. She could order them, but it would undermine her with the officers. It was a bizarre way to run a military but his was not to judge.

Paul shook his head. He knew Jennings. Whatever they thought couldn't happen, she would *make* happen. No doubt.

The auto door slid aside and an army private stepped in. He wore the armband of their communications corps.

"Comandante Ruiz?" he asked, his voice high pitched and squeaky.

Ruiz, to her credit, sat across the room, sipping an espresso while she went over the training exercises for the day. Even while practicing for war, they were continuing the daily training. Five thousand Cordoban soldiers learning from 200 marines. It was a learning experience for all of them.

"Yes, Private?" Ruiz replied, glancing up from her coffee.

"Hands up," Jennings said as she pushed the private into the CP. Corporal Naki, Lance Corporal Owens, and PFC June stormed in behind her, clearing the room ahead of Capitán Javier Martinez. The older man stood in the doorway with openmouthed shock.

"She said we would walk right in and take the place... but I didn't believe her," Martinez said.

Paul resisted the urge to let out a laugh. Of course, she found a way to do just that.

"Comandante, I think Gunny Jennings just pointed out the need for 100 percent security at this time of day, don't you think?"

Ruiz had stood, hands up, while Jennings checked the rest of the room.

"I couldn't agree with you more, Captain," she said with a grin.

———

After taking the CP, Jennings and her squad were excused for the day. It wasn't as if they could go to town and live it up, so instead they hit the chow hall and settled for some hot food after three days of field rats. The line for breakfast stretched around the tent. She didn't mind waiting. Owens grumbled about starving, but she ignored him. They stashed all their gear in the Mudcat that Captain Bonds brought down. They wore just their combat uniform, vest, and sidearm.

Her muscles ached, and she was bone tired from their trek through the woods in the middle of the night, and her squad felt the same way. Smells of peppers and fried meat wafted out of the mess tent.

"My stomach is gonna revolt if we don't get some chow, Gunny," Naki said.

"We all ate at the same time, Naki, simmer down," Jennings said.

The line moved at a snail's pace, moving forward centimeter by centimeter. Jennings took the time to scan the men ahead of her. Something about the soldiers was off to her. They were all a little heavy, a little slow. Were they not full-time soldiers? That thought boggled her mind. How could a planet as big and wealthy as Cordoba not have a full-time army?

Jennings, not one to dive too deep into any thoughts, decided to let her subconscious chew on the matter for a bit. Whatever it was, would come to her in time.

"Gunny," Javier said as he approached with his squad. "You

don't have to wait in line, Jennings. We're the enemy, we get to go right in." He clapped her on the back, as friendly as can be.

"Oorah," she said. They cut out, went right into the tent. The food was as good as it smelled and she dished herself an extra heap of eggs and bacon, wanting to pack on the protein for the next training exercise that started first thing in the AM. The Marines found their own table away from the locals, and dug in.

"Gunny," Owens started around a mouthful of richly spiced potatoes. "Why are we playing stone-age soldier? No drones, no orbital cover, no nothing."

Jennings finished her mouthful before setting her spoon down and glaring intently at the red-headed lance corporal. "Naki, you wanna answer his question?"

"To be honest, Gunny... I was thinking the same thing."

She shook her head. Her Marines were excellent fighters, some of the best. Better, she thought, than even the special forces team they served with... which made her think about Danny for a few seconds, which in turn made her *feel* something that she didn't like.

"June?"

The PFC ducked her head sheepishly. "Yes, Gunny. Same."

Jennings worried about June. She'd spent the last four months at fleet medical getting her back and legs repaired and rehabilitated. The wounds she suffered, though, hadn't seemed to deter her desire to serve.

"Look around, tell me what you see," she said.

Owens took a moment to scan the full mess hall. It wasn't at all like the Navy or Marines would have, more of a well-structured tent with a serving line on one side and tables taking up the rest of the space. The food was cooked somewhere else and brought in.

"Three exits, two obvious places for cover, and one exit via knife," Owens said.

"Good, but not right. June?"

Determined not to get it wrong, she took even longer than Owens had, really looking around. "Sixty military-age males, though that's a bit questionable because Cordoba has access to genetic aging tech... they have facial hair, uh... their uniforms aren't great... sorry Gunny, that's all I got."

Naki raised an eyebrow at Jennings. "For real?" he asked, understanding dawned on his face. "Is that why we were able to walk through the whole base?"

"You got it. They don't know the basics of soldiering. Maybe they rely too much on tech, maybe they never knew the basics, but like with the Raptors, if you don't know how to fight outside of them—"

"You can't fight in them," they finished as one.

Jennings had noticed it with Javier over the last week. None of the soldiers were in top shape, they weren't quite slovenly, but they certainly weren't sharp. She figured it was her job to push home the point that they needed to get squared away.

Captain Bonds would take care of that once she finished killing them over and over again. That thought brought a wicked grin to her face. By the end of the month, they would have these soldiers whipped into shape.

CHAPTER EIGHTEEN

Mendez stepped back from the grill, sweat seeping down the crease of his back. He had to resist the urge to wipe his forehead. The galley wasn't prepared for twice the normal crew, certainly not ones who wanted to come back for seconds. He couldn't even hear himself think over the din of the mess.

"Mendez, we need more food pronto," Bosun Sandivol said.

"I'm on it, Bosun."

An hour earlier, the Bosun had alerted him that *Interceptor* was going to dock with *Estrella* and have a joint dinner. After twenty missions, she had finally landed a blow against *Kidd* in the last operation. A monumental achievement, even if they ultimately lost the battle. The skipper, however, didn't want to waste the opportunity to reward the Cordoban crew.

"Head in the game, Perch," Mendez said.

Perch froze as his bare hand was about to grab the hot pan off the laser cooktop.

"Thanks PO," Perch said.

———

Jacob's ears rang from the cacophony of the mess deck. Over a hundred spacers from the *Estrella* were aboard *Interceptor*, enjoying their food and especially their soft-serve ice cream machine. According to Castro, such luxuries didn't exist on their ships, but they had plenty of alcohol. Alcohol they were liberally sharing with his crew.

He spied Bosun Sandivol moving to intercept a spacer on his first deployment about to take a drink. Jacob waved Sandivol off, deciding that the celebratory spirit warranted some drinks.

"COB?" Jacob said to the dark-haired woman next to him.

"Skipper?"

"Can you quietly let the crew know that as long as they don't get out of control, we can be a wet ship for the duration."

Chief Suresh raised an eyebrow. "All right, then," she said, effecting a mock attention.

She walked to the nearest Cordoban, taking the offered flask, raised it to the crew, and drank deep. "The captain says have at it—" Cheers erupted along with raucous smiles. "But keep it reasonable or the Bosun will have your hide!"

Someone raised a borrowed flask. "To the captain!" Flasks went up.

Jacob waved graciously at his people before ducking out of the mess and heading for the bridge.

"Commander?" Capitán Castro said, as he made his way forward.

"Capitán, your crew sure knows how to have a good time," he said with a smile.

Castro didn't miss a stride as she stepped up to him, walking shoulder to shoulder. "What they lack in discipline they make up for in good spirits."

Jacob had wondered about that. He wouldn't call them sloppy, but their uniforms were about as well tailored as their salutes were crisp—which was not at all. However, it wasn't for him to judge. They operated their equipment with proficiency, and they worked hard.

There was more than one way to pluck a tree-duck, he supposed. While his navy worked hard to maintain discipline and tradition, he could see the advantages of a laxer approach.

The briefing room hatch stood open, with PO Cartwright manning the bridge hatch, including his sidearm. Jacob didn't have him come close the briefing room... it taxed most everyone but Jennings.

"How can I help you, Capitán?" he said as he took his normal seat at the far end.

Castro stood at the end where his XO would normally be. Her expression showed little; he didn't know her well enough to know for sure what she was thinking. Pensive was the word that came to mind.

She put a hand on the chair as if she were going to sit down, then changed her mind.

"Commander Grimm," she started, but stopped with her mouth open.

"Capitán—"

Castro raised her hand. "Helena, please," she said.

"Jacob," he returned. "Helena, I'm not familiar with your people's customs, but I know when someone has a question. How can I help?"

She shook her head, finally deciding to take a seat. "This is the problem, Jacob"—his name sounded odd with her accent, but not unpleasant—"you're too kind..." Her pause spoke volumes. "Which is part of the problem. Commander Grimm—Jacob, my world is going through a lot right now. Perhaps your home is similar? I don't know much about Alexandria."

Jacob thought about the upheaval of the last five years. A

war that very few people believe they can win, scant allies, corruption—yes, they were going through a lot. He wasn't about to air his home world's dirty laundry to a stranger, though.

"I think it's the nature of man to face adversity. When people come together to form something greater than themselves, there is always going to be conflict revolving around exactly what that looks like. Despite some unrest on Alexandria, almost all of our disagreements are how to proceed in a way that's best for everyone. I imagine it's similar here on Cordoba?"

Castro's eyes widened, and she looked at him, really looked at him, as if she hadn't seen him before. "That's exactly what's going on. I thought..." She glanced away. Did he see shame on her face? "Well, I guess I thought it was unique to Cordoba, that our problems were somehow special."

Jacob resisted the urge to laugh or chuckle. "I think everyone experiences that belief. We are, after all, living in our minds. I'm sure a lot of problems in the galaxy could be solved if people just took a moment to view things from another perspective. It's a vain hope, though. That's just not who humans are. Inherently, we're selfish, elitist, and power hungry. Only our desire to do good, to rise above our natural inclinations, is what elevates us."

He paused for a moment, heat rising on his neck as he realized he'd slipped into the tone and voice he used to lecture the crew.

If Castro noticed, she said nothing. Her eyes were lost in thought.

"Your view is a noble one, and enviable. I'm afraid I don't have the luxury of that. I wish I did."

Confused, Jacob decided not to press the matter. For him, right and wrong weren't foolish pursuits. He wasn't naïve.

There were situations where those two concepts didn't come into play. However, every thought, every action, needed to be evaluated on that scale. If he didn't, then it would be too easy to use *duty*, or something else, as an excuse for evil.

"Helena, I feel like there is something else you want to talk to me about. Is everything okay?"

She shook her head. Standing, she started walking for the hatch. "I'm afraid I have to get back to my ship, Commander. Thank you for the talk. It was... enlightening."

Just like that, she was gone, leaving Jacob alone in the briefing room wondering what had just happened? Command was a lonely calling. One could never really open up to subordinates about feelings or frustrations. Yes, anything involving the crew, of course, but not about one's own personal thoughts and feelings.

A close relationship with an exec can help, but to really understand what is going on in the mind of a captain, another captain was needed. Jacob felt like she had attempted to communicate something to him, more than just the words she used, but he couldn't figure out what.

Castro's performance in the games was as good as one could expect. Better even, considering the technological disadvantage her navy was at. Though, he would rather be on the frontline, fighting the Caliphate. Goodwill missions were important, too, especially when they might lead to bringing in a new member planet. The Alliance could use all the help they could get.

Jacob leaned back, rubbing his face for a moment. The list of things he needed to do never seemed to diminish. He pressed the button on the table, activating the comms.

"Bosun, Skipper."

"Bosun here, Skip."

"What is the status of the fabricators and supplies? I want to make sure—"

He lost himself in the management aspect of command, letting his worries vanish under the weight of responsibility.

CHAPTER NINETEEN

Lieutenant Commander Yuki leaned back in her chair, marveling at the ease her computer tracked the hundreds of contacts coming into and departing Cordoba. The outer system was a plethora of small to medium sized transport ships.

"How many on screen right now?" she asked her astrogator's assistant.

PO Metzer held the noise-canceling headphones to his ear, listening for the telltale sound of gravity waves as they were translated by the lasers in the hull of *Apache*.

"One hundred and ninety-three, within thirty-three light-seconds, ma'am."

"Wow," she muttered. "Xavier, what do you think? Sit and watch or pick one at random?" she asked her XO.

Xavier Thompson's height almost rivaled Commander Grimm's, but he was far skinnier than the skipper, to the point his uniform always seemed loose on him. She liked him, though. He never complained, spoke up when he thought he should, and worked hard.

"One second, ma'am," he said. Reaching down, Xavier

tapped a few keys on her MFD, transferring the readout to the main viewer.

Kim loved *Interceptor* and would never forget her time aboard the destroyer, but *Apache* was only five years old. Her tech, reliability and armament outweighed her old ship three to one. Of course, she wasn't as fast as the Hellcat. Acceleration on the Apache peaked at 520 g's.

The main viewer mixed all the ship's sensor data together. Every ship *Apache* could see appeared, along with an arrow showing their current direction, acceleration, velocity, etc. All she had to do was point and the computer would bring up a more detailed info box. Along with that information, ghost lines showed the probable destinations. The longer her sensors tracked a ship, the accuracy of the probability improved.

"Remove everything heading for Cordoba. They have their own customs," Kim ordered.

"Aye, aye, ma'am."

A few seconds passed and suddenly one-third of the ships vanished.

"Now take away M-class ships flagged in the Alliance or the Iron Empire.

"That's odd," Xavier said.

"What?" Kim asked.

"There are none for the Iron Empire, or the Terran Republic, but there are a few for the Alliance. Far fewer than I thought there would be," he said with a shrug.

"Could be the time of year. Carry on," she said.

The remaining ships were all small and medium sized freighters flagged with the Terran Republic or other independent systems.

"Eight M-class ships are currently heading for Alliance space, three for the Republic," her XO said. "About... two dozen small freighters going in either direction and..."

Kim gave him a moment to continue, not wanting to be one of those commanders who said the obvious.

"Sir?" PO Metzer said to get his attention. "Is this what you're looking at?"

A ship highlighted on the main screen. A circle appeared next to it, showing all the relevant sensor data.

"Thank you, PO," Xavier said.

Kim leaned forward, enhancing the view of her MFD. "This is a little odd, don't you think?" she asked.

"Aye, ma'am. Want me to hail them?"

Kim played with the sensor controls, rewinding them to where they arrived in their current position eight hours before. At no point did the ship engage her gravcoil.

"No... let's inspect, shall we? Astro, set a course. Keep it casual, though. I don't want to spook them if they're up to no good."

The young lieutenant astrogator grinned big as he replied. "Aye, aye, ma'am, setting a casual course. Helm come to—"

Kim let them do their job as she examined the odd contact closer. Something about it seemed familiar, but she couldn't place what. She was sure it would come to her.

———

Former supervisor and current captain in the new TFG's intelligence division, John Hopper rotated in his seat. Bored, didn't begin to describe what he was. When the Guild switched over to its more military approach, he'd found a way out of the front line. He'd seen the footage of what one out-of-date Alliance destroyer had done to four top-of-the-line Guild ships.

What he hadn't realized at the time was how dull intelligence gathering was. Cordoba was busy, yes, but all he had to do was sit and let the computer form a picture of the system.

Once every twenty-four hours it asked him to move, and he passed that order to his crew, who moved the disguised freighter. Rinse and repeat. He could hardly blame the four other crew on the bridge for not paying attention to their screens. It was a little odd, he thought, that the TFG Intel would assign such a small crew to a ship and only one officer? If the rumors were true, their human resources were stretched thin.

The Board... Admiralty, he wasn't sure what to call them, weren't obliged to tell him why they weren't fully crewing the ships they sent out. Maybe it was because there wasn't anything to do and having a hundred men with free time on their hands was much worse than eight. Enough for two watches and no more.

Unfortunately, his command chair was the only station on the ship that couldn't play movies or games. Hell, his helm/navigator slept at his station, boots on the console. Hopper couldn't exactly discipline them. They were stationed in Cordoba for at least two more weeks, and he didn't need the headache. Things were certainly a far cry from how they used to be, where if one of his subordinates failed there were immediate and painful consequences.

An alarm rang out on the bridge followed by a flashing red light on the astrogator's panel.

Hopper waited ten seconds before demanding what was going on.

"Uh, I'm waiting for the computer to tell me, sir," Chesire said.

Maybe the Guild had cut training costs a little too much in favor of using the less expensive computer assisted packages.

"By all means, *wait for the computer* to explain the flashing red light. It's not like our lives will depend on it."

"Yes, sir," Chesire said, the sarcasm flying over his head.

———

"I think they spotted us, Skipper," Xavier said. Sure enough, the ship they were closing in on suddenly fired up her gravcoil and headed for the closest starlane.

Kim examined the power curve of the ship. Something about it sparked a kernel of a memory.

"XO…" She debated her next words. She was about to take the ship from casually looking around to something far more deliberate. "Action stations."

Lieutenant Xavier glanced her way before reaching up and grabbing the mike. "All hands, set Condition Zulu, Action Stations. I say again, Action Stations. Condition Zulu." He placed the mic back in the cradle.

"Xavier, you have the con. I'm going to change. If they do anything hinky, use your discretion."

"Aye, aye, ma'am. I have the con."

Kim had *Apache* well trained. Two minutes and seventeen seconds later, they had their ship in action stations. Crews manned turrets, torpedoes, and radar.

"Weapons," she said as she racked her helmet on the command chair. "Live track the ship."

"Aye, ma'am, live track," Lieutenant Hernandez replied.

Kim pulled the fleeing ship's silhouette up. Something about it bugged her.

"Do we have a thermal reading on their reactor?" she asked.

"Aye, ma'am, one second," PO Metzer said. The main viewer flickered, and an outline of the fleeing ship appeared. The reactor flashed in the middle of the ship. "Uh, thermal is off the chart for a ship that size. I don't get it?" Metzer said.

Realization hit Kim like a slap across the face. "Battle stations! Drain the can," she shouted. Her helmet slammed down on her suit, hard. "Comms, get me *Justice* and send an update to the skipper," she said.

"Aye, aye, ma'am," her comms officer said.

Commander Marsh's face appeared on Kim's MFD.

"Sabrina, there are Guild ships in the system. I'm tracking one right now. They have a superweapon called a gravity laser. Do not, I say again, *do not approach* the ships from the front. If they so much as adjust their yaw by a single degree, you blow them out of space. Understood?"

"Aye, ma'am, understood."

Kim killed the connection, refocusing her efforts on the current tactical situation. While the Alliance wasn't directly at war with the Guild, they were under orders to apprehend any of their ships that came to Alliance space.

"Comms, get me on the chip."

"Aye, aye, ma'am. On the chip."

———

The woman looked pissed. Even though Hopper could only see her face through the helmet she wore, her words were crystal clear. Heave-to and prepare to be boarded. She knew all about their gravity laser. If he tried to run, change course, or so much a rolled his ship, she would open fire and obliterate them.

He had no intention of following the Guild's asinine death before capture policy. However, his options weren't self-inflicted destruction or capture. They had the right papers, the correct ID tags, there wasn't any reason he couldn't just do as they ordered and not come out on top. The Guild had paid a lot of money making sure their intel ships were survivable and somewhat secure. It wasn't like they had any legal authority this far away from Cordoba. Maybe if a local ship was with them... as it was, though, the only authority the Alliance had was that of their guns.

Which for him was the same thing. "Put me on," Hopper said.

"Link established."

"Captain Yuki, this is Commander Hopper of the Terran Trading Vessel *Monitor*. We will come to a stop and await your order." He killed the link, then waved for his helmsman to stop the ship.

―――――

"That's a little too easy," Kim said. "Chief Fletcher, keep us on their six."

The short man in the Pit repeated her command as the *Apache* slowed along with the *Monitor*.

Kim wondered if the name referred to the lizard, or the action? Were they a spy ship?

"Skipper," Xavier asked over the comms, "are you sure it's a Guild ship? The frame doesn't match what we have the database."

"The power output does, though," she replied. Was she sure? Her instincts, or gut, as Commander Grimm would say, told her it was. Why else would a small ship have a fusion reactor of such size? No, it was a Guild ship. Crossing their bow would mean death for her crew. "Until I know otherwise, I'm going to assume it is."

"Aye, aye, ma'am."

Kim watched the plot carefully as *Apache* closed in on the suspected ship. Every piece of information that could be detected was displayed on an overlay of *Monitor*.

"Weps," she said without taking her eyes off the plot, "if

their power spikes, or they change direction, do not wait for orders. Just fire everything."

"Ma'am?" her weapons officer asked.

"Lieutenant Bricker, they have a weapon called a graser. It's a gravity laser with enough power to turn *Apache* into a floating field of shattered nano-steel. Understood?"

"Aye, aye, ma'am."

He sounded scared. *Good,* Kim thought, *fear will keep him sharp.*

Distance dropped steadily until Apache came to a full stop one kilometer off the stern of the ship.

"Comms," she said again. "Open a channel to *Monitor.*"

"Aye, aye, ma'am."

Kim waited for a few seconds for her comm to give her the thumbs up.

"Monitor, *Apache.* Transmit your identification and prepare to be boarded." She cut the line. "Xavier, take Gunny Hicks and Delta over and secure that ship. I want them in mag cuffs and on their knees before we search the ship. Don't take any chances, the Guild likes to blow themselves up."

Xavier blanched at her concern. "Aye, ma'am."

CHAPTER TWENTY

Jacob shook his head as he watched Kim's report. A Guild ship? In Cordoba? But not one willing to fight or blow themselves up. So far Kim's boarding party hadn't found anything but weeks of recordings. The ship had sat in the outer system, watching traffic, and recording the comings and goings of every ship.

"What do you think, Carter?" he asked.

"Intelligence gathering?" he asked.

It made sense. Jacob manipulated the controls on his NavPad showing the data they'd collected. Months and months. He scrolled through the information, looking for some sign of what they were looking for. It would be one thing if they were close to the planet, monitoring communications and observing the people of Cordoba, but only if there was something worth monitoring.

Jacob liked the people of the planet below. He liked their military, but they were woefully, hilariously underpowered compared to the galaxy at large. How could they not be? One planet, no matter how financially successful, couldn't hope to compete with dozens of planets all working together.

The Guild, though, defied that rule since they were an unknown quality. How many planets like Wonderland did they have? As far as Jacob knew, they had infinite resources; they were just spent in the wrong direction.

"Commander Yuki did say they weren't outfitted like a Guild ship, though. Something about..." Carter paused as he scrolled through the report. "Pseudo military ranks?"

Jacob skipped to the section Carter referenced. Sure enough, they were using generic navy ranks. It was a lot to take in. Had the Guild changed since the last time he'd run into them?

"Regardless of what they're planning, and I think we have no way of knowing what that is, if it's anything at all, let's move the squadron to Condition Yankee, even if we're in orbit."

Carter frowned as he added the notes. "That's going to add a lot of wear and tear to the systems. An extra..." He paused, doing the calculations. "...thirty hours at least."

Jacob understood where Carter's concern came from. They were already a month into the mission with hundreds if not thousands of extra hours on the equipment from the travel and the war games. Every hour of use had a number of minutes of corresponding maintenance. Once they were back in their port and the minutes turned into hours, hours into days, paperwork mounted, and the yard started questioning everything.

"True, XO, but at the same time"—Jacob held out his hands like a scale—"maintenance or death from lack of preparation?"

Carter's face tightened. "You make an excellent point, Skipper."

Jacob shrugged with an easy smile. "It's why they pay me the big bucks. Okay, let's get on to the leave requests. I know with us orbiting a foreign port, the crew's slamming you with requests?"

"Aye, Skipper. About one a day."

Jacob checked the calendar. They had another week of war

games with Cordoba. Assuming they weren't asked to stay longer, or the ambassador didn't need him, they could depart. If they headed for home immediately, it would be another five weeks before the crew had a real leave. That seemed wrong to Jacob. All it would take was one request for an extra seventy-two hours and he could grant leave to half his crew at a time. While Cordoba wasn't as exotic a port of call as a Consortium world, it would still be worthwhile.

"Let them know I'm working on it. If it's up to me, then yes, leave will happen before we start the trek back to Alexander."

A knock on the hatch interrupted them.

"Sir?" Spacer's Apprentice McKnight entered with a look that told Jacob the young man would like to be anywhere else.

"Yes, Spacer?" Carter replied.

McKnight entered the room and came to attention. "Chief Redfern would like to request water for the fusion plant, sir. He said it needed to be watered daily."

Jacob held his tongue, desperate to avoid laughing at the earnest young man.

Carter managed to look away, a grin spreading on his face as he hid his guffaw.

"Talk to PO Mendez in the galley, Justin," Jacob said. He figured the embarrassment of the wild-goose chase would be lessened by having the "old man" call him by name.

"Sir, thank you, sir." McKnight spun around like he was on review and marched out of the room. Jacob and Carter listened for the sound of the young man's boots on the ladder before breaking out into a laugh.

"Oh man, I needed that," Jacob said. "Tell Redfern well done."

"Aye, sir, on it," Carter said.

He glanced back at the NavPad with Kim's report. There was something going on out there, but this simply wasn't their territory. His authority was limited. Kim pushed her luck demanding the Guild ship heave-to. He stood behind her decision, though.

Carter stood and stretched. "Sorry, sir," he said covering up a yawn.

"No need, XO. I'm glad you're working hard, but don't work yourself to the point of uselessness."

After Carter departed, Jacob turned back to the NavPad.

The Guild was a problem. He hadn't really heard any news about them since they lost Wonderland... other than their purchase of two state-of-the-art battleships from the Terran Republic.

They wouldn't need battleships unless they were planning a battle. Perhaps they had learned from the one-sided engagement with the Alliance. You don't take a freighter to a warship fight. They just aren't suited for it. Beyond weapon systems, energy, and materials, there was mass and construction. Freighters didn't have quadruple redundancy on compartments, or the same density of materials.

He tapped his fingers on the shark logo while thinking about what to do. The chances of the Guild attacking the exact system he inhabited seemed small to none. Not zero, but infinitesimal.

The image of the small freighter Kim seized the day before popped up on his NavPad. If they weren't planning on attacking, then why have an intelligence gathering asset in-system?

Curiouser and curiouser. Also, above his pay grade. He finished his report to the Admiralty, along with a recommendation to put a permanent squadron out in the general area. Once he finished writing it, he put it in queue for the next packet.

———

"I don't see a problem with that, Commander Grimm," Ambassador Nguyen said in reply to the request for leave.

Nguyen leaned back, glancing at the holograph of his wife placed carefully on his desk. His days on Cordoba were packed with meetings, lunches, and tours. The few precious hours he'd spent with her each night were all he could spare. Six months out of every year, though, his duty demanded this of him, and as the amazing companion she was, she stuck with it.

"I'm having lunch with the president, and I'll run it by him. I don't think he will complain... if you haven't noticed he's a bit—"

Commander Grimm coughed, his cheeks turning slightly red from the ambassador's words.

"Interested?" Grimm asked.

Nguyen chuckled as he spoke. "Captivated would be my word. He's an armchair admiral and has read or watched everything about you he can."

The *Interceptor*'s CO raised an eyebrow at that. "When we were at the welcoming gala, he did seem overly interested in how the Alliance Navy functions and our traditions. I assumed it was professional interest. Wanting his own navy to improve. Are you saying it was about me?"

It was Nguyen's turn to chuckle. "Commander Grimm, you might not be aware, but you have something of a famous career. I'll make sure he knows about your request for leave. The day you're supposed to depart is right after the election, so they're going to be busy down here. I don't think a handful of... *excited* spacers are going to interfere with that."

———

"...interfere with that."

General Perez scraped her fingernails along her desk like a

cat clawing at a tree. Anger burned within her, but she kept it under control. Everything the Guild had told her was happening and it infuriated her.

Six months ago, her plan was working. Their candidate screamed ahead in the polls. She and her sister controlled the military, as meager as it was, and President Santiago was on his way to being a one-term president. Her extreme backup plan, the coup, wouldn't be needed.

With zero logic, Lady Franceska Divine had fallen twenty points in the polls, despite massive crowds at rallies and vocal support from the public. It was as if the media were simply making up the poll numbers and statements.

Just like the Guild told her would happen when they offered to help her win. She had foolishly turned them down. They would win with honor and follow the duly elected official, after all, and it would be her side that won.

What sway did her oath have when the man elected was a fraud? What power did she have when all those around her were blindly following a man who corrupted their sacred system? She couldn't, that was the only answer.

Just thinking about a coup, let alone planning on as she had, violated her oath. Her soldiers would follow her, of course, they had endured much together—too much not to. While they faced no domestic threats, several pirate raids had created a unity with them that would last.

If only she had a massive standing army instead of the 5,000 regulars and 25,000 reserves. There simply was no need for a large ground force when the only threats came from space.

Still... her army trained with the foreigners even now, and if they were still on the ground when the election happened, they would need to be dealt with.

Could her men do that? Two hundred Alliance Marines were nothing to shake a stick at. Decision made, Perez stood and moved to the life-sized painting of Cordoba's founding father on the east wall. She pushed it aside revealing the RF secure safe embedded in the wall. She was no fool, Falcon had handed her a surveillance device. She kept it, but in a place where it would do them no good.

The safe opened, she retrieved the card. Once she did this, there was no going back. Was she trading one master, Santiago, for another, the Guild? Would they demand considerations from her?

Perez placed her thumb over the falcon logo and spoke. "Juanita Angelica Pérez. I need you to deal with the destroyers. Commence your plan, Mr. Falcon."

She could only pray that no one ever found out.

CHAPTER TWENTY-ONE

J ennings ducked under the clumsy right hook and brought the back of her hand against Sergeant Tizen's face, knocking him back two eye-crossing steps. He shook his head, trying to clear his vision.

"I'm small, Sergeant, but that doesn't mean you can leave yourself open. Never trade hits with your opponent."

Jennings lectured the men while inside a clearing fifty klicks north of the main force. She had Capitán Javier and his grunts in a semicircle on one side while her Marines were on the other. Tizen, the largest of the locals with plenty of mass and muscles, volunteered first.

"I'm confused, Gunny," Tizen said, holding one hand up to pause the attack. To his credit, to all their credit, they didn't seem to be offended that the Marines were just better at everything than them.

"Go ahead," she said.

"You all speak of aggression, attack, and kill, but now you're saying don't?"

She relaxed, returning to a stand. "That's an excellent point, Tizen. Naki, you want to handle this?"

"Aye, Gunny." The taller Marine unfolded from his cross-legged position, essentially popping up without having to lean or push himself up. "Pure aggression is like fighting angry. If you want to lose, be angry. A Pyrrhic victory is no victory at all."

Capitán Javier raised his hands. "Could you explain that, Corporal?"

Naki glanced at Jennings who gave him the go ahead.

"PFC June, up," he said.

June leaped up.

"Did you bring it?" Naki asked.

A look of confusion bounced around the Army grunts as they watched the exchange between the Marines.

June blushed but maintained her forward visage. "Yes, Corporal."

"Well, get it," he said with a gesture.

Jennings watched bemusedly. During their last deployment, things had gone south in a hurry and the Marines had ended up in close combat—something they trained for but wasn't likely to happen. Except for Bravo-Two-Five.

PFC June reached down and opened her pack, pulling out the point-seven meter long tomahawk. While it looked like her people's ancestral weapon, it was as modern as could be, with a monomolecular blade and near unbreakable haft. The grin on her face spoke volumes about her love of the weapon.

"En guard," Naki said.

June dropped into combat stance. Naki pulled his Marine-issued bayonet. He charged forward, using his superior reach to force her back. June surprised him, slipping under his attack and slamming the sheathed blade down on his foot.

However, he dragged the length of his bayonet down her back.

"Break," Jennings said.

The two Marines fist bumped before sitting down.

Jennings pointed at Naki. "He killed her with the back strike but lost his foot. That's a Pyrrhic victory. Naki won, but he lost."

Heads nodded around the circle. Jennings instructed the grunts the rest of the long, hot day in melee combat. While there were always detractors of physical combat, she was of the belief that any form of discipline sharpened the mind.

By the time the sun set, everyone, her Marines included, were covered in bruises and sweat.

Nighttime on Cordoba came quickly. The warm air switched to a cool breeze the instant the sun vanished behind the horizon. Jennings sat atop a large boulder, her MP-17 in sniper mode, cradled on her lap.

"Gunny, can I speak to you for a moment?" Capitán Javier asked. The rock jutted out two meters and overlooked a green valley below that led to the army's encampment. After sacking it the first time, they were told to leave it alone as part of the war game parameters. Jennings was okay with that. She hated repeating tricks.

"There's room for two," she said as she scooted over. The uneven rock wasn't the most comfortable guard watch, but it worked. She peered downrange; scope pressed to her eye. Javier scrambled up the rock side, using different handholds than she had, but he made it. The locals impressed her. They learned quickly and didn't condescend, a bonus in her opinion. Her scope lit the night up, showing what lay beyond the small reticle as if it were bright as day. While Javier got comfortable beside her, she swept down range looking for any surprises one Captain Paul Bonds might send her way.

When Javier didn't speak, Jennings simply continued. Silence was her old friend. Back when she was an idiot private, she'd spent many extra hours, weekends, and countless nighttimes by herself. Either because she didn't fit in with the Marine culture or from volunteering for extra duty.

"How does your husband feel about you being off on such long missions?" Javier asked out of the blue.

Jennings cocked a sideway look at him. Putting down her rifle for the moment, she gave the Cordoban Army captain her full attention. "If I had a husband, he would need to find a way to be fine with it. My boyfriend is in uniform, so he understands. I don't even know where he is right now. At least he knows where I am." She didn't understand why she had suddenly opened up to the man. Maybe it was Danny's influence. Always telling her to speak more.

"I'm sorry," Javier said, "that was rude. I was trying to say something else and that just came out. On my planet... here, a woman would never leave her man, and vice versa, for so long without incredible cause. If he joined the army, she would work on the base. Of course, I have the luxury of saying that, given the size of our army."

A flicker of light in the far distance caught her eye. The sun was over the horizon, but the sky itself held the purple hues and wasn't fully dark. Jennings made a note of it on her range card. Giving herself time to check it out later.

"I wondered about that. You have what we would call a brigade, maybe three to four battalions. I gather that's all you got, am I right?"

She studied the area where the light flickered, looking for any other signs of activity while Javier gathered his thoughts. It didn't take a military intelligence genius to figure out that Cordoba had a small military. What would they even use ground forces for? Hell, even the Alliance's standing army size was considerably reduced. Ships secured systems, and Marines controlled the ground. Army was more for logistics, rear echelon, and of course the special warfare people.

"You are perceptive. Yes. What need do we have for a large army? We are one people, no borders, no other planets in-system to fight with. The army exists to stop larger threats like pirates, terrorists, and the like. It's why we aren't..." He looked around trying to say the right words.

"I get it," Jennings said. "You're part-time warriors. When there's no threat, there's no need to be hard."

Javier nodded emphatically. "That's it exactly. How do you stay ready, you can't possibly fight enough aboard ship to justify your level of preparedness?"

Jennings lifted the scope, peering through again. The computer noted movement, but the distance of two kilometers was too great for it to narrow down what it could be. She shifted the scope to maximum enhancement. There were people down there, moving slowly and in her direction. About twelve of them. A shimmer of a smile ghosted her face. Bonds was trying to take her by surprise. Good for him.

She snorted at his comment. The people of Cordoba lived in relative peace. Sure, pirates sucked, but they weren't fighting a war for survival. "You would be surprised how often we fight. Marines live to train, fight, and thrive. It's baked into us. Part of a century's long tradition."

Javier looked up at the stars. The man had something to say, even Jennings could tell that.

"Don't judge my people too harshly, Gunny. We all play the hand we're dealt."

She cocked her head to the side. Judge? She wasn't the judgey type. The first year in the corps tended to weed out those who didn't belong. Usually. There were always those that slipped by. The Marines spent most of their time assigned to shipboard duty. It was a smaller community than the old-style corps that had bases and camps. The only permanent Marine locations were on Blackrock, where the corps sent recruits for basic training and other schools, like Raptor school.

"No one can do any more than that, Captain."

Javier hopped down without another word. Jennings watched him go, a sense of unease growing in her gut. What would there be to worry about, though?

The captain would know.

"Charlie-One-One, this is Bravo-Two-Five-Alpha, you on station?"

"Roger, Bravo. Go ahead."

It was nice having their own Corsair to ferry them around the battlefield. It certainly made up for her being outnumbered.

"Is there any word from Actual?"

The radio crackled for a second. With the ionic activity in the atmosphere, the channels weren't as crystal clear as they normally would be.

"Sorry, Bravo-Two-Five, Actual is out of range. They're due back on Echo plus 7."

Jennings checked her NavPad to see when that would be.

"Roger, Charlie-One-One, out."

———

Captain Bonds walked through the field with his adjunct, Lieutenant Lia. She held her MarPad in front of her, following closely behind as she listed the different requests from the four platoon leaders under his command.

"They're asking again for advanced technology to train the army on, sir," she said.

Bonds shook his head. Since they landed, the locals had asked for more tech. On the surface their requests made sense. Their army was woefully unequipped to take on anyone other than pirates and raiders. If they did join the Alliance, and he hoped that was the case, they needed to jumpstart their training on the TOE. However, their soldiers were... pathetic. Most of them were overweight. They lacked basic soldiering skills. They were enthusiastic and eager to learn, but not what he would call frontline troops.

Which was why he and his officers had made the decision to limit tech on the op. None for the locals or the Marines. MP-17s, comms, and regular kit. No drones, no advanced sensors. The Corsairs were only for transport and not for CAS. He wanted to whip them into shape. Once they were in the Alliance, there would be plenty of time to bring them up to speed.

"Tell them the same thing we did the last five times. It's not up to me. Our orders are basic training. We're not technical advisors, and we certainly don't have a deep TOE on *Coughlin* to start handing out space armor and Raptors."

"Roger, sir. One other thing. Apparently, there is a dinner at the Presidential Palace tonight—"

Bonds shook his head, one hand massaging the bridge of his nose. "Tell me I don't have to go."

"You don't have to go," Lia said with a smile.

"Then why are you mentioning it?"

"Commander Grimm is going to be there and—"

"He will need a Marine escort," Paul finished for her. "Oh, I have a really good idea."

CHAPTER TWENTY-TWO

The last rays of the system's primary splashed against the side of the transport as Jacob stepped off, ducking down to avoid the nearly silent spinning rotors above his head. Cordoba used conventional aircraft in many respects. He thought back to Rod Beckett's words when he upgraded *Interceptor*. Power, and how to move it, was always the problem. Cordoba had few fusion reactors, and no fusion batteries to speak of.

Hopefully, that would change if they ended up joining. He'd met these people, grown to respect them. They had a truly free spirit and, as far as he was concerned, belonged in the Alliance.

"Sir?" A young woman waved him over. "You need to clear the pad."

Jacob jogged over to her, careful not to split the seams on his mess uniform. They weren't exactly delicate, but running in one would ruin it.

The familiar wail of plasma engines lit up the evening over the capital city. Jacob couldn't help but smile. He recognized Corsair engines anywhere. Sure enough, not five seconds later, Charlie-One-One arced overhead, her engines flaring blue in the dwindling light as she took a lazy turn, circling the landing pad once. He couldn't see Boudreaux from his spot on the ground through the canopy, but Jacob had no doubt she flew the bird.

As the bird finished circling, the engines tilted back, her nose lifted, and she sat down gently on the pad. With a whirr, the large side hatch slid open. A very disgruntled looking gunnery sergeant and a smiling PFC June disembarked.

Jacob waved to Boudreaux who stayed in the cockpit. Her feet were up on the console before the two Marines joined him.

"Sir," Jennings said curtly.

"I just want you to know, Gunny... this was all Captain Bonds. I had nothing to do with it."

"I figured, sir."

The two women cut quite a figure in their Marine mess dress. Jacob would never admit it aloud, but Marine uniforms beat the Navy hands down.

"This way," the young woman said as she turned to lead them in.

As palaces went, it was resplendent. Not that Jacob had seen a great many. The Palisade back on Alexandria was really the only capitol building he'd ever seen. Cordoba's was a seven-story, T-shaped building surrounded by immaculately kept lawns filled with hedges, pools, and fountains. The walls of the palace were a deep-red brick with white on the corners. Four massive pillars that stretched the entire height of the building greeted them, along with an eight-man security detail.

They weren't hiding weapons; they carried them in plain sight. Sleek, beige-colored slug throwers with short barrels and large magazines. Jacob and the Marines stopped as they were scanned, then patted down.

"What's this?" The man searching Jennings pulled a twenty centimeter straight-edged blade from her boot.

"A knife," she said.

"And this?" he said as he lifted a bandolier of three throwing knives from her waist.

Jacob closed his eyes and took a deep breath. He knew what she was going to say before she said it.

"Three knives."

"You're not allowed to have weapons in the presence of the president, didn't anyone brief you?"

"Does that mean I can't go in?" she asked.

"You can go in," the guard said, trying his best to push down his exasperation. "Just not with weapons."

That resolved, their guide led the trio into the main hall, which had them walk through another, more advanced security screen. Jacob breathed a sigh of relief when it didn't pick up any more weapons. He glanced her way, but her neutral expression said nothing. Either she didn't have more weapons, or they didn't find the ones she had... He bit back a groan as he realized it was the latter.

From there, they waited in a small foyer decorated with wooden furniture, oil paintings of generals, and past presidents. Their guide sat across from them. She held the local version of a pad in her hands, thicker than what the Alliance used, but it did the job.

Suddenly, she stood up. "The president will see you now."

The far door opened. Cooked meat and spices assaulted his nose, and it occurred to him he hadn't eaten all day. The inside of the dining room was every bit as luxurious as the rest of the mansion. A long table, with twenty chairs for guests filled the center, but left enough room around the edges for servers to comfortably move around.

"Jacob, over here," President Santiago said from the head of the table, waving like a madman.

"Someone has a fan, Skipper," Jennings muttered.

Jacob plastered a smile on his face. Not that Santiago wasn't pleasant, but the man had an insatiable appetite for war stories, something Jacob had no desire to share. Next to Santiago sat a woman of beauty and elegance, with braided black hair and dusky skin, and large violet eyes. Even on Cordoba, genetic age treatments were available, so it was impossible to tell her age. He guessed older rather than younger, since she held herself with a regal air that the young couldn't duplicate.

"Jacob," Santiago said, "this is my lovely wife, Ines."

"A pleasure to meet you, ma'am," Jacob said, taking the offered hand and bowing over it. Her cheeks flushed slightly at his gesture.

"And my three girls..." Santiago looked around not seeing them. He shrugged. "Are around here somewhere?"

Jacob turned and gestured for his two Marines. "This is Gunnery Sergeant Jennings, and PFC June. They are both Marines from *Interceptor*."

At the mention of his ship Santiago's eyes widened, and Jacob could almost see the questions forming.

"*Osito*," his wife said lovingly. "Allow our guests to eat before you badger them with questions. Please, sit," she said.

Jacob waited for his Marines to take positions next to him. He glanced at the rest of the table, an eyebrow going up at the emptiness.

"Will there be more people joining us?"

Both their faces fell. "I invited our military commanders to join us, but they declined," President Santiago said.

"I'm sorry to hear that, Mr. President, I know—"

"Please," Santiago said, holding up his hand to stop Jacob. "Roberto will be just fine when in private."

Jacob nodded. "Roberto it is, then. I'm sorry they won't be joining us. The general and admiral are quite the pair," Jacob said.

Ines scowled.

"Please, dear, not in front of the guests," Roberto cautioned his wife.

It didn't take a genius to pick up on the political problems the planet was having. The ambassador had warned them that there were some issues happening.

"Far be it from me to comment on matters of state," Jacob said. "I'm just pleased to be here, and in good company."

Servers entered with food, cutting off whatever the president was about to say. The aroma of cooked ham, spices, potatoes, and what was surely olive oil made his stomach growl.

Once the food was in place, a second set came in with a bottle of white wine. As usual, Jacob covered his glass. The server raised an eyebrow at him.

"I'll take his," Jennings said, snatching his glass and offering it to the server. Jacob just chuckled.

Ines waved at the waiter. "If you don't like white, I'm sure we have a deep red around here... Manuel, can you—"

"No, ma'am, I don't drink alcohol. Water is just fine."

Both husband and wife looked at him like he'd grown a second head. "You don't drink..." Ines said.

Jacob shook his head. "No, ma'am. Really, though, it's fine. Please enjoy yourself."

He hated this part of dining out. People weirded out when they found out he didn't drink. Well, except for Jennings. She was happy to drink his share. *Marines.*

"May I ask why?" Ines inquired.

"Religious reasons, ma'am. Nothing too exciting, I'm afraid."

She nodded. "We are nominally Catholic, as is most of the people, but it's more functionary, expected, than for a deep religious reason. I have to say, it's refreshing to meet someone who actually practices their beliefs more than once a week."

Jacob's cheeks heated. He wasn't used to praise about his religious beliefs. There were days he felt like most people would be happy if he sat down, shut up, and never prayed, ever.

"Thank you, ma'am."

"Ines, please," she said.

He noticed June tentatively holding her wineglass.

"PFC?" he asked.

"Sorry, sir, this is all a bit over my head. But... am I allowed to drink this?" she asked.

Jacob let out a hearty laugh. "Yes, PFC. You're old enough to die for your country, and you have almost done that multiple times now. You're old enough to drink."

They dug into the food. Jacob savored every moment of the lovingly cooked Jamón Iberico ham. PO Mendez was a hell of a cook, but the food here was special, something just beyond good.

"Whoever your chef is, you don't pay him enough," Jacob said.

Ines' smile spread wide. "It is my brother. I will tell him you said so."

Roberto, in between bites, slipped in a technical question about *Interceptor* that Jacob happily answered. Anything other than the battles they fought.

"How do you like training with the army, Gunnery Sergeant?" Ines asked Jennings, who froze with her fork halfway to her mouth. Unsure of what to do, Jennings put the fork down and looked Ines in the eye.

"Fine, ma'am."

"They're an interesting bunch," June added. The flush of her cheeks told Jacob she'd drank maybe a little too much. "They certainly love their world."

Roberto nodded. "That is something we all have in common, a deep abiding love of our world and our culture.

There are some, I won't mention names, who think we should join the Terran Republic."

Surprise washed over Jacob. He was certainly no expert, but as far as he knew, once a planet joined the Republic, they were given a governor to rule them from Earth. A duly elected governor but elected by all the people of the Republic and then a blind ballot was cast to see who governed where. They considered it a fair system. He did not.

"That's certainly a route you could take. They have a large fleet, plenty of financial stability, and you wouldn't have to worry about having a standing army."

Ines threw him a questioning glance. "I'm surprised to hear you say that."

"The captain is being polite," Jennings interjected. "The TR is a steaming pile of crap."

Jacob put a hand to his forehead. Leave it to Jennings to cut through the veneer.

Roberto laughed long and loud, and the rest of the table joined him, except for Jennings.

The far door opened and three dark-haired little girls ran in. The oldest was maybe eight, the youngest probably four. They were filthy, having clearly played in the mud until recently. Jennings' hand went to her side until her brain registered that they weren't a threat.

"Bella, Grace, Sandra, this is Commander Grimm, Gunnery Sergeant Jennings, and PFC June."

The little girls waved. They were immediately drawn to Jennings, her blonde hair so different from their own. "Were you born with hay for hair?" the youngest asked.

Ines' cheeks flushed with embarrassment.

"It's fine, ma'am. I'm from MacGregor's World. Most of the colonists have blonde hair and blue eyes. We're also very strong. Want to see?" she asked. The girls nodded emphatically.

To Jacob's surprise, Jennings stood up, walked over to the girls, and held her arms out straight while kneeling. "Hold on," she said. They did. She stood, lifting all three girls off the ground, and spinning them around.

"She's quite the woman," Ines said.

"Indeed. She's saved my life... you know, I think I lost count," he said with a grin.

After the dinner was over, and the girls had dragged Jennings off to show her their doll collection, the party moved to a room with stuffed recliners. The president pulled out a box of cigars, which Jacob declined.

"Your loss," he said as he lit the odorous thing.

"PFC June, would you like to see our art collection?" Ines asked.

"Sure?" June said, a little unsure of herself. Jacob nodded for her to go.

"Did you want to speak to me in private, sir, or is this just a coincidence?"

Roberto looked at him for a long moment. Gone were the eyes of an enthusiast, replaced by the statesman.

"I know my military thinks I'm making a mistake. My people have always wanted to be left alone, to develop our own way. We trade with other planets, we have embassies, but the idea of sending our young men and women to die in a war that has nothing to do with us, is abhorrent."

Jacob leaned back and thought about what the man was saying, and about his own mother. Master Chief Petty Officer Melinda Grimm would still be alive if the Alliance hadn't joined the Terran Republic in their war against the Iron Empire. A war Jacob knew was a mistake to begin with. He'd met people from the IE. They were hardworking, dedicated, and forthright. It was simply bad politics that embroiled the two nations. Bad politics and distance. It was no coincidence that the Consor-

tium and Terran Republic were allies with the Alliance. Not that
he thought they could ever ally with slave traders, no matter
the proximity.

"I can't say I disagree," Jacob said.

"So you think we should stay out of the war, stay out of the
Alliance?"

He needed to measure his words carefully. He didn't want to
sound biased, though he undeniably was. "No, not that, sir. I
emphatically think you should join the Alliance if that is right
for your people. Humanity has fought wars for as long as we've
existed. Before there were armies, tribes fought. Once we *civi-
lized,* it became about land, food, and finally power. If we fought
the Caliphate for any of those things, we wouldn't be the
United Systems Alliance. This is a war for the future of the
galaxy. If the Caliphate wins, my people go into slavery, as does
the Consortium. You really think they will conquer half the
galaxy and stop at your borders?"

Roberto puffed on his cigar, staring at a statue against the
far wall. "If what you say is true, wouldn't it make more sense
to join the Republic?"

He had a fair point, and it wasn't one Jacob could refute. If
only the Ambassador was with him, he could handle this much
better.

"What good is your survival if you lose who you are as a
people?"

Santiago leaned back; eyes closed. "This is what weighs on
me, my friend. Until the election is behind us, I cannot decide.
But my heart tells me the Alliance would be the only way
forward. If the polls are anything to go by, I will win by a landslide. Then I will talk to your ambassador and begin the formal
request. Thank you," he said, holding out his hand.

———

"...I will win by a landslide. Then I will talk to your ambassador and begin the formal request. Thank you."

General Perez swore up and down as she walked around her office. She'd hoped, prayed, begged for it not to come to this. Either her people were blind to the president's obvious corruption, or he had the system rigged. She bet on the latter. There was no way they didn't see his frolicking with the Alliance as anything but a betrayal of their trust.

What choice did she have? None, that was what. Perez slumped into her chair. No matter what happened next, she was the one who broke her oath. But it was for the greater good. If the people didn't see that, she would show them.

CHAPTER TWENTY-THREE

Jennings' eyes opened, instantly taking in the surrounding scene. The sky was dark, but not dead-of-night dark. Someone didn't wake her for watch.

"Dammit, Naki, I'm going to skin you alive," she muttered. She climbed to her feet, cradling her MP-17 as she marched for the designated watch spot. They were hunkered down in a forested area at the end of a valley. The boulder she liked to sit on during the evening was the perfect spot to keep a lookout.

With the ROE being what it was, she didn't expect the *enemy* to attack their position. It never hurt to reinforce basic training of security. Having a percentage of troops on security at any given time was an honored tradition that kept Marines alive.

She made it to the rock. The empty rock.

Something was wrong. Jennings dropped the training mag from her MP-17 and loaded a real one. She would use trigger discipline to avoid shooting friendlies, but she would be dammed if she took an empty weapon into a fight.

"Charlie-One-One, Bravo-Two-Five, copy?" she asked in a hushed tone.

She crouched down, moving to the shadows. The moonless night helped her vanish.

"Go ahead, Bravo," an exhausted Boudreaux replied.

Maybe she had overreacted. Maybe Javier hadn't woken Naki up.

"Everything okay?" she asked.

"Other than you waking me up, oui. Now go back to bed."

Jennings relaxed a little. If there were a real attack, they would have started with her or the Corsair, not the others.

"You've seen too much combat," she muttered to herself. Her nerves were getting the better of her. Desper had told her more than once to seek counseling beyond the mandatory minimum, but it always seemed such a waste of time.

Wood snapped. She spun, bringing up her weapon. A line of blue light reached out and hit her in the chest. Electricity crackled through her, sending her muscles into spasms. The ground came up fast and she let out her breath to break the fall.

She gritted her teeth and forced her muscles to work.

"Get her," Javier yelled.

Three men jumped on her, struggling to get her hands. Adrenaline kicked in, clearing her mind and the effects of the stunner. Jennings bucked her hips and knocked the man on her into another, then pulled her hand loose, grabbing the third man and slamming him face-first into the ground.

She rolled to her feet, grabbed the one on the ground, and yanked him up as the stunner fired again. Blue light hit her makeshift shield, and he screamed in pain. Her fingers went numb from the transfer of electricity.

"Naki," she yelled. Hefting the man, she charged forward toward the stunner. The man spasmed uncontrollably, spittle flying from his mouth. She let go at the last second, sending him careening into the stunner.

Jennings turned, her knife appearing in hand, and she froze.

Javier had Naki, Owens, and June on their knees, hands and feet bound. He held Naki's head with one hand and a curved knife against his throat.

"Please, Gunny. We mean no harm. We just need you subdued for the next twenty-four hours and then you can go. I swear. But if you make me, I will kill you and your people. Get down on your knees and let my men cuff you."

She took a step forward.

"No surrender, Gunny," Naki yelled, knowing it would mean his death.

Jennings took in the tactical situation for an additional five seconds before deciding. With a jerk of her wrist, she buried her combat knife into the ground at her feet and held up her hands.

"You and I are going to have words, Javier."

"I promise you, Gunny. No harm. Tie her up and don't take your eyes off her."

Jennings had to admit, they had learned their lessons well. If the Cordoban Army wasn't using them against her team, she would feel something akin to pride. Part of her still did.

Within minutes they had Bravo-Two-Five bound and secured, along with a swearing French woman in a jumper as they pulled Boudreaux out of the Corsair.

"Mon Dieu, you surrendered? I thought you were dead," Boudreaux said as they pushed her down next to Jennings.

"Not yet."

Javier rounded up his men and the Marines equipment, accounting for everything.

"Good job," he said. Three of his men were holding their heads, one had a bloody rag pressed to his face. Javier keyed his radio, looking up at the black sky as he did so.

"*La Operación Arintero es una oportunidad,*" Javier said.

Jennings waited as the men she thought of as allies settled down. If she observed and showed patience, then she would win the day. Escape would come, but like the captain, she wouldn't willingly lose people to do it. Right after capture, everyone's adrenaline was high, alertness spiked. If she exercised some patience, the moment would arrive.

"Sorry, Gunny," Naki said. "Javier was just talking to me and the next thing I knew, I woke up like this."

She shrugged. "There was no warning, Corporal. I'm actually impressed." She pitched the last bit louder.

Javier glanced her way. He handed his man the radio before walking to her and crouching.

"I'm very sorry, Gunny. We were hoping you would be gone when the time came. I want you to know I hold you Marines in the highest regard."

"I wish I could say the same thing about you."

————

"Uh, sir," PO Collins said over her shoulder to Lieutenant Roy Hössbacher who occupied the center seat.

Roy glanced up with his red-rimmed eyes. He hadn't slept since his last watch because of the Guild ship *Apache* had discovered, and now it was the middle of a very long day for him. Not only was he the OOW for morning watch, but Commander Yuki had also sent him all their computer files and he was busy trying to crack them.

"Yes, PO?" he replied.

Collins glanced into the mirror that allowed the CO to see the occupant of the Pit's face. "I think you want to see this, sir."

Roy stood up. His whole body ached from the twelve hours he spent hunched over the computer node.

Kneeling down, he nodded for her to go ahead.

"This is our current position above Cordoba. We're offset from the capital by eighteen degrees south, by their reckoning. Our orbit is high to avoid their traffic, a little under one hundred thousand klicks."

Her hands flashed across the keys as she brought up a two-dimensional map of the planet. Glowing green dots represented every ship in orbit. Two blue dots were *Interceptor* and *Kidd*. Multiple white dots were satellites, stations, and other objects that were navigational hazards for shipping.

"Got it," he said.

"This is *Estrella*, the cruiser that runs the fleet for Cordoba," she said, pointing. *Estrella* and her four companion ships, barely corvettes by Alliance standards, flashed and turned red.

"Why did you flag them as tangos?" he asked.

"I didn't, sir, the computer did when this happened."

As Roy watched, the six ships spread out in a star pattern. Little trails of light indicated their direction, and while they weren't heading directly for *Interceptor,* they moved in their direction.

"Can you pull up—" Before he finished, Collins had the probable trajectory on screen.

He grinned, clapping her on the shoulder. "Well done. The only question is, why are they trying to flank us? Astro," he called over to Spacer Filoni, manning the station. "Keep an eye on them. I'm going to get the captain."

If he had to guess, this was another war game and Castro wanted the upper hand. Though the skipper slept, Roy was sure he would want to know.

————

Jacob arrived on the bridge, a yawn escaping him as he settled into the command chair. Roy had filled him in while he dressed.

"Any updates?" he asked.

"Yes, sir," Spacer Filoni said.

Jacob grinned when the spacer didn't elaborate.

"Filoni," Roy urged.

"Right, sorry. They're maintaining speed and heading. No deviations detected."

"Very good. Jen, what's our status?"

This was the morning the crew would begin taking leave in shifts. He hated to do anything to interrupt that. However, while the official war games had concluded, he couldn't begrudge Castro a chance to even the score. She was going to have to do better if she wanted to sneak up on his crew, though.

"All systems are nominal, Skipper."

The blips continued to move, ever so slowly, toward his ship. Their current range was a little under a hundred and ten thousand klicks, spitting distance for his armament. Cordoba's directed energy weapons and missile systems were best used under one hundred thousand klicks. The computer knew this, so if they fired, it would simulate the correct damage.

Something nagged at him, though. He didn't know what. His interaction with the Admiralty of Cordoba hadn't left him with a sense of alliance, but Captain Castro was nothing but welcoming.

"Roy, if our simulation system is off and they fire simulated weapons, will the computer tell us?"

Hössbacher stepped over to the Ops console. He brought up the status of the simulation and shook his head. "No, sir. They would need to establish a laser link with us. That way, all the computers are synced. Without it, we wouldn't even know they fired."

"That's damn peculiar, then," Jacob said. Why try to sneak

attack them if the simulation wouldn't show it? Maybe it had nothing to do with *Interceptor* at all. Perhaps they were moving for some kind of election celebration? By *The Book*, he should bring the ship to Zulu, and gain some distance. Cordoba was a foreign port of call, not an ally, despite the war games. It wasn't like a friendly ship had never taken fire in a supposedly friendly foreign POC.

Jacob waved to Spacer Abbot who, like everyone else on the bridge, looked his way. "Abbot, signal *Kidd,* tell them to go to Zulu."

"Aye, sir. Signal USS *Kidd* to Set Condition Zulu. Relaying."

Roy's eyes widened. "Sir, does that mean…?"

"I don't know what's going on, Roy, but let's not get caught without an ELS on. Sound Condition Zulu, battle stations."

Throughout the little ship, the klaxon wailed to life. Crew sprang groggily from their bunks, rushing to the ELS storage. From sheer force of habit, they donned their suits and charged off to duty stations. Hatches were closed and dogged, equipment made ready. Within two minutes of the alert sounding, *Interceptor* was ready to fight—real or simulated.

Jacob pulled on his gloves but carried his helmet under his arm. "Roy, prepare to drain the can—"

"Weapons fire!" Brown yelled.

"Helmets on," Jacob ordered. Training kicked in and the crew slammed their helmets over their heads. "Drain the—"

Interceptor shook as multiple directed energy weapons struck the ship's flank.

"Flank speed," he ordered.

"Flank speed, aye," PO Collins replied as she slammed the throttle forward.

As captain, he didn't have time to process the little things that needed to happen throughout the ship. He had to rely on his crew and their training to do the job. It was his job to worry about the big picture.

"Brown, they'll fire missiles next, bring up the giga-pulse."

"Aye, aye, sir. Giga-pulse laser online and tracking," Brown said. "Missile launch, multiple launches. They're tracking for *Kidd.*"

Jacob finished buckling in his harness and glanced at the plot. *Kidd* was closer to them giving less time for the weapons track.

"Helm, starboard ten degrees, five degrees down bubble. Brown, target those missiles."

A chorus of acknowledgements filled his ears. Interceptor rolled as she adjusted course.

"Giga-pulse tracking and—" Brown's words were cut off by the obvious.

Too late. The leading edge of the barrage ripped into the aft of *Kidd. Interceptor*'s computers fired the single laser atop turret one. Heat buildup flooded the bridge, but it wasn't nearly as bad with a single laser firing.

"Did we get any?" Jacob asked.

"About half, sir," Brown replied.

Cordoba fell in the distance as *Interceptor* sped away at 540 g's.

"Comms, get me the *Kidd,*" he ordered.

A second later, Commander Carlos' face appeared, a somber expression through the faceplate. Smoke blurred the image.

"We're under way, three hundred g's. Their DEWs are crap, but those missiles ripped up our aft coil housing. If we push too hard, we might lose the coil entirely. Thanks for coming to our aid."

Dammit. What was going on? Why would Castro fire on them?

"Sir," Abbot interrupted.

Carlos' face vanished, replaced with static.

"Jamming?" he asked.

"Aye, sir," Abbot replied. "Establishing laser."

Carlos' face reappeared. "They're pursuing, sir. Chief Donley says we can't get more accel without a couple of Gorillas going out and clearing the debris."

Jacob checked the plot. Every passing second, *Interceptor* stretched out her lead. They were already out of weapons range for Castro, if not their own weapons. *Kidd,* though, couldn't outrun them, not at 300 g's. Unless...

"Commander, is your coil stable enough for starlane travel?"

"It should be, sir, but we're not leaving you."

Jacob shook his head. "Commander Carlos, you are to head to the starlane leading home, gather up the rest of DesRon 12 and RTB ASAP. Understood?" Carlos' jaw clenched in response to the order. Jacob hated to give it and knew he himself would have a hard time following it. He could see the conflict on Robert Carlos' face. "Whatever's going on here, Commander, we can't get involved. The squadron must depart, but I'm not leaving without the Marines on the ground."

"Understood, sir, and... good luck."

"To us all," he replied and cut the line. Jacob pulled the plot to the main screen. It showed a fairly accurate rendition of local space. *Kidd* accelerated away twenty degrees to port with Cordoba's navy in pursuit. Jack *Coughlin* hadn't budged, which meant they probably couldn't. It wasn't as if the ship had any real weapons. The smart thing would be to signal surrender the moment the shooting started.

The only ship in real danger was *Kidd.* He needed to get those ships off his tail without destroying them.

"Collins, throttle back 250, and change course fifteen degrees to port. Brown, prepare a barrage that will fall short of their ships, but should wake them up."

"Aye, aye, sir," they both responded, repeating back his orders. *Interceptor* rolled, the gravity fighting with the main gravcoil, forcing her crew to hold on as the ship changed course. Fifteen degrees was the absolute most a ship could change course without an unacceptable acceleration loss.

Jacob silently counted while he watched the plot. If his estimate was right, *Kidd* would pass under him in less than a minute. Sure enough, the screen updated, and the ships were doing precisely what he thought they would.

"Turrets are locked and loaded, Skipper," Brown reported.

"Load a MK XIV in tube two. Program it for wide area jamming. If they're going to follow someone, it will be us," Jacob ordered. The torp would blind them and force a follow of *Interceptor*.

"Loaded," Brown said.

"Open the outer doors," Jacob said. "Abbot, relay to Kidd. Change course fifteen degrees port and proceed to two thousand KPS. Cut engines for one hour, effect repairs, and bug out."

"Relayed, sir," Abbot said.

Jacob looked to Brown and pointed with his hand. "Fire."

The torpedo burst from the fore tube and instantly flooded space with massive amounts of EMI. Enough that even *Interceptor* couldn't see through the jamming and completely concealing *Kidd*'s course change.

At the same instant, all four turrets fired a single shot. Interceptor shook from the recoil. While the Cordoban ships weren't as advanced, they weren't blind. Their acceleration cut.

"Message from *Estrella*, sir. She's demanding our surrender."

Jacob glanced down at the blinking light of *Jack Coughlin* and thought about the two hundred and four Marines on the planet, not to mention his Corsair and pilot. He owed it to them to find a way to resolve this peacefully.

"Put her on," he said.

Captain Castro's face appeared. Her hair was back in a severe bun, and she wore a clunky version of an ELS suit. It made them look like they were hunkering down for the winter.

"I see you're wearing your helmet, well done," Jacob said with a genuine smile. It was one of the lessons they had impressed upon the Cordoban Navy.

"Surrender," she said in a no-nonsense tone.

"And if I don't? We both know I could destroy your entire fleet within thirty seconds of the engagement."

"You're no murderer, Grimm. You value life too much to throw it away, even if they are the enemy."

Someone's been paying attention, he thought. "You're right, Castro. But I value the lives of Alliance citizens more than your crew. So tell me, why?"

"Surrender, or the two hundred Marines on the planet will be executed."

"I won't surrender my ship. I will, however, return to orbit under your watchful eye and oversee the evacuation of my ground forces. Once they are safely off the planet, we will depart the system. Which, for the record, we would have done had you asked."

There was something akin to shame in her eyes. She tried to hide it, tried to pretend it wasn't there, but Jacob saw the truth.

"It's no longer about your departure. If you resist, I will destroy the *Coughlin* and kill all of your people on the planet."

"Understood. Filoni, plot us a course back to the planet." No matter what happened next, Jacob wasn't leaving without his Marines.

———

Paul woke up with the urgent need to pee. He stumbled into the head, his mind half awake, thinking about Boudreaux and their night together before the assignment started. That woman brought a smile to his face.

As he exited the head, his hatch burst open and two men in all black pointed guns at his bed and fired.

Not guns, stunners. The sheets whipped around in a frenzy.

The Marine in Captain Paul Bonds took over. Wearing only his Marine Corps boxers, he charged the two men. He hit the first one, barreling him into the other. Aggression and surprise were on his side.

The first one crumpled as his breath was knocked from him. The second fought to bring his stunner around. Paul reared back and slammed his fist into the soft part of the man's nose, breaking it.

They all tumbled to the ground. Paul snatched a stunner out of a flailing hand. He wasn't sure whose, and he didn't care as he fired from point-blank range, three times.

He knelt and searched the men. They didn't wear masks.

"Ortega?" Bonds whispered. He remembered the NCO from their first meeting. The man didn't seem to like the Alliance. But... this was akin to the sergeant major of the corps trying to assassinate someone. He glanced at the weapon; well... not assassinate, but capture.

He had little time. They would send more when these two didn't report back... whoever they were. Bonds had so many questions. He leaped over the bodies to his ruck and pulled out a fresh combat uniform. Years of training let him dress in less than thirty seconds.

In his mind, he saw where he was: not three hundred meters from the CP and the radio he would need to alert the ships. Maybe this was an isolated event, or maybe the start of a war, but either way the captain needed to know.

Between the two weapons, he had enough charges for thirty more shots. He wasted two on the already unconscious men. Once outside, he stayed in the shadows. Ears open for any sound that would alert him.

Ducking from building to building, he arrived at the CP only a few minutes later. There were no guards, no one outside waiting for him. After Jennings marched into their camp and took it from them, he would have thought they would post extra guards. Ten meters separated him and the entrance. The CP's lights illuminated the surrounding area, but with no watch they were useless.

He could run for it or walk like he belonged. He ran. His big feet pounded the dirt as he headed right for the door. A shout from behind, followed by the whine of stunner fire echoed through the night.

Bonds crashed into the door with earth shattering force. The reinforced plastic shattered under his assault. Inside, Comandante Ruiz leaped up in alarm. No one else was present in the CP. He sighed with relief. For a moment, he thought it wasn't an isolated event.

"Ruiz, Ortega tried to stun me in my sleep. I need to report to the *Interceptor* what's going on," he said as he moved to the comm unit.

"What is going on?" she asked.

"I don't know. But—"

"Paul, I'm sorry. Don't move or you will be hurt," she said.

Paul turned around ever so slowly. Ruiz held a compact pistol in a classic grip, the barrel unwavering and pointed right at his chest. "Good stance," he said.

"Thank you. I know this is confusing, and believe me, I didn't want it to come to this. But we all must follow our orders."

Bonds nodded and placed the stunners down on the floor. "And my people?"

"With any luck, this will all be over in a few hours. You, the crews of the ships, and your Marines will be returned to the Alliance."

Crews of the ships... they're planning on keeping our ships. Ha. Like the captain will let that happen.

"Ruiz, if any of my people are hurt or killed, I will personally guarantee we will glass this rock down to the magma," he growled.

"That's up to you. Have them lay down their weapons and don't resist."

It was against everything Paul Bonds believed. Marines were the definition of no surrender. However, he had 200 men and women on planet, and they were mostly asleep. Some of his people would be killed, but they would surely kill many more of them... and start a new war in the process. That was the last thing the Alliance wanted or needed.

"Very well, Ruiz. For the sake of your people, and to prevent a war, we'll stand down."

CHAPTER TWENTY-FOUR

Jennings watched Javier move back and forth while talking on his radio. Every moment he spoke he grew agitated.

"Any of you speak their language?" she whispered.

Her Marines shook their heads. It was a rookie mistake keeping them together. Javier should have separated everyone.

"A little. It's based on Latin, like my own, much superior French," Boudreaux said.

"And?" Jennings asked.

Boudreaux focused hard on Javier, his mouth, and what he said.

"This is a coup, but it's not going to plan. The foreign ships... our ships, got away."

"Pshaw," Jennings said, "I'd bet my left arm the captain isn't running."

Boudreaux continued. "The military fell in line, but there are civilian agencies defending the president. There's fighting in the streets and—"

Javier turned suddenly, glaring at Boudreaux before walking further away.

Jennings pictured the three little girls she'd played with at the president's dinner. She had no loyalty for the planet, or for their current leadership, but coups were bloody and violent. Leaders and their families ended up executed in public or lined up against a wall and shot. History was full of legitimate coups ending in a bloody reign of terror.

"The longer this goes on, Gunny, the worse it will be. If they're hoping for a peaceful turnover of power, that ship sailed," Owens added. "Someone's going to see the bodies piling up in the street."

Javier returned, a scowl deep on his face. He spoke to two of his men and sent them off.

"It seems," he said as he approached them, "the rest of the Marines surrendered peacefully. Captain Bonds ordered them to stand down."

Jennings raised an eyebrow at the revelation. Of course, Bonds had a bigger picture to worry about than herself.

"You best be thankful that he did," she said. "I don't think the Alliance would take kindly to us killing a few thousand of your people."

"A few thousand?" Naki scoffed. "Try all of them. You people aren't soldiers, you are civilians playing dress-up."

Naki wasn't wrong in Jennings' estimate. As much as she liked the people of Cordoba, they lacked discipline.

Javier glared at Naki before speaking. "Be that as it may, we might not be able to let you go as quickly as we hoped. Get comfortable."

"Javier," Jennings said, "do you really think this is going to turn out for the best? You attacked Alliance personnel, ships, Marines. What about the ambassador and his wife?"

"That is outside my scope. We were to deal with you, that is all. Others are taking care of those matters. I assure you, Gunny, you won't be harmed."

Jennings wasn't so sure about that. If the tables were

reversed, could she make such a promise? What if the situation became such that it was her or them?

"What about the president?" she asked.

"Why do you care? This isn't your world."

"Humor me."

Something in the man seemed to relent. His shoulders sagged. "If everything had gone according to plan, the people would have woken to the news that Lady Divine was the new president. However, his security detail was more prepared than the general understood. The fighting there is fierce. He will be tried for his crimes against the people and publicly executed. You have to understand, he cheated. He used his power to alter the polls and the votes. We have the evidence, but no court on the planet will hear it. This is the only way."

"Right," Naki said.

"He's a nice man," June said. "His wife too. Will you kill her?"

That simple statement brought Javier up cold.

"No—"

Jennings fumed. It was one thing to know you were doing something horrible, but to be willfully ignorant? That was inexcusable.

"We're you born a dumbass, or did you work at it?" she growled.

Javier frowned, narrowing his eyes in rage at her. "This is not your world, Gunny. You don't know us."

"I'm sure you're different from every other civilization. I'm sure your rebellion will be different. Don't pee on me and call it rain, Javier. Your people are about to start a massacre, and it starts with the president and his family getting lined up and shot."

Javier shook his head emphatically. "No one wants to shoot

a bunch of little girls. We're going to do this with the least amount of bloodshed possible."

"Like I said: dumbass."

She closed her mouth, having had her say. *Danny would be proud,* she thought. After all, she'd spoken more in five minutes than the last five days.

———

Commander Yuki stared across *Apache*'s briefing room table. The ship's symbol, a bow and knife crossed, rested between her and John Hopper. He wore his civilian clothes, but every item he had was confiscated and under lock and key. She put a prize crew aboard the Guild ship in the meantime.

"You want to cut the crap, *Mr. Hopper?*" Her tone made it clear she didn't believe that was his real name.

"If I had anything to tell you, I would. It's not like it used to be," he said, a wistful look on his face appearing for just a moment. "When I was a supervisor, I had real authority. I was in the know... Now? They put me on a ship and said go watch the traffic in Cordoba. Nothing else, I swear."

It was the same story, or a variation of it, from the rest of his crew. She had her best people trying to crack their software, but so far they hadn't made a dent. Why, though? They hadn't heard hide nor hair from those corporate bastards for over a year and now they pop up in Cordoba of all places.

It's too convenient to be a coincidence. Are they planning on coming after the captain?

Yuki's thoughts were interrupted by the comm.

"Skipper, *Kidd* just popped on the screen. They're signaling Condition Zulu."

Her hand hit the button before his words left the air. "Put me through. Route in Commander Marsh as well."

"Aye, aye, ma'am."

Frustratingly long seconds passed by.

"Commander Yuki, Cordoba is having some kind of internal strife. A civil war or coup, I'm not sure. Commander Grimm ordered us to RTB to Alexandria with all haste. *Kidd*'s gravcoil is cracked and our speed is limited."

The sheer audacity of them to fire on her skipper pissed her off to no end. But leave? He wanted them to leave?

"Marsh, take lead, head for the lane. I'll escort *Kidd*," she said.

"We're not really going to leave, are we?" Commander Marsh asked.

Yuki wished to her ancestors she could have some clever plan that would allow them to stay. "This isn't a debate, Marsh. The captain has given his orders and our job is to follow them."

The younger woman's eyes went wide. Yuki could tell Marsh knew exactly what would happen to *Interceptor*.

Yuki glared one more time at John Hopper. "If I find out you knew more, you're going to wish I'd thrown you out the lock."

The desperation on his face made her feel better about the situation as she jogged for the bridge. "Set Condition Zulu, battle stations," she yelled before she got to her chair.

———

Ambassador Nguyen jumped as his door crashed open. His chief of security, a man from Rōnin with a steely gaze, rushed in.

"Sir, we need to get you to the vault," Ozaku said.

"Sara," he said, shaking his wife awake. Like the levelheaded woman she was, she took the whole thing in stride. They both leapt out of bed, dressing as quickly as their fingers would allow. While they had drilled several times for this scenario, it was still a shock.

Ozaku's companion held a hand to his ear. "They're at the gate demanding entrance."

"We have to hurry. Go now," Ozaku said.

"Who's at the gate?" Nguyen said as he hustled out of the room, holding his shoes, but otherwise dressed.

"Cordoban Army, Mr. Ambassador. I don't know why, but there's fighting in the streets and the presidential palace is under assault. They're rounding up off-worlders and arresting them... Alliance citizens included."

Nguyen shook his head. That made no sense. This was unlike the people he knew. There had to be a mistake. Gunshots from chemically powered weapons rang out. Sara ducked, and Nguyen put one hand over her shoulder.

"They're firing at the gate," Ozaku said. "Charles, go reinforce them. I've got the package." The second man nodded with a curt movement and darted through the hallway.

Ozaku led them to the lift, activating the special mode with his security ID. "Sir, once you're in the vault, do not come out unless I or the Marines give you the all-clear.

Nguyen nodded his understanding. He kicked himself for agreeing to let the embassy guards partake in the war games now. All they had were the embassy security services, which were only armed with low-powered small arms.

The lift dinged its arrival. Ozaku hustled them in, standing between them and the hall until the doors closed. An explosion rocked the building, shaking the lift. Nguyen hugged Sara tightly. "It's going to be okay."

She looked at him. He didn't think he'd ever seen fear on her face before, and it broke his heart. "What about the staff? They're not Alliance citizens, but if the government is arresting people...?" she asked.

He wished there was something he could do. History was

replete with violent changes of power; collaborators were rarely treated kindly, even if they did nothing wrong.

"We'll do what we can," he assured her.

More gunfire sounded through the building. Another explosion sprinkled them with dust.

"Almost there," Ozaku said.

The lift doors opened onto the hallway that had only one door. Pistol out, Ozaku pulled Nguyen behind him to the vault door.

"Are the comms working? We can call *Interceptor* for evac?" Nguyen asked.

Ozaku hit the door, gun pointing back the way they came. "Open it," he ordered.

Nguyen pressed his palm to the scanner, and the door slid instantly aside. He glanced at Ozaku to answer his question and the grim look in the man's eyes told him there would be no rescue. No one was coming.

———

President Santiago sheltered with his wife and children inside the bunker, a thick metal wall between them and the outside world. Cordoba simply didn't have a reason to have extensive underground survival capability for anyone. They were one people, at war with no one, surrounded by allies. Their biggest threat were pirates, and the military had dealt with them over the last twenty years to the point they weren't a threat anymore.

He knew the election was a contentious one. How could he not? But the polls were so clearly in his favor, and early voting showed him leading in every territory. Why would Perez, of all people, lead a coup?

She's had dinner with my family, played with my children... She is going to destroy us.

An explosion, all too close, shook the room. His children cried out, holding onto their mother.

Santiago glanced at his wife, who gave him a smile of confidence. He was blessed to have such a woman in his life.

"Friedo," he said, getting his security man's attention. "Get me a radio, something, anything, I can use to talk to Perez. There has to be a way to resolve this."

While the security man tried the radio, Santigo stopped to do something he hadn't since he was a child: he prayed. A slight smile ghosted his lips as he remembered something his father had told him. *There were no atheists in a crisis.* Whether it was something innate in humans, or learned, it seemed reaching out to a higher power for help was instinctual.

"I have her, sir," Friedo said, holding the receiver up for him.

"Juanita—"

"*General Perez,* and don't address me like a friend," Perez's voice crackled out of the speaker like a lightning bolt.

"Fine, *General,* why?" he asked. None of his security people saw the coup coming... or they were in on it. Despite the call, and the need to stay focused, Santiago found himself looking at the four-man detail in the room with his family. If he had so badly misjudged Perez, who could he know was loyal?

"You know why. Surrender and you will not be harmed. Abdicate to Lady Devine and spend the rest of your days in prison or face a firing squad." The line clicked dead.

Santiago shook his head. The pure vitriol in her voice shocked him. She was beyond reason if she thought he could just quit and appoint a successor. That wasn't how their country worked. She wasn't just planning on replacing him, she wanted to overthrow the whole system and use Devine as her puppet.

In that moment, Santiago lost hope. His security forces were no match for the whole military. An idea popped into his head. Maybe if he couldn't count on his military...

"Get me Ambassador Nguyen," he ordered.

CHAPTER TWENTY-FIVE

Jennings squinted as the sun crested the ridge to the east. Her butt ached from sitting on the ground and she needed to pee. From the way her squad squirmed, they all did.

"Javier," she said.

"Capitán Javier," he scolded her.

"Whatever. We need to pee," she said bluntly.

He crinkled his nose in disgust. Clearly, they hadn't thought it through. Maybe they planned on handing the Marines over before too long. Bravo-Two-Five was out in the woods, klicks from the main base, and she could imagine picking up a handful of foreign soldiers in the middle of a coup was low on the priority.

"Tizen, get Rodrigo and Senna, take them one at a time and don't let them out of your sight."

"Yes, sir." Sergent Tizen pointed at the two other soldiers, and they approached Naki, heaving him up.

"You brutes ever hear of ladies first?" Naki said.

"Do you want to go or not?" Tizen said.

"Fine."

They heaved him up, not unbinding his hands, as they marched him off into the woods.

Jenning bid her time. She'd tried the captain's way. There was no talking them out of their foolishness. Whatever possessed them to forsake their oaths and abandon their duty had to be severe, or very, very misguided.

She twisted her wrists, testing the reinforced plastic cuffs. They weren't the magnetic, metallic cuffs her Marines used, but they were strong enough. Tensing her muscles, she braced her wrists together and pulled—nothing. Repeating the process over and over stretched the plastic bindings ever so slightly. Enough, she thought, maybe there was room to yank on them.

The three soldiers returned with Naki, pushing him forcefully down to the ground. Next, they yanked up Owens and shoved him stumbling toward the woods.

Naki, with his head down, winked at her. With a nod, he showed his hands and had a rock in one.

"Good man," she whispered.

Javier was at least organized. He had his men gather all their gear, including the spare equipment from the Corsair, and pile it up for inventory. Jennings got the idea that the man thought they would be able to use it. Some, like the soft body armor and knives they could, but the MP-17s and the Corsair itself would only work for authorized Alliance personnel.

She glanced at June, who nodded. *Good, we're all on the same page.*

Gunfire erupted from the woods. A rapid fire of the local weapons, cracking in the air like two sticks hitting together. A second later, Tizen came barreling out of the woods. "He's gone. Owens. He headbutted Rodrigo, knocked him right out, and took off running."

Javier scowled. "Why did you untie him?"

"We didn't!"

"Bring Rodrigo back and take four more and go after him... ándale!"

Tizen charged back into the woods. Seconds later he dragged a bleeding and unconscious Rodrigo into the clearing. Four more of Javier's men left with him, leaving just Javier, a man named Filipi, and the unconscious Rodrigo to watch over three Alliance Marines and a navy puke.

Jennings tensed her muscles, readying herself to attack, when Javier realized his mistake. His hand went to the pistol on his side when she struck. Arms like coiled metal expanded, breaking her plastic restraints while she dove forward.

The pistol barked, the bullet ripping through Jennings' side as she barreled into Javier, knocking them both to the ground. She smashed her forehead into his face. He howled in pain, one hand going to the bloody mess that used to be his face.

Javier tried to bring the pistol around, but she used his own momentum against him, snatching the gun and rolling with him. The roll ended with him flying away from her.

On her feet, she held the gun in one hand, pointing it between Javier's eyes with an unshakable grip.

Naki had Filipi down on the ground, powerful legs wrapped around the man's neck as he choked the life out of him. June freed herself by sticking her tomahawk in the soft dirt and cutting her bonds. She had one in hand while she ran to Boudreaux to cut her free.

"Don't make me kill you, Javier," she said.

He looked at her hard in the eyes, and she knew what he saw: a killer.

"You would, wouldn't you?" he asked. "Despite my promise not to hurt you..."

Jennings only nodded. There was no need for words. Javier was fooling himself if he thought his promise was valuable.

Boudreaux massaged her wrists back to life. June ran to Naki to free him.

"Get the Corsair fired up and call the captain."

"Aye, we're going to bug out, right?" Boudreaux said. When Jennings didn't respond, she repeated her question. "Right?" Boudreaux ran for the Corsair, June trailing behind her as security.

Naki went to their gear and dug out three mag cuffs, securing all the men with them. "Never rely on your enemy to be weak," she said as he slapped them on Javier.

"Still teaching us?"

"Don't worry, Capitán Martinez, I promise we won't hurt you," Naki said with a smile.

"Somehow, I don't find that comforting."

Once they were all secured, Naki made them lie face down on the ground. By then, Jennings swapped her stolen pistol for an MP-17. She tossed one to Naki. "Stun setting," she told him. "Less-than-lethal unless we have to."

MP-17s were versatile shipboard weapons, ones the Marines of the Alliance favored. With their nanite reserve, they could take the form of pistols, SMGs, carbines, rifles, and sniper rifles; fire anywhere from semi-automatic to hyper-velocity flechettes capable of cutting an unarmored human in half; on top of all that, they also could fire 10mm balls at subsonic speeds that would break bones and knock targets unconscious. They could be lethal, but used correctly, they were less-than-lethal.

"Naki, take one to June, then get back here. We need to set up a welcoming party for when Owens returns."

Javier banged his forehead into the dirt in frustration.

———

Lance Corporal Owens ran through the trees, leaping over fallen logs and ducking under branches. In his mind, he kept a running tally of steps as he moved away from the camp. Zigzagging, he put the sun on his right for one hundred meters, then turned into it, running another hundred meters, before turning right again.

A commotion off to his right, which was the way back to his camp, caught his attention. The men that came after him charged through the underbrush like bulldozers, breaking everything in their path and making enough noise to alert a squirrel-bat. The deaf possum-like flying critters that inhabited his homeworld.

He slowed his pace, scanning for the right place as he switched to stealth from speed. A fallen tree, its stump exposed above ground, provided the perfect cover for him.

"Okay, Owens, you led them away. Now time to break these bonds," he told himself. Standard E&E instructed the runner to keep his morale up, free his hands, find weapons, and keep moving. Placing his back against the overturned tree, he felt around for a strong root until he found one and held on with one hand. Using his body weight, he leaped up and came down on his other hand, snapping the ties around his wrist.

He bit his lips to keep from crying out from the pain in his wrist. Cradling it to his stomach, he got up and headed back in the general direction of the camp. A gunshot snapped in the air from ahead of him.

"Don't die on me, Gunny."

———

Boudreaux climbed into the cockpit, settling into the leather chair like the comforting embrace of a lover. Paul's face flashed through her mind and she pushed down the worry that filled her heart. If they made it through this, she could chew him out then. The Corsair was completely powered down to avoid any electronic signature, which wouldn't do them any good if Javier had told his people where they were.

"PFC," she yelled down to June. "Get on the door with your rifle and make sure no one boards."

"Aye, aye, Chief," June yelled back.

Viv flipped the switches to begin the generator startup. The fusion battery powered the craft's basic systems, but she needed the plasma engines fired up for the EW to work. Lights flashed green on her console. She stabbed the transmit button.

"Indigo-Actual, this is Charlie-One-One, how copy?"

A glance at the EMI told her they were being jammed. The needle pegged to the maximum. Broad spectrum interference flooded the airwaves. If *Interceptor* was in range, they wouldn't pick her up unless she made it to the upper atmo, maybe not even then.

She flipped over to her laser, scanning for her ship—nothing.

"June," she hollered down. "Get Gunny on the comms. We need to talk."

CHAPTER TWENTY-SIX

Jacob tapped his fingers pensively on his armchair. Things weren't going as planned. This was supposed to be a straightforward assignment. It was turning into something not.

"High orbit, Skipper," PO Collins said.

"Thank you, Jen," he replied.

What to do? His Marines were on the planet. The *Jack Coughlin* was a sitting duck for their orbital weapons. The Cordoban Navy wanted him to hand over *Interceptor*, or they would start killing his people, starting with the troop carrier.

There were two things he couldn't do: depart without all his people and hand over his ship.

"Did we get a casualty report from *Kidd* before they were out of range?"

"Aye, sir," Hössbacher said. "Fourteen casualties, no KIA."

Thank you, Lord, for small favors.

If any spacers were killed, his position would be far more inflexible.

"Any word from the ambassador or our ground teams?"

Spacer Abbot shook his head. "I'm sorry, sir. Their jamming

isn't elegant, but it's powerful. They must have a fusion reactor powering an antenna farm with enough EMI to cook a saber-shark whole."

Jacob could only imagine. "Get me Castro," he said.

Abott keyed in the laser and activated the comm at Jacob's chair.

"Commander, we're in orbit, as agreed. I want to talk to the ambassador immediately."

Castro's haggard face appeared, far more tired looking than she had seemed thirty minutes before.

"When you agree to turn over your ship, you will see the ambassador and your Marines and not a minute before."

They were putting him in an awkward position. Standard naval doctrine was to comply until forced otherwise. Turning over one's ship wasn't ever in the cards. Castro had to know.

If he could talk to Nguyen, he could figure a way out of this mess without starting a war or an interstellar incident. In the grand scheme of things, Cordoba wasn't a threat. At the same time, boat commanders who obliterated foreign navies and took sides in civil wars weren't favored by high command.

He leaned back, taking a deep breath. A civil war. That's what it was. They could dress up the language, but the people on that planet were fighting a war for domination. Under no circumstances could *Interceptor* get involved. Regardless of the side. If he helped those defending or attacking, it would be a de facto endorsement by the Alliance.

Things were about to get bloody on the planet, and all he could do was watch and wait. He didn't even have a Corsair to go down with.

"PO Collins, make sure we have an angle to cover the *Coughlin*. I don't want them thinking they can just blow her up if they want. They need a reminder of what our guns can do."

"Aye, aye, sir. Changing orbit to cover MTS *Jack Coughlin*."

He knew what would happen next.

"Sir," Spacer Abbot said, "Hail from *Estrella*."

"Put her on."

Jacob's MFD flashed, and Castro's face appeared. She wasn't in her suit anymore, which to him meant they weren't planning on combat. He wore his.

"Commander, return to the designated orbit immediately or—"

Jacob looked away in the middle of her demands. "What was that, Roy? Yes, I would love some tea, thank you."

Lieutenant Hössbacher returned his look with open-mouthed wonder that quickly turned to a grin.

"I'm sorry, Helena. Whenever I get into these pissing contests, I get thirsty. Let me be clear: I'm here for my people. Not because you or your admiral have any leverage on me. If you kill any of my Marines or if Ambassador Nguyen or his family are harmed, I will rain down hell from on high." Without waiting for her response, he thumbed the disconnect on the screen. "Abott, if they call back tell them I'm in the head."

"Aye, aye, sir," Spacer Abbot replied with a grin so large it looked painful.

They needed to stew for a few minutes. If he made it abundantly clear they had no bargaining power, then maybe he could de-escalate this. He felt for the people of Cordoba, he really did. They were in a tough spot. Join the Republic and lose their identity or join the Alliance and go to war. He could tell them all day long of his confidence in the Alliance's ultimate victory... but there were still men and women on the planet below who would die in a war they had no say in, a war that would likely never touch their borders.

Unless we lose.

Jacob tapped a few keys on his MFD, pulling up the file on Cordoba plus his own log on the military members he'd met so far. The two sisters who ran the military, Admiral Perez, and General Perez.

He suspected, though he couldn't know, that it was General Perez behind the coup. Of the two, she was more... impressive. The admiral wasn't anything like Villanueva or DeBeck. Those two titans commanded respect with their very presence. Admiral Perez tried too hard to impress her underlings with her power and presence. The general, though, with her plain desk and spartan office, no, she was the leader.

"Sir?" XO Fawkes interrupted his musing.

Jacob looked up, surprised to see him out of DCS while they were still on alert.

"Carter?"

"I figured while we were in orbit it would be a good time to survey the ship. We took some hull damage, but nothing penetrated. The armor Captain Beckett installed at Kremlin really came through for us." Carter glanced around the bridge while he spoke. "Also, sir, I wanted to report on crew morale." Despite them wearing their ELS and connected via a closed radio, Carter leaned in. "They're with you, sir. They know you'll go to hell and back for them, and they for you... Skipper."

Jacob blinked at the unexpected emotion welling up in him. He loved his ship and crew. Almost in the way a father loves his children, but children he'd gone to war with.

"Thanks, Carter."

"Sir," Carter replied with a semiformal bow before departing to check on the rest of the bridge crew.

It was a good XO who made sure every station was staffed, and the crew were taken care of. It was tempting, especially with a CO they admired, to stay longer or hide an injury. As the captain, he could tell them to report injuries or take breaks, but for an honest response, it needed to come from the XO.

Abbot waved to get his attention. "Sir, there's an Admiral

Perez on the line. She's demanding to speak with you."

"Demanding, eh? Tell her I'll be just a minute. Then, Abbot, could you find PO Mendez and have him break out the sandwiches and orange drink? I'll take the call in the briefing room."

Jacob stood, stretched, and let out a big yawn. "Roy, you have the conn."

"Aye, sir. Ops has the conn."

It was important for the crew to see him as relaxed, calm, and in command.

Roy took the seat from him. He strolled out of the hatch, nodding at PO Cartwright who had his sidearm and manned the bridge hatch. Once in the briefing room, he left the hatch open. He took his seat at the table. After he was comfortable, had his NavPad out, and situated, he keyed in Hössbacher. "Roy, fill the can. Helmets off but maintain Condition Zulu," he ordered.

A moment later, air hissed into the ship followed by Roy's voice on the radio, "All hands, maintain Condition Zulu. Helmets off, helmets off."

With the atmosphere returned, Jacob pulled off his helmet and took a moment to stretch his face and neck. Once he was situated, he keyed the comms switch and put the admiral through.

Her holographic visage appeared in the air before him, projected by his NavPad.

"Admiral, thank you for taking the time out of your busy schedule to speak with me."

She scowled. "Don't patronize me, Grimm. Open your outer airlocks and—"

Jacob held up his hand to stop her. "No. Let me be clear. There is no way we are handing our ships over to you. The rest of DesRon 12 is already out of your reach. Not that I need them to mop up your navy. I'm only here to ensure the remaining personnel, including the Marines, Ambassador Nguyen, his family, and every Alliance citizen is transported up to MTS *Jack Coughlin* and evacuated. Then you can continue with over-throwing your government."

She smiled coldly at him, casting doubt on his read of the situation.

"You don't have all the cards you think you do," she said.

The line terminated.

What is going on here?

"Gun!" a shout from the bridge echoed down the passageway.

Jacob leapt to his feet, charging for the hatch before the sound faded. A sharp crack of repeated weapons fire deafened him. Solid slugs pinged off the hatch next to his head. Jacob ducked instinctively. He ran, legs pumping hard as he headed for the bridge.

Cartwright was slumped to the side, a bloody hole in his chest, his MP-17 on the deck. Jacob slid to a halt, picked up the MP-17, and dashed to the open hatch.

He glanced in. A man had his back to him and repeatedly fired into the captain's chair. Jacob brought up the MP-17 to the assailant's head and squeezed the trigger. Cartwright had it set to a three-round burst. Silicate flechettes accelerated out of the barrel and exploded through the man's head, showering the command chair with his remains. The lifeless body slumped to the floor.

"Medical emergency to the bridge," he bellowed. Jacob turned and knelt next to Cartwright. His ELS readout showed his life signs. They were weak, but he was alive. "All hands, intruder alert. All hands, intruder alert. Roy, get me—"

As Jacob turned to finish his order, his command chair rotated, showing the bloody remains of Roy Hössbacher's body, riddled with bullet holes.

CHAPTER TWENTY-SEVEN

Gunny Jennings finished outfitting her armor, replacing her knives, grenades, and extra ammo. Owens had returned a minute earlier. Other than his sprained wrist, Bravo-Two-Five was ready.

"What about them?" Naki asked, nodding at the Javier and the men they had subdued.

"Leave 'em. The rest will come back soon. We have a place to be."

Naki gave her a raised eyebrow but complied. He climbed into the Corsair as the engines powered up. Plasma burned from the exhaust, blackening the soil underneath as the drop-ship lifted off. The trees in a fifty-meter radius shook and swayed from the blast. A few seconds later and the Corsair skirted the tree line heading north.

"What's the plan?" Boudreaux asked over the comms. It was far too loud inside to have a normal conversation.

"What's their SAM capabilities?" Jennings asked as she made her way to the cockpit. Owens manned the EW suite with one hand. June acted as his backup since she was the most trained on the equipment besides Owens.

"Uh," Boudreaux said, hesitating. "I guess we'll find out."

"Whatever it is, Gunny, they got nothing on our EW," Owens added.

Jennings left it to him, then. She understood SUT, and she knew the importance of EW, but operating the actual equipment wasn't her skill set. She had a decision to make. Attempt a rescue of her CO, head for orbit, or...

Dammit. While she had every ounce of confidence in her four Marines, they couldn't take an army. Not without their Raptor suits. If they broke for orbit, no matter how good their EW was, they were still in a dropship. It was no match for a warship, regardless of tech level.

They couldn't run. They couldn't hide.

The image of those three little girls popped into her head. Dark haired and messy, running around trying to outflank her. She wasn't exactly the most personable human being to grace the universe. But those little girls...

No one wants to shoot a bunch of little girls... Javiers voice came back to her. He sounded so sure of himself. Jennings wasn't what one would call educated. She'd read a few books, knew the history of the Marine Corps. But she knew, without a doubt, it was rare for coups not to turn bloody, especially when they weren't over quickly. Maybe they had the best of intentions. She doubted that, but whatever ideas they started with would fall by the wayside as power came within their grasp.

"Ah damn. The captain's going to be pissed," she whispered. "Boudreaux, set a course for the presidential palace."

"Say again, Gunny?"

"You heard me. Marines, we're going on a rescue op."

———

Bonds smiled as he heard the unmistakable roar of plasma engines in the distance. He wasn't naïve enough to think they were coming to rescue him, but Jennings certainly had thrown a monkey wrench in the works.

Ruiz sat at the comms station of the CP, listening intently to a report. Her face went from a facade of calmness to a mask of anger.

"Captain Bonds, it seems some of your people didn't get the memo. Call this gunnery sergeant and tell her to stand down?"

Bonds let out a laugh. "I would if I thought it would do any good. Maybe if she were here in front of me... maybe. But on the radio? What am I going to do, threaten to court-martial her? If you wanted to keep Gunny Jennings out of the fight, you should have sent fifty men with her."

Ruiz scowled at him. "They will kill her, you understand? We lost the ship on radar, but once they pick it up again, there are fighters coming to kill her. If they don't, then our SAM sites will surely get her. I'm trying to save lives here."

"You keep telling yourself that, Ruiz. You say to yourself, 'this is all about saving lives. No one is going to get killed that didn't deserve it.' I'm curious how long you can lie to yourself."

His words hit home, and he could tell she knew he spoke the truth. There just wasn't anything either of them could do about it.

———

"RWR, fifteen klicks, one o'clock—altitude angels plus ten," Owens shouted. "June, press that button and turn that nob to full."

Boudreaux acknowledged him. From her position in the cockpit, she had excellent visual reckoning. The bulbous canopy gave her a full field of view, and the deck below her feet was transparent for when she needed to land in tricky situations. Or fly below radar. With one hand on the stick, the other on the throttle, and her feet firmly placed on the rudders, she edged the Corsair closer to the ground. Her altitude warning light already blinked at her.

"Three hundred meters," she said more to herself.

"Another one, ground level, looks like a SAM," Owens said.

"Mon Dieu," she exclaimed. Pushing forward slightly on the stick, the nose dropped, and the altitude dipped below two hundred meters. The trees below were so close, she felt like she could reach out and touch them.

Her own systems alerted her to the same information Owens had. She just didn't have the bandwidth to split her attention.

"Naki," she said over the comms. "Get up here and man the weapons console."

A minute later, the lanky Marine climbed into the backseat, strapping in.

"What do you want me to do?" he asked.

"Activate the weapons systems. Switch the radar to track-while-scan, but keep it off."

"Roger, TWS but off."

Below her the 10mm coilgun unfolded, stretching out and locking in position. While they were flying faster than 125 meters per second, the gun was locked onto the ship's beam.

Her hands were like iron on the controls as she guided the Corsair along the nape of the planet. The RWR quieted as she lost the threat. It wasn't that they couldn't see her on radar; it was the systems couldn't distinguish between her and the ground. If they had look-down radar or some other form of satellite tracking, they might see her. Maybe.

"Capital city in five mikes," she said.

"Roger, Chief," Gunny Jennings replied.

She thought the Marines were crazy under the best of circumstances. Hell, she had helped them with their crazy stunts in the past but... assaulting a presidential palace of a foreign power to rescue a family...

"You know this is going to get us involved in their civil war, right, Gunny?" Boudreaux asked.

Jennings' voice came back as calm and nonchalant as ever. "They involved us when they started it. I won't sit by and let those kids get killed, Boudreaux. I can't."

Boudreaux had pulled the trigger personally, ending life with her decisions. She couldn't fault Gunny for wanting to save those kids.

"I can drop you on the roof or the grounds. You'll have to do a rolling debarkation. I can't stop or they'll hit us with a heavy weapon, or even concentrated small arms, understand?"

"Aye, aye, Chief."

Boudreaux let the gunny worry about her decision while she focused on flying.

"Naki, on your right you will see a countermeasures panel..."

"Got it," he said.

"Good. When we get to the palace, I want you to depress the flare and chaff buttons and hold them down until you have to go, understood?"

"Aye, aye, Chief."

It wasn't exactly a smoke cloud, but at such a low altitude it would do the—

Tracers erupted in front of her as they cleared the last ridge before the city. She banked hard to port, kicking the tail around and pointing the nose at the ground.

"I thought you said they didn't see us," Jennings shouted.

"They can still hear us," Owens replied.

The frame shook as the *tack-tack* of rounds hitting metal echoed. Boudreaux jammed the throttle forward. The ground came up fast. She yanked the stick back, leveling the nose with rooftops of the metropolis.

"What about power lines?" Naki said.

"We'll slice through them," Boudreaux said. The Corsair shook again as it plowed through several lines, snapping them in half. "See?"

She glanced at her airspeed. They were too fast. A building came up, and she rolled the ship while applying rudder, causing it to go over the roof upside down.

"Threat!" Owens yelled. "Fast mover. Six o'clock, twelve klicks and closing."

A radar image appeared behind her. Were they really going to engage her over the city? That was foolish. The debris would take out buildings and start fires.

"Are they locking?" she asked, unable to take her eyes off the obstacles before them.

"Negative, our ECM is too good, but if they have guns..."

"Thirty seconds," she said. Whatever fighter they had in the air wouldn't be there before she could drop the Marines.

———

Major Iglesias frowned as he put down the receiver. He'd started his day shooting his CO in the head, and it had only grown worse from there. His battalion of light armor had the presidential palace surrounded, but they refused to surrender. He'd shelled the residence, hoping to kill the president, but to no avail. Now he was told an enemy dropship was coming in to reinforce the president... but his army didn't have dropships. Did they mean transport?

A howling roar echoed through the city from the west. He turned in time to see a black-as-night ship, with a massive turret on the nose and missile pods slung under the wings, thunder overhead. Hot air slammed down on him, forcing him to the ground and sending his hat flying.

Flares burst to life from her stern in an explosion of white light and heat. Glittering silver canisters erupted out, spraying the area with radar diffusing chaff.

"What the holy hell is that?" someone yelled. Then a noise that would haunt him till the end of his days bellowed from within the smoke. Tracer fire flying faster than his eyes could register ripped through two of his tanks and the mobile artillery gun, shredding metal and rendering them into burning hulks.

The artillery battery's ammo canister cooked off. The shockwave hit like a hammer, knocking him along the ground like a can in a storm.

"Fire," he yelled. "Somebody fire!" His men were as stunned as he was. Air and smoke swirled, and the demon ship shot out like a bullet, trailing blue flame behind her engines.

———

Boudreaux couldn't spare a thought to her Marine friends. In the thirty seconds it took her to drop them, smoke the armored vehicles, and depart, the fast mover traveled eleven klicks. It was on top of her, and she had no EW crew, no back seater for support.

"Dammit, Stawarski, that's the last time I leave the ship without you. I don't care how secret the OP is."

She jammed the throttle all the way forward, pushing the plasma engines to the max. A hundred meters above the city, the dropship broke the sound barrier. The shockwave rolled out behind her, shattering windows, and setting off alarms.

Radar screamed at her as the enemy fighter tried to lock her up. If he got close enough, he might be able to, even with her ship's advanced systems.

She pulled up on the stick, craning her head to look behind as she gained altitude. An arrow-shaped fighter with a single rudder and triangle wings followed her at less than half a klick. As she gained altitude so did it.

"Yeah, you think you can follow me," she muttered.

RWR rang to life as the fighter's primitive radar systems tried to lock on. The Corsairs advanced paint and passive ECM systems protected it for the moment. Boudreaux drew the fighter in, pulling back on her throttle just enough that it closed the distance until she could see the shape of the pilot.

Her fingers flew across the controls, unlocking the swivel on the cannon.

Bullets rang out from the cannon mounted in the nose of the aircraft and pinged off the dropship's armored hull. While it wouldn't stop coilgun fire, regular old chemically fired bullets were no match.

Chief Boudreaux swung the coilgun around to face her six, lined up the fighter, and squeezed the trigger. Six barrels shot to life, spinning like a tornado and spitting a volley of 5mm, steel-coated, nanite-hardened tungsten slugs at a rate of 1,500 meters per second.

The fighter disintegrated in a cloud of fiery debris.

RWR flashed all over her HUD. She realized the ground stations were tracking her and probably had held off to avoid hitting the fighter. With it destroyed, they were going to launch and hope for the best.

Threats turned to launches as missiles actively sought her out. She kicked the rudder over, bleeding off energy and pointed the nose at the ground. Plasma turbines fought with the atmosphere, but with gravity on their side it was no contest. By the time the enemy missiles were in the air and seeking her, the Corsair sped along the surface at Mach 3, heading for the nearby mountain range to wait for Bravo-Two-Five's signal for pickup...

If it ever came.

CHAPTER TWENTY-EIGHT

As the men surrounding the palace fired uselessly at Charlie-One-One, Jennings and her squad hoofed it for the pillars that guarded the front entrance. Two of them were blown in half, the marble ruined with scorch marks and fire. The other two were pitted with gouges and shrapnel.

Jennings ducked behind the first pillar, spinning around and shouldering her MP-17 to face the enemy. As her people ran by, she counted them, making sure they were all present. In the heat of combat, even experienced Marines had trouble recognizing faces. Numbers and equipment, though, were easy.

Wind from the east picked up, scattering their impromptu smoke screen. Jennings had seen the Corsair in action on multiple occasions. It never failed to impress. Two low-slung armored vehicles were burning wrecks and a third mobile gun emplacement was nothing more than a crater in the grass.

Naki patted her on the shoulder as he passed. She fell back, weapon pointed toward the enemy, through the large doorway that one of the tanks had blasted open.

The foyer where she had entered the night before was gone. In its place was a war zone. The walls were burned, the tile on the floor cracked, and everything that could be turned over and used for cover was. To her, it looked like the president's security team put up a hell of a fight, until the army decided to shell the place. A glance up showed where the roof had partially collapsed from artillery fire.

"They really know how to build 'em to last here," June said as she spied the huge hole in the ceiling.

"Naki, mine it," Jennings said while pointing at the door.

Three Marines turned and knelt behind cover, aiming their rifles at the doorway and beyond. Naki pulled two of his grenades out and held them up. "Proximity detonation, emplace." They beeped once, letting him know they were active, and he slid them on the floor to the doorway.

"Now where?" he asked as he backed up.

"Their internal security is probably shot, Gunny. But if you get me to a console, I can find the president," Owens said.

She stood, pointing to the doors leading deeper into the palace. As silent as a whisper, the four of them exited the foyer and headed deeper into the palace.

Gunny remembered how to get to the massive dining room, but that was the only place she had seen in her time there. Besides the little library the girls had shown her.

"Owens, libraries have computers, right?" she said.

"Usually."

"This way." She took a left into the kitchen.

"It almost looks untouched," June said.

She wasn't wrong. A pot on the stove was filled to the line with cold soup. Vegetables were cut but left on the counter where the cooks dropped them. As they moved through the kitchen, a chill ran up Jennings' spine, like her brain knew that something was wrong but couldn't tell her what.

"We might run into friendlies in here, make sure you verify contacts before firing," she told them.

Out of the kitchen and into the immaculately decorated room with its long table and red velvet curtains. She led them to the right. Through the door, the girls had entered from the night she and the captain had eaten with the president's family.

It took her a couple of tries to find the right door leading out of the dining room but eventually they ended up in the children's library. Several terminals dominated the right side of the room opposite six kid-height bookshelves that were only partial cover for the Marines.

"Owens, get to it," Jennings ordered. She took up position facing the door and ordered June and Naki to flank her.

"This isn't exactly what I was talking about, Gunny," Owens said as he knelt in front of the child's computer. He slung his rifle and went to work.

————

President Santiago resisted the urge to pace. It wouldn't help and it would make him look nervous, upsetting his wife and girls. Something he didn't want to do. How had Perez so thoroughly infiltrated every level of government? Was he really that bad of a leader that virtually the entire military would betray him?

He'd hoped he could speak to Nguyen, but Perez's madness knew no end. She'd bombed the embassy, likely killing the ambassador and starting a war with the Alliance. Why would she want war with the Alliance?

"Sir?" Friedo called.

His faithful security man watched the monitors outside, what few remained. Short of a nuclear bomb, Perez couldn't get into the vault. After the brief skirmish in the halls of the palace, she had ordered them shelled. Killing all the men who had held the line so he and his family could escape.

"What is it?"

Friedo pointed at the monitor showing the outer vault doors. Four Alliance Marines in combat gear with their hi-tech weapons knelt, facing the only way in. One of them—

"Jennings!" Bella yelled, causing everyone in the room to jump.

"Hush child," her mother said.

"Bella?" Santiago asked his oldest daughter. "Are you sure?"

"You can see her straw for hair peeking out of her cap."

Sure enough, if he squinted, he caught sight of a strand of blonde hair. How the child had seen that from across the room boggled his mind.

"Let them in, Friedo."

"Sir, if it's a trap and I open the door... you know how heavy it is. I won't be able to close it right away."

Santiago knew all too well how long it took to close the door.

"I won't leave them out there to die, not when they obviously came here for shelter or to help. Open it."

Friedo opened the shielded button on his console and depressed it for a solid ten seconds.

Alarms wailed, and yellow lights flashed. Massive hydraulic pistons activated, pushing open the door centimeter by centimeter. Santiago didn't know all their names, but he recognized the—what did they call her? A PFC? The one with dark hair. June. She entered first, followed by a man with bright orange hair and then a tall fellow with high cheekbones. Once they were all in, Jennings entered, walking backward, keeping her rifle pointed toward the entrance.

"Close it," she said.

"We have to wait for it to open all the way, then I can reverse it," Friedo explained.

She muttered something too quiet for Santiago to hear, but her Marines chuckled. Seconds inched by while he held his breath, waiting for the inevitable attack.

None came. The door sealed shut, and they all breathed a sigh of relief.

"How can we help you, Mr. President?" Gunny Jennings asked.

Those simple words filled him with so much joy, he collapsed into his chair. Bella and the girls giggled with delight as they ran to Jennings. All he could do was look over at his wife and smile. Ines smiled back.

"You don't know how glad I am to hear that, Gunnery Sergeant. I wish there was more you could do, but unless you're willing to commit your Alliance to my aid—I'm not sure what you can do?"

"As long as you're with me, sir, I can defend myself. If that means defending you and your family, then so be it," Jennings said.

Friedo snorted. "I don't care how tough you think you are. You can't defeat an army." He shook his head in disgust.

"Friedo!" Santiago snapped.

"No, it's okay, sir. He's right. We can't," Gunny Jennings said. "However, we also don't have to. I just need to speak with the ambassador and call my ship—what?"

How did he tell her?

"It's not just the army, Gunny. It's the entire military. They bombed the embassy within minutes of the coup."

———

Jennings frowned at the president's revelation. More than likely, though, the ambassador would have made it to his safe room, which would survive any bombing short of an orbital strike.

"Lance Corporal Owens, do you have today's codes?"

"Yes, Gunny." He pulled a card-sized object from his uniform pocket and handed it to her.

She glanced at them for a second, making sure they were indeed valid. "Owens, you and I are going to make our way to the embassy and secure the ambassador. Naki, you and PFC June will remain here. You are to shoot anyone who points a weapon in your general direction."

"Oorah!" all three said.

"Oorah," Jennings echoed.

Santiago looked at her with stunned disbelief in his eyes.

"You can't be serious?" Friedo asked. "Didn't you hear him? Your embassy was bombed. Your ships are likely destroyed."

Jennings didn't have to answer. The grin on Naki's face did it for her.

"*Interceptor*, destroyed? I'm afraid the captain wouldn't let that happen," Naki said. "Listen, I know you hear a lot of bravado from military types. Trust me, though, we know what we're doing. Commander Grimm is up there and he's working on a plan to rescue all of us, or I'll eat my gun, barrel first."

Jennings pulled out her spare pistol and handed it to Naki. "Just in case."

"Aye, Gunny."

"Open the door," she ordered.

Friedo let out a sigh of exasperation, but the door opened.

Jennings charged out the door, moving swiftly, stopping at the corner five meters away to make sure Owens followed her. They had worked together enough that they both understood how each other moved and operated. It wouldn't take them long to find their way to the remains of the embassy. As long as nothing else went wrong, maybe they would be back on the old girl in time for chow.

———

Kimiko Yuki had learned much from her time as Grimm's XO, and even more under his command of DesRon 12, though they hadn't actually performed as a squadron for very long. *Apache* hummed like a well-tuned coilgun. If there was one lesson she took away from her time with Grimm, it was everyone has a duty to perform.

Whether they liked it or not.

She hated leaving him. It felt too much like betrayal. Too much like she was leaving him to his fate. Orders, as he would say, were orders. They weren't for her to judge or to interpret, just to follow. If he wanted her out of the system, it was for a good reason. If only there was a way for her to stay? Her knowledge of the regs was as good as anyone's, better even since she spent months memorizing them. Disobeying a CO's orders without just cause violated her oath of uniform, and of the constitution she swore to protect.

"Skipper, we're ready. Do you want to give the order?" her XO asked.

There simply wasn't anything for her to do.

"Close the aperture and prepare for starlane egress."

Her crew went through the motions they had done a thousand times. Starlane travel tested both mind and body. The better they did their jobs, the easier it would be for the crew. A rough transition could put people in sickbay.

"Ready," her XO said.

"Helm... execute."

The screen went white as the ship's gravcoil latched onto

the invisible strand of gravity connecting Cordoba's main sequence star, with their target over fifty light-years away.

"Contact!"

Then they were through, blazing along a trail with *Kidd* and *Justice* in front of them.

"What did you see?" Yuki asked when her head cleared.

Her gravity man shook his head, trying to clear the fog. He pointed at his screen. "For a minute, ma'am, I thought I saw a massive signature coming out of the starlane. It might have been a freighter out of Rygel but..."

Yuki focused on the PO, urging him to continue. "But what?"

"The power signature was massive. Freighters don't run large reactors. Only warships packed that much juice."

She slammed her hand down on the command chair's arm in an unusual show of anger.

"Astro, how long to Rygel and back?"

"Assuming there's no traffic? Thirty hours... minimum."

Lieutenant Commander Kimiko Yuki had seen Grimm overcome much more than a destroyer had any right to. But with a coup brewing, and the Guild involvement, she hoped he had enough luck left to survive...

CHAPTER TWENTY-NINE

Jacob didn't move—couldn't move. He cradled Lieutenant Roy Hössbacher's lifeless body in his arms like a bear held a cub. Pain flared to life in his heart. He'd lost people before, people he cared about. This was different. Roy was... like a younger brother. He'd served with Jacob as a midship. And now... he was gone. Killed.

No.

Murdered.

"Skipper," PO Desper said from his shoulder. She stood with Spacer Whips, a nanite preserver body bag in hand.

He wanted to let go, to let her do the job. The grisly job of removing the body followed by the Bosun sending men to clean up the bridge. That's what it was. Naval combat felt different. It was a chess game. Him matching wits with another captain, another crew. This wasn't combat, this was an assassination. The very act tainted his bridge, made it dirty.

His grief vanished, replaced by cold, hard rage. Admiral Perez did this. She had known it was going to happen; not only that, but she'd also set it up. The assassin wasn't one of his crew. Couldn't be.

"Skipper," Desper whispered. "It's time to let go," she said.

Jacob opened his eyes, not having realized he clutched Roy's body.

"Go with God, my friend," he whispered before gently laying down the body.

Silence permeated the bridge. The main viewer had three holes in it, peppered by the assassin's gun. Jacob turned to the other body. Without care, he jerked the body over and searched the suit.

For the first time, he looked around the bridge. The crew, mostly kids who were working the midnight to 4 am watch, were wide eyed with terror. Combat wasn't supposed to be like this, so up close and personal.

While the man's face was unrecognizable, thanks to Jacob's MP-17, the uniform under his ELS suit wasn't. Cordoban Navy. He likely slipped aboard when they had their joint celebration. The bitter stab of betrayal stung all the worse, knowing it was his lax security that allowed the assassin aboard. He should never have agreed to it.

"PO Collins, take Ops please and call a relief," he ordered.

"Aye, aye, sir."

She unbuckled and climbed out of the Pit, her back and hair covered in blood from both Roy and the shooter.

"Belay that, PO. All hands are relieved. Call your reliefs and report to sickbay."

A chorus of aye, ayes followed. Jacob watched as each one departed, thanking God the tragedy hadn't been worse than it was. Had Cartwright not fought with him and warned everyone, he could have walked onto the bridge and killed the entire watch.

For two minutes, only Jacob Grimm and the ghosts of fallen crew inhabited the bridge. When the thud of boots on metal filled the O-deck, he dragged his arm across his eyes and regained his feet.

Chief Suresh arrived first, nodding to her captain as she took her seat in the Pit.

"Orders, Skipper?"

"Maintain for now." Jacob went to the opposite side of his chair and pressed the comm stud. Thankfully, it wasn't covered in blood. "Sickbay, Bridge. How's Cartwright?"

"Chief Pierre here, Skipper. Commander Freydis is operating on him as we speak. I can't guarantee it, but it looks like the bullet tore through his aortal artery. He lost a lot of blood, but he's got a good shot at pulling through. The commander is a top-notch surgeon. If anyone can do it, she can."

"Understood, captain out."

Unwilling to take his chair, he walked behind it. His hands went to grasp the back, but he pulled up short. Anywhere he touched his chair would get more blood on him. Instead, he grasped his hands behind his back and stared straight ahead. He needed to think. While he stood like a statue, the rest of the relief showed up. McCall took comms, Tefiti Astro, and Ignatius on weapons. A minute after that, Bosun Sandivol arrived and sat at Ops.

"The fabricator is building a new chair, Skipper, and—"

"Negative, Bosun. Send them up here to clean this one."

He wouldn't have the only reminder of his stark failure removed. It felt... wrong. Like a betrayal of Roy's memory.

"Skipper... there are holes in the chair. We need to replace it—"

"No. That's an order."

Jacob turned away from Sandivol and glanced out the hatch, seeing the blood still cooling on the deck. Everywhere he turned was the evidence of his failure. He was so damn arrogant.

"Skipper," Mac said. "Admiral Perez is on the line. She wants to speak to whoever's in charge?"

She didn't know I wasn't on the bridge when I spoke to her?

"Bosun, have the backup man at arms up here ASAP. Have him grab whoever's available. I want two people on that hatch at all times, body armor and weapons."

"Aye, aye, Skipper," Sandivol said.

"Mac, tell her that the CO will be with her in a minute."

"Aye, Skipper."

If she had another assassin, he would not be caught unawares a second time. Reaching down, he scooped up the MP-17 he used to stop the assassin and stuffed it in the small of his back under his waistband.

Spacer First Class Teller and Carona showed up shortly after, both outfitted in soft body armor and carrying pistols on their hips.

"Put her on, Mac. Speaker."

"Speaker, Skip?"

"Aye, Mac. Speaker."

Sound crackled to life as the bridge speaker broadcasted the radio signal.

"*Interceptor*"—Admiral Perez's voice dripped with sarcasm —"congratulations on your promotion. I trust now that you know I can reach you no matter where you think you are. Surrender your vessel and I won't destroy it. You have thirty seconds to comply."

Jacob slashed his hand across his throat, telling Mac to mute it.

"PO Ignatius, get on the gun camera and find a large open area devoid of buildings near their military command center. When I flew in, there were large expanses of open spaces all around it."

"On it, Skipper." Ignatius pulled up the camera and bent over the station, peering through the eyepiece.

Jacob waited until Perez spoke again.

"Your time is up. What say you?" She sounded so confident that whoever was left in charge of the *Interceptor* would capitulate.

"I'm afraid the reports of my death are greatly exaggerated, Admiral."

Dead silence filled the bridge, broken only by the crackling radio.

"Is he dead, then?" she asked.

"Your assassin? You sent him on a suicide mission, Admiral. Don't pretend you thought he would live. You betrayed our trust, sent an assassin to our ship, murdered one of my officers, and you have the audacity to worry about his life?" Rage boiled his blood, heating his neck and clouding his vision. He wanted nothing more than to let the shark loose and pummel Cordoba into the stone age. "Ignatius, do you have the target?"

"What target?" Perez yelled. Her voice cracked at the end, going high.

"Aye, sir. Target locked."

"Fire."

Ignatius flipped the shield up on the firing stud and depressed it flat. Turret number one rotated four degrees to port, elevated eighteen degrees, and fired. A 20mm nano-hardened tungsten penetrator, wrapped in a steel shroud, exploded from the barrel at 10,000 KPS. It hit a field two kilometers from the military command building, but they felt the shockwaves for klicks beyond that. An explosion of dirt and topsoil shot a hundred meters into the air.

"I trust I have your attention, Perez?" Jacob said.

"You bastard. What if there were civilians in that field?"

Jacob glanced at Ignatius, who shook his head negatively.

The reason he had the PO use the gun camera was to visually make sure no one would be harmed. However, Jacob didn't want the admiral thinking he cared if civilians lived or died, even if he did.

"I don't care, Perez. I wanted you to know what I could do, four times every thirty seconds for six hours... if I wanted." *If the regs permitted me, I already would have.*

"The Treaty of—"

"Only refers to orbital bombardments with weapons of mass destruction. NBC. Nuclear—Biological—Chemical. It says nothing about tungsten. If any of your ships so much as turns on their search radar—" he took in a deep breath and blew it out noisily, "The next round will land on your head."

The line clicked dead.

"Yeah, that's what I thought."

"Skipper," Carter called from the hatchway. "A moment?"

It was late. Exhaustion weighed heavily on him. He suddenly found it hard to breathe. Jacob exerted monumental effort not to stumble as he made his way out of the bridge. "What is it, XO?"

"Adrenaline is crashing in you, sir. You've operated on alert status for almost twelve hours. The emergency has passed. Let me take the ship and you get some rack time."

Jacob started to argue, but he knew Carter was right. On the surface, they were scrambling to evacuate the command building. Perez would search for a place to hide, and there was no way *Estrella* and her consorts would attack him now. It was as good a time as any.

"You're right, XO. You have the conn."

Jacob moved like a zombie, each foot falling hard on the deck. His hatch opened and his bunk called him. The small, empty stateroom had never seemed lonely before. Until now. He crashed face-first on the bunk and passed out.

———

Carter watched to make sure his captain made it to his bunk. After that, he got to the work of cleaning up the ship. He'd known Roy since Zuckabar. He stopped at the center seat. Still covered in blood and riddled with bullet holes.

"Bosun, we're going to need this replaced," he whispered, so only Sandivol would hear.

"The captain said not to, XO. He was adamant about it. I've got some of my boys coming up to clean and repair it as best we can."

Carter frowned as the Bosun spoke. That captain seemed pretty shook up. Hell, they all were. Maybe he just needed time? He only wished they had it. Whatever was happening on the surface escalated by the second. If they waged war against the Alliance for their coup to take place, then they would kill anyone who stood against them.

Including Alliance citizens caught in the middle.

"Comms, is there any way you can cut through the jamming? They've got to have a mechanism, otherwise they wouldn't be able to talk to us."

"Fair point, sir," Mac replied. "They might be using a ground-based synchronization system that allows their frequency to broadcast while jamming others. I know they've put a hell of a lot of power into the EMI in order to blanket half the planet. Hell, anyone stationed at... the..." Mac paused mid-sentence.

Despite the somber situation, Carter grinned as an idea blossomed in Mac's mind. "What is it?"

"Sir? Oh, nothing... maybe. I was just thinking if they're pumping out that much juice, I might be able to locate the fusion reactor and then—" He glanced at PO Ignatius.

Ignatius shook his head. "Can't do it, PO. Orbital bombardment of nuclear or fusion reactors is forbidden the same as dropping them as bombs."

Mac frowned. "Oh, I hadn't thought of that."

"Wait..." Carter interjected. "Mac, what do you think the odds are that the antenna farm will be at the same location as the reactor?"

He thought about it for a moment. "Technically, it could be anywhere on the planet. However, the farther away it is, the more power they lose in the transfer. Entropy and all that. For efficiency's sake, I would put it as close to the reactor as possible but not so close that losing one would impact the other, sir."

Carter slapped his hands together in a burst of excitement. "Mac, find that reactor and relay the coordinates to weps. PO Ignatius? Once you've got the coordinates, get on the gun camera and find the antenna farm. If there are no civilians present, then—"

"There's nothing stopping us from sending a present," PO Ignatius finished. "On it, XO."

Lieutenant Fawkes had to catch himself from sitting in the bloodied command chair. It was a stark reminder of the danger they were all in and not to get too comfortable.

CHAPTER THIRTY

Sweat dripped down Jacob's forehead and pooled in his eyes. Exhausted as he was, he couldn't sleep. He punched up the galley on his NavPad.

"Can you please send a large orange drink to my cabin?"

"Aye, sir," Spacer Perch replied. "I'm on it."

Jacob cut the line. Stripping off his ELS, he hit the head for a hot shower, hoping the water would wake him up and give him some clarity. It wouldn't hurt to pray as well.

By the time he exited the shower, feeling refreshed, if not alert, Perch arrived with his drink in a bottle.

"Here you go, sir."

"Thank you, Perch."

The spacer left and Jacob downed half the contents. It wasn't suggested to drink that much, that fast, but he needed his brain clear and his emotions in check. Anger fueled him and it was the wrong emotion for decision making.

Roy...

What was he going to tell the boy's parents? It was one thing to die in battle, but murdered on his own ship? He would need to get with Carter, change some policies aboard *Intercep-*

tor. Two guards on the bridge at all times while not in Alliance space. No matter how friendly the port is.

Thank God they pulled this stunt before the men went on shore leave. He shuddered to think what would have happened if half his crew was down on the planet when the coup kicked off.

Jacob finished dressing in his service dress blacks. They weren't the most comfortable, but his day uniform was laid out on his bed when he collapsed, and it wasn't presentable. He swiped his blood-red watch cap and placed it carefully on his head, making sure the lines of the cap were parallel to the deck.

There was much to be done in the next few hours, and he needed to look his best.

"Captain on deck," Spacer Teller announced.

Bosun Sandivol's boys were good at their job. Other than the bullet holes in the chair, it was as clean as the day it was new. The main viewer was a loss, though. Frustratingly so. The viewscreen acted as an information center, letting him delegate information to it instead of using the limited space available on his MFD.

"I have the conn," he said.

Bosun Sandivol replied. "Captain has the conn."

Instead of sitting, he stood behind his chair, hands grasping the headrest. He needed to think, and the bridge was the best place for that. For the moment, Cordoba's ground and naval forces were on the defense. Eventually, though, they would try to force his hand again. If they started shooting Marines, he wasn't sure what he could do? Certainly not turn over the ship.

Somewhere down there were members of his crew. Gunny Jennings and Bravo-Two-Five along with Chief Boudreaux. He wouldn't leave them behind.

Jacob's NavPad beeped for his attention. A quick look told him about Carter's plan and what Mac was up to on comms.

It was a solid start. He just wished he could get down there and help them. At this point, he could care less about who won what. He just wanted his people home, safe and sound.

"PO McCall, I know you're busy trying to find the source of their jamming, but is there any way you could put a laser on *Estrella* and let me talk to Captain Castro?"

PO McCall glanced over his shoulder and nodded. "Aye, aye, skipper. One sec and I'll have a secure line."

True to his word, five seconds later the laser connected, and Castro's face appeared.

"I'm not supposed to talk to you," she said.

"Then why are you?"

"I want to know why you fired on that field. I would've bet money you would never risk civilian lives like that." Her countenance spoke the truth, but Jacob was second-guessing his people instincts after the blindside of Cordoba. Though, in hindsight, it seemed Castro had tried to say something. She was either a fabulous liar or she didn't know.

"Captain Castro, we talked about duty in my briefing room. I feel like you were trying to tell me something then. Let me ask you this, did you know?"

"Of course, I knew. The entire officer corps of the military was in on the coup. We—"

"Not about the damn coup. About the assassin your admiral planted on my ship during our celebration. About him murdering my Ops officer because he thought it was me." Jacob's voice echoed down the hatchway. None of his crew had ever heard their CO shout like he just had.

Castro's face turned ashen. She blinked several times, slowly shaking her head back and forth. "No, you're lying. She would never—"

He swiveled the video pickup, showing the bullet holes. One in the headrest, two in the back.

"I don't ever lie, Castro. I might bluff, exaggerate, stretch the truth in order to save my ship, but we are naval officers and lying is beneath us." He wanted to drive home to her how disgusting he thought her actions were.

"I swear to you, Commander Grimm, on my mother's life, I didn't know."

"If you had, would you have warned me?"

She shook her head. It disappointed him to know that she would have let it happen anyway. He wanted to think more of her, to think she held herself to a higher standard.

"If I had known, I would have resigned."

Her words lifted his spirits slightly. She was the officer he hoped she was.

"Now that you know, what can you do to help us? I don't think my bluff with threatening the admiral will last longer than she takes to get to a new location. One that we can't find. I need to get in touch with my people, and I need my Marines off planet."

As Jacob saw it, there were multiple problems to solve. Some more pressing than others. The safety of the ambassador was paramount, followed by his Marines, including Paul Bonds' men.

"I didn't know it would be this bad," Castro continued. "When they briefed us about the election issues, and how the president's security teams rigged the polls and ballots, they made it sound like it would be over in an hour. The presidential palace would be seized by the army. Your ships would be held until we were certain our position was secure." She dropped her chin to her chest. "I was a fool to go along with this. As soon as Perez ordered me to fire on you, I should have resigned on the spot. I'm sorry, Commander Grimm, truly."

Her heartfelt apology meant something to him. It wouldn't undo Roy's murder, but it was something.

"No one aboard *Kidd* was seriously injured. By now, DesRon

12 is out-system and heading for Alexandria. They're beyond
the reach of your admiral." Jacob took a deep breath, held it for
a few seconds, and let it out along with his rage. He could be
furious with Perez, but Castro wasn't at fault. Not for Roy's
murder. "I would truly like to resolve this without any more
death—on either side."

Castro looked off screen for a moment, and her expression
darkened. "I'm afraid that might not be possible... I—"

"What is it?"

"I just received word that General Perez ordered the army to
shell your embassy. They've gone insane, Commander Grimm. I
always knew the sisters were ambitious, but this... this is
madness. It's like they want a war with the Alliance. I don't
know what to say."

Jacob's gut twinged. He understood the coup; he didn't
agree with it, but he understood their motives. A war with the
Alliance to avoid joining the Alliance's fight against the
Caliphate made no sense at all. Unless there was a missing
piece. Some third-party actor pulling strings. Who could
possibly benefit from this? Not the Republic. Certainly not the
Caliphate.

"Reason and logic often go out the window where emotion
is concerned. If our embassy people were killed, then that's a
problem, but one we'll have to deal with when we know for
sure."

He felt far less reasonable than he sounded. He knew that.
The truth was, there were very few Alliance citizens in the
actual embassy. Most of the staffers were locals. Maybe fifty or
so card-carrying citizens. He hoped they all made it out.

"I don't think anyone on *Estrella* will give me any trouble.
The other ships, though, are loyal to Admiral Perez. I don't want
to hurt them, but..."

"Do nothing for now. Make sure you're safe. If she planted

an assassin aboard my ship"—Jacob's throat tightened— "who knows what she did on yours."

Castro gave him a heartfelt nod and disconnected the line.

Jacob leaned against his chair, using it for strength. "PO McCall, as soon as you know the location of that antenna farm, alert me. I don't care where I am. I want to know."

"Aye, aye, skipper," Mac said.

He came around the chair and thumbed the comm button to notify Carter. "XO, round up five or six crew members who are proficient with MP-17s. We might need an impromptu boarding party, and I want to be ready."

"Aye, skipper. Will do. Oh, and Captain? PO Cartwright is going to be okay."

Jacob sighed inwardly, thankful for the good news amongst the tragedy.

Without a Corsair, there was no way down to the planet, so the first order of business was to get in contact with the ground team. They could only do that once the jamming was lifted, or if Boudreaux managed to find them with a laser. If they were where they were supposed to be, she might. The woman was a wizard with that thing. However, they weren't.

"PO McCall, prepare a packet for *Coughlin*'s skipper. Let him know what our plan is and the current situation. We should be able to hit him with a laser and deliver it... discretely."

"Aye, aye, sir."

———

Carter went to the mess first; he knew exactly which PO he wanted in the lead.

"PO Mendez," he called out. Josh Mendez was far from the kid who'd come aboard all those years before. He'd blossomed into a good man, and a leader of note, even if he didn't realize.

"Yes, sir?" He stuck his head out from behind the galley window where he busily prepared food.

"It's 0345, Josh, who are you making food for?"

"Skipper, sir. He hasn't eaten in twelve hours. With what... happened, I figured he could use a bite."

Carter smiled genuinely at the young man, who in truth was only a few years younger than himself. "If the captain ever leaves the Navy, I hope I can snag you on my ship!"

Mendez grinned, his hands a flurry as he chopped fresh onions. "With all due respect sir, if the skipper ever leaves the Navy, I'll be right behind him. It wouldn't be the Navy without him."

"That aside, when you're done here, I need you to form a shore party. No more than six hands, yourself included. All of them need to be certified with the MP-17 pistol and boarding practices. Can you do it?"

Josh looked up, pausing his knife work. "Shore party? Can do, sir."

"Good man. Report back to me when you have your list."

That checked off his list, Carter decided to hit his rack and sack out for a good forty-five minutes before there was another crisis to deal with.

CHAPTER THIRTY-ONE

In her time with the Marines, Jennings had seen heavy action since she was a private. She'd fought smugglers, pirates, and the Caliphate. The streets of Cordoba were another thing entirely. Whatever plans the military had for an orderly transition of the coup, went out the window when they shelled parts of the capital city.

Citizens were desperately trying to evacuate. The army was busy rounding up off-worlders and taking the opportunity to seize anything of value. A third of the capital burned. The very part Jennings and Owens were navigating.

"This sounded like a great idea when we were in the bunker with the president," Owens said.

Jennings had her rifle configured for midrange, including a foregrip and a 2x sight for quick target acquisition. Both she and Owens held them in combat position, tight against their shoulder and barrel out.

"Quit your whining, Lance Corporal, or I'll send you back," Jennings said. "Where are we now?"

Owens paced her by two meters and offset by a meter. He held his NavPad in one hand, with the map displayed.

"Two klicks in the direction we're going." An explosion rocked the street a hundred meters in front of them. Jennings jerked to the side, kneeling as she braced herself against the wall.

The street could be anywhere in the galaxy. A series of shops with brightly colored displays lined the east side, while doorways to apartments were on the west. The sidewalks were wide and ground cars lined the streets. If it weren't for the fires, rubble, and partially collapsed buildings, Jennings wouldn't mind living there.

"They really messed this up," she muttered. They were connected via comms; at close range, they were virtually undetectable.

When there were no secondary explosions, she used her hand to signal Owens to move. Fast walking, they stuck to the sides, near cover, darting from obstruction to obstruction.

"You hear that?" Owens asked.

Jennings cocked her head to the side. A rumble from a gas-powered engine echoed down the wide avenue.

"Military vehicle?" she asked.

"You wanna find out?"

She shook her head no. While there was plenty of cover fore and back, a passing vehicle could spot them easily.

"Into the shop," she said, pointing at the clothing store with a broken window. She leaped over the edge, catching some of the glass on her pants. Her boot hit a sign proclaiming, Don't Forget to Vote. She thought it was cosmic irony.

She ducked behind the wall, using the broken glass as a mirror showing the street. Owens hid opposite her. The rumbling engine came to a sputtering halt outside their hiding place. A heavy metal tailgate fell, and a dozen men jumped out armed with local weapons. She pointed at Owens and knife-handed to the back of the store. Maybe they could take the regular soldiers, but not without killing them.

Owens nodded, twisting around so the barrel pointed at the opening, carefully walking backward. She did the same. They ducked behind the counter, crouching to stay hidden as they moved. Boots on glass alerted her that the enemy soldiers followed them through the broken window. Because they detected the two Marines, or for looting, she didn't know.

Owens pointed to a door. The glowing red words above it could say anything, but the fact that they were red and glowing meant exit. She hoped. Leading the way, she pushed the lever down and opened the door five centimeters. It led to an ally in the back. No guards cried out. No shots.

She pushed through, turning on her boot hard to the right. Owens bolted out left, sticking his boot in the doorway to prevent the metal from banging. Once out, he gently closed the door.

Two klicks of this. It would be so much easier if we could just shoot them.

"Can we use the alleyway all the way to the embassy?" she asked Owens.

The red-headed Marine checked his pad, examining the city map he'd downloaded when they first landed. He'd done it to find good places to drink, but it ended up proving far more useful.

"Hey, Gunny, have you noticed how these soldiers are more... military?" Owens asked as he scanned the map.

She crouched down behind a dumpster, keeping her rifle pointed downrange. "Yeah. We were duped. The ones we've spent the last few weeks training were the reservists. They kept their real forces concealed from us."

"I knew no soldiers were that out of shape, no matter how much they loved their country."

She signaled him for silence. Inside the store they vacated came the sounds of shattering glass and crashing debris.

"They're looking for us," Jennings said. She glanced up, an utterly useless gesture but a universal one indicating satellite surveillance.

"Stick to the buildings, then," Owens said. "Under the awnings. If we use the side streets, they won't be able to see us."

She knife-handed the direction and they took off, sticking to the walls and narrow streets.

A sheen of sweat built up on her as they hustled, narrowly avoiding one patrol after another.

"Gunny," Owens whispered. "How did they know we were heading for the embassy?"

She shook her head. That was a level beyond her. Her job today was to find the ambassador, keep him safe, and initiate communications between him and the president. Others could handle logistics.

———

June fidgeted with her pack, making sure her dual tomahawks were limber and ready for close combat if need be.

"You're just making yourself anxious," Naki said from the leather couch adorning one side of the presidential bunker.

In the bunker with them was President Santiago, his wife Ines, and their three children. His chief aide, four security men, and several staff members. All in all, it was a load of civilians. She glanced at the security people. They were quiet and stayed opposite the Marines.

Did they resent their presence? How could they not? If she were guarding her president, and outside forces came to assist, she would have failed.

"Do you think they're going to make it?" she asked Naki.

He glanced at her. "You remember when we were on that ship?"

She suppressed a shiver from the memory. How could she forget? If it wasn't for the advanced medical science of the Alliance, she'd be dead many times over. On the Caliphate ship from close range plasma burns, and then later on the planet when her Raptor was shot down and she broke her back. There were some things nanite medicine worked exceedingly well on, and so far, that was in her favor.

"I remember."

"That was a challenge. This is a walk in the park. Gunny will be just fine."

"But we don't have air cover, the ship, or anything. We're down here training them on the basics. How's she—"

"PFC, she's going to be fine," he said with more emphasis. Naki looked at her hard, then used his eyes to motion to the civilians in the room. June got it. She needed to be strong for them. Even though they were all older and more experienced than her, she was the one wearing the uniform. The one they would look to for leadership.

A loud boom shook the room. The youngest girl screamed.

June hefted her rifle, spinning around to face the door. Whatever the local army called their explosives, she knew a breaching charge when she heard one.

The door didn't budge—yet. Eventually, they would get through. When they did, it would be a slaughter.

"Mr. President," Naki said, standing up, "You should move to the back of the room. PFC, help me make a barricade."

Santiago ushered his wife and children to the back.

"If they breach that door they will kill us," Friedo said with a fear-tinged voice. "If you surrender now, you can negotiate with them. Surely, they won't kill you if you surrender?"

Naki pushed the couch he'd lounged on a moment before to

the center of the room. It wouldn't stop anything fired at them, but it would conceal their exact location.

"Surrender, Friedo? They bombed the palace, declared war on the people, and you think they will stop just shy of murdering me?" President Santiago said.

Friedo glanced at Naki, which June thought odd.

"I... I know they will. If you surrender, General Perez will guarantee your safety. Just turn over the keys to her and—"

"How do you know this?" Santiago demanded.

Friedo looked at Naki again.

"She told me. None of this was supposed to happen. This was all supposed to go down while you slept. If we hadn't cheated in the election—"

Santiago stood violently. June looked at Naki to take her cue from the older Marine. He did nothing, so she held her ground.

"I didn't cheat. I have no idea where she even got such an idea. The only thing I did was invite the Alliance here because her party insisted I'm too much of an isolationist. And look where that got me?"

June barely paid attention to her own planet's politics. Trying to understand a foreign world's politics was too much. Cheating, though, she understood.

"They have no such evidence." Santiago stood, face red as his anger rolled off him. "I didn't cheat. I have no reason to cheat."

When she was a kid, and her parents would argue, June wanted nothing more than to run outside and hide in the woods. Exactly like she wanted to do now, but the door was locked, and an enemy army was outside.

Santiago looked at his wife. "I swear, mi amora, whatever evidence they have is made up. I didn't cheat."

"I know you didn't. That's not the man I married," Ines said while she comforted her littlest.

June shoved a chair into the center, adding it to the makeshift barricade.

"I saw it, Roberto. I don't know why you didn't tell me, but I saw it. Otherwise, I would never have—" Realizing he'd said too much, Friedo froze, as did the rest of the room.

Before the president could respond, another room-shaking explosion detonated outside. The massive door trembled. June dropped to one knee. Naki kept his feet, but the rest of the room fell.

Taking advantage of the moment, Friedo crawled for the computer. Confusion flashed through June as her mind processed what she saw. Naki figured it out first, running right at the man.

Friedo hit the keyboard—Naki plowed into him, both rolling over the table. Naki landed on top and brought his fist down hard against the man's face. June had sparred with the muscular Marine. He hit Friedo, and Friedo hit the floor, eyes rolling up.

"Oh no," Ines whispered. Gears ground to life as the titanic metal door rumbled to life.

Naki struggled with the man. June acted. While she wasn't an expert with the local computers, she did no electronics. She had seconds to act. The doors wiring ran on the inside through a conduit.

Leaping up, she pulled a grenade from her waist. "Shape charge, twenty degrees, contact," she said to the grenade. It beeped its understanding.

June, with the practice of a hundred sessions with DI's screaming at her, placed the charge right where she needed to. A split second after she took her hand off, it detonated.

All the explosive force went into the wall, obliterating the conduit and wiring. The door, only a sliver past its housing, ground to a halt.

Naki looked up at June from where he held Friedo down face first.

"Quick thinking, PFC," he said.

She shook her hand and smiled.

CHAPTER THIRTY-TWO

P O McCall stared at the screen until he lost focus and had to force his eyes away and blink several times. He'd looked at power readings and surface scans for hours. He was exhausted, not just from the searching, but from the emotional turmoil of the events of the day. He was thankful to not be on the bridge when it happened.

Poor Lieutenant Hössbacher. *What's the captain going to tell his family?*

Mac shook his head, clearing his thoughts of what had happened. There would be time enough for grief and anger later. He needed to put it all in a box and focus on the mission.

The only problem was, the screen at his station was just too small, and there was a lot of ground to cover. Cordoba's absolute land mass was, well, massive. The southern continent the majority of the populace favored was 6.3 million square kilometers.

The ground-based fusion reactor could be anywhere... anywhere flat and...

Mac leaped up, forgetting to take off his headset, then turned around and hung it on the console.

"Ensign Brennan, permission to relocate to stellar cartography?" he asked the OOW.

"Permission granted, PO," she replied.

Mac practically ran off the bridge. He hit the ladder and slid all the way down. Deck by deck, he ran, yelling, "Make a hole!" when spacers occupied the passageway. By the time he hit deck five, his chest heaved and his legs burned.

"I've got to get more cardio," he muttered as he stumbled into the fore compartment.

Stellar cartography was a fancy name for a holographic interface that displayed a highly filterable map of the known galaxy. The ship's astrogator could use it before missions to plot out very precise courses and have them ready at the touch of a button.

He pulled up short as the hatch opened. PO Tefiti stood in the middle of the room surrounded by sparkling lights from Cordoba's many large bodies.

"PO," Mac said. "I'm sorry, I didn't realize you were using the room."

Tefiti waved away his apology. "It's not like you can't come in, Mac. I was just finishing up. What does commo need with the cartography room?"

Mac closed the hatch behind him and joined the older man. While they were both POs, Mac's promotion was still fresh. He was a PO3 and Tefiti's next promotion would make him a chief.

"I'm trying to find the source of the jamming. We're pretty sure it's on the planet. Intel says they only have a couple of modern fusion reactors. One is on *Estrella,* but the other ships are all running fission piles. I think they're using the others to power an antenna farm that's jamming everything under the sun. Except their comm's, of course. Only a moron would jam their own comms," he said with a laugh.

Tefiti put his NavPad down and gestured to the controls. "You wanted to use the holo to find the reactor?"

Mac moved the panel and typed in the coordinates he needed. "Yes, but the reactor is on the planet's surface so..." Mac rerouted the gun camera from the bow to the room.

"Engineering, this is PO McCall in stellar cartography, can you give me priority access to computer node one?"

"Chief Redfern here, Mac. What's it for?"

Mac glanced at the controls one more time, making sure he'd configured it the right way.

"I'm working on a special mission for the captain. I need the extra processing power to run the guncam through the thermal filters."

Redfern didn't respond right away but Mac's console lit up.

"Good idea, PO. You've got it. Engineering out."

Mac moved the camera to face the planet, centering the southern hemisphere before he zoomed in over the capital city.

"I didn't know the cameras were that precise?" Tefiti asked.

"They're not usually. We're in a stable orbit, which helps. Not to mention, I'm running the image through the most powerful computer node on the ship. It's doing most of the work." Once the image showed the capital city from three hundred meters up, Mac slowly moved the camera along its axis to the west.

The slightest bump in the controls caused the camera to leap wildly off course. It took him several tries to get it just right, but eventually he managed to find the military HQ building. Displayed in the room from the same altitude, was the multistory headquarters. Two hundred meters to the west, a massive still-smoking crater loomed.

"Is that where the skipper fired?"

"Aye, PO. He was pissed to say the least. I don't think I've ever seen him that angry before and I've served with him since he took command at Zuck."

Tefiti only nodded, watching Mac work with interest.

"What's your plan?" he asked.

"If you had a rare power source capable of running an entire continent, would you restrict it to just an antenna farm with a narrow use? Or power your entire military infrastructure off of it?"

Tefiti stared at McCall with open-mouthed amazement.

"That's genius, Mac. Of course, they would. Since the power from the reactor will come from a hidden source, all we have to do it switch on the thermal and follow the lines that lead away from civilization."

"That's the plan, PO. Here we go."

————

Admiral Lucia Perez briskly walked from her armored ground car into the elevator that would take her to the underground complex. Her sister, General Juanita Perez, ran the liberation from the command room. After Grimm's stunt with the field, neither was safe in the military HQ.

Though... everything Castro had reported on him, including the publicly available information, said he wouldn't kill innocent people. If only her assassin had worked! Dammit. Then they could focus on eliminating President Santiago and get on with the business of running the planet.

She should have known a forced surrender wouldn't work. Not after the showing her pathetic navy gave in the war games. Castro did the best she could, but Grimm's destroyer was just too advanced, too powerful for her planet's navy.

The lift ground to a halt. Of course her sister hadn't decorated the bunker, only made it as functional as possible.

"Juanita, we need to talk," she said, striding across the circular room. Heads turned as she spoke. Twenty-five patriots manned the consoles that controlled all the communications, power, and infrastructure on the planet.

Juanita Perez, her older sister with her fine features and classic, turned to glare at her.

"What did you do?" Juanita demanded.

Lucia frowned. "What are you talking about?"

Juanita stalked around the command console, her black leather boots clomping on the metal grating. Lucia noticed, for the first time, how imperious her sister looked. Fire burned in her sister's face. She came to stand before her. While they were the same height, Juanita's boots made her five centimeters taller, leaving Lucia staring at her sister's chin.

"I'm talking about your ham-fisted attempt to murder Grimm."

"Oh, that," Lucia said. She unconsciously took a step back.

"Yes, that." Juanita's eyes were merciless and filled with ice. "You turned a noncombatant into an enemy."

Lucia pushed down her fear response, the same way she always did when her sister scolded her.

"You're one to talk. Tell that to the ambassador and the city block you annihilated." Her words emboldened her, and she stepped back into her sister.

"That wasn't me, you fool. That was an over-eager army general who won't be in the way—ever again."

Lucia felt her temporary courage flush out of her system with her sister's announcement.

"You killed him?"

"No. His second-in-command did the actual killing. I ordered it. Between him and you, we're dangerously close to war with the Alliance."

Lucia wasn't worried about the Alliance but about the war

they had with the Caliphate. The Alliance couldn't afford a war on two fronts.

She leaned in closer to her sister since what she was about to say wasn't public. "Once we join the Republic, war with the Alliance won't be a problem." No one in their right mind would want a war with a nation that had hundreds of member star systems?"

Juanita's eyes flickered to the side. "We're not talking about that right now or here." She grabbed Lucia's arm, escorting her to the side of the room.

"You're hurting me," Lucia hissed.

"I'll do more than hurt you if you mess this up. I gave you specific orders. Seize their ships. That was it. Now you've put me in a position that I didn't want to be in."

"What's that?"

"Executioner."

CHAPTER THIRTY-THREE

J acob strode onto the bridge wearing a fresh uniform, with four hours of sleep. He wasn't quite a new man, but he was good enough for government work. The position *Interceptor* found herself in was unusual to say the least. They weren't in a shooting war with Cordoba, but after the crap they pulled, he wanted to be.

Kidd took damage, Roy was dead, and they had the audacity to demand he surrender his ship. The only leverage they had on him was the Marines and the ambassador. If Castro were correct, they already bombed the embassy. That just left the Marines.

He stood behind his seat, unwilling to sit. The memory of the young man who occupied it was still too fresh in his mind. It hit him hard, harder than any loss he'd endured since his mother. It was something he would have to deal with later. Probably with Nadia's help.

"PO McCall," Jacob called out. "I hear you have a firing solution for me?"

"Aye, aye, sir," McCall said with a toothy grin. He beamed

with excitement. "With PO Tefiti's help, I found their antenna farm. I have it highlighted on the plot, Skipper."

Jacob reached over and brought up the plot on his MFD. With the main viewer destroyed, it was his only option other than leaning over one of the crew stations.

"Clever," he muttered. Jacob wasn't a comm's expert, but like every shipboard officer, he'd spent his time at the station. Despite advances in encryption, broadcasting, power, and the like, radio waves couldn't pass through a planet. In order to give their antennas the best range, Cordoba flattened the top of a mountain and filled it with antennas. "What's the altitude there?" he asked.

Tefiti manned astro next to Ensign Brennan. "Roughly eight thousand meters, Skipper. It's the tallest mountain in the continental range. They probably used a nuke to excavate, then went to work flattening it. Quite the accomplishment."

Jacob couldn't agree more. It was an engineering marvel. "Too bad we're going to obliterate it. Weps, target the coordinates. I want one shot from each turret. If that isn't enough, we'll drop a Long 9 on them. Understood?"

"Yes, sir," Lieutenant Brown said with a grin. "Locking target."

"I'd warn them," Jacob said to no one in particular, "but all our comms are jammed."

A light chuckle broke out around the bridge.

"Gun crews report ready," Brown said.

Jacob let go of the chair, sending it softly spinning. He leaned over Brown and flipped the fire control shield up.

"I've got this one, Lieutenant Brown."

"Aye, aye, sir."

Jacob closed his eyes for the briefest moment, sending a prayer to the almighty for Roy.

He depressed the button flat.

Interceptor's orbit quivered as four, 20mm turrets fired as one. Leaving the barrel at 10,00 KPS, the tungsten rounds impacted the antenna farm before the barrels finished reloading.

———

Raymundo Rodriguez sipped his rich southern coffee from the comfort of his office. He'd spent five years as a low-level engineer when the *Cresta de Nieve* project began. Five years of climbing along the mountainside, through tunnels, and over ridges. Five years of his idiot supervisor, Carson Madrigal taking credit for all his hard work.

Thankfully for Raymundo, Carson had retired the year the project finished. As the next senior engineer, he took over and finished the excavation for the mining nuke. Then it was ten long years of installing housing, antennas, and wiring. Not to mention the power runs all the way down the mountainside to the fusion reactor under the *Lago Prístino* hydroelectric dam. He was particularly proud of that. It was a genius way to hide the power runs. Only a close inspection from, say, an orbital satellite with a high-resolution thermal camera would reveal the deception.

His office, buried inside the mountain, had a fantastic view of the antennas that ran his planet's military and kept foreign invaders from communication. He was a patriot.

A well-paid patriot.

The flash of light caught his attention.

Followed by the deafening roar.

His beautiful view turned into a hellscape as four projectiles struck his antenna farm, each with the force of a 5,000-kilogram bomb.

The energy of the explosion tore through the antennas,

turning fragile material into hypervelocity shrapnel. What wasn't destroyed by the initial impact blew apart from the fragments burning through the air. A massive shockwave shook Carson's office, rolled down the mountain, and terrified small cities for kilometers around.

When the dust cleared, and Raymundo could see again, there wasn't a single standing antenna remaining. No trace of his decade of hard work existed at all.

————

Jacob watched the devastation from the nose camera feed. "Good impact," Lieutenant Brown said.

"Sir, we got comms," PO McCall said with a big grin.

"Excellent. Get me Captain Bonds—"

"Chief Boudreaux is calling us already, sir."

"Put her on."

"Indigo-Actual, this is Charlie-One-One. How copy?"

There was residual static on the line. Either from the bombardment or Cordoba's energetic atmosphere, Jacob couldn't tell.

"Charlie, this is Indigo-Actual. We're five by three here. That's as good as we're going to get."

"Roger, Actual. Corsair is 90% and Bravo-Two-Five is with the local leadership, defending them."

Jacob froze. His mind raced to understand what Chief Boudreaux said. Defending local leadership? What did that even mean?

"Can you clarify?" he asked.

"We escaped captivity from the turncoats and Bravo-Two-Five went to the aid of the president. Or more precisely, his daughters. I don't know their status as of yet. I'm at angels two-two approximately thirty-seven kilometers from their location.

Local SAMs were taking potshots at me and I didn't want to wait for them to get lucky."

Jennings. She'd taken it upon herself to defend the president. She was an Alliance Marine. Which meant the Alliance was defending the president.

Which meant he was.

This changed *everything*. He could no longer be a neutral third party in the coup.

"Dammit," he muttered. "Comms, see if you can get Bravo on the line?"

"Aye, aye, Skipper," McCall replied.

"Charlie, maintain position and wait for my signal. We're going to try and sort this without any more violence than is necessary."

The Alliance had protocols for this sort of thing. It was rare, but violent changes of government power happened. He was supposed to stay uninvolved as much as possible and only intervene on behalf of Alliance citizens.

What the hell is Jennings thinking?

————

The patrol caught them by surprise. Gunny Jennings flipped to her side, firing the 10mm stun rounds rapidly downrange. Two men folded with cries of anguish. Owens took down the next two.

"Is that all of them?" he asked.

"You have the same kind of eyes I do, Owens."

She got to one knee and scanned the area. They were one block from the embassy. Just one. Once it was clear, she went to the first downed man and mag-cuffed and gagged him.

"I don't want them alerting their compatriots. Got it?"

"Aye, aye, Gunny," Owens said as he went to work.

She heaved each one into a blown-out bookstore, hiding them behind a fallen rack. "No offense at all, but you're lucky you're not dead." Patting the only awake one on the head, she climbed back out the broken window.

"This way," Owens said, looking at his pad. He led them to the next alley, then through to the block over. Jennings resisted the urge to whistle. The Cordoban artillery blew the hell out of the embassy. The once tall building was reduced to a quarter of its height, three of the four sides collapsed.

"How in the hell could anyone survive that?" Owens asked.

"Bunker," Jennings replied. "Watch the street."

With Owens covering her, she dashed across the rubble-strewn lane, sliding into cover on the other side. She immediately rolled over and covered Owens as he did the same.

"Now what?" he asked.

Jennings clicked her radio over to the embassy frequency and fished out the code card.

"Echo-Three-Whiskey, this is Bravo-Two-Five calling on Sierra-Seven-Alpha coded emergency channel. Does anyone copy?"

Owens kept his eyes peeled, scanning the street back and forth. "Gunny, they should be able to respond this close. The jamming shouldn't impact our close-range broadcasts."

"Bravo-Two-Five, Echo-Three-Whiskey copies. I have Big Bird and Little Bird with me."

Jennings checked the card and sure enough, those were the ambassador and his wife. "Echo, are they operational?" She didn't think for a second the yokels could defeat her NavPad's encryption, but comsec was life.

"Roger, Bravo. All primaries are undamaged."

She gave Owens a thumbs up.

"Wait one, Echo." She clicked her radio over to Charlie-One-

One's channel. "Dammit," she muttered. "They're still jamming. Owens dig in. We might be here a bit."

Owens nodded and went about finding a suitable spot with both cover and concealment.

Jennings clicked back over to the embassy. "Echo, is your egress clear?"

"Wait one, Bravo."

Jennings rolled over onto her side, eyeing the street, then over to the other side. Crouching, she shuffled deeper into the ruins, not wanting to risk an accidental discovery by a passing patrol. Owens climbed his way up to the bombed-out second floor and found himself a place to hunker down. He grinned at her and flashed a thumbs up as she passed underneath. Sometimes she found his insufferable optimism annoying, but most of the time she appreciated the carrottop.

"Bravo, our egress is blocked by debris. I'm working it from our end. Our secondary egress is clear, though. Do you have that on your map?"

Jennings switched her NavPad to map mode and punched in the embassy. She had to sit with her back to an internal wall and focus on the pad while she navigated the functions and found the escape tunnels from the bunker. Every Alliance embassy, of which she had guarded a few, had a bunker or safe room for emergencies the Marines couldn't handle, but ideally could hold out until reinforcements arrived.

She found the tunnels on her map. The primary exited into the basement. Using her pad, she found where it should be and shook her head. Barring a ceasefire and heavy equipment, they weren't getting out that way.

"Echo, negative on primary egress. You won't be able to clear it from your side. I have eyes on it now. Proceed to secondary escape and we'll meet you at the exit."

"Roger that, Echo out."

At least the secondary tunnel would take them away from the active combat zone and deposit them a kilometer south of their current position. It wouldn't be fun for the ambassador. The embassy tunnel connected to an existing sewer two hundred meters from the foundation.

"Movement, two hundred meters, twelve o'clock," Owens whispered over the comms.

Jennings slowly put away her NavPad, securing it in her pocket. Carefully, she brought up her rifle and scanned the direction Owens indicated. Movement turned to contacts as a six-man patrol appeared around the corner of the far building.

"That's just great," Jennings muttered. These looked like Army regulars, with their generic blue uniforms and aged equipment. Despite their lower level of tech, the rifles they carried were deadly as an MP-17. If she had to fight them, people would die. Six were too many to catch by surprise with stun rounds.

In the distance, she heard the heavy beats of rotor blades.

"Gunny—"

"I hear it. Bug out—south. Secondary egress. I'll be right behind you."

She needed to make sure they weren't followed before she could head out. If the Army found the ambassador, she had no doubt they would finish the job they'd started with artillery.

"Roger that." Owens vanished a second later, as noiselessly as a bird flying through traffic. The wiry Marine constantly surprised her. He was probably a better fighter than her, certainly with the curved knives he carried.

Pushing Owens out of her mind, she trusted him to Charlie Mike. She carefully moved to his abandoned position, lying down on the ceracrete floor with her rifle beside her while she pulled out two grenades and set them next to her for easy access. If things went sideways, she wanted to be ready.

CHAPTER THIRTY-FOUR

Comandante Sofia Ruiz put the line down, her hand shaking. She missed the cradle twice before successfully landing it. She loved her world. Considered herself a patriot. Which was why, when presented with irrefutable evidence the president had violated his oath of office, she was willing to go along with the general and attempt a coup.

A coup that should have completed before the sun came up. Now there was fighting in the capital. The president wasn't in custody. The Alliance ships had fled, except for the Marine's transport ship and one destroyer.

And now....

Sofia gripped the small pistol at her hip and pulled it out. The sleek, black pistol had served her well, fighting pirates when they raided the planet a decade before.

She had once used it to shoot a man in the head as he charged her with a glowing machete. It was the first—and only —time she had killed a man. As a young, idealistic lieutenant leading her first patrol.

And now...

General Perez wanted her to execute Captain Bonds with it.

That was never part of the plan. The Marines were to be held until passage could be arranged. Their ship and equipment would be seized, but they would be unharmed. Only a fool sought a war with a technologically, numerically, and in every other way, superior opponent. The only thing that would stop the Alliance from swatting them like a fly was their ongoing war with the Caliphate. Did the general think that the Alliance wouldn't act against them once the war was resolved? Did she think they would lose the war?

Ruiz was no expert on intergalactic politics, but she knew the Alliance and the Consortium had a good chance of defeating the Caliphate. After meeting Paul Bonds, she was fairly certain they would win by a large margin.

She hefted the pistol in her hand, feeling its weight. The .45-caliber round it fired was considered an antique by modern standards. Slow and heavy. It did the job, though. Not once in her long career had she ever considered disobeying an order. Not once.

Standing, she slid the weapon back into its well-worn leather holster, grabbed her cap, and marched out of the command tent and headed for the parade ground where the prisoners were kept.

Two hundred Marines milled about inside an electrified chain fence. Paul had trusted her. More than that, he had tried to save their lives. He knew his Marines were outnumbered, but how many of her people would have died trying to subdue them? Especially if they fought to the last man. Outside the parade ground, four Corsairs were parked, locked, and inaccessible. They had tried to cajole the codes out of the Marine aviators, but the stubborn pilots wouldn't give them up. It seemed pilots of any culture were the same.

She marched past the sentry and waved at the makeshift gate. "Open up," she said.

"Ma'am?" the sentry asked.

"Do you have a hearing problem?"

"No, ma'am." He hurriedly unlocked the gate, sliding it open.

She strode in, two guards immediately unslinging their rifles and falling-in behind her.

The Marines, as if unconsciously understanding something was happening, stood up. Bonds lazily rose, like a lion with no need to hurry. His young lieutenant stood beside him.

Ruiz pulled her radio out and keyed the comm. "General, I'm with the Marine contingent commander, a Captain Paul Bonds." She held the radio out to Bonds.

———

Inquisitively, Paul took the radio and held it up to his head. He eyed the unstrapped sidearm Ruiz carried. Her stiff gait, and the way she clenched her jaw. He'd bet that these people weren't murderers. Bet his people's lives on it. He prayed to God he hadn't bet wrong.

"This is Captain Bonds," he said, his deep baritone rumbling across the field.

"Captain Bonds, this is General Perez, leader of the people's transitionary army. You are to order your men to turn over all technology and codes to Comandante Ruiz immediately."

Paul frowned. He'd already told Ruiz that wasn't going to happen. The only Marine gear they could use without authorization were their uniforms. The MP-17s, Corsairs, hell, even the grenades wouldn't work without an authorized Marine holding them.

"As I explained to the Comandante, we can't do that, ma'am."

"Is that your final answer?" Her voice crackled over the radio.

Paul glanced at Ruiz who wouldn't return his look.

So that's how this is going to go.

"Lieutenant Lia," he said.

"Yes, sir?" she replied. His Marines were tough. Half of them had served on *Enterprise* when they took Medial. He had faith in them.

"No matter what happens. No matter what they threaten or do, we are not turning over any codes. Understood?"

Lia's fear was evident in her eyes, but the set of her jaw spoke of determination and courage.

"Aye, aye, Skipper," she said.

Paul keyed the radio. "Yes, ma'am, it is. There isn't anything you can do to change that."

"We shall see."

Paul went to hand the radio back, but Ruiz shook her head.

———

"Skipper?" PO McCall asked to get Jacob's attention.

"Go ahead," he replied.

"General Perez for you," McCall said with a grin.

Jacob had expected the call. They'd taken out the jamming fifteen minutes before. It cleared the space-to-ground traffic, but there were still pockets of localized jamming. He could talk to Charlie-One-One but couldn't get through to Bravo or the *Coughlin*'s Marine contingent. At least they were able to communicate with Commander Estaban on *Coughlin*. His crew were fine, no casualties. The Cordoban Navy hadn't chosen to fire on the ship. As far as Jacob knew, and from what Castro had said, they wanted the Alliance's equipment.

"General, what can I do for you?" he asked.

"You destroyed millions of dollars and a decade of work. You killed thousands of people. Don't pretend to be some moral paragon." She practically spat the words out.

She lied, though, and Jacob knew it.

"Thousands of lives? That's funny. Our sensors showed no one at the point of impact. Were they hiding under an invisibility shield?" He mocked her. It was a dangerous game to goad her. The sisters, though, had pissed him off. His anger was cooler than the molten rage it had been after Roy's murder.

"You are a war criminal, Commander Grimm. I order you to command your Marines on the ground to turn over all their equipment to my army. You have five minutes to comply or there will be consequences."

Jacob could only imagine what those would be. She couldn't hurt *Interceptor*. She'd already killed the ambassador. The only card she had left was *Coughlin's* Marines. As much as it pained him, as much as it would haunt him for the rest of his life, he couldn't do as she asked.

"Perez, think this through. Right now, you've already committed an act of war against us. Maybe we can walk out of this without a shooting war if you release my Marines immediately."

There was a long moment of silence. "You have four minutes and thirty-two seconds."

"Dammit Perez. I can't do as you ask. No one can. If you shoot them, I will fire on you in earnest. If you think what we did to that antenna array was bad, imagine what our Long 9 would do to your capital?" She didn't answer. "Perez?"

Jacob gripped the headrest and squeezed like it was Perez's neck.

"Skipper?" Fawkes asked from beside him.

"Yes, XO?"

"We're not going to bomb their city, are we?" The look on his face told Jacob how much he needed the answer to be no.

"No. But she doesn't know that," he said. Relief flooded Fawkes' face. "What I want you to do is get with Lieutenant Brown and work out a firing solution for every military installation they have. Every single one. Prioritize them by value and plug it into the computer."

"On it," Fawkes said, grinning.

Jacob looked back to his MFD, willing Perez to come to her senses. Surely, she wouldn't execute his Marines. Right?

———

Boudreaux's Corsair circled the capital at a distance of twenty-two kilometers, twenty-two thousand meters up. Well out of range of their SAMs, if not their radar. Though she doubted their radar could see her with active ECM up. She had no EW officers below, forcing her to set the computer to automatic.

It would do in a pinch, but she sure wished Owens had remained behind to run it.

Her radio crackled to life, and she listened intently to Perez's demands of *Interceptor*. Corsair equipment included extensive comm equipment. She was no expert, but it was her bird and she knew every system, at least at a basic level.

She scrambled, trying to remember the procedure.

"Alpha five to radio intercept," she recited as she pushed the buttons in the correct order on her panel. The MFD had a dozen modes she could use, one of them allowed her to triangulate radio signals.

The makeshift army base outside the city where the war games were happening lit up on her map. A red blinking dot from where the radio relayed. If she went full burn, she would scream overhead in fifteen seconds. Her hands twitched on the controls. If Perez were going to shoot anyone, even if she tried to shoot someone else, Paul would make sure he was the first to go down.

———

"Marines, fall in," Paul bellowed.

Two hundred men and women scattered in organized chaos as they lined up by platoon and height, with Captain Bonds at the center just in front of them. Each platoon had two Marines in front, an LT, and a sergeant. Standing behind Bonds, Lieutenant Lia came to attention and spun in a perfect about-face.

"Company, report."

"First Platoon ready, Oorah," the LT bellowed. A second later, his entire platoon followed with a shouted "Oorah!" of their own. Each platoon repeated in order.

"Sir," Lia said, spinning around and snapping to attention. "Alpha Company, 2nd Battalion, 11th Marines reporting ready."

Bonds saluted her in turn, then did his own about-face and dropped into parade rest. At which point the entire company, as one, did the same. Bonds knew the impact such perfect coordination could have.

"Comandante Ruiz, you and I both know the captain will not give that order. If you're going to shoot anyone, you start with me and you look me in the eye when you do it."

Sofia Ruiz shook her head. "I—"

"Comandante," General Perez said over the radio. "If Commander Grimm hasn't given the order or Captain Bonds hasn't turned over the codes in thirty seconds... shoot Lieutenant Lia in the face."

In disgust, Bonds chucked the radio to the ground. There

was no point in having it. It's not like he would let them shoot
his Marines, then decide to give up the codes. It was all or none.

"You start with me. You work your way down. Better call for
more ammo, because you're going to be shooting all of us," he
said. His barrel chest expanded as he declared what she would
have to do. Paul didn't want to die any more than the next
person. There was a pride of sorts in knowing he met his end
like a man of honor doing his duty.

Ruiz pulled her pistol out and pointed it at Lia. "I'm sorry,
Paul. I have to obey my orders... I don't want to, but I have to. If I
don't she will order one of these men to and then I'll be dead
and so will you."

A rumble, soft at first, and so distant Paul thought he had
misheard, but then he knew.

A grin spread across his face as the rumble grew louder by
the second.

"Times up, Sofia," he said.

She pulled the hammer back and—

Plasma engines roared overhead, drawing everyone's attention. Paul lunged for the pistol, getting both large hands on it.
Ruiz brought up a foot to kick him, but at 109 kilograms, Paul
out massed her by almost half. Her foot connected with his
thigh, and it just bounced off. He grunted, lifting her off the
ground by her wrists. She cried out as something popped. He
took one step back and flung her aside, ripping the gun out of
her hand.

"Marines, kick ass!" he yelled.

Two hundred voices roared in a primal cry of promised
pain. They broke formation and charged the guards. Sporadic
gunfire erupted. Paul didn't have time to feel the pain of his
Marines, for he knew each shot was likely a dead Marine.

———

Boudreaux pulled up hard on the stick, converting her speed to altitude. RWR wailed at her as ground stations desperately attempted to lock onto her ship. She flipped the ECM to automatic mode. Switched targeting to the AGM computer and let it do its thing.

As soon as the RWR switched from a warble to a steady tone, chaff pods jettisoned from the sides of her ship, confusing their radar. Missiles were launched, and she was their target.

Boudreaux looked up as the ship continued its vertical loop. The ground was above her now and she pulled hard to bring the nose back into alignment with the makeshift military base. From where she was, three thousand meters up, she couldn't make out the people. The Corsairs were easy, and so were the Cordoban Army vehicles. Using a hat switch, she marked six trucks in a line.

The Corsair shook as missile pods locked into position. Her computers beeped at her as they lined up with the six vehicles and then—

She hit the button. Six plasma engine–propelled, fusion battery–operated AGM 101 Comets streaked one after the other out of her pods.

"Rifle," she said over the comms.

Six was overkill. Each Comet held the equivalent of twenty kilograms of conventional explosives.

She pulled up, rolling to the side as the SAM streaked by her. Its proximity explosion showered the Corsair in metal debris but left her otherwise unharmed.

———

The roar of plasma turbines clued Paul into what was about to happen. "Incoming," he yelled. The order was repeated as the Marines all hit the dirt. Boudreaux's missiles streaked hot and true, slamming into the trucks one after the other. Heat rolled over the field as the AGMs flattened the armored vehicles.

"Fight," he yelled.

They jumped up, continuing the fight with the stunned soldiers.

Paul made his way to the downed Ruiz, lifting her up with one hand. She clawed at his hand and he punched her hard in the face.

"I don't want to kill you and you don't want to be dead. Order your men to stand down."

She shook her head. "I deserve to die," she said. To him, she looked beaten, not just from the pounding he gave her, but from following orders she knew in her heart were dishonorable.

"Sofia, it doesn't have to be this way. We don't have to fight. Save the lives of your soldiers and my Marines. Surrender, now."

———

"Dammit," Boudreaux muttered as another missile fired at her. She rolled the ship to the right, dropped the nose, and put the incoming missile on her right side. She scanned the terrain with her forward-looking infrared and found the SAM site.

The missile streaked above her, failing to track at all. She slaved the nose turret to her helmet and locked the pip over the sight. "Hold this for me," she said. Her finger squeezed the trigger. Hundreds of 10mm tungsten balls spat out of the barrel. They streaked toward the SAM at fifteen hundred meters per second. Dirt blasted in a line, running right through the SAM. A second later, it exploded in violent fire.

CHAPTER THIRTY-FIVE

Juanita Perez wanted to scream at the walls. These idiot Alliance people had screwed everything up. Everything.

She wanted to shoot them all herself. Ruiz missed her chance. When this had all started, she'd hesitated to commit violence against them. As they interfered with the smooth transition of power, she wanted more and more to execute the lot.

"Juanita," Lucia whispered. "The army surrendered to the Alliance Marines, and Captain Castro isn't answering my calls. I think she may have surrendered as well. What do we do?"

If the president had died, then this would be moot. How could everything go so wrong so quick?

She glanced at the private safe, identical to the one in her office in every way. If she called him, then all bets were off. Would they even have a planet left?

Even if it cost her everything, she would win this day.

"I have to make a call. Get out."

Lucia frowned but did as her sister asked.

Once she was alone, she opened the safe and activated the comm device.

"Mr. Falcon?" she said.

Nothing.

"Mr. Falcon, I know you're there."

"Ah, Juanita. To what do I owe this pleasure?"

"Dispense with the nonsense, you know why I called. Can you do as you promised? Destroy the Alliance ship?"

He waited an infuriatingly long time to answer. "Of course. And when we have orbital control, you will be the new leader of the planet."

"No!" Juanita shouted. "Lady Devine. I'm not worthy to—"

"Spare me your drama. If you were concerned about honor, you wouldn't have attempted a coup. You want power, General. Admit it and do us both a favor. After all, all it took were some rigged elections, and you tried to overthrow your government."

She wanted to shout more at him. "He cheated and—"

"How do you know he cheated?"

"You... you showed me the evidence. My own people confirmed it. We saw the raw data and—"

Understanding began to dawn on her. She never trusted the Guild, but she wanted what they offered. Power. Control. Falcon had said it himself. Who better to lead than her?

He'd infiltrated every level of her planet. He'd never hidden that fact. Never hidden that he could listen in on every conversation. Access any computer. Even the election ones that were supposedly secure.

He'd rigged it to make it look like it was rigged... so I would...

She would do what she wanted to do all along. Unseat the hated *man* and put herself in charge. She'd spent her entire life preparing for the moment, seeding the military with loyalists who felt the way she did.

"You did this," she whispered.

"No, General. You did. I was but the tool. The question is, do you have the balls to finish what you started?"

Jacob let out a long, low breath as Captain Bonds reported in.

Finally, some good news.

"I've got twenty casualties. Thankfully, no KIA. I'm loading them up on the Corsairs for evac to *Coughlin*. Are the skies clear?"

"For now. Any word from Gunny Jennings?"

"Not yet. Comms are still spotty down here. You took out the planetary jamming, but they still have control of the airwaves in the city. Sir, I'd like to take my Marines and—"

"Negative, Captain. Arm up, secure your position, and hold tight. Until I can speak to the ambassador, we can't do anything except defend ourselves."

"Understood," Bonds growled. "Out."

Jacob felt the captain's frustration all the way up in orbit. He wanted nothing more than carte blanche to open fire and shred the planet's defenses. He could no more commit the Alliance to a war than he could turn over his ship. He really needed to talk to the ambassador. Soon.

"PO McCall, have Chief Boudreaux try to find our missing gunny."

"Aye, aye, sir. Charlie-One-One, this is Indigo. Actual wants you to establish contact with Bravo-Two-Five."

Jacob tuned out his message as he went over the tactical situation in his head. Castro was on his side. The rest of the ship commanders were probably waiting to see how it turned out on the ground.

Still... something nagged at him. Like he'd forgotten an important message or missed an appointment. He hated the feeling. Hopefully, it would come to him soon.

Jennings closed her left eye as the soldiers hit the hundred-meter mark she had memorized. Far enough away that they wouldn't be able to quickly identify where the shots were coming from, but close enough for her to fire accurately. She wasn't averse to killing, but she certainly didn't want to if she didn't have to.

Her scope let her see the soldiers as if she were twenty-five meters away. Breathing steadily, she hovered the red dot over the rear man's arm. The selector switch was set to single shot, flechettes, not stun. They would slice through him like a ship through water. He might lose his arm, but he would live.

Letting her breath out, she repeated the Marine mantra in her mind: *slow is smooth and smooth is fast.*

The silicone sliver accelerated to supersonic speeds and ripped through the air. The soldier screamed as he spun to the side, a spray of blood hitting the wall next to him. His squad instinctively turned to the sound of pain.

She hovered the dot over the lead man's shin. A second shot sliced through his ankle. He fell backward, shouting from both the pain and surprise of the hit.

As one, they realized they were under fire and dodged to the left and right, trying to find cover. She shot another who was slower than the rest of his squad. He fell, holding his hip to try and slow the bleeding, mewling as he crawled to cover.

"That should do it—"

"Bravo-Two-Five, this is Charlie-One-One. How copy?"

The sudden communication startled her. Jennings picked herself up, glanced once more at the slowed patrol, and climbed over the rubble, heading south.

"Three by three, Charlie. We have comms again?" she asked.

"Roger. Indigo took out their jamming."

Jennings smiled at the thought. Of course, the captain worked the problem from his angle.

"I'm sending you the coordinates of the secondary egress for Big Bird. He will need a pickup ASAP."

"What about you?"

"Either I'll meet you there or you can pick me up on the way," she said. "Bravo-Two-Five out."

Jennings hustled out of the bombed building. Her legs were cramped from prolonged stillness, and she was eager to move a little faster.

———

PFC June braced as the next explosive detonated. The room shook, people screamed, dust rained down. The door held, but only just. The next one would blow it open; she was sure.

She held a finger up to Naki and mouthed *one more*. He nodded in understanding.

The makeshift cover they had rigged would protect them from the blast and, for a little while, bullets. The rest of the presidential staff were in the next room behind a far less sturdy door. It was here that she and Naki would make their last stand.

What was she doing? It was one thing fighting against the Caliphate for the Alliance, but she didn't even know these people. They weren't allies... they weren't friends... just a random planet they were on.

She shook her head. This was her duty. If her time on *Interceptor* had taught her one thing, it was everyone did their duty. At least this time, she was pretty sure death was the likely outcome. Far better than getting her back broken and spending a few months in rehab.

Someone shouted from the other side.

"Here we go," Corporal Naki said. "When it blows, just stay down. They will expect fire immediately. We wait for ten seconds, then—"

"Close the loop, got it."

He nodded. "Just remember, slow is smooth—"

"And smooth is fast. You know this isn't my first action."

Naki's smile was regretful, not happy. "I know."

She didn't have time to ponder why it saddened him. The door blew and a chunk of wall the size of a man flew across the room, smashing the desk that controlled the door.

"Surrender," a man yelled.

June glanced at Naki who held a finger up to his lips.

"Maybe we killed them," a second man added.

"Go," the first said. June closed her eyes, taking a deep breath. Here it came. Fear and uncertainty warred within her. She would either make it through or join her ancestors. Either way, she was a warrior, like so many of her people before her.

Naki held up three fingers. Two. One.

They rolled out from opposite sides of the cover, only revealing as much as they needed to shoot. MP-17s spat out ten-millimeter stun rounds in a fusillade of pain.

Three men in combat gear fell backward, trying to get back out of the hole they had just walked through.

The Marines recovered, taking cover again.

"What the hell was that?" the first man yelled. From the moans and groans, June could tell they'd scored solid hits.

"Stun rounds," Naki yelled. "Don't make us switch to lethal."

While politics were far above his paygrade, he knew enough not to start some kind of incident.

———

"Mr. Ambassador, it's good to hear your voice, sir," Jacob said. Nguyen, his wife, and half of Bravo-Two-Five were on board Charlie-One-One.

"Same to you, Commander. When the fighting started, we feared the worst."

"It hasn't been easy, sir. We've lost people... good people. But I think we can still come out of this on top if we pull out all our forces now and—"

"No. This is the perfect chance, Commander. The Alliance wants Cordoba. If we make a deal with the president, we can end this civil war and bring them in all together."

Jacob truly liked most of the people he'd met on the planet. Even the ones like Castro who had betrayed him. He feared, though, that taking any side would lead to more discontent. If they exited the battle now, and left it up to the locals, whoever won couldn't blame the Alliance for the outcome.

"I understand the desire, sir. This is a textbook military emergency, which means I'm in charge. I want my people off that planet now."

"Captain, I understand this is difficult. But please, this is a golden opportunity."

Jacob's hands clenched around the headrest until his knuckles were white and his neck red.

"Difficult doesn't begin to describe what we've endured, Ambassador."

"Please, Captain. I know what I'm doing. Let me talk with the president. If I can get this situation peacefully resolved, it will be good for everyone."

Jacob purposefully relaxed his fingers. His thumb brushed the hole left by the assassin's bullet. If they left now, then Roy's death would be for nothing.

"One hour, Mr. Ambassador. One hour."

———

"You want me to what?" Boudreaux asked.

"Land in front of the presidential palace and drop the ambassador and me off," Jennings said.

"I know what you said, Gunny. I'm just making sure you know what you said."

Jennings cocked her head to the side, the way she always did when trying to decide if the person she was speaking to was a dumbass or not.

"I know what I said. Land it."

Boudreaux let the Marine slide down the ladder with no further argument. She had too much else to worry about. RWR lit up her board, but that was Owens' problem, and he did a marvelous job spoofing them.

The Corsair came in low and mean, hugging the rooftops, blowing loose debris aside as her plasma engines pushed her past 400 KPH.

"Ten seconds," she said. "When I drop you off, I'm going full burn for orbit, everyone else stay buckled in."

———

Jennings switched her MP-17 to pistol mode. Nanites flowed out of it back into the reservoir, converting the large rifle to a manageable pistol. With her other hand, she gripped Ambassador Nguyen's shoulder.

"You move when I move, sir, and you do as I say. Understood?"

"Yes, Gunny," he replied.

His lack of argument raised her respect for him. It was pretty low to start, with him being a career politician.

As the Corsair came in for a landing, she noticed the lack of small arms fire. Maybe there was a ceasefire?

"Out!" Boudreaux yelled over the comms.

Jennings shoved Nguyen out, leaping right behind him.

They stumbled forward, her strong arm keeping him from falling as she covered his back. Once they were clear of the blast zone, Boudreaux pulled up on the nose and rocketed into the sky.

By the time the Corsair disappeared, Jennings had Nguyen through the burned pillars and headed toward the president's location.

The dust from the combat landing cleared. Two dozen soldiers stood in the burned-out foyer, all of them looking at her. She tightened her grip on the pistol but didn't fire. Their weapons were lowered, and they stood nonchalantly like they were on a smoke break.

"Who's in charge here?" she yelled out.

An overly robust man came out of the stairway that led down to the bunker. His right eye was swollen shut from an impact that Jennings guessed was a 10mm stun round.

"I'm Capt—Major Jorge, my previous commander has been relieved. We tried to tell your men—"

"Marines," Jennings corrected.

"Yes, your Marines, but they're shooting anyone who even sticks their face in." He gestured to his black eye.

"I take it, then, the coup is over?" Ambassador Nguyen asked.

"Mostly. Only the top commanders were in on it."

Jennings didn't believe that for a second. All militaries ran on their noncoms. They were the ones who would make the coup work. Officers might have planned it, but they didn't carry it out.

"What about Captain Bonds?" Jennings asked.

Jorge snapped his fingers and was handed a radio, which he gave to Jennings.

"This is Bravo-Two-Five, go ahead," she said.

"Bravo, good to hear your voice. I'm here with Comandante

Ruiz, who's agreed to surrender the army. We just need to talk to the president."

She tossed the radio back to Jorge. "Good enough for me."

Leading Nguyen down, she walked by memory back to the bunker. The hall leading to it was almost unrecognizable. Massive burn marks and blown-out walls were signs of the explosives used to break down the door.

"Naki, get your butt out here," she said.

"Gunny?" he replied. "How do I know it's you?"

She stuck her head in the hole. "I'm gonna give you ten seconds to get your dumbass out here before I drop you until your grandchildren are smoked."

CHAPTER THIRTY-SIX

J acob relaxed for the first time in days since the whole mess started. The pain of Roy's loss would haunt him forever. But as far as outcomes went, this wasn't the worst.

"They still don't know where the Perez sisters are," Captain Bonds said from the holo. "Once Ruiz ordered the army to stand down, they mostly did. The majority of the fighting happened in the capital. I think the coup leadership thought it would be quick and painless. Head of the snake and all that."

So far, the debrief lined up with what he knew. There were a few things he couldn't figure out, though.

"I had dinner with President Santiago. While I don't know him well, I wouldn't think of him as a cheat."

Paul rubbed his impressive jaw. "It's possible he's a good liar—he's a politician, after all. But—" He held up his hand to forestall Jacob's complaints. "He insists he didn't. I'm having Owens and the *Coughlin*'s computer people go over the data and see if they can figure out what happened. If this were some kind of misunderstanding, or PSYOP, it would go a long way to helping these people heal."

Jacob couldn't agree more. For most of the population, it

would be a distant memory, but millions were affected by the fighting in the capital. If it were Alexander, he had no idea how they would mend.

"Very good, Paul. How are the wounded?"

He grinned, his face splitting apart from his enthusiasm. "Ready for fortune and glory, Skipper. Heartbreakers and life-takers, every one of them. They fought well."

He'd read the report of how the unarmed Marines had charged armed guards on their captain's orders. It was an impressive feat of heroism; one he would make sure was rewarded.

"That's great. Now we can—"

The comm light on the table flashed red. "Skipper, Ensign Brennan, can you come to the bridge, sir? It isn't urgent, but it might be important."

Brennan was the OOW, and Jacob had every confidence in her. If she thought it was urgent, so did he.

"On my way," he said. "I'll message you if I have any more questions, Paul. I'm glad you made it."

"Me too, Skipper. Me too."

Paul's holo blinked out. Jacob headed for the bridge. Cordoba would begin the process of joining the Alliance. The people of the planet got to keep their freedom and identity, and the Alliance would gain access to their manufacturing and population. It worked out.

"Sir," Brennan stood from the center seat.

"I'm going to grab chow after this, Ensign. Keep the conn," he said.

"Aye, sir. I called because I noticed something odd. We've had our hands full with the coup, so I wasn't paying attention to local traffic."

"I can forgive you, Ensign Brennan. We've had a busy week," Jacob said.

"Be that as it may, sir, no traffic has come to Cordoba in the last seventy-two hours. None."

Jacob looked over at the plot and frowned. She had the data pulled up on the chair's MFD, and sure enough, the time lapse showed nothing.

Tefiti turned in his chair and waved the captain over. "Sir, do you remember when we came in-system and we thought there was something funny about the traffic?" he asked.

Jacob gestured for Brennan to follow him over to astro. "Yes. Go ahead." The feeling of missing something grew and Jacob's gut started to hurt.

"With Brennan's discovery, I thought we might take another look."

"What do you suggest we do differently?" Jacob asked.

Tefiti shook his head. Manipulating the controls, he pulled up the traffic. "When you said something seemed off, I couldn't see it. I've looked at this data the entire time we've spent in orbit. Between the coup and the constant threat of Naval attack, I had put it out of my mind until Brennan said something. I can compare it to a previous scan of the system. Maybe then something will jog loose."

"Do it."

Tefiti ran his fingers over the console, typing in commands quickly and efficiently. The display flickered and a timestamp appeared from three years before, the last time an Alliance warship passed through. Traffic scrawled across the screen. Designators blinked in and out of existence from the time lapse.

"It looks like a regular busy system," Jacob said with a sigh.

"Here's since we arrived," PO Tefiti said.

The image blinked. A new timestamp appeared, showing the date they arrived in-system. Hundreds of ship designators blinked into and out of existence at the time they were in range of the starlanes. More when the data dump from *Apache* arrived. If anything, it looked even busier.

Jacob frowned, though. He was missing something, and it felt just out of his grasp.

"I know something is wrong," Jacob said. He rested his hand on the console, leaning over, taking the weight off his legs. "I just don't know what."

"You're right, sir. I can almost feel it, but I can't see it," Tefiti said with a sigh.

"Wait," Brennan said. "These designators—" She reached over the display and paused the screen. "They're the ship's IFF. Port of Origin, mass, hull number, and heading." She pulled up one that read T1410-344. "That means Terra, a hundred and forty-one thousand tons."

Jacob glanced at the display again. He'd forgotten that Brennan was a comms specialist by trade. This was her area of expertise. However, officers needed to be well rounded, which was why she wasn't on comms.

"Go ahead, Ensign."

"Excuse me, PO," she said, making a little shooing motion with her hand.

Tefiti stood up, abdicating his seat to her, waving her in like a gentleman.

She quickly pulled up a list of ships, organizing them by port of call. "A few hundred ships from the Terran Republic come through daily."

Tefiti pointed to the screen. "The nearest Terran Republic planet is only three starlanes away. That makes sense."

"Yes, PO, I understand, but... look." She put both lists on the screen and pointed at the top ship on each list.

Three years ago, the largest ship was the *Yíng Cái Shén*. T131185-072. "It's registered to the Luna-Trading Company. It was a thirteen-*million*-ton freighter. The next smallest one was twelve million, so on and so forth."

She pulled up the current sheet. "T1410-344's POC is Terran space, but she's registered as independent."

"Okay?" Jacob said, still confused.

"Skipper, the largest ship to come through since we arrived is an independent freighter with a mass of 140,000 tons.

None of these ships," she said as she scrolled through the list, "are registered to corporations. They're all independent and small."

"Have you ever gone fishing, Skipper?" Tefiti asked suddenly.

He shook his head. "Not really. Hunting, but not fishing."

"On Ohana, when you're out on the water fishing and all the fish disappear, it's because—"

Realization hit Jacob like a hammer. "A predator," he finished for Tefiti.

"I think, Skipper," Brennan said, "that Cordoba's about to be invaded, the TR knows it, and warned their major corps, which are all owned by the state anyway. They don't care about the independent traffic."

"Who, though?" Tefiti asked.

"I know who," Jacob whispered. Admiral Villeneuve's briefing came back to him in vivid clarity. "*Apache* caught a Guild ship spying on the system. That's the missing piece."

Jacob turned around, stretching to his full height as he walked around the bridge. "If I had to guess, President Santiago didn't cheat. The Guild just made it look like he did. Perez's ambition did the rest."

Brennan stood up and gestured to the main screen. "Then why go through all this just to invade anyway?" she asked.

"The Guild's plans are always overly complicated. They can't seem to do anything straightforward. Maybe they figured if there was a coup, they could justify their invasion. Regardless, my gut tells me this is right. The only question is, are they bringing the hammer?"

"Sir?" Tefiti asked.

"Before we left Alexander, I was privy to a general fleet briefing. The Guild purchased two battleships and several smaller screening units from the TRN."

They needed out of the system and fast. *Interceptor* was tough but... not that tough. There were no reinforcements coming, no one to warn, no good by squaring off against an unbeatable foe. Cordoba was lost. All he could do now was save his people. It burned in the pit of his stomach, the thought of what was about to happen to these citizens of the planet below. The Guild was brutal in the treatment of their *employees*.

"General recall. Get everyone back on board. Ensign Brennan, take comms while PO McCall does the recall. Get me a line to *Coughlin*'s CO, Commander Esteban and Captain Bonds. Then cross me to Ambassador Nguyen, President Santiago, Captain Castro, and anyone else they think is relevant."

Brennan gulped. "Aye, aye, Skipper. On it."

Jacob double-timed it back to the briefing room. He pulled up his NavPad and placed it on the table, activating the holographic feed.

One by one they appeared. He hadn't actually met Commander Estaban in person. He was a thin man with a thinner mustache and he looked impeccable in his Navy uniform.

Jacob began. "I have some unfortunate news. I know you're all still dealing with the coup, but..." He sighed. "I think the Guild is in the system and heading for the planet." He spelled out his evidence and revealed the classified information about the Guild's recent purchases.

President Santiago sunk in his chair, exhausted and beaten. Captain Castro shook her head.

"What kind of force are we looking at?" Castro asked.

"That we don't know. I wouldn't bring anything less than a battleship and a half dozen screening units. I'm sorry, Mr. President, there's nothing we can do. I need all my people off planet—"

"Commander Grimm," Ambassador Nguyen interrupted. "We're on the verge of these people joining the Alliance... surely we can?"

Jacob wanted to say yes, come up with some brilliant last-minute tactical maneuver. It wasn't even a matter of strategy and tactics, though. There simply wasn't anything to achieve. Even if he faced them down with his full squadron, it wouldn't change the outcome. His ships would be destroyed, and the planet taken all the same.

"Ambassador, Mr. President, Captain Castro, I truly wish there was something I could do. I can't throw the lives of my crew away. If there were some chance of victory or... a goal we could achieve by delaying them, I would do it in a moment. There isn't, though. All I can suggest is you get your people to shelter, prepare your defenses, and pray."

Santiago nodded solemnly. "I understand."

"Commander Grimm," Commander Esteban said, "I believe we have enough Raptors on this ship to outfit a platoon of Marines. All the ammo and ground-based firepower we need to win a war. Isn't that right, Captain Bonds?"

"That is correct, commander," Bonds said.

"Commander Esteban, I appreciate the sentiment, but I can't authorize that—"

"I can, Commander." Ambassador Nguyen looked straight into the camera, gave them all a stern look. "President Santiago — as an official representative of the Alliance—"

Jacob ground his jaw as the ambassador spoke. He was about to commit the Marines and his crew to a fight that couldn't be won. Worse, it would achieve nothing. He didn't want his crew to die for these people.

"Ambassador—"

"I'm sorry, Commander. You can only do what you think is right. As I was saying, if Cordoba agrees to a unilateral joining of the Alliance, ratifies the joining, then I'm authorized to accept it forthwith on behalf of President Axwell."

Santiago glanced between Jacob and the other two men. "Surely it can't be that simple."

"It's not," Jacob said. "Ambassador Nguyen, they *murdered* my third officer in cold blood while on my ship. I will *not* condemn the rest of my crew to die for these people." Hot, unreasonable fury bubbled up in him. He knew it was irrational. It didn't make it any less real. What was he supposed to tell Roy's mom? *Oh, sorry, ma'am, they murdered your son and then we defended them.*

"So you'll condemn my people to death and slavery because one of them killed your officer? I read the report, Commander. Didn't you kill the assassin? How many Cordobans must die for the scales to be balanced?"

Shame replaced anger as the ambassador dressed Jacob down. Shame, not because the ambassador was right, but because of Jacob's instinctual response: *all of them.*

He didn't really want them all to die. Roy's face popped in his head, and he knew what the young man would say.

"Captain Bonds, you need six hours to offload your entire armament?"

"Yes, sir," the Marine replied.

"Get to it. Ambassador, I need that formal ratification on my ship ASAP. If we're going to do this, we're going to need to hurry. We're also going to need the *Coughlin* to take on refugees. I won't leave any Alliance citizens behind. "

"If President Santiago can sign it, I can have it to you within the hour."

"Good. Captain Castro, I don't want to assume your forces will join us, but we could use the help."

Castro glanced off camera for a moment, as if she were confirming something. "We have much to repent for, my friend. We will help in any way we can, unto death if need be."

Jacob sighed. He hated this, but he also knew in his heart, it was the right thing to do. "We have a plan, let's execute it."

CHAPTER THIRTY-SEVEN

A cratered wall and scattered debris of napkins, glass, and broken china didn't stop Jennings and the Marines of Bravo-Two-Five from raiding the palace's kitchen. They were starving, and a little thing like artillery wouldn't stop them from finding chow.

Naki came out with a handful of donuts. June found bread and made sandwiches, and Owens—bless his Irish soul—found coffee. From there, they went back to where the president and his family were and took up residence in the room, albeit on the far side to avoid interrupting his calls.

Jennings paid peripheral attention to the conversations taking place. It looked like Bonds' Marine company would remain behind and defend the planet from a Guild attack.

She scoffed at the notion of the Guild. She'd faced them before, and it felt like killing children. Not that she knew how that felt exactly, but the Guild were so poorly trained it couldn't be much easier. The four of them, well three plus Private Cole—God rest his soul—had taken out an entire Guild military base on Wonderland.

Bonds appeared, marching through the blasted-out door.

Jennings leapt to her feet. "Captain on deck," she bellowed. Her Marines, in the middle of stuffing their gob, jumped to.

The large man waved his hand. "As you were," he said.

Bonds approached the president, ignoring the security men who stood guard, and spoke to him directly. "Sir, do you know where General Perez and her sister might be? There are pockets of the military that are refusing to follow Comandante Ruiz, and we need all your forces on board if we're going to mount a defense against a ground attack."

President Santiago, sitting behind a massive oaken desk, shook his head. "Believe me, Captain, if I knew... I still can't comprehend what compelled her to do this."

"If the Guild is involved, anything is possible," Bonds said.

Jennings opened her mouth to speak but thought better of it. Surely the president's men had thought to look in the obvious places, like old C&C centers?

"Commander Estaban says five more hours. Is there anything we can do to help?"

"You're already doing it. Those of your people who can find shelter are. We'll try to keep the fighting to where the Guild lands, but there's always the possibility of bombing and mass executions. I know that's difficult for you to hear, and you can still surrender—"

Santiago slammed his fist in a fit of anger. "They did this. Whatever Perez thought she would achieve; the Guild was behind it. I won't surrender to them. My people won't surrender. They can't kill us all."

Comandante Ruiz entered the room, and Jenning noticed the massive bruise on the side of her face. She glanced at Bonds' fists and knew exactly how that bruise came to be.

"Mr. President, we have seventy percent of the military reporting ready. There are some holdouts who are receiving their orders from General Perez, but we don't know where she is and no one who has... come to their senses knows."

Santiago rested his hands on the desk, regaining some semblance of control. "I know her evidence was convincing, but it's time we all were on the same page. The Guild isn't coming here to restore order, they're coming to destroy us."

"Sir," Paul said, "if we could capture her, it would go a long way to telling your army that you are in charge. Is there no place she would go? An old home, a former military post?"

Jennings found herself talking before she realized it. "A home won't work. It has to be a base. She needs the C&C to talk to her people." She forced herself to keep quiet by stuffing a dinner roll in her mouth.

All three looked at her and she decided she didn't care if they thought she had spoken out of turn.

"The old HQ under Castillo Mountain," Ruiz said with a burst of enthusiasm. "It's the only place that would have the necessary infrastructure."

Santiago nodded with her assessment. "No one's used it in twenty years. It would be perfect."

Bonds glanced her way with a wink. She frowned. The El-Tee was constantly trying to promote her. He was as bad as the captain. She was happy as a gunnery sergeant and felt no need to seek a higher rank. Plenty of Marines spent their twilight years in the Corp as a gunny.

"Psst." Naki made the sound to get her attention.

"What?"

"They're going to need someone to go get her." The grin on his face was unnerving.

"So?"

"Watch," he said.

Bonds grabbed a knocked-over chair and righted it. He offered it to Ruiz who, after a demure nod, took the seat.

"Mr. President," Ruiz said. "I want you to know you have my full support. I appreciate you allowing me to make up for my mistake. I wish I could say to you that whoever we sent to get her would be loyal as well, but..."

Santiago deflated somewhat. His expression was more of sadness than anger. "I love our world, Comandante Ruiz, as do you. I just wish she would have spoken to me, asked me, but then again, maybe it wouldn't have made a difference." Santiago looked at Captain Bonds, an unasked question on his lips.

Slowly, all eyes in the room turned to Jennings.

Who shot a grin at Naki.

"Yes, sir. Can do," she said.

Captain Bonds slapped his hands together.

"With your permission, sir, I'll get with Comandante Ruiz" —he nodded to the woman beside him—"and we'll plan the op with Bravo-Two-Five."

Jennings waved to her people, twirling her finger in the air to round them up. She followed Bonds and Ruiz out of the office. The leader of the security team guarding the president nodded at her as she left. Smiling wasn't in her nature, but she felt right about helping the president and his family.

"Jennings!" Bella, Grace, and Sandra darted out from behind their security team, dodging grasping hands as nimble as a hypersonic fighter jet. All three girls ran to the Marine and leaped into her arms, hugging her.

"You girls taking care of your mamma?" Jennings asked.

"Yes, Gunny," they replied.

She put the girls down, taking a knee to talk to them at their level. "I've got to go do a mission. Don't give your mamma any trouble, understood?"

"Yes, Gunny!"

The youngest girl, Sandra, hugged Jennings fiercely. "Will we see you again?"

"Of course," she said, returning the hug. "Now git."

The girls ran back to their mamma, who gave Jennings a large smile. Allison had never wanted kids before, but those three girls triggered something in her. She was right to protect them, even if the larger ramifications were more complicated because of it.

"Captain Bonds? A moment please," Ruiz said.

"Gunny, Charlie-One-One is outside. Get your people on board. Wheel up in five mikes."

"Semper Fi, sir," she said. "Bravo-Two-Five, move out."

———

Paul Bonds watched Jennings lead her team out. Pride swelled in his chest. He'd known her since she was a wee lance corporal. He liked to think his influence had something to do with her success. The truth was, though, she was one of those people that would make it no matter what. She was just so damn driven.

"Captain Bonds, I—"

Paul turned to the comandante. "Ruiz, listen, you did what you thought you had to do. Do I like that you pointed a gun at me? Hell no. I'll get over it. What matters is that I can trust you now, right?"

Her eyes brimmed with tears, making him supremely uncomfortable. His throat tightened, and he resisted the urge to swallow.

"You won't ever know what your trust means to me, Captain. I will do my best to live up to it."

"Good enough for me. You've got my comms. Get me the

location and blueprints while we're in the air. Time is of the essence."

"Can do, Captain," she said, mimicking Jennings.

Paul decided that if these people made it through the Guild invasion, they were going to be all right. If they made it through. With his indomitable spirit intact, he spun on a heel, jogging for the Corsair. He wasn't about to let Jennings have all the fun. His XO, Lieutenant Lia, could handle the details of the fortifications.

———

From the bridge of the *Interceptor*, Jacob monitored the progress of *Jack Coughlin*'s evacuation. With four Corsairs, and the vast majority of the Marines on the surface, the unloading of the ship's equipment was slow going. Their first run was bringing half the Marines back to organize the departure.

The mission clock showed a little under five hours remaining to complete the task. Five hours in which any minute a Guild battleship and escort could show up. He'd fought the Guild before, beat them even. When they were in civilian freighters armed with a one-shot-kill weapon they relied heavily on. Too heavily.

He doubted they would make that mistake again. The Perez sisters sold Cordoba out. The Guild wasn't coming to install them as leaders, but to enslave its population and strip-mine the world. They were the worst kind of corporation, driven only by greed and almost five hundred years of isolation and profit.

While there were plenty of companies in the Alliance who were driven by greed, there were also plenty who looked after their employees and tried to do the right thing. People, after all, were people. There were good and bad everywhere.

His fingers ached from gripping the headrest. With a

supreme effort of will, he released the chair, turned, and walked the two steps to Ops. The empty station where Roy worked this cruise was like an open sore, reminding him what had happened.

"PO McCall, can you have the Bosun assign somebody to Ops? I think POs Collins or Oliv would be fine," Jacob said.

"Aye, aye, sir. Call the Bosun, have him assign a PO to Ops."

"Skipper?" Carter stood behind him, for how long Jacob had no idea. Carter's NavPad showed a bevy of orders needing the CO's approval. Leaving the Marines behind wasn't covered by the mission brief. He had to write those orders himself. The ship's JAG, PO Filipe, checked them against regs to make sure they were legal, and here was Carter, ready for him to sign them.

"Thanks, XO." Jacob took the orders, approved the changes, and handed the NavPad back.

"Skipper, a word?"

"Lieutenant Brown, you have the conn."

Jacob followed Carter out into and down the passageway to stand next to his cabin door.

"What is it, XO?"

"Sir, there's a crewman who's exhibiting signs of depression. I'm worried he's heading for a disaster."

Jacob frowned. Crew welfare was the XO's domain. He appreciated Carter bringing it to his attention, but it was up to him to resolve these things.

"Have you talked with his PO?"

"Yes, sir. He concurs. Since it began, the crewman has distanced himself from his crewmates. He's become formal, using full ranks and names, even for the most casual conversations."

He's talking about you, dummy. It was his own thoughts, but he heard them in Nadia's voice. Damn, did he miss her.

"I get it," he said with a tight grin. "Tell the Bosun—Juan, I appreciate his and your concern, but it's misplaced. Yes, I'm angry about Roy. Dammit, I liked that kid, XO. He had a bright future ahead of him and he didn't deserve to die that way."

Carter put his hand on Jacob's shoulder. "Deserves got nothing to do with it, Skipper, and you know it. Sometimes, no matter what decision we make, people die. That's our duty. You taught me that in Zuckabar and every time I serve with you."

Jacob covered Carter's hand with his own. "Thank you." He patted the hand. "I just need some time, XO—Carter, that's all. I'm only human."

Carter vehemently shook his head. "No, sir. You're not. You're the skipper, the right hand of God, the man on high. You don't have time to be human, not to the crew. They can't lose faith in you, Jacob. I hate to say this to the captain, but... get your head out of your ass and get to work... sir."

There were several conflicting emotions running through Jacob's heart. Surprise was at the top of the list, anger, and guilt below, and a dash of shame. He hadn't let his crew down, not yet. He could see where Carter came from, though. Watching his captain spiral down the drain, eaten by anger.

Words weren't what Carter needed from him. Action was. He clapped the young man on the shoulder, looked him in the eyes, and nodded. Patting him one more time, he turned and headed back to the bridge.

They were going to win this battle, punch the Guild in the nose, and bring back a force that would make them regret ever facing off against the *Interceptor*.

CHAPTER THIRTY-EIGHT

Corsairs were loud. Jennings, unperturbed by the noise, rested in the crash chair, head back and eyes closed, even if she wasn't sleeping. When they first boarded the dropship, Captain Bonds disappeared into the cockpit for a minute. She pretended not to know what he was doing. Before she met Danny, she would have scoffed at the very idea of a boyfriend. Since then, though, she had learned to appreciate a companion. She certainly wouldn't deny Captain Bonds a little piece of happiness.

"Gunny," Bonds said. "The intel just came in. Gather round, people."

Her band of Marines pulled themselves up, walking shakily to surround Captain Bonds as he placed his MarPad on the deck. Once in a circle, they held onto the overhead straps to keep their balance.

"This is the old C&C for the military. They built it under a mountain for protection against an orbital strike. *Interceptor* could fire multiple Long 9 rounds into it, but the president would really like prisoners. If we can capture either of the Perez sisters, he can use them to bring in the rest of the military.

You've fought the Guild before, but we're going to need all the help we can get."

He hit the button on the Pad, bringing up a holographic projection of a twin-peaked mountain top covered in snow. "The peaks are at six thousand meters. There are several access shafts we could infil through, but—"

"Those will be the most guarded," Owens said, adding "Sir." At the last second.

"Right," Bonds said.

The Corsair dropped several hundred meters suddenly.

Boudreaux's voice broke over the radio. "Sorry, they have some funky weather patterns on this planet."

"What about the main entrance?" Naki asked.

"Three meters of ceracrete and steel," Captain Bonds replied. He pulled up the schematics, showing the blueprints of the front door. Naki let out a whistle upon seeing the specs.

"Back door?" June asked.

Bonds shook his head. "They have an emergency exit, but it's seven kilometers long and exits out into a quarry on the other side of the mountains. It would take us hours just to get there and they would know the moment we entered."

Jennings spotted something in the schematics. "The front door... it's not deep in the mountain." Jennings pointed at the way the road lead right to the side of the mountain. There was a twenty-meter-long tunnel, then the massive door.

"If we had time, we could bring the Raptors down and burn it," Owens said.

Jennings shook her head. "I have a much better idea." She triggered her comms. "Charlie-One-One, put me through to Indigo."

———

Lieutenant Brown shook his head. "You want me to do what?"

The radio crackled as Jennings spoke. "Send a 20mm turret round through the door, maybe two. I don't know the math. That's your department."

Austin Brown, who hailed from the same planet as Jennings, looked at the schematics they had sent him. A four-meter-tall door made of reinforced steel sunk into a ceracrete wall protected the entrance to the mountain. Her idea was sound, he admitted. A round from the turrets could penetrate the door, maybe... the angle would need to be exact.

"I don't know," he said after a long delay. "It gets iffy when we're talking about ground strikes. Assuming everything stays somewhat constant, one round should do it. Just don't be within a half klick of the impact." He pulled up the computers targeting system and fed in the coordinates Gunny Jennings wanted hit.

He turned over his shoulder and made sure the captain was paying attention.

"Do it," Commander Grimm ordered.

"Aye, aye, sir. Jennings, give me ten minutes to do the math."

Austin Brown stared at his console for a moment, trying to figure out the protocol for a ground strike. He'd done it before but firing four turrets at a football field–sized target was far easier than a precision strike on a single door.

"Uh, Ensign Brennan, a little help please," he asked.

Brennan unbuckled and moved to sit beside the broad-shouldered lieutenant.

"Yes?"

"Your math's better than mine. Help me calculate this please," he asked.

She blushed and silently went to work. The two of them

created the orbital path, angle, and worked out the degrees the turret would have to point at in order to hit.

"At the projectile's speed, atmospheric drag shouldn't factor," Brennan said as she adjusted the calculation.

"Skipper," Brown asked, "I think we've got it."

"Good job, you two," Commander Grimm said. "It's the Gunny's ball game, let her call it."

———

Inside the mountain, Perez studied the image of the Corsair landing. *What were they doing?* Five Marines disembarked, and she had to cover a snort of derision.

The Alliance, with all their technology and money, relied heavily on both over numbers. Sending five Marines to assault her mountain was an insult. The automated defenses alone would protect them.

She turned her attention back to the situation at hand. The Guild ships were hours away. All she had to do was hold on until they arrived, and the problem would go away. Cordoba would be under her control. Once that happened, things would change. No more trading with the Alliance, no more kowtowing to the Republic. So, what if it cost a few people in trade to the Guild? Better some be indentured servants than all her people be drowned under the controls of a foreign government.

"Sister," Lucia said from the doorway. "The sentries tell me the Alliance has located us?" Was there a terrified edge to her voice? The last thing Juanita needed now was a breakdown.

"Yes, but it doesn't matter. Go back to work."

Lucia didn't budge. "They've found us... it's over, then. Will you surrender?" Her voice broke as if she were a child again.

Juanita Perez examined her sister in a new light. Had she made a mistake pushing the woman into the navy? Lucia had a mind for managing people, but never the guts to do the hard things. She always looked for the easy way—like trying to assassinate Commander Grimm. If only it had worked.

"Lucia, it doesn't matter," she repeated. "They won't get through the doors and help is on the way."

Her sister frowned. "What do you mean, help is on the way? Our troops aren't responding. The ships have surrendered. Your Comandante Ruiz is working with the president—it's over, Juanita. We need to get out of here." Lucia marched across the office. Her hands slammed down on the simple desk, and she looked Juanita dead in the eye.

All Juanita Perez saw in her sister was fear and cowardice. How had she not seen it before?

"What I mean, *Admiral Perez*, is that at this very moment, a Guild battleship and ground troops are heading here to help. Once they arrive, they will destroy all the traitors, and then I will be president of Cordoba."

Lucia jerked up. "You? That wasn't the plan. Lady Devine is our candidate and—"

Juanita scowled. "She was nothing more than a puppet. I was always going to be the real person in charge. Me. Not her. Don't pretend like we were going to overthrow our government, then replace it with the exact same corrupt institution? We might as well surrender."

"Better to live in prison than under the heel of the Guild. What were you thinking, making a deal with them?" Lucia's fear gave way to anger. Juanita leaned back and examined her sister more closely. To this point, she had loyally followed her. Had that time come to an end?

"Look," Juanita said. She pointed at the large monitor on the wall. The Marines had taken up a position three hundred meters from the door. The only reason she knew they were there was the thermal cameras. They were otherwise hidden.

"They can't get in. We're not going to prison and the Guild is only putting me in charge. They're not taking over."

"How would you stop them if they did?"

She knew the answer: she couldn't. She wouldn't need to, though. The Guild wasn't interested in Cordoba, beyond a fresh source of workers. No. This was all part of the plan.

"They won't."

"But how do you know? You can't trust them," Lucia said. Fear quavered the younger woman's voice. Juanita's eyes darted to the sidearm her sister wore. The sidearm Lucia's hand slowly moved to.

Betrayed at every turn.

Juanita Perez had asked much of the people who followed her. They turned on their government, their friends, even the people themselves. All for the greater good. Only she had the vision—it seemed—to see what Cordoba could be.

With speed born of practice that a naval officer would never have, Juanita drew her pistol and shot her younger sister through the heart. Lucia's expression froze in shock. Her hand came up from her pocket, holding a kerchief, not her gun, which she used to stem the blood flowing through her tunic.

"Why?"

Lucia Perez stumbled back. Her mind dimming as her heart pumped blood from her body out the open wound. She collapsed against the wall, sliding down centimeter by centimeter.

"Why?" she asked again.

Her eyes closed for the final time.

"Guards," Juanita said. "Remove the traitor."

———

Jennings ducked behind the berm they used for cover. Odds were the enemy had thermal cameras. No drones in the area, though, thanks to the Corsairs ECM. She did a last visual check, making sure her Marines were properly covered.

"Sir," she said to Captain Bonds, "I would like to protest your participation."

Bonds grinned like an idiot. "I'm sure you would, Gunny. However, privilege of rank."

At least they had the TOE onboard the Corsair to outfit him properly. Soft body armor, along with the nanite energy dissipation in the uniforms, would protect him from any stray bullets.

"Fine, have it your way. Squad, helmets on," she said. The Marine standard helmet fit snugly over their heads, not only covering their skull, but providing them with vision, hearing, and facial protection. Along with several vision modifications.

"Indigo, this is Bravo-Two-Five. We're ready. Commence firing."

"Roger, Bravo-Two-Five. Indigo firing in five..." Brown's voice sounded steady. She sure hoped he was better at his job than he was at unarmed combat.

The second he said "one," thunder rolled through the air. A streak of fire, so fast their eyes didn't register where it came from—it was just there—impacted the side of the mountain. Dirt, debris, and smoke filled the air.

Jennings crawled up to the crest of the berm.

"Negative impact, Indigo. Decrease elevation by one percent," she said. After they answered, she scurried back down.

A second later, another streak of fire and thunder boomed off the mountain.

"Down one more," she said into the radio.

"Roger that," Brown replied.

Fire rained down from the sky and slammed into the tunnel.

"Good hit," Jennings said. "Fire for effect."

"On the way," Brown replied.

Another 20mm steel-wrapped, nano-hardened tungsten penetrator blasted the door, and another after that.

"Cease fire, Indigo."

Jennings waved her Marines up. They split up into two columns, five meters abreast with three meters between them, darting from cover to cover until they reached the tunnel—or where the tunnel used to be.

Kinetic energy from the impact excavated the side of the mountain. The tunnel, overhead, and reinforced door were just... gone. All that remained of the door was the glowing edges, where it connected to the reinforced concrete buried in the mountain. While the precision strike had hit the door, it also wiped out the upper levels.

"Down," Bonds said. He pointed at the sheared-off top of an elevator shaft.

"Naki, clear it."

"Frag out," Naki said as he dropped a proximity grenade down.

Jennings silently counted. At five, she heard the boom echo up.

"What, 100 meters?" she asked.

June looked up, doing the mental math. "122," she said.

"Break out the harness."

It took them less than sixty seconds to prepare to descend into the tunnel.

"Gunny, we won't have backup down there," Bonds reminded her.

"We don't have it up here," she replied.

Naki went first, dropping down the nano-filament line, bouncing like a Pong ball. His rifle pointed down as he disappeared into the darkness. June followed, then Owens, Jennings, and Bonds brought up the six.

Jennings dropped into the darkness. Her helmet automatically switched between vision modes until she could see. A glowing white outline shone around her Marines.

"Status?" she whispered.

"They wired the door," June replied. "One mike."

"Get on it, PFC."

Naki maneuvered to one side, covering the door with his rifle. Owens held the opposite side, while Jennings and Bonds waited above.

June worked her wand under the lift door, allowing her to see beyond.

"Five soldiers, projectile weapons. Simple mine on the door, but it's trigger activated."

Jennings scowled. That meant they would detonate it upon the door opening.

"June set a charge, blow the door. Everyone else, up ten."

They did as she ordered. When June finished rigging her makeshift breaching charge using her grenades, she joined them.

"When the door blows, it should take out the mine," June explained.

"Good. Naki, you and I. Owens, then June and the captain. PFC June, your job is to keep Captain Bonds alive at all costs."

"Aye, aye, Gunny," she said.

"Now wait a damn minute, Jennings I—"

"Sir, you're an officer on a dangerous op. You're not going in unprotected. Period."

Bonds deflated somewhat, but his indomitable smile returned. "Okay then. Marines?" he asked in a whisper. "Who are we?"

"Killers!" came back their united, if subdued, reply.

"Damn straight. Gunny, take them in."

Inwardly, Gunny Jennings was proud of her old CO. She was glad he got to participate in his favorite ritual one more time.

"Oorah, sir. June, blow it."

June's accurately placed breaching charge detonated. An excessive, explosive force hit the doors, rending them inward like a freight train had blown through them.

The explosion blew the mine backward. Splinters of metal shredded the two soldiers standing closest to the door. The other three dropped to the ground, the concussive force blowing out their eardrums and shaking their brains.

Jennings swung in first, detaching her magnetic line, the second her boots passed the threshold. She hit the ground, rolled behind cover, and popped up and fired two bursts into the closest man. The silicate projectile cut through his body armor and heart, killing him instantly.

Naki, right behind her, fired a full-auto burst, stitching the last man from stomach to neck, showering the wall with his blood.

"Clear," Jennings said. She moved forward, head swiveling, making sure she didn't miss anything.

"Clear," Naki said. He knelt to check the two bodies on his side.

Owens rushed forward, past them, to kneel in the hallway and cover their twelve o'clock. June and Captain Bonds swung through last.

"Movement beyond the next door," Owens said.

Jennings checked her HUD. Sure enough, thermal readings fluctuated through the forward door.

With their six covered, she motioned for Naki to follow her up to Owens. They formed a firing line anchored around Lance Corporal Owens. Unlike the lift door, or the outer door, this one was made of simple materials.

"Full auto, six seconds," Jennings whispered. They both gave her a thumbs up.

She held up two fingers. One finger.

Their volume of fire shredded the door and the six unarmored men behind it. Naki pulled a grenade from his harness and chucked it. "Frag out," he yelled.

The *boom* blasted through the door, forcing the Marines to shield themselves for a second.

"Screamer," Jennings ordered.

Owens snatched his grenade, switched it to sonic screamer, and threw it in the room.

Audio-dampers clamped down on their ears as the screamer blasted 200 decibels in a twenty-meter radius.

Charging into the room, the three Marines sliced the pie of the room, Jennings going left, Naki right, and Owens forward. A dozen unarmed soldiers clasped their ears, writhing in agony. Blasted computer components, dead bodies, and collapsed ceiling tiles littered the floor. Two men on the right maintained their composure, firing solid rounds right at Naki.

He went down as the kinetic energy blasted him backward. Owens spun, firing two quick bursts. The first man slumped to the floor as his chest exploded. The second burst, kicked higher by the slight recoil, caught the man in the face.

"I'm okay," Naki yelled into the radio.

Jennings followed the oval room around until she hit the doorway into the office. According to the blueprints the president provided, this was the room she needed.

She lifted one booted foot and kicked the door as hard as she could. Wood splintered, the frame shattered, and she followed the door in. General Perez, using her simple desk as cover, fired her pistol. A half dozen shots rang out. Two hit Jennings. Her armor absorbed the impact, preventing penetration.

It still hurt.

She growled through the pain, charging the woman. It was stupid; she knew that. But they needed a prisoner to talk the army down. It was all for naught if she killed herself.

Perez fired until her gun clicked empty. Three more rounds hit Jennings, one bouncing off her helmet. The rugged Marine charged through. Perez desperately tried to reload, slamming a new magazine home just as Jennings leapt over the desk.

Ninety-five kilograms of Oorah hit the traitorous general in the face.

CHAPTER THIRTY-NINE

Jacob tapped the back of his chair while examining the plot. There were a dozen ships in orbit. Six of them were Castro's. Two were his. The other four were civilians. He made sure Mac called each one and informed them of the situation. To his relief, all the ships volunteered to load up with refugees and head for the exit lane.

Even the Guild wouldn't destroy civilian ships trying to escape, so they should be safe.

"Skipper," Lieutenant Fawkes handed him his NavPad showing the outgoing inventory. "All four Raptors, the extra armor and MP-17s, along with three cases of grenades the Bosun managed to fabricate before *Coughlin*'s Corsair departed."

"When is Bravo-Two-Five scheduled to come back up?" Jacob asked.

Carter breathed in, nervously glancing around. "Well, about that, Skip—"

Jacob handed him back the NavPad, peering at him. "What?" Jacob didn't mean to sound cold. The last thing he needed was more bad news.

"Nothing bad, Skip. Close the outer doors," Carter said waving his skipper down.

Jacob put a hand to his temple, massaging them for a minute. He was on a hair trigger, for sure.

"Sorry, XO. What does the Gunny need?"

"They're wrapping up the operation to nab General Perez. You'll be interested to note they found Admiral Perez's body. Apparently, her sister killed her. Once the news was made public, the holdouts surrendered. President Santiago gave them a blanket pardon if they choose to fight the Guild."

Jacob was about to ask what this had to do with Jennings when McCall interrupted.

"Skipper, Captain Bonds would like a word."

Carter looked like he wanted to say something else, but he didn't.

Jacob grabbed the offered earpiece and held it up.

"Go for Actual," he said.

"Actual, we have things wrapped up down here. We're moving our focus to setting up the defenses. Gunny Jennings will be leading the—"

"What?" Jacob asked.

There was a pause.

"That's what I wanted to tell you, sir. Bravo-Two-Five is remaining behind with the rest of the Marines," Fawkes said. He had the sheepish look of a man who didn't want to be delivering the bad news.

Jacob glanced at his XO before returning to the conversation.

"Go ahead," Jacob said.

"Uh, like I said, Jennings will lead our QRF. She wanted to know if *Interceptor* can use the gun cam to record a detailed map of the hundred square klicks around the capital?"

"One mike." Jacob handed the earpiece back to McCall. He

stormed by Carter. "Mr. Brown, get the Gunny what she needs. XO, you have the conn." He exited the bridge, heading for his cabin. Time was a commodity he didn't have, but he needed a minute.

The assassin had killed Roy, but he also killed the sense of security and safety aboard ship. He'd hoped that when Jennings returned so would the feeling of safety. He couldn't deny her desire to stay and fight with the other Marines. No doubt they would be better off having her with them.

"Don't be a selfish jerk," he muttered to himself inside his cabin where the crew couldn't hear him. He really had come to rely on her. Just her presence made all the difference.

Jacob sat on his rack, back against the hull. On his NavPad, he pulled up the system map, tying it into the main computer and displayed all the information they had so far in a holo.

An unknown number of Guild ships were on their way to Cordoba. He had just enough civilian ships to evacuate every Alliance citizen off the planet along with a few thousand Cordoban civilians. The government chose to send as many children as possible. They were loading up the civilian freighters with them.

Jacob closed his eyes, relieving those awful moments when he fell into the Caliphate trap and fired on the ambushers in Pascal. The discovery of those tiny bodies threatened his career, even his life.

He'd more than redeemed himself, though, for something that wasn't his fault to begin with. It was all part of the Caliphate's propaganda. This wasn't that.

Though he knew they had murdered children before and would again. The Alliance couldn't clean up the galaxy. Even if they wanted to put an end to the Guild, the military had their hands full taking on the Caliphate. Who knew if the Alliance would even want to fight another war, or if they even could?

While the rules for fighting a galactic corp might be unknown to Congress, he knew what the ROE was for his ship. A foreign navy heading right for him meant only one thing. Would the Naval Review Board see it that way? Could he open fire on them first?

There was no beating them, that was obvious. He just needed to get past them. If he slowed them down, great, but really, survival was the key.

He also needed to officially convey to them that Cordoba was Alliance space. It was a paper threat only, though. It wasn't like they could enforce Alliance law this far out without a fleet. It would be like the Caliphate declaring that Alexandria belonged to them. Meaningless.

Spinning the map slowly on its axis, he examined the different celestial bodies in the system, checked the tags of ships, and looked at the distance to the starlanes. A lot could be gained by using one's terrain—such as it was—when fighting a numerically superior opponent.

The twin asteroid belts, each about three hours away at max acceleration, were highly magnetic with a dense cluster of rare elements. Useful, if the Guild decided to fight in the asteroids. As a rule, navies tended to avoid navigation hazards. He reminded himself that it was doubtful the Guild was actually operating the ships they were sending. Maybe a PMC, or even another nation under their flag. Possibly the Terran Republic? Regardless, he couldn't count on the lazy ship handling they had in Zuckabar and Wonderland.

That just left the moons. Two of them orbited Cordoba, a third one orbited the fifth planet in the system. There were more, but those three were the only ones of the right size to properly obscure a gravwake.

Ideally, *Interceptor* would have a full head of steam before engaging the enemy ships, and they would be sitting still. Even a kinetic strike would do significantly more damage with an added 6,000 KPS.

Expanding the holo, he focused on the area around Cordoba. He played with the map, accelerating the timeline, moving the moon around in its orbit... an idea hit him. It was risky, but it just might work. All he needed was for the Guild ships to come in peacefully and assume a parking orbit.

Jacob slapped the comms button next to his bunk. "Comms, get me Captain Castro, please."

"Aye, sir," Spacer Abbot replied. "One mike."

Jacob liked the new comms man. Mac's training turned a raw eighteen-year-old kid into a competent spacer.

"Captain Castro, Commander. What can I do for you?"

Jacob quickly explained his plan, sending over the relevant maps to show her exactly what he intended to do.

"If it works," he said, "they will be completely caught off guard."

"And if it doesn't, it will leave you with your ship swinging in the wind and nothing to protect you," Castro replied.

Jacob had considered the downsides of his plan. Regardless of the risk, or how much he personally wanted to abandon the planet to its fate, his duty was clear: defend Cordoba as long as he could.

Once it was no longer possible to defend, or if his ship's level of damage prevented defense, he could return to Alliance space. Hopefully to bring back reinforcements. Even so, that would take at least two months. Two months that the Marines would have to hold out against a superior force with no backup.

That, though, was a worry for future Jacob. The immediate concern was the incoming fleet and defending the *Jack Coughlin* until it could depart. They would need to take a circuitous route. Though the Guild wouldn't likely fire on civilian ships, if they were here to do violence, an Alliance MTC would be fair game.

"No risk, no reward, Captain. The battle goes not to the strong, but to the skilled. We just have to time it right and take our chances."

Her expression grew pensive as she thought through what he said.

"Okay, Commander, we'll do it. Just be ready because if you don't show, we're going to have to engage them at point-blank range... and that will be the end of us."

Jacob understood all too well what he asked of them. He asked the same of himself and his crew.

"We'll be there, Captain. You can count on us. *Interceptor* might be old, but she's got it where it counts."

————

Captain Bonds accepted the last of the transfers with the press of his thumb against the MarPad. The rain had finally abated, and he could venture outside their makeshift CP without the water soaking through his uniform.

"Thank you, Top," he said to his Marine company first sergeant. They were but a single company, Alpha, 2nd Batallion. They were some of the best, though. Even though the training with the Cordoba Army ended up being a ruse, it turned fortuitus. In the time they trained them, the Marines of Alpha company turned 5,000 out-of-shape irregulars into lean, mean, fighting machines.

A hefty local sergeant, his gut hanging out over his belt, came up the path to the CP. "Message from Comandante Ruiz, sir." His heavy accent, while thick, wasn't as hard to understand as when Paul had first arrived. "All necessary civilians have been evacuated."

"Thank you, Sergeant."

Maybe not lean, but certainly mean.

"PFC Vicker, get me Commander Esteban."

Resting on a stump, a PFC in Marine camo held the portable radio with its micro-fusion battery. The radio would outlive humanity if left alone. Small, compact, and made of nano-reinforced steel, it weighed hardly a kilo, yet could reach the moon if need be.

"Commander Esteban for you, sir," PFC Vicker said, holding out the handheld.

"Esteban here, Captain."

"Are you ready to depart?" Paul asked. They had discussed this, and Esteban wished he could stay. In the end, though, it simply wasn't an option. Esteban kept a skeleton crew and loaded the ship up with as many people as he could.

"I am. Commander Grimm's astrogator sent us over the course five mikes ago. It's solid. We'll depart at a right angle to the incoming forces. Despite that, we'll be at the starlane in ten hours. After that, it should be clear sailing..."

"I know, Commander. Believe me, if we didn't have civilians to evacuate, I would welcome your presence. We all have our duty to do, though."

He heard Esteban sigh, an unexpected emotion from the man. "I know. I know," he said. "Good luck, Captain. And as an ancient forbearer said: give 'em hell."

"Oorah," Paul replied.

This fight was going to be long and nasty. His Marines were going to be guerilla fighters while the Cordoban Army fought the straight-up fight. One hundred sixty Marines with soft armor, comms, and plenty of ammo for their rifles would attack the enemy from the flank—wherever that flank ended up.

Forty-four more wearing Raptors was their QRF. Wherever

trouble popped up, Bravo-Two-Five and forty Marines would be there, wreaking havoc.

He knew that the captain's battle upstairs would be far more dangerous. The Guild would land troops and round up the population, as monumental a task as that was. The captain would have to fight his way through their ships, not even knowing what he faced until it was too late to abort.

"Vicker, get me *Interceptor*."

"Aye, aye, sir."

A moment later, he was speaking with Commander Grimm.

"We're about to pull out of orbit, Paul. I wish there was more we could do for you," Grimm said over the crackling comms.

"You've done more than enough, Skipper. Take care of that ship and hurry back. We'll hold out as long as we can, but if you take much longer than six months, we're in trouble."

Grimm's laugh filled the little CP with much needed light-heartedness. Paul knew very well that they wouldn't last six months, not against a determined foe. Two months, though? They could do that.

"We'll be back before you know it. Take care of my Marines," Grimm said.

"Take care of my ship," Paul countered.

He handed the handset to PFC Vicker, who stayed with the comms and the captain. Paul looked out over his command and wished that he didn't lose a single Marine. The next few months would be the hardest battle they ever fought. It would be a long-drawn-out, desperate fight every day. He looked up to the sky, pretending that one of the stars twinkling in the twilight was *Interceptor*.

"Godspeed, Skipper," he whispered.

CHAPTER FORTY

Draining the can of air was a matter of securing the atmosphere regulator and shutting off the valves to the oxygen. Once that was complete, micro airlocks around the ship opened and *whoosh* went the existing air. Replaced after a moment by inert nitrogen harvested from the crew's own exhales. Every breath went somewhere. The heat bled into the hull, which in turn ended up in the carbon-fiber heat sink. Moisture was wicked out of the air, absorbed into filters, purified, and turned into ship's water. Carbon dioxide and other chemicals were filtered out by scrubbers.

Spare nitrogen tanks existed on the ship, but unless they drained the can repeatedly, there wasn't a need for them.

"All departments report ready, Skipper. Two minutes, forty-six seconds," PO Collins said from Ops. There weren't any backup officers on a destroyer. With Roy—gone—he filled the position with whoever he could. The Bosun would work, but Collins was more than capable. The crew's assignments were as tight as their shifts. If Collins was on the bridge, that meant Spacer First Class Perch was promoted to turret #1 gunner, which further meant a spacer's apprentice moved from engineering to the Long 9.

XO Fawkes took care of the details. He made sure every station that needed a pair of hands, had them.

Jacob looked around the bridge. Roy's death had dampened his spirit, but it remained undaunted. Lieutenant Brown and PO Ignatius ran weapons on his left. Opposite of them to his right were Ensign Brennan and PO Tefiti on astro. PO McCall and Spacer Abbot were on comms. Chief Suresh sat in the Pit like she faced impossible odds every day of the week and twice on Sunday.

The coming battle would come down to who saw who first. There wasn't any point in shooting at a battleship, but her escorts, if caught by surprise, he could damage.

He looked to the main viewer, wishing for the hundredth time that they could fix it. Instead, he pulled up the plot on his MFD to check on *Jack Coughlin*'s progress. Her symbol blinked along with the fading gravwake. Another ten minutes and it would be out of sensor range and free to head for the starlane.

They only had the two choices, back the way they came or toward the Terran Republic. With the proximity of the starlanes to each other, he could head for one, then divert for the other if needed. They were only a few hours apart at max acceleration.

"Chief Suresh, execute course Lima-Sierra One."

"Aye, aye, Skipper, low and slow one."

Interceptor rumbled as Chief Suresh pushed forward on the throttle ever so slightly. While the gravcoil acted as the main propulsion, it only moved the ship forward. Reaction thrusters venting gas from the fusion reactor maneuvered the ship. With *Interceptor*'s relatively low mass, the thrusters could whip the ship around.

Gravity fought between the gravcoils, forcing the crew to lean fore as the ship dove "down" toward the planet. Of course, there was no up and down, but Jacob had always eschewed that attempt at thinking. It was much easier to train people to think in relative perception than try and force an abstract thinking on them.

The ecliptic was the plane, and anything "below" it was down. Anything "above" it was up. Below and above were set by the ship, which in turn could be interpreted by the crew. Sure they could orbit a planet and look up at it, or sideways, or point the fore of the ship toward the surface. It made no difference in the end. He chose to keep things in such a way that made the crew's job easier, not harder.

Cordoba passed above them. Jacob resisted the urge to look up. He closed his eyes and whispered a prayer for his Marines and Alpha Company. They were going to need all the help they could get. That was out of his hands. His only concern was making sure the civilians exited the system safely, and doing as much damage to the fleet as he could—without losing his ship. That last part was very important to him.

"On point in two mikes, come to course two-nine-five mark two-eight-seven, maintain twenty-five g's," Ensign Brennan said.

Chief Suresh repeated the order. With a steady hand, she guided the ship along the course.

Spacer Abbot turned excitedly in his chair and started speaking before remembering to turn on his comms.

"Sorry, sir," he said after they were on. "Comm call from *Coughlin.* They got a clear look at the incoming force. Putting it through now. He's too far for a response sir, it's recorded."

Jacob pressed the screen on his plot to accept the communications.

"Captain Grimm," Esteban said, his face an emotionless mask. "We picked up a brief gravwake, but there's no doubt it's the Guild. At least one battleship-sized wake and several smaller ones. Their formation appears to be line-a-breast, which of course makes no sense. But they're the Guild, what do they know about ships? Regardless, I hope this helps. Good luck, Commander Grimm. *Coughlin* out."

Jacob correlated the data from *Coughlin* with what they knew. One battleship or two, it hardly made a difference. Between the six local ships and Interceptor, they couldn't take any battleship out.

"Mac, send the signal. It's time."

———

Captain Castro, in her much more primitive ELS suit, closed her eyes when the signal came. She asked a lot of her people for this mission. More so than for the coup. *The failed, unjust coup.* It was one thing if he had really cheated and stole the election... but he hadn't. He was framed by the very people they were about to fight.

No amount of sacrifice could ever remove the stain of her broken oaths. However, facing down the Guild to give *Interceptor* a fighting chance was a good start.

"Helm, bring us to three-three-zero, one hundred g's."

"Aye, aye, ma'am."

Estrella shot out from orbit, followed by her five corvettes. They would play their part to the best of their ability. She just hoped the Guild believed them. Otherwise, her ships would be so much confetti.

———

Mr. Falcon frowned. He'd tried calling General Perez repeatedly over the last hour to confirm with her the military control. When they setup the operation on Cordoba, he'd made sure that no military jamming would impact his comms. He should be able to reach her. She resented him and the Guild, so she might just be acting petty. Still, he wanted to confirm her control and, if she didn't have it, warn the approaching ships who thought that the planet was secure.

There was no accounting for the Alliance using their own EW equipment, which was far more advanced than Cordoba's. He couldn't even communicate with his people. Once they landed, he could identify himself and request transport.

The sooner the better. He had no desire to be on the mudball any longer. If he never saw rain followed by heat again, he'd be happy. So far, the operation went better than the last attempt at a system takeover. The plan, if not a little convoluted, had worked. Theoretically, the military answered to General Perez, which meant the Guild ships should make orbit without a fight.

His only concern was the reports of the Alliance Marines coming down from orbit. If they planned on fighting on behalf of Cordoba, it could slow things down.

Population assimilation took months. Longer if there was armed resistance. Once they accepted their fate, the Guild could begin setting up the mining and farming operations. Cordoba was far more than just a mudball, but what they didn't know, and the reason the Guild wanted the planet, was the naturally occurring osmium deposits. Millions of metric tons. Enough to build gravcoils on a level beyond any other manufacturer in the known galaxy. The amount of money they would make selling those to the Caliphate was almost incalculable.

Letting the Alliance have the planet wasn't an option. They also couldn't glass the surface. It would bring far too much attention to their operation. Once the Republic or Alliance found out about the rare elements buried in the mantle, there would be a fight over the resources. One the Guild couldn't win.

However, if the planet was already conquered and ruled by one of their own... then who could argue. It was a nice plan.

Something told Mr. Falcon that not everything had worked out the way he wanted it to. Still, even if Perez ended up dead, they could find some other puppet to sit in the big chair.

No, this time next year, the Guild would have trillions in new income, and Falcon would be sitting in a corner office.

Things were looking up.

————

"Admiral" Mike Arnold sipped his bland coffee as he watched the plot. His assignment to *Revenge* was the easiest job of his life, but one he took seriously. The Guild had rushed him through naval training school, promoted him to admiral, and put him in charge of a fleet. As a former director in charge of a cargo ship, he had the most space-going experience... of the people that were loyal to the Guild.

He wouldn't say he loved the Guild. That was going too far. But there was no escaping it.

"Any word from our operative?" he asked.

A man whose name he didn't know replied. "No, sir. Not since the initial communications. He signaled all clear, and that was it."

Mike checked the packet with his orders, bringing them up on the holoscreen. There was a plethora of regulations, contingencies, and the like for him. His primary mission, secure orbit around Cordoba and land ground troops, was the priority. He wasn't to seek out conflict—as if he would—but he was allowed to defend himself or take out targets of opportunity. No orbital bombardments... *yadda, yadda, the usual crap.*

He sighed. They had planned to enter the system if it was hostile, friendly, or neither. Nothing about losing comms after the all-clear was signaled. He didn't know the details of the ground plan, other than they were installing a puppet leader. Odds were, in the chaos that usually followed a sudden, violent change in leadership, they weren't able to call.

The ships guarding Cordoba were a joke. His light cruisers could take them with their eyes closed. Hell, the two transport ships and the mobile manufacturing center could take them—if they were armed.

"Admiral," a man called his attention.

What was his name? Jones... Johns... Joker... "Yes, uh, Private?" he said.

The man looked away suddenly before responding. "Lieutenant, sir. Lieutenant Joshua."

Mike snapped his fingers. "Right. Joshua. I knew it was a J something. What is it?"

Joshua pulled up a screen that showed six slow-moving blips.

"Ships, sir. Six of them. From the output, they look to be the Cordoba System Patrol. We have details on their schematics and crew. According to the op order, a Captain Castro should be in charge. If she is, then the operation succeeded. If not, we blow them up."

Mike frowned. "That seems wasteful."

Lieutenant Joshua looked up at him and blinked as if he was wondering how this man was in charge of him.

"Those are the orders, sir. I can forward them to you if you like."

"No, no, good enough. Can we talk to them?"

"Yes, sir, I'll have comms put it through to your screen... over there," Joshua said, gesturing back toward the admiral's chair.

"Right. Well done, Jones." He clapped the man on the shoulder and went back to his chair.

The screen attached to it, one of many large screens, blazoned to life with a dark-haired, dusky-skinned older woman. Mike had seen women before, obviously. Mostly in illicit vids and on the occasion, he had visited the pleasure centers. He had yet earned the privilege of procreation from the Guild, but if this mission were a success, he was sure he would.

However, she might be the most beautiful woman he'd ever seen in his life. She had a look about her that the women of the Guild never did, not even the gene-engineered ones.

"Hello," he said with a false smoothness. "How are you?"

She blinked, eyes going a bit wide. "I'm fine? Are you the man in charge of the Guild ships?" she asked formally.

"Yes, I am. I'm Directo—I mean, Admiral Arnold. Are you Captain Castro?"

"I am. I'm here to escort you to the planet. Our leader, General Perez is eager to meet you."

Perez, that was the name.

"Right. As much as I would like to, I'm not going to be going down to the planet. However, I have an excellent lunchroom here. They serve dinner that is to die for. Perhaps you could come aboard...?"

Was she confused by his offer?

"No, thank you, Admiral. I appreciate the offer, but there is much work to be done. If my astrogator has calculated the course correctly, we should match velocity in the next thirty minutes. We will then escort you to the planet and serve you however you might need."

Mike could think of several ways she could serve him.

"Of course. I think a meeting would be in order. Perhaps you and one or two other female officers?"

Again, a look he didn't recognize. "Sure," she said. "I can arrange that once we're in orbit," she said.

"I look—" The screen went dark.

Maybe the assignment was better than he thought. All those years of kissing ass and brownnosing had finally paid off. He was loyal, the Guild knew he was loyal, and he would complete the mission. If he were lucky, he could do so much more while stationed on the planet.

CHAPTER FORTY-ONE

Interrogations didn't interest Gunny Jennings in the slightest. For some people, no amount of physical pain would pry the truth from them. Hours and hours of questions and answers under the influence of certain drugs would reveal a far more accurate result, but even then, it had to be checked and double-checked.

"I don't get why they wanted her alive, Gunny?" Naki said from beside her. He cradled a cup of joe in one hand and a dry ham sandwich in the other.

"Answers," she replied.

Owens and June were in the room with them, also eating if the smacking noises were to be believed. Jennings had eaten already, a meal bar from her kit and a swig of water.

General Perez sat handcuffed to a chair while two men from the president's security detail badgered her with questions.

"I don't think"—June started while still chewing—"that they're going to get the answers they want."

Jennings agreed. The woman had shot her own sister. Murdered, who knew how many of her own people. Life wasn't a vid. The villain didn't just throw their hands up and surrender, telling the hero all their dastardly plans. Part of her wished she'd gotten to shoot the admiral. If Jennings had remained on *Interceptor*, Lieutenant Hössbacher would still be alive. She was going to have to live with that. When she did get back to the ship, she was going to have a word with the captain about leaving the bridge hatch secured, instead of open.

One of the security men slapped Perez across the face hard enough to leave a welt. Jennings felt Naki stiffen beside her.

"Easy, Corporal. Not our circus, not our monkeys."

"It's not right, Gunny. You don't hit women."

She scoffed. "I'll remember that next time we spar."

He sat back down, defeated. "You know what I mean."

"I do. But it's not our call."

Perez broke out in a laugh, maniacal and cackly that bordered on screeching. She ranted for a solid minute about how she would lead her people to a glorious future. The two men looked at each other, shrugged, and exited the room. A second later, the taller of the two entered the viewing chamber.

"She's either the strongest woman I've ever met, or she's mentally unfit," he said.

Jennings shook her head. "Commitment gives your blood the strength of steel," she told him.

"Si, señorita. I don't think we're going to get the answers we wanted. We still don't know who her contact is in the Guild. The last thing we want is them warning their coming ships."

She thought about it for a second. Standing up, she asked, "Mind if I take a crack?"

"Be our guest. Just don't kill her."

Jennings grinned. "I won't lay a hand on her."

———

Corporal Naki liked Cordoba, and he felt bad for what the poor people were going through... but he detested violence against women. He didn't really think of Jennings as a woman so much as she was a Marine. It was his moral code; he didn't have to justify it to anyone.

The entire situation made him think of lovely Sakura. Lag between the Consortium and Alliance hadn't stopped them from trading comms messages almost daily. She'd returned to school and pursued a teaching career. He was saving up all his leave, even forgoing the last round of time off from June's extended stay at the medical center. He wanted a few months off so he could spend some real time with her.

Jennings walked into the next room, intentionally slow. In fact, he'd never known her to move with speed unless it was Marine business or combat, which were pretty much the same thing.

The diminutive Marine walked around the table and sat with one hip on the surface. She leaned over and whispered something in the prisoner's ear.

"You know what she's saying?" Owens asked.

"No," Naki said. "June?"

"You've known her longer than I have."

Perez's eyes went wide. She shook her head rapidly and began rapid-fire speaking in her native tongue.

"I hope they're recording this," Naki said.

A moment later, Jennings patted Perez on the shoulder, stood and walked out, replaced by the two men in suits.

"How did you get her to talk?" Naki asked when she came back into the room.

"I'm persuasive," Jennings said. "Gear up, we got ourselves an op."

———

The Corsair rumbled over the city, skirting the building tops to avoid detection. Jennings wasn't worried about sensors, so much as their target seeing them coming. Not that "Mr. Falcon" knew they were coming. Perez had located him early on in their relationship just in case she needed to know where to find him.

He lived in the lap of luxury, in the largest skyscraper in the city, well outside the combat zone.

Jennings triggered the side hatch and it hummed open. Wind rushed in, blowing strands of her hair loose. She hadn't slept in over twenty-four hours and in that moment realized she had to smell something awful.

Of course, the next few months wouldn't have a lot of time for baths and showers.

Naki stepped up next to her, toe edging the yellow-and-black line.

"Hook up," Jennings said. The four Marines reached up and grabbed the tether, clipping it to their harness.

The ship banked hard, and they all had to hold on to the grab bar above them as they looked down at the luxurious condo rooftop.

"He'll know we're here now," Jennings yelled over the gale.

Roaring plasma engines drowned out any response as Boudreaux flipped the wings and brought the ship to hover.

"Go!" Boudreaux yelled over the comms.

Jennings and Naki leapt out. The line pulled tight, slowing them down at the last second. Their boots hit the terracotta roof with a crunch. Right behind them, so close they were touching, Owens and June hit.

Gunny waved the second pair to the right, while she and Naki headed for the lift. If it was guarded, or booby-trapped, she wanted to know. If there were cameras, they would be too small for visual, and she would rely on the electronics in her helmet to warn her.

"Blow it," she said.

Naki went right to the lift, placed a magnetic grenade on the door, and keyed it.

"Fire in the hole," he said as he backed away.

Binary chemicals mixed and exploded inward, vaporizing the door and emitting a deafening boom that shook the rooftop.

Without stopping, Jennings ran into the lift, tossing her magnetic line to the opposite side and free-falling to the penthouse suite fifteen meters below. Naki followed. Owens and June hit the stairwell to block any escape attempt, and as a flanking move if need be.

She stopped outside the lift door and pulled a grenade from her side. "Shaped charge, elevator door." The computer inside the grenade auto configured the blast. All she had to do was stick it to the outside.

Despite being in an enclosed space, the blast went entirely inward. The doors peeled open like tinfoil.

———

Falcon worried something had gone wrong. No matter how meticulous the operation was planned, the human element always managed to screw it up. He'd expected fighting in the streets, even the explosions—after all, unseating a president never goes smoothly. Regardless of the outcome, his fleet would arrive to seal the deal. If Perez were still alive when they arrived, great. If not, they would find someone else to install as head of state.

All they really needed for the plan to work was a population of males to work the mines and equipment, and a local to pretend to be in charge. Once the system started producing gravcoils, the powers that be would look the other way.

Shockwaves rocked his soundproof windows, rattling the

room. He frowned. His luxury apartment was in the richest district in the capital. There wasn't supposed to be any fighting near him.

Falcon stood, unease filling him with an unusual feeling... the feeling of not knowing what was happening.

Maybe it was nothing... No one on this mud ball knows my location. Even if they knew what I looked like, they wouldn't be able to find me, right?

Fear and uncertainty warred in him. Fear won. Falcon headed for the bedroom. Next to his bed, in a biometric-sealed safe was his comms gear for contacting the approaching ships. If they were close enough, he could alert them to possible danger even through the jamming from the Alliance. Halfway there, he stopped, realizing he'd left his pistol in the kitchen. If attacked, he was defenseless. Falcon turned to get his gun—

The elevator doors exploded inward, sending sharp pieces of the doors burning through the air. He screamed as several cut him, tracing lines of blood across his face and chest. Panicked, his body followed its last order, running for the kitchen.

"Where?" he shouted as he searched for it.

The drawer on the left. He yanked it open, grabbed the pulse pistol, and raised it up—only to see a diminutive Marine in full combat gear pointing her rifle directly at him.

"Drop it," she said. Her rifle barrel didn't waver. Something about her made his blood run cold.

Falcon never considered himself a coward. Quite the opposite. He was on a deep cover mission in enemy territory. He was doing the kind of mission that made legends... all from a luxury apartment with an unlimited budget.

With the crystal-blue eyes of a real killer staring him down over the barrel of a rifle, Falcon did the only thing his mind would allow...

Threw the gun away and raised his arms.

"Don't kill me!" he cried out.

————

"Secure this POS," Jennings said to Naki. She didn't take her barrel off him for one second. Her finger was already depressing the trigger, not enough to fire, but enough to eliminate any delay if she shot.

Naki moved past her, careful to stay out of her line of fire. He slapped a mag cuff on one wrist, then the other, and yanked them both down behind them.

A second later, Owens and June entered through the stairwell, rifles at the ready.

"Owens, get Charlie-Actual on the line and let him know we have the Guild spy."

"Aye, aye, Gunny."

————

Captain Bonds sighed in relief when Jennings told him the good news. She was in the process of handing Falcon off to the president's security forces. The president, a brave man in Paul's opinion, stayed behind. He'd sent his family off on the *Coughlin,* but he was determined to lead his people through the coming trials.

"Good job, Gunny. Now RTB with the Corsair. We need to get all our equipment shielded. Once the Guild lands, we can start our counterattack. If they see us from orbit, though, it will be all for naught."

"Aye, aye, sir. Any word from *Interceptor?*"

"She's radio silent. They picked up the incoming fleet, and the captain initiated his plan. That's not our concern. Grimm's got that. We have this. Just get back here ASAP."

"Affirmative. Bravo-Two-Five out."

He sat the radio down and looked out from the cave where he'd set up his CP. The same valley they had trained with the locals in. He was grateful for it. Far enough away from the city that they wouldn't be easily seen, shielded by the surrounding mountains, and with plenty of natural caves for them to hide in.

They had the Corsairs parked in the woods covered with sensor-dampening netting. Even if they walked troops through the valley, they wouldn't see them after the way his Marines camouflaged them.

Two hundred Marines, all the equipment and ammo they could ask for, six Mudcats, a command Mudcat, and an MRAV, along with enough electronic warfare systems to fry an egg.

It's almost not fair.

He chided himself for thinking like that. The only fair fight was the one he lost. The United Systems Marine Corps wasn't about fighting "fair," they were about winning.

CHAPTER FORTY-TWO

Captain Castro looked at her crew with pride. They knew the odds of survival were almost nothing. Like her, though, they also felt the shame of what they had done. How were they so easily manipulated by the Guild and by Admiral Perez. In retrospect, upon examining her feelings, she realized she held no love for the now-deceased admiral. It was her duty to obey orders, but more than that, she wanted Santiago to be corrupt because she didn't like him. Cordoba needed to embrace the galaxy, not be an isolationist nation. If he had made overtures to the Alliance before the election, she would never have gone along with the madness of the coup.

When the admiral showed her the evidence, though, the irrefutable evidence of his rigging the election... what was she supposed to do? Their plan would minimize bloodshed. The sisters said nothing about bombing embassies and assassinating navy officers. If they had, she never would have agreed.

It was time to make up for that mistake.

"Let me know the moment we're in a stationary orbit," she said.

"Aye, ma'am. Fifteen minutes, three-four seconds to full stop."

The Guild had brought what she considered a massive force. A battleship, three light cruisers, and two troop transports. Each of the transports had five thousand Guild soldiers, with technology far more advanced than even the Alliance had. The ships were straight off the ship builders on Terra. How the Marines planned to fight them was beyond her.

Not that she would be alive to see the fight.

Her viewscreen showed the massive battleship, a kilometer long, as it floated beside them. Her little cruiser was lost in the behemoth's shadow. The Guild chose an odd formation. The admiral had his ships all flying abreast, troop transports on either side, flanked by two LCs on one side, and the single remaining one on the other. If they were a wet navy, it would make sense, but this was space. Attacks could come from any direction. Tactics dictated separating the ships out in a line, making sure only one or two ships could be taken by surprise.

She shouldn't complain, though. Their poor ship handling might just buy her people time to live.

"All ships, when the time comes, focus fire on the light cruiser on our right flank. If we can destroy one of them, we can strike a blow for our people. Castro out."

What she did next, she did for her people. Eyeing the mission clock, she waited. *Interceptor* hid behind the moon. There was no way to communicate with them. They'd planned the mission out to the last detail. It would work.

It has to work.

———

Jacob wanted to walk the ship, but there was no time. The Guild had come too quickly for him to partake in his ritual. With the can drained, everyone sat snugly in their ELS suits. He still had yet to sit in the command chair. It was time, though. They were about to embark into combat, and he couldn't do it standing up.

With a deep breath, he spun the chair around, really looking at it for the first time. He refused to let them replace it. They would eventually. They would have to. Bosun had patched the holes, but they were obvious to him.

He sat. Roy's smiling, always-optimistic face appeared in his mind. It was time to put it behind him. He would remember the young man, honor him, but letting Roy's death embitter him would just lead to a path of self-destruction.

This is why people in the Navy drink, he thought, a genuine smile gracing his lips.

"Chief, you ready?" he asked.

"Aye, Skipper. It should be interesting. There's something odd about the planet's gravity and the moon. It's like flying through a storm, almost. PO Tefiti and Ensign Brennan have mapped me a good course, though. We shouldn't slam into the moon's surface."

Jacob started to laugh and realized there was no mirth in Suresh's voice. Was she doing the thing?

"You're joking, of course? Right?"

She looked at him through the mirror they shared and shook her head.

"Great," he muttered. "Mac, give me all hands."

"Aye, aye, Skipper. All hands." Mac pointed at him, letting him know he was on.

"Attention crew of the *Interceptor*. This is your captain speaking." He paused for a moment, making sure to have everyone's attention. "We've taken a hit. The loss of Lieutenant

Hössbacher is a blow, but not a mortal one. Roy died doing his duty to his ship, his fellow crew, and to the Alliance. We—"

He wanted to say more about Roy, about the impressive young man and officer. The future admiral he saw in him, but he also wanted to inspire the crew against what was likely to be far more dangerous than anything they'd survived to date. Which was saying a lot for his crew.

"We are the *Interceptor*, though. We bare our losses on our hull. Every pit mark, every scratch, every burn is a crewmember who didn't return with us. We honor them by continuing on. We celebrate them by doing our duty. We mourn for them in the night, and we take care of their family with our blood, sweat, and tears.

"This is the story of the *Interceptor*. She's old, scarred, and bruised... but never beaten. There's no mission she can't accomplish. No job too tough. No adversary she—we—can't beat. Keep your heads, watch out for each other, and we will be victorious. First to fight, captain out."

All he had to do was wait for the mission clock to tick down.

"Skipper," Lieutenant Brown called him on the private channel.

"Yes?"

"I've got the turrets locked and loaded. Two questions for you, sir. Do you want to risk having the Long 9 preloaded?"

Jacob thought about the risk for a moment. If they waited to load the main gun until right before shooting, they knew for certain it would work. However, if the round was preloaded, he could shoot faster. The only concern was that if the bow took a hit, then the coils would lose alignment and the weapon wouldn't fire.

"I think we can risk the preload. We should be close enough to fire before we take fire."

"My thoughts as well, sir."

"And the other?"

"I want to open with a pair of MK XIVs. They should sow confusion and delay their return fire."

Jacob smiled at the idea. It was an excellent plan. He'd wanted to fire as much ordnance downrange as possible. There was simply no escaping return fire. However, the advanced EW torpedoes served them well against the Caliphate and would likely work just as well against the Guild ships.

"Do it. Also, Austin, make sure the giga-pulse laser defense is up. I know it's a significant heat source and power draw, but if they are loaded with the Guild's torpedoes, we're going to need it running."

"Aye, aye, Skipper. Will do."

His officers were well aware of the Guild's advanced torpedoes. Alliance MK XIIs accelerated at 700 g's for the duration of their drives. When *Interceptor* raided Wonderland, their space elevator fired torpedoes with an acceleration of 2,000 g's.

According to the briefing, the Guild recently acquired their ships from the Terran Republic. Loading it with new torpedoes would be much simpler than refitting their weapon systems.

Jacob breathed in a deep breath, holding it for a few seconds before exhaling. He'd never engaged the Terran Republic before. They were allies, but the fact that they sold battleships to the Guild may mean that was all about to change.

Why they ever would was well outside his pay grade. What mattered to him was the reality in front of him. A battleship, three light cruisers, and two troop transports.

"We're not going to hurt that battleship, but we have a real shot at disabling or even destroying the transports. Make sure you do your best to target them first, understood?"

"Aye, aye, sir," Lieutenant Brown confirmed.

He eyed the mission clock as it continued to count down. He felt like he'd forgotten something, something critical. The plan was laid out. Everyone involved had the information. The can was drained, weapons loaded. Was it his nerves?

With an audible chuckle, he remembered the last thing he needed to do.

He prayed.

———

Admiral Mike Arnold looked down at Cordoba from high orbit. On either side of his ship, tucked within the shadows of their fire control was his fleet. He knew it had to be impressive looking. A kilometer-long, state-of-the-art battleship, three light cruisers, and two troop transports. This was his mission. Establish orbital control, make sure the ground was secure and then await orders.

The leader of the ground team, who was certain to have more fun than himself, would handle the rest of the mission. A mission Mike wasn't privy to.

All he had to do was keep the system secure while they did their business. Sometimes the Guild's paranoia and secrecy annoyed him to no end. He could probably do his job a lot better if he knew the whole scope. Instead, they relied on very detailed op orders. Under no circumstances could he bomb the planet from orbit. He wasn't to destroy any civilian ships, *especially* any flagged from the Terran Republic.

"Admiral?" Lieutenant Joshua called him.

"Yes?"

"Our commanders all report the orbit is clear. General Finlay would like to begin deploying to the surface. It requires your authentication."

Mike looked down at the screen attached to the command chair—his chair. Other than the friendly cruisers there were no other ships in orbit. Though the large moon could be obscuring one or more. However, their man on the planet would have warned them if things were still contested.

"Any word from the planet?"

Joshua shook his head. "Only the comms with the other ships, sir."

Mike wasn't the most tactically minded person in the Guild, but he was loyal. He wanted the mission to succeed. If the Guild thought it was important to have this planet, then he thought it important. Of course, he also didn't want to be the guy who went over budget on the mission. Time was money, and every minute the troops weren't on the ground was a minute they were paid to do nothing.

"Are we sure everything is as it's supposed to be? I don't want to get halfway to landing and find out there's a minefield or something the locals forgot to tell us about."

Joshua, whose name he could now remember, turned to his panel. "Sensors, go full fidelity on scans. I want to see everything in orbit. The admiral is worried it's a trap."

Mike pondered the situation, and the attractive captain on the other ship, while he waited for the results of the scan.

"Sir," Joshua said interrupting his daydream. "All stations are active. No gravwake, no radar returns, nothing. The only possible place anyone could be is—" Joshua pointed at the main screen displaying the large moon. "That seems unlikely."

"All right. Tell the general he's free to begin his operation." Mike leaned back, a satisfied smile on his face from a job well done. He liked his position. If he succeeded here, who knew, maybe he could even get promoted to the board of directors.

CHAPTER FORTY-THREE

Timing on the modern battlefield came down to planning. Was there enough time to plan, inform, and commit? Could the allied forces be coordinated in their attack? When line of sight became an issue, and there was no way to relay communications, how did they pull off a simultaneous assault?

The answer? A twenty-seven-hundred-year-old invention: the clock.

Jacob watched the mission clock run down to zero. If he were right, and if Castro lived, when *Interceptor* came out from behind the moon, he would have a target-rich environment.

There were too many *ifs* in the plan for him, but this was the hand he was dealt.

"Chief Suresh, execute prearranged maneuver. Weps, open the outer doors. Fire tubes #1 and #2 on apogee, then reload with standard MK XIIs. Ops, drop the heat sink."

All replied in the affirmative.

Here we go.

Interceptor's gravcoil revved with energy as the MK III fusion reactor pumped giga-joules of power through the ship. Hyper and supercapacitors throughout the ship charged, holding power in reserve for critical systems. As the ship moved, the cumulative stored heat of the vessel ejected out the stern in the form of a carbon-fiber sphere that exploded into a million pieces upon hitting the surface of the moon.

The shark-nosed ship charged forward a mere one hundred meters above the barren moon's surface. Debris from her passing gravwake scattered behind her like a wall racing to catch up.

"Approaching point alpha," Chief Suresh said.

"Execute," Jacob ordered.

Bow thrusters fired, raising the nose. In response, the ship flew upward and away from the moon. Their velocity ticked over to 14 KPS, a slug's pace for the destroyer, but necessary to prevent the wake from warning the enemy. It also allowed them enough time on target to engage with accuracy. They could go flank speed and rev up to 560 g's and hit 300 KPS in that same time, but their chance of hitting anything would drop to not zero.

Interceptor kicked up, rocketing for high orbit. Like the sun rising in the east, she came over the horizon with blinding speed.

"Fire torpedoes," Jacob ordered.

Brown pushed the firing stud flat. Two MK XIV EW torpedoes launched out of the forward tubes. Just like *Interceptor*, their velocity was set low to keep them in range long enough to do them good.

Castro's eyes were closed. She knew this was the end. For her, a lifetime of service and commitment boiled down to this very moment. She wouldn't fail her people like she already had.

"It's time, ma'am," her XO informed her.

"Thank you, Justin. It was a pleasure serving with you."

"Aye, ma'am, you as well."

Castro inhaled deeply and let it out slowly.

"Weapons lock all batteries on the closest light cruiser. Use the passive sensors. We don't want to give away our hand. Helm, prepare for flank speed on my order. Confirm all ships are in sync."

A series of replies came back informing her they were ready. Her cruiser, and the five smaller ships with her, would all fire at the same time. Because of their range and relative motion, she hoped to do some damage before they destroyed her.

"All ships report ready, ma'am," her XO said.

With a finality and resolve she had never felt before, Captain Elenna Castro gave her last order. "Fire."

———

Running a Guild task force might have been even cushier than his last job. While Mike Arnold wasn't a hundred percent sure on the specifics of combat, he did know how to run a ship efficiently. Mostly it meant leaving his people alone and filing paperwork. Despite his laid-back exterior, he did keep an eye on the numbers, if not the people. He found in his life, the closer he watched the underlings, the more he missed and the less work they did.

Instead, he watched the numbers. Fuel consumption, stores, reports, etc. They all told a different story that was far more reliable than hovering over a crewman's shoulder while he looked at radar returns.

"That's funny," Joshua said.

"What is it?" Mike hopped up, eager to interact with

A GRIMM DECISION 323

someone to escape the boredom while he waited for the landing to begin.

"Gravwake, but weak. Low power and maybe diffused through the planet... no, that doesn't make sense." Joshua looked up at the main screen showing Cordoba and part of their moon.

The admirals bridge held a half dozen crew, but Mike didn't know their names. Joshua he knew, so Joshua he spoke to.

"Why is that odd?" Mike asked.

"All the traffic is accounted for, sir. There shouldn't be any gravwakes unless—"

Mike frowned. *I knew this was too easy.*

"Better go to red alert," he said.

"Battle stations, sir, not red alert."

He shook his head and grinned. "Okay, battle station—"

Alarms wailed as a wall of electronic noise slammed down on the *Revenge* and her consorts.

"We've lost sensors, no comms, I think we're being fired on," Joshua said.

Before Mike could give any orders, one of his three light cruisers, the *Covenant,* exploded in a massive fusion-powered fireball. Only three kilometers away, it was perfectly visible on the screens that mimicked windows around his bridge.

"Open fire," Mike yelled. He turned and ran for his chair, not wanting to risk a hit throwing him across the compartment.

"On who?"

———

Castro ordered her ships to accelerate. Gravity surged through their coils shooting them forward toward the planet.

"That worked better than I thought," she said. "Fire on the next cruiser."

Estrella's directed energy weapons, traditional lasers and grasers charged with a hundred megawatts each, opened fire. Invisible energy ripped across space, striking the second cruiser, *Order*, on the flank just as she began to move. *Order*'s active gravcoil mitigated the energy weapons, bending and refracting their power. Large burns appeared across her hull, but they didn't penetrate.

———

Jacob only had a moment to take in the scene. It was unlike anything he'd prepared for in the past. Battles at slow relative velocity in orbit around planets weren't common. It didn't change the outcome if he stuck around. That monster would eat *Interceptor* for breakfast. They had surprise and subterfuge going for them.

As they finished their arc, lining up with the troopships, the plot blinked and one of the cruisers vanished. "Way to go, Castro!" he said, unable to hide his jubilation. "Weps, fire on target Golf-Tango-One."

"Aye, aye, skipper. Golf-Tango-One."

Turrets rotated minimally, adjusting for the actual range. As one, they fired. Four 20mm tungsten penetrators ripped out of the barrels at 10,000 KPS. A mere three-second flight from the moment the order was given.

Golf-Tango-One weighed 100,000 metric tons. She carried a crew of thirty-five and five thousand Guild ground soldiers. The box-shaped transport had powered up her gravcoil right behind the cruiser when *Interceptor* struck.

State-of-the-art composite armor, reinforced with nano-ablative panels did much to stop the four rounds. Each one struck hard, blasting away at her flank, exploding through multiple layers of armor before their kinetic energy was spent.

The second volley, though, burned right through the weakened armor. Twenty millimeters of death burst into the interior, shattering bulkheads and splintering into deadly fragments.

Turret number one hit just above the gravcoil, killing five men instantly and severing the main power runs.

Two hit three meters higher, deflecting up and into fusion #1. Eight men, including the transport's chief engineer, died in a horrific burst of radiation so powerful it burned them to ashes, fried the consoles, and sent the reactor into emergency shutdown.

Three impacted at a right angle, spending all her energy against the hull.

Four, though, was murder itself. Punching through the already weakened hull, it lanced deep into the transport's launch bay where five thousand Guild troops lined up in neat rows, waiting to disembark. Twenty-millimeter's of tungsten had the energy of a fireball. It ripped into the landing bay. Five hundred men died from the shockwave, another thousand from the fragmented hull as it exploded inward, and the rest when the outer hull exploded and ejected the remaining troops into space.

Golf-Tango-One listed hard to port, fire briefly illuminating the holes *Interceptor* punched in her.

Jacob opened his mouth, ready to give the order to fire again, when *Revenge* returned fire.

Still blinded by the MK XIVs, *Revenge*'s attack was indirect and poorly aimed. However, sixty-four gigawatt grasers firing pulse beams traveling at the speed of light didn't need to be as accurate as a coil turret. Like an angry porcuswine, *Revenge* bristled with death.

At near point-blank range the beams of gamma-powered lasers sliced through space, cutting four of *Estrella*'s consorts in half. The little ships came apart in violent explosions, the lasers so powerful they continued on after obliterating their targets.

The three surviving ships accelerated away, riding their gravcoils as they continued to fire on the remaining cruiser to no avail.

Then *Interceptor* fired again. Her torpedoes flew toward the last troopship, but it was too late. The ships were on alert, laser defense turrets fired, detonating the warheads mere milliseconds after they exited the tubes.

Jacob grimaced as the ship bounced, riding the exploding warheads. "Fire the main gun," he said.

Lieutenant Brown triggered the button. Nine kilograms of steel-wrapped nano-reinforced tungsten penetrator accelerated down the twenty-nine-meter-long coil at a third the speed of light. The unstoppable weapon shed its steel case in a blink of an eye and the tungsten arrow slammed into the stern of the last troop transport. Energy like a miniature sun vaporized the armor, fire and death atomized eight compartments killing seventeen crew and crippled her ability to move. With the control runs to the gravcoil destroyed, the ship floated inert on a heading it couldn't sustain.

"Flank speed," Jacob ordered.

Chief Suresh jammed the throttle all the way forward and past the *full* icon until it read *flank*. *Interceptor*'s gravcoil produced 560 g's slinging her away from the battleship in the opposite direction that Captain Castro took her ships.

Jacob tapped his fingers calmly on the arm of his chair. The blinding EW torpedoes would run out of charge soon and the battleship would see them.

"How long until we're out of range?" he asked.

"Nine minutes, three-seven seconds," Tefiti said. "Assuming they don't come after us immediately."

Jacob prayed fervently they didn't. "Start the clock."

Ensign Brennan put the countdown on the bridge clock.

"MK XIVs have terminated," Lieutenant Brown informed him.

"Five degrees down bubble and twelve degrees starboard. Let's angle to put the planet between us and them."

"Aye sir, five degrees down bubble and twelve degrees starboard," Chief Suresh replied.

Seconds passed. Jacob willed the *Revenge* not to move, and if she did move to pursue *Estrella*. While powerful in every way, battleships weren't fast. Each passing second allowed his ship a better chance of survival.

CHAPTER FORTY-FOUR

Mike Arnold was a dead man. Forget being an admiral. He'd lost half his command in half a second. One cruiser obliterated, one transport utterly destroyed, the other in need of rescue.

"Status," he said, forcing his voice to work through dried lips.

"Uh, I'm not sure," Joshua said. "Comms is trying to get the remaining transport, but their bridge may be in trouble."

Mike fumed. This was going so well and then... he replayed what had happened over the course of less than thirty seconds. Cordoba betrayed them. They would pay for that.

"Tell the helm to pursue that cruiser. I want them dead, dead, dead!"

"Yes, sir. And the other ship? The fast one?"

The ship that had appeared from behind the moon was clearly part of the Alliance. Fast and nimble, but not enough firepower to hurt his ship. At the same time, with its head start, he didn't think catching it was likely.

"After our remaining troops have landed groundside send *Disclaimer* after her and turn it to scrap."

Ensign Brennan monitored the sensors with every ounce of her focus. The merest blip could mean the difference of life and death, and she was determined to give her captain the best she could.

At close range, radar and lidar worked perfectly, and she recognized the movement before the gravwake registered.

"Sir, movement. Golf-Bravo-One is moving on a heading of —zero-nine-three relative. She's going after the *Estrella*!" Despite meaning another ship would be destroyed and all lives lost, Brennan couldn't help but be excited. Battleships were things of nightmares. More movement, no, not movement, fragmenting showed on her screen. She adjusted the resolution scan, focusing on the troopship. Was it breaking up? A hundred smaller objects appeared around it, heading for the planet and—

"Oh," she said. "Golf-Tango-Two is landing troops, sir." She wanted to look at her captain, see his face and know that he understood, but her job was the radar screen. She would have to leave everything else up to the rest of the crew.

"Good catch, Fionna," Commander Grimm replied.

Her face blushed with the praise. Despite her rocky start, or how she felt it was, Commander Grimm had done more to bolster her confidence than any other officer she had met.

Maybe even more than PO Mendez.

"Mac, notify Captain Bonds that he's about to have company. Wish him well."

"Aye, aye, Skipper. Sending the message now."

It would be months before they returned with reinforcements. Jacob hated the plan. Hated the idea of leaving his people behind. Everything in him screamed to turn and fight. Everything but logic. There was no victory against a battleship. The most they could hope for was a clean escape. Which they might not even achieve if the cruiser came after them.

His visual on the ships vanished as Cordoba moved to obscure the view. At least they had some time before they would face the enemy.

Jacob keyed the comms to engineering. "Engineering, Captain."

"Engineering, Chief Redfern."

"Chief, do you know the max accel on a Terran light cruiser?"

Redfern didn't respond right away. "One moment, Skipper. I'm going to check with Lieutenant Kai."

Jacob waited, watching the plot as the distance from the planet slowly climbed along with their velocity. After five minutes, they were hitting 823 KPS and were only 1000 km and change away. Not even far enough to avoid their main gun... except they had put a planet between them.

"Sir, Lieutenant Kai. I have info on them, but it's not through official channels."

That piqued Jacob's interest. "Explain?" he asked.

"I read a lot, Skipper. All the engineering papers and books that I can get my hands on. It takes time, but the larger volumes make their way to the Alliance eventually. I make sure to update my NavPad whenever I'm in port."

Jacob shook his head, a wry smile forming on his face. Leave it to an engineer to geek out on books about other nation's ships.

"Lay it on me Kai, what are we looking at."

"They're more advanced than us, but not by much. Grav-coils are five to ten percent more efficient and their reactors produce twenty to twenty-five percent more power. Overall, they compare in mass to our light cruisers but are twenty percent faster. I can't give you a specific number, but I would guess 380 to 420 g's acceleration, Skipper."

Jacob let out a whistle. For a man whose info was sparse, he was awfully thorough.

"So once they're in weapons range, they'll fire and we'll have to stay in it for a while, then?"

"Yes, sir. Not to mention, they use heavy-duty grasers and grav torpedoes for long range. Plasma missiles for short. Generally speaking, the TRN favors more diverse firepower than we do."

That wasn't good news. Jacob knew about their diversity in attack philosophy. Energy weapons, projectiles, short and long range. Their speed, though, surprised him. Clearly the Navy's book on TRN ships was out of date.

Bringing up the plot, Jacob examined the map of the star system one more time. He had a plan for if they chased him, but he'd hoped they would all go after Castro's ships. Cordoba's two asteroid belts were his only real option for cover. But which one? They were both thick, but only one of them was positioned near a starlane... but it was the wrong starlane.

It led to an empty system with no easy path back to Alliance space. Which was the entire reason Cordoba was important to the Alliance at all. They were the bottleneck between the Terran Republic and Alliance.

Examining the map, he spun it around, looking from different angles, marking waypoints and trying out virtual navigations. It could be all for naught. It was entirely possible the enemy ships wouldn't pursue *Estrella* and stay to guard the remaining troop transport. *No, you know that's now what's going to happen. That's not how the Guild operates. They wouldn't give a damn about the landing troops.*

Their plans were overly complex, but their skippers have no experience. They charge forward like bulldogs with little care for losses.

"Contact," Tefiti bellowed over the comms. "Golf-Charlie-One. Light cruiser, accelerating at four-eight-zero gravities, Skipper. She's approximately four-nine-zero thousand klicks behind us."

Damn.

Brennan's Irish-accented voice broke in. "Radar return, their outer doors are open—"

"Launch, launch, launch. Torpedo in space," Lieutenant Brown announced. "Correction. Four—six— wait one."

Jacob glanced Tefiti's way. "Tefiti, weapon acceleration?"

The PO looked back at him, his eyes heavy from the knowledge. "Their gravwake matches the torpedoes from Wonderland, Skipper."

Brown popped up from his station, half turning to the center. "Eighteen torps in space, sir. They're fast. I've never seen anything like this."

Jacob nodded, setting his jaw—he had. Destroyers were poor torpedo targets—because they were fast enough that torpedoes ran out of fuel before catching them. If that were nullified? *Interceptor* was in real trouble.

"Weps, spin up the stern giga-pulse laser defense system on turret four. Time to impact?"

Brennan, Tefiti, and Brown all worked their consoles fervently, gloved fingers tapping away as they fed the computer the information and worked the math.

"Initial wave will hit in four minutes, twenty-seven

seconds. Each additional wave will come in every four-five seconds after," Tefiti said.

Tefiti's numbers came on his screen, showing the math. Golf-Charlie-One would fire on them for the next eighteen minutes. Jacob looked up at Brown. "I really hate the Guild."

"If we weren't out of effective range of the grasers, we'd already be dead, sir," he said.

Jacob understood all too well what a graser would do. The Consortium used something similar as their main gun, and one of their vessels had nearly ended his command before it really began.

A sick, cold feeling washed over Jacob. He pulled up the ship's library and scanned for his log entry from when they fought the Guild in Wonderland. Back then, they had relied on their gravity laser. However, the space elevator had fired a pair of torpedoes which had hit 2,000 g's acceleration.

He found the relevant entry and forwarded it to Brown. Technically, the young man didn't have the clearance, but Jacob had more important things to worry about.

"Austin, make sure you feed that into the giga-pulse firing solution," he told him.

"Yes, sir, and... 2,000 g's... why don't we have that?"

"You can ask when we see them."

The clock counted down as the torpedoes closed. It boggled his mind how fast they moved.

"Should we return fire with the torpedoes, sir?" Brown asked.

The enemy cruiser wasn't closing. Unless they scored a hit on *Interceptor*, they weren't likely to catch them. At the same time, could he risk a tail all the way to the starlane? Two torpedoes wouldn't ultimately make a difference.

"Stand down the stern torpedo rooms."

"Aye, sir."

By the time the torpedoes were in range, *Interceptor*'s aft torpedo rooms were clear. Eight crew sealed the compartments and were distributed by Lieutenant Fawkes to assist elsewhere. While they had a full roster, it never hurt to put an extra pair of hands where it was needed most.

"Ten seconds to giga-pulse engagement," Brown said.

Jacob tapped his fingers rhythmically on the arm of his chair. With no atmosphere, no one heard, but it comforted him to tap out silent music. The last time they'd used the giga-pulse laser, the ship's heat systems had overloaded and he'd almost lost the ship.

"Laser engaging... now!" Brown said. Lights flashed on his panel. Within one second, all eight torpedoes vanished.

Jacob looked around the bridge. No panels exploded, no lights flashed, and the temperature didn't increase.

"Looks like our solution worked," he said with a smile. As long as nothing went wrong... "Chief, bring us ten degrees to port, two degrees down bubble."

Chief Suresh repeated his order as she turned the ship. "Are we heading for the asteroid field?" she asked.

"Unless we want them on us all the way to the starlane, we've got to lose them."

Asteroid fields were a vast area of space with remnants of unborn planet spread out around them. They weren't crowded clusters but spread out from millions of years of orbital drift. With the highly magnetic nature of Cordoba's asteroid belts, though, Jacob might be able to hide his ship in them. He needed to break contact first, then he would worry about hiding.

There were still a lot of ifs in his plan.

Captain Castro's bridge shook as more hits poured into her little cruiser. "That thing's a monster," her XO said. Another volley of graser turret fire lit up the screen. Alarms wailed from concentrated radiation surges. Thankfully, they had managed to avoid the worst of it. She couldn't say the same for the rest of her fleet. *Estrella* was all that remained.

Had she not gone along with the Perez's sisters terrible plan, maybe they could have warned the Alliance sooner. Grimm would have brought more ships if he knew. She understood that now. Maybe not every commander in the Alliance was like him. But... he was the ideal. The man was like a legend and he didn't even know it. She wouldn't let him down now.

"Weapons, recharge time?"

"Thirty seconds."

If only—no. She stopped herself. The technology she had was what she had. What ifs were a waste of her time.

"Helm, bank port thirty degrees on my mark. All weapons, focus the battleship's prow. We might not be able to destroy her, but maybe we can hurt their gravcoil."

Her XO looked up at her, a thin smile on his lips. "It should work," he said. "But you know they will have a clean shot at us."

The distance was close enough that if she gave them a full broadside, there was a solid chance it would work.

She hoped.

"Five seconds to weapons recharge," weapons informed her.

"Mark," she said.

Estrella violated the rules of combat one last time. The ship banked hard to port, her thrust generating a new vector. For a split second, she had no acceleration in either direction.

All her directed energy weapons fired at the battleship's prow. From *Estrella*'s perspective the enemy ship simply hung in space making no attempt to dodge.

"Direct hit on—"

Captain Castro never heard the rest of the statement. Six grasers smashed into the cruiser's hull. Armor exploded inward as kinetic energy transferred, shattering the metal like ceramic under a hammer. Every crew aboard died in a violent explosion that rendered the ship to atoms in a split second.

A moment later, *Revenge* passed through the remains of the ship as if it never existed.

CHAPTER FORTY-FIVE

Interceptor shook as the giga-pulse laser demolished the last torpedo, six thousand kilometers off her stern.

"They're getting closer," Jacob said.

"I know, sir," Brown replied. "Heat buildup in the fore computer node is impacting the targeting computers performance."

Five minutes until they were out of range and two hours after they would hide in the asteroid field. They just had to hold on.

"Tango status?"

"Still pursuing. They are making evasive course corrections as they do so, but it's not enough to significantly impact their pursuit."

Jacob almost laughed out loud about that. It seemed the Guild wasn't hopeless. He'd defeated their last ships because they charged straight ahead without making even the smallest course change. In the end, he'd destroyed half their fleet with turret fire initiated well out of range.

"Let's stay focused on the goal. We're not trying to beat them, just outrun them. Something *Interceptor* was born to do."

Part of him wanted to turn around and fight, even though the odds of taking out a light cruiser were low in a straight-up fight. Even if he could, the battleship would still be over the planet. There was no going back.

"Two minutes," Tefiti said.

"Giga-pulse engaging next volley," Brown announced.

Come on, girl, you can do it.

On his MFD, green lights blinked torpedo after torpedo disappeared. Alarms flashed on Brown's console.

"Malfunction in the forward node. PDL offline," Lieutenant Brown said.

"Fire the turrets," Jacob ordered.

As fast as Brown was, it took him ten seconds to switch the turrets to fire. Three and four opened, firing 20mm tungsten. Two torpedoes exploded from the impact, only a hundred kilometers from *Interceptor*.

The last sailed through the explosions, her onboard targeting computer zeroing in on *Interceptor*'s gravcoil. Magnetic fusion bottles exploded inside the weapon, sending nearly incalculable amounts of energy through the miniature gravcoils focal, creating a microgravity laser. A ten-centimeter-wide laser of condensed gravity shot out, smashing into *Interceptor*'s top deck. New reinforced ablative armor absorbed much of the energy but didn't stop it from blasting through deck one at frame thirty-five, obliterating computer node #2 and Spacer McKnight who manned the station.

Lights flickered on the bridge as the ship violently heaved, jerking Jacob against his harness.

"Status?" he asked hoarsely.

"Damage to the deck, comp node two is out, one casualty," PO Collins said from Ops.

They got lucky. That could have hit the gravcoil or any number of critical systems.

"Austin, time to reengage the GPLs?"

Brown shook his head. "The targeting computer is fried, Skipper. I would need to get in there with engineering and do a BDA to know."

"We're out of range, Skipper," Brennan said.

"Fantastic. Brown, get on it. We need those defense lasers operational."

"Aye, aye, sir." Brown unbuckled, leaping for the hatch.

Jacob eyed the plot as Golf-Charlie-One fell farther and farther back. If they continued to pursue, they would eventually catch him. He couldn't stop at a starlane for the ten minutes he needed to find it with a LC running him down. Nor could they use the planets to hide and wait them out. All it would take was a few more ships and they could lock the system down.

Interceptor had to go, and she had to go now. Even if the only lane they could risk was the wrong one. He checked the distance to Rygel and the math just didn't work. As much as he willed it to. They weren't going home.

"Fionna, set a course for Orion's starlane. Make sure to set the origin point after we pass through the asteroid belt. I don't want to give them a whiff of what we're up to until they're already looking in the wrong direction."

"Aye, aye, sir. Course for Orion's starlane. Origin point beyond asteroid belt."

Her nerves echoed in her voice and Jacob couldn't blame her. Going through Orion would add weeks, maybe months to their journey home—time the Marines would spend facing the Guild on their own.

Life was never easy. If they tried for the correct lane and died, then the Marines would never get the reinforcements they needed.

Even if he went through Orion, *Jack Coughlin* and the other merchant ships were heading for Alliance space as fast as they could. It might not make a difference at all for *Interceptor* to get there. It wasn't worth the risk.

Two hours passed as the ship continued toward the asteroid belt. Forty-five minutes after the engagement ended, Golf-Charlie-One fell off their screen as the distance surpassed ten million klicks.

"Full astern, let's slow her down," Jacob ordered.

Interceptor flipped end over end as the gravcoil worked to decelerate her at the same speed she had accelerated at. If there were any ships within ten million klicks, they would see the gravity cavitation like a beacon. As it was, the waves would still go farther than normal.

It wouldn't help the enemy, though.

He didn't need them to come to a full stop, just take the edge off their acceleration and allow them to alter course enough to make the Orion starlane.

"Passing through outer edges," Ensign Brennan said.

"Switch to active radar and lidar. I don't want to slam into a moon while going 6,000 KPS," Jacob ordered.

"That would make it a short trip," Chief Suresh said.

"Skipper, Damage Control."

"Go ahead, XO."

Jacob's MFD popped to life, showing Lieutenant Fawkes strapped into the damage control station.

"Report from the forward computer room. It's not looking good, sir. The temperatures spiked and literally melted the housing. Chief Redfern and Lieutenant Brown are up there now trying to clear it, but... I don't think we can count on the GP for the rest of the trip."

Jacob set his jaw and nodded. It fit with the rest of the mission. Nothing went right since they left Alexandria.

"Any good news?" Jacob asked.

Fawkes looked off screen for a second before answering.

"The main fire control is unaffected, if that helps." Fawkes gave him a stoic grin. "I'll see if there's anything else we can do."

The next question Jacob hated to ask, but he had to. "Who was the casualty in computer two?"

His XO was many things, but a poker player he wasn't. A beaten expression passed over Carter. "Spacer's Apprentice McKnight, Skipper. I had him manning the computer station when we closed out the stern torpedo rooms..."

Jacob understood all too well what Carter felt, since he felt it as well. He'd ordered the evacuation of the torpedoes. It was on him. Otherwise, no one would have died—unless the stern rooms took a hit.

"You don't carry that weight, XO. We'll toast to him when we return, but for now, Charlie Mike."

"Aye, aye, sir. Understood."

The line died, leaving Jacob staring at an MFD of statistics showing everything from the current KPS to the levels of heat on the hull.

"Jen," he said as he turned to her. "Fill up the can. Helmets off, but keep them handy."

"Aye, aye, Skipper," she said. Her voice sounded full of relief as she passed the announcement to the rest of the crew.

———

PO Mendez scrambled down ladder three, sliding the last eight rungs. His boots impacted the deck with a clang. He ran as hard as he could for the mess, Perch and Zack right behind him.

"Don't prepare anything complicated. Ham and cheese sandwiches and premade coffee packets. I'll take care of the bridge. Perch, you take engineering; Zack, the turrets."

"That's a lot of ground to cover, PO," Zack said.

Josh keyed the mess deck hatch with his NavPad. It

whooshed open with a rush of cold air. Josh charged ahead for the galley hatch while Zack and Perch bolted for the coffee machine.

"It is what it is, Zack. Get it done."

"Ain't no thing but a chicken wing, PO. We're on it," Zack drawled.

————

Chief Redfern took the offered coffee, downing the self-heating plastic mug in ten seconds. He let out a burp and tossed the cup to an astonished Spacer First Class Perch.

"That was hot coffee, Chief..." Perch said.

"I ain't got time to burn, Spacer. Thanks for the go-juice."

"I brought two. I thought Lieutenant Brown was here."

He looked at the spacer like he'd said something funny. "An officer making repairs is about as useful as a screen door on a destroyer."

Perch chuckled. "Yes, Chief."

Redfern turned back to the melted mess of wiring that used to be a targeting computer for point defense. He didn't have time to write a report for the captain, but he had some choice words for the engineers who installed the computer. They'd gutted two torpedo rooms in the fore of the ship to install six nitrogen-cooled servers. On paper, it worked great. No one had used the system before *Interceptor*. The tremendous surge of heat as the guidance computers calculated math that was frankly beyond his pay grade melted the housing. All four turrets firing destroyed it in seconds; one turret firing over the course of twenty minutes had the same effect. They either needed to install liquid-nitrogen cooling, or an additional heat sink and use... the torpedo tube... the idea hit Redfern like a thunderbolt.

He glanced at the sealed torpedo hatch. It would be simplicity itself to jury-rig a mechanism to auto eject a heat sink. They just needed to install the heat transfer mechanism and... a loose hot wire sparked next to him, jerking his attention back to the matter at hand.

"Save that for later," he muttered to himself.

———

"It's the magnetic properties of the heavier rocks, Skipper," Ensign Brennan said. The screen she showed him blinked madly with static. "Generally, it wouldn't be this bad, but..."

Jacob glanced over at Tefiti who nodded in confirmation.

"That's the whole reason the system doesn't have asteroid mining. The rocks in this belt are full of low value magnetic materials. It's dense enough it's impacting the radar systems. Not just the waves, but the detection apparatus itself. It makes navigating them at high velocity tricky."

"Good work, you two." Jacob clapped them both on the shoulders. He'd wondered about putting Brennan on astro when her scores in comms were stellar. However, he had a good feeling about her and he was happy to be right.

"Chief Suresh? How long until we can initiate our turn?"

She had the numbers already pulled up and ready to go. "Once our velocity hits 500 KPS, we can change course to follow along the asteroid belt. Should be another... ten minutes and change."

Ten minutes. The Guild cruiser hadn't shown up yet, so either they gave up or they were about to make an appearance.

"Contact, extreme range," Tefiti announced. "I can't be sure, but it looks like Golf-Charlie-One. Grav readings are the same. I doubt they see us yet, though."

Jacob grasped the science behind how the gravity detection worked, but only just. Masters like Tefiti knew it inside and out.

"Start the turn now, COB. Flank speed for thirty seconds, then run silent."

"Aye, aye, sir. Starting turn," Suresh repeated.

"All hands," PO Collins announced over the shipwide, "prepare for silent running. I say again, prepare for silent running." Throughout the ship, crew closed hatches, secured electronics, and ran for their new stations. A crew might be assigned to engineering during battle stations, but then switch to a computer node for silent running. It depended on the need of the mission. Right then, Jacob needed his ship to disappear. No electronic emissions, no heat, no magnetics. A black hole in a black hole.

"Thirty seconds, shutting it down," Chief Suresh said. She eased the throttle back to zero. Her fingers flew over the console in the Pit as she shut power down to the helm, finishing by clicking the throttle and stick in place, preventing accidental movement.

She took her hands off, visually showing them to the captain. "Dead stick," she said.

"Dead stick," Jacob repeated. They were in the hands of fate. If they plotted the course right, *Interceptor* would sail through the worst part of the belt completely powered down. Seeing *Interceptor* normally was hard enough; surrounded by giant radar disrupting rocks? Impossible. Or so he hoped. The part he didn't like was not seeing them.

CHAPTER FORTY-SIX

Captain Seren frowned as his prey vanished from the screen.

"Are you sure that was them?" he asked his XO, Venice.

Venice shook his head. "Not a hundred percent, sir. There's some odd interference. The grav readings were weak, but... who else would it be?"

Who else indeed, Seren said to himself. Admiral Arnold sent him after the Alliance destroyer, hoping to take him out before reaching the starlane. Whatever they could do to stop any interference while they instituted their plan, the better.

It was his job to help Admiral Arnold secure the system, and he was going to do just that.

"What's this field?" he asked. It would be easier to do what the Guild asked if they properly briefed their commanders. He didn't even know he was coming until a day before they departed. The Guild barely had their own warships, and here he was, a newly minted captain in battle, watching ships around him explode. *It wasn't us, that's the important part.* They should never have trusted Cordoba. He was still shocked that their pathetic ships had even damaged the state-of-the-art Terran ships.

"Looks like one of two asteroid belts in the system," Venice said. "From the way our radar is going nuts, I'm guessing highly magnetic?"

"Weapons, fire a volley dead ahead. Set the torpedoes to go Pitbull at a hundred thousand. Maybe they're hiding in that mess. If they light up their grav drive, they'll be in trouble."

———

"Launch, launch, launch," Tefiti said.

"Launch?" Jacob repeated lamely. He glanced at Brown who shrugged.

"I can't see anything on the tracking passive, Skipper."

Tefiti held one hand to his ear, listening intently to the confusing symphony that was space-time.

"Torpedoes, full acceleration. They're going to pass eight-six thousand klicks astern. If our gravcoil were running, they would track, but instead—" He shrugged.

"They're taking pot shots and hoping to get lucky," he mused aloud. Even if the torpedoes tracked him, he doubted they could turn hard enough to come at *Interceptor*. They're practically ninety degrees astern. The plot updated, showing an entire volley sail right by where they were a few minutes before. "It's a good thing we made the turn. Those would have hurt," Jacob said to no one in particular.

"Sir," Brown said to get his attention. Everything had happened so fast, Jacob hadn't yet drained the can again. He likely wouldn't for at least another hour. Jacob moved over to lean against the weps console, arms folded to listen to his weapons officer.

"I still don't see how they can possibly shoot torpedoes that accel at 2,000 g's. That's insane."

Jacob felt Brown's pain. The burly lieutenant from McGregor's World hadn't arrived aboard until after their adventure in Wonderland.

"The Terraforming Guild, or just the Guild as we call them, advanced beyond most nations' levels of technology. They did this by charging exorbitant fees for their services and collecting on them for centuries. A couple of years ago, we found a hidden starlane outside Zuckabar and discovered a Guild base there. The GP lasers come from their ships." Jacob looked up as if he were seeing the defense turrets through the hull. "We captured some of their ships, but they didn't have torpedoes aboard. Just something called a glaser—"

"You mean graser?"

Jacob chuckled, recalling the exact same question from himself when Kim Yukio told him about it.

"No. That would be easier. These are gravity lasers. I don't think we're dealing with them."

"Why not?" Brown asked.

"Because we would be dead. They were one-shot-kill weapons."

Suresh guffawed from behind him. "Not on us, they weren't."

"No," Jacob said with his own smile tinged with sadness. They'd lost good people in those engagements. "They weren't. Long story short, Austin, I don't know how or why their torpedoes can accelerate the way they do or for as long as they do. Just that they do. However, their detection ability doesn't seem any better than ours."

Tefiti broke in. "Another volley, sir. Golf-Charlie-One continues to accelerate at flank speed."

Jacob quirked an eyebrow. "They're not slowing down?"

"No, sir," Tefiti replied. "Still charging ahead at approximately 6,150 KPS, Skipper. The max of what their particle shielding and gravwake can take."

It was a tactical risk, Jacob admitted. Maybe if he were desperate, he'd make the same decision. They needed to stop him and the only way to guarantee he was stopped was blow him up. Still... these asteroids were tricky. It wasn't just that the radar returns were confusing, the radar itself wasn't operating correctly.

"What's the minimum we could put on the gravcoil and safely remain undetected?" he asked Chief Suresh.

She looked up at him from the Pit.

"I know that look," she said.

He shook his head. "I don't have a look. What acceleration, COB?"

"Normally? None. But the way they're barreling in, we could sneak up right behind them and they wouldn't know it until we lit them up. Call it 50 g's until they pass and flank after they're gone."

That's what Jacob thought. If it were an Alliance vessel going by *The Book*, they should reverse engines, reducing their overall velocity, then cut engines to look around. From what he could tell, they didn't even have their towed array out.

"Once they're past us, go full reverse and pursue. We'll follow to the starlane and give them a taste of their own medicine."

"There it is," Suresh said with straight face. "Aye, aye, Skipper. Follow and do something crazy."

Jacob couldn't help but grin. His crew knew him well. He didn't think it was crazy, just good tactical sense. Never let an enemy's mistake go unrewarded. In a way, he was teaching the Guild important combat lessons.

In a deadly way.

Captain Seren eyed the radar returns as the static grew with each passing second.

"What's going on here?" he asked. Like most Guild commanders, he was assigned to the ship mere minutes before departure and hadn't time to learn his crew or the ship.

"The magnetics of the asteroids are interfering with the radar in an unusual way."

"You knew this already, though, can't you compensate?"

Seren considered slowing down, flipping the ship and going full reverse. However, they needed to find the Alliance ship and destroy it. They had to have the system secure. The enemy ship had to be in front of them. There were only two starlanes they could go to, Rygel or Orion. Rygel led to their home, though. That's where they were going.

"I compensated for the magnetic fields, sir, but... there's something else. It's like the arrays are malfunctioning..."

Damn idiotic Terran Republic technology, he wanted to say aloud, but it wouldn't look good to bash their new partners. On a Guild ship, everything was recorded and observed.

"Lidar?" Seren asked.

Venice shook his head. "We can for short range, but anything else is unreliable. I'm having engineering see what they can do."

"Fine, fine," Seren said. A cold pit formed in his stomach. He didn't know much about space combat. Though he'd operated a ship for years, they were freighters, not fighters. He was out of his depth, but too stubborn and proud to admit it.

"Continue on flank speed, then. We'll get to the Rygel star-lane behind them or ahead of them. Regardless, they won't stand a chance once we're in range and they're sitting still."

———

"Drain the can," Jacob ordered. Multiple shifts on alert, wearing most of the ELS, and sleeping with a helmet on wasn't easy for the crew. Exhaustion set in faster, nerves wore on. The actual battles tended to last mere minutes, maybe an hour at most, but the lead-up always took the longest.

The problem for the most part, was that the battle could happen at any second. The tables were easily flipped, and he couldn't risk losing half his crew to explosive decompression. The choices were draining the can and wear the full ELS suit, or restore atmo and keep the suits on but take the helmet off. The Alliance had performed numerous studies that showed crew morale lasted longer with the helmet off.

It also made common sense. As someone who had spent days of his life inside the ELS, he knew as well as anyone how claustrophobic it could be. Today, though, they had no choice.

"Helmets on, helmets on, helmets on," PO Collins' voice rang throughout the ship. During the last stages of pursuit, he'd rotated the bridge crew for chow and rest. They were back after a solid forty-five-minute nap. One he hadn't taken.

"Helmets are on and can is drained, Skipper," Collins said.

Jacob silently confirmed her. She was as solid a PO as he had. All his crew were above average. However, having her at Ops reminded him of Roy's death at the hands of an assassin. He couldn't help but glance over his shoulder and make sure the hatch was sealed.

"All right, Chief Suresh, she's in your hands. When they decelerate, we decelerate."

"Aye, aye, Skipper."

What they were attempting to do was risky. Follow a ship too close and a sudden acceleration change could lead to a collision. Too far away and they would detect them.

This was akin to a minnow riding along with a shark. Or in *Interceptor*'s case, a shark riding along with a much larger shark.

His MFD blinked, showing the course they were on, along with a cone where *Interceptor* could theoretically *hide* from enemy sensors. The entire reason ships came with towed arrays was to prevent him from doing exactly what he was doing. It was the Guild's ignorance of their own hardware that allowed it. Buying advanced ships didn't mean they would work as well for the unskilled.

At the same time, their ship was far superior to his. If it weren't for the asteroid field combined with the poor ship handling of his adversary, he wouldn't be able to get away with it.

"Weps, ready everything. We might get two volleys, maybe three, before they know what's going on."

"Aye, aye, sir," Brown replied. "All turrets switch to local control and fire on my mark. PO Ignatius, ready the Long 9. Torpedo rooms one and two, load the tubes."

Jacob's fingers tapped away on the arm of his chair of their own accord. The comforting pattern of his mother's favorite song beating out in silence.

If everything went right, they would come to a stop at the starlane. The moment the gravcoil shut off, he'd open fire.

———

Seren scowled, the wretched feeling grew to encompass him entirely. He'd forgotten something important, or he was late... it wasn't a feeling he liked, he knew that. It was akin to showing up without pants on. The terrible dream he'd experienced over and over again whenever the Guild sent him to a new post.

"Venice, something's wrong. We should have seen them by now."

With the starlane quickly approaching, and the ship decelerating, they were almost at a standstill.

Venice looked up, his face clouded with insecurity. "I don't know, sir. This is the closest lane back to Alliance space. It's the direction they were heading when we lost... track..."

Venice looked at his station as if it were alive and fighting him.

"What?"

"They turned. When they got out of range of our sensors, I don't know how, but they turned. Maybe those asteroids but... we're at the wrong lane, sir."

It all came together for Seren. Venice was right. Those bizarre asteroids had masked their presence and now his ship was sitting at the wrong lane at near zero velocity.

"Astro, how long to reach the other lane? Not stopping, just a flyby?"

His young astrogator worked feverishly on the controls. "Uh, five hours, sir?"

Seren's helmet stopped him from slapping his own face. "Are you telling me or asking me?"

The astrogator blushed furiously. "Telling, sir. Five hours, fifteen minutes, seven seconds from full stop."

Seren could do that. Come to a full stop, make sure they're not hiding anywhere, and then off to the right lane.

He cursed himself for a fool. Why did the Guild always jump headlong into these overly complex plans with no preparation?

―――――

"Thirty seconds," Ensign Brennan announced.

Jacob watched the plot religiously, which reminded him to say a quick prayer with the little time they had left. When he opened his eyes, ten seconds remained.

The Guild's light cruiser out massed *Interceptor* by a factor of three. She had more weapons, more armor, more crew to make up the gaps.

None of that changed what would happen in a knife fight.

"Range?" Jacob asked.

"Seven-one thousand klicks," Tefiti said.

Jacob made an involuntary fist.

Closer, just a little closer. Jacob willed with his every fiber.

"Six-five—" Brennan said.

"They're approaching zero, gravcoil strength fading," Tefiti said.

"Keep going. Two-zero-zero gravities," Jacob ordered.

His bridge was a high-speed superconductor. Everyone hit the right note, at the right time.

"Five-zero," Brennan said.

"Grav output zero. They'll see us any second," Tefiti said with an even, calm tone.

While the cruiser had turrets, and main guns, and torpedo tubes, Jacob was certain there would be some sign they were about to fire. Every second he waited increased their chances of success.

"Cut acceleration," he said.

Suresh pulled back on the throttle to zero. Their gravcoil shuddered as the last of the power ran through it. They coasted at their last velocity, and would forever if nothing hit them.

"No energy spikes," Brown said. "Turrets are locked forward... I don't think they see us."

"Four-seven," Brennan said.

Jacob glanced at the radar screen. It blinked wildly, snow filling it. If his radar didn't work right, theirs wouldn't either.

"Four-two."

Jacob inhaled deeply, pulling on his harness to make sure it was as tight as possible. *Just a few more seconds.*

———

"That's strange," Venice said.

"What is it?" Seren asked. Instantly alert, he leapt out of his chair and stormed over, eager to have a hand in the man's work.

"Radar is still down, I'm not picking up a gravwake, but for a split second I thought I saw one. It wasn't long enough for the computer to give me a clean read, but... it was there."

"Go active on everything. Helm, bring us around ninety-degrees. Weapons—"

———

"They're coming around," Suresh said.

"Fire!" Jacob ordered. The range dipped below three-zero thousand klicks and it was as close as they were going to get.

Interceptor shook as four turrets, two torpedoes, and the Long 9 fired at once.

The Long 9 hit first. Its nano-hardened tungsten penetrator barely had time to free itself of the steel shroud when it slammed into the starboard stern of *Disclaimer,* ripping through her advanced armor and obliterating the crew quarters on four decks, leaving a burning, jagged hole where the crew slept.

Seconds later, four 10mm tungsten rounds peppered the forward sections. One hit at high aspect, slamming into a turret as it powered up. Secondary explosions opened the weapon like a can, spewing fire died out into space.

The next one impacted at a seventy-degree angle, burrowing into the ship like a tick, rupturing conduits and fusion batteries.

Turret three hit below the bridge, exploding inward and lighting up the lift mechanism in a ball of energetic fury.

The final round smashed dead center in the ship, slicing

through armor and crew until it passed through main engineering. Shrapnel and heat pulled with it like a wind from hell, burning, slicing, and killing everyone in its wake.

———

Captain Seren's lifeless eyes stared back at Venice. The fool had unbuckled to stand over his shoulder, and when unquantifiable amounts of kinetic energy impacted the ship, he'd flown around the bridge like a rag doll, smashing into everything and everyone.

"Weapons, fire," Venice croaked out. A crack in his helmet's faceplate hissed as his oxygen escaped. He had to fix it, but first he needed to make sure the ship lived to do it.

"I don't have a lock," the man at weapons replied.

"Can you see the target?"

"A little..."

"Then fire!"

———

Five turrets swiveled on automatic, firing their grasers at full power back the way the ship had come. Weapons had a fuzzy idea where the Alliance ship was, but space was big. Without their radar, or a solid gravity lock, hitting anything was a crapshoot.

Even a broken clock was right twice a day.

Four mega-joule grasers missed with a wide margin.

———

Radiation warning alarms spiked on *Interceptor*, but the electromagnetic fields she used to protect the crew from solar and cosmic radiation held.

Then her luck ran out. The fifth turret's one-meter-wide beam lanced through space and struck the port of the shark's nose.

Energy impacted with deadly kinetic force. Nano-steel and ablative armor absorbed as much as they could before giving way, and the entire forward firing node exploded inward. One second the front of the ship was there, the next, a massive hole ripped down her port side and from frame #1 to #30 ceased to exist. Two engineers' mates, including Spacer Fantino and PO Harper died instantly.

Radiation alarms wailed as the spent gamma ray laser flooded deck's two through four with lethal amounts of energy.

———

Jacob tried desperately to shake off the hit, but *Interceptor* had tossed around like a bone in a sabershark's mouth.

"Flank speed," he managed to spit out.

Suresh, still holding herself together, slammed the throttle forward and the little ship shot through space.

"Damage?" Jacob asked.

"Propulsion and weapons are online," PO Collins said. "Working out where we got hit."

The two lights on his plot representing the torpedoes they fired sped toward Gold-Charlie-One at seven hundred g's. Either the cruiser didn't see them or couldn't stop them.

She was still alive, though. Wounded, turning and listing, but alive.

"Ten degrees down bubble, let's go beneath them. Weps, rapid fire, all batteries."

"Aye, aye," Suresh and Brown said together.

Two Alliance MK-XII torpedoes, each loaded with nano-hardened tungsten BBs sped toward the lamed ship. With all the power they needed, they homed in on the ship's gravity emissions, made all the worse as the cruiser attempted to maneuver. Sixty seconds after the battle started, the two weapons detonated, sending their warheads slamming into a full broadside of the Guild cruiser. A dozen different holes erupted in her. One found the fusion reactor and *Disclaimer* vanished in a brilliant fusion ball.

Jacob heaved a sigh of relief. They had done it. Barely, but they had done it.

"Astro, belay that last. Get us to the lane and out of here."

CHAPTER FORTY-SEVEN

Ambassador Nguyen watched his wife sleep on the Marine rack in their room. As small and cramped as *Interceptor* had been, it felt like a lived-in ship, like a home. *Coughlin* was far more regimented, stricter, even with the company of Marines gone and only the Navy crew remaining, along with every single one of their people from the embassy who lived.

He knew he had to put his thoughts down soonest. The longer he waited, the more convoluted they would become. Making Cordoba an emergency member of the Alliance was a massive political risk. Despite his assurance to Commander Grimm, President Axwell might just say no to his agreement and that would condemn the Marines who stayed behind to a long, slow death.

Despite the political machinations and deal-mongering that ruled his home, he was confident that Axwell would make the right decision and ratify the treaty.

While it would take the ships months to return to Alliance space, his packet would arrive in a week, maybe less. If everything worked out the way he wanted, then Navy ships would pour into Cordoba in less than two months.

The Marines just had to hold out for that long. After what he'd seen them do, outnumbered and outgunned, he was confident they could.

He just hoped and prayed *Interceptor* survived.

Mr. President. I have used my emergency powers to formally offer full membership to Cordoba. I know this is unexpected, but let me explain. The Guild conspired with their military leaders to overthrow the elected government and kill all witnesses, myself included, along with Commander Grimm's and Captain Bonds' respective commands. The Guild may be inept, greedy murderers, but they must have a reason for wanting this planet. I think it's worthwhile to find out. Therefore, I recommend initiating an intelligence gathering mission to their homeworld immediately upon receipt of this message. I also wish for a full task force to be sent to Cordoba to secure the system and reinforce the Marine company that remained behind to defend our newest member...

There was so much more he wanted to put in the message. About the heroism of the Marines, the Navy, and the dedication of Cordoba's leadership. However, this wasn't the time. He'd make his full report upon returning to the capital. For the moment, this would have to do.

Nguyen looked once more to his sleeping wife and wondered how many Marines and Navy had loved ones who were sleeping blissfully unaware of the peril they were in. The coup on Cordoba had happened fast. Faster than he could have imagined. And now Alliance military were in the crosshairs.

"Godspeed, Commander Grimm," he said.

———

Commander Jacob T. Grimm, the Marines of Bravo-Two-Five, and the *Interceptor* will return in...

TRADITIONS OF COURAGE

THANK YOU FOR READING A DECISION GRIMM

We hope you enjoyed it as much as we enjoyed bringing it to you. We just wanted to take a moment to encourage you to review the book. Follow this link: A Grimm Decision to be directed to the book's Amazon product page to leave your review.

Every review helps further the author's reach and, ultimately, helps them continue writing fantastic books for us all to enjoy.

———

Check out the entire series here!
(tap or scan)

―――――

You can also join our non-spam mailing list by visiting www. subscribepage.com/AethonReadersGroup and never miss out on future releases. You'll also receive three full books completely Free as our thanks to you.

Facebook | Instagram | Twitter | Website

Want to discuss our books with other readers and even the authors? Join our Discord server today and be a part of the Aethon community.

Looking for more great Science Fiction and Fantasy?

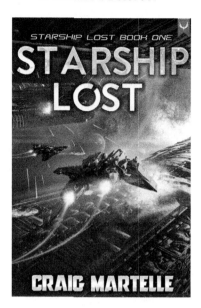

A crew born to end the war. A determined enemy. A fight for freedom.

The ship survived, but over time the original crew died out. Their children were left to continue the fight for their home against their sworn enemy, the vicious alien Malibor.

They've lived their whole lives in space. Their idea of heaven is open air, blue skies, and the quiet of peace. But they'll never have that if they don't take it by force.

Captain Jaq Hunter and Commander Crip Castle lead this new generation against the Malibor. For now the time has come to re-enter the war and reclaim what is should be theirs.

The crew returns to fulfill their destiny and honor their parents' legacy.

The battle is joined.

This is the first book in the Starship Lost Military Sci-Fi Series from Military Sci-Fi Dragon Award Finalist and

Amazon International Bestselling author Craig Martelle. It's perfect for fans of Rick Partlow, JN Chaney, and Joshua Dalzelle. Read it today!

Get Starship Lost Now!

Find them, kill them, or die trying.

When the Solus Hegemony's profit margins are threatened, expendable soldiers are called in to foot the bill—one bloody conquest at a time.

Noah Rivers is one such soldier. Raised from birth with a single objective; obtain eternal glory through death in service to the galaxy's most notorious corporate empire.

Rifle in hand, Noah arrives on the distant world of Kilmori ready to fulfill his ultimate purpose, but not even the Solus could have predicted what lay hidden in the sands of the harsh, desolate, alien world.

This baptism by fire changes everything Noah thinks he knows about the galaxy, and himself. To snatch victory from this devastating new calamity will require blood, sweat, tears... and a brutal edge.

The Kilmori War begins.

Don't miss the start of this action-packed Military Sci-Fi Series from author Pacey Holden. It's perfect for fans of Rick Partlow, Joshua Dalzelle, and Marko Kloos.

Get Calamity's Edge Now!

A war hero gone rogue. The Frontier worlds threatened. Only one man can protect them.

Hard times make for strong men, and Antonin Murdock's childhood was as rough as it gets. Now, he's a Ranger, the only law for colonists seeking their fortune far from home.

Murdock's investigation into a missing freighter takes him to Coracaesium, a world he discovers has been turned into a stronghold by brutal pirate forces. They are more organized than anything he's seen before, equipped with advanced weaponry, and led by a tactical and strategic genius.

Sanya Baretto.

She was once one of the Fleet's elite fighter pilots, holding the line against a ruthless alien enemy. Until the Commonwealth gave her reason to turn against it.

In her cold fury, Baretto may manage something even the entire might of the Tahni Empire couldn't.

The destruction of the Commonwealth.

Don't miss the start of this new Military SciFi Epic from the bestselling duo of Rick Partlow and Ralph Kern. Two legends in the genre bring you a new story filled with pulse-

pounding action, realistic battles, and a soldier you can't help but root for.

Get Pirate Wars Now!

For all our Sci-Fi books, visit our website.

ABOUT THE AUTHOR

Join me in whatever way works for you. I love talking about my work, about how to help other's succeed, and sci-fi in general.

Mailing List: https://goo.gl/LJdYDn

Haskell's Heroes (New FB fan group): https://www.facebook.com/groups/731572934942029/

YouTube: https://www.youtube.com/c/JefferyHHaskell_Author

Twitter: https://twitter.com/jeffery_haskell

Email: jeffery.haskell@gmail.com

Website: www.jefferyhhaskell.com